PENGUIN TWENTIETI

OFFICERS AN

Evelyn Waugh was born in Hampstead in 1903, second son of the late Arthur Waugh, publisher and literary critic, and brother of Alec Waugh, the popular novelist. He was educated at Lancing and Hertford College, Oxford, where he read Modern History. In 1927 he published his first work, a life of Dante Gabriel Rossetti, and in 1928 his first novel, *Decline and Fall*, which was soon followed by *Vile Bodies* (1930), *Black Mischief* (1932), *A Handful of Dust* (1934), and *Scoop* (1938). During these years he travelled extensively in most parts of Europe, the Near East, Africa, and tropical America. In 1939 he was commissioned in the Royal Marines and later transferred to the Royal Horse Guards, serving in the Middle East and in Yugoslavia. In 1942 he published *Put Out More Flags* and then in 1945 *Brideshead Revisited*. *When the Going was Good* and *The Loved One* preceded *Helena* (1950), his historical novel. *Men at Arms*, which came out in 1952, is the first volume in 'The Sword of Honour' trilogy, and won the James Tait Black Prize. The other volumes, *Officers and Gentlemen* and *Unconditional Surrender*, were published in 1955 and 1961. *A Little Learning*, the first volume of an autobiography, was published in 1964. Evelyn Waugh was received into the Roman Catholic Church in 1930 and his earlier biography of the Elizabethan Jesuit martyr, *Edmund Campion*, was awarded the Hawthornden Prize in 1963. In 1959 he published the official *Life of Ronald Knox*. He was married and had six children. Since 1937 he and his family had lived in the West Country. He died in 1966.

Waugh said of his work: 'I regard writing not as investigation of character but as an exercise in the use of language, and with this I am obsessed. I have no technical psychological interest. It is drama, speech and events that interest me.' Mark Amory called Evelyn Waugh 'one of the five best novelists in the English language this century', while Harold Acton described him as having 'the sharp eye of a Hogarth alternating with that of the Ancient Mariner'.

EVELYN WAUGH

OFFICERS AND GENTLEMEN

PENGUIN BOOKS

PENGUIN BOOKS

Published by the Penguin Group
Penguin Books Ltd, 27 Wrights Lane, London W8 5TZ, England
Viking Penguin, a division of Penguin Books USA Inc.
375 Hudson Street, New York, New York 10014, USA
Penguin Books Australia Ltd, Ringwood, Victoria, Australia
Penguin Books Canada Ltd, 2801 John Street, Markham, Ontario, Canada L3R 1B4
Penguin Books (NZ) Ltd, 182–190 Wairau Road, Auckland 10, New Zealand

Penguin Books Ltd, Registered Offices: Harmondsworth, Middlesex, England

First published by Chapman & Hall 1955
Published in Penguin Books
with *Men at Arms* and *Unconditional Surrender*
as 'The Sword of Honour' trilogy 1964
23 25 27 29 30 28 26 24 22

Set, printed and bound in Great Britain by
Cox & Wyman Ltd, Reading, Berks.
Set in Monotype Times

CONTENTS

BOOK ONE

Happy Warriors

1

THE sky over London was glorious, ochre and madder, as though a dozen tropic suns were simultaneously setting round the horizon; everywhere the searchlights clustered and hovered, then swept apart; here and there pitchy clouds drifted and billowed; now and then a huge flash momentarily froze the serene fireside glow. Everywhere the shells sparkled like Christmas baubles.

'Pure Turner,' said Guy Crouchback, enthusiastically; he came fresh to these delights.

'John Martin, surely?' said Ian Kilbannock.

'No,' said Guy firmly. He would not accept correction on matters of art from this former sporting-journalist. 'Not Martin. The sky-line is too low. The scale is less than Babylonian.'

They stood at the top of St James's Street. Half-way down Turtle's Club was burning briskly. From Piccadilly to the Palace the whole jumble of incongruous façades was caricatured by the blaze.

'Anyway, it's too noisy to discuss it here.'

Guns were banging away in the neighbouring parks. A stick of bombs fell thunderously somewhere in the direction of Victoria Station.

On the pavement opposite Turtle's a group of progressive novelists in firemen's uniform were squirting a little jet of water into the morning-room.

Guy was momentarily reminded of Holy Saturday at Downside; early gusty March mornings of boyhood; the doors wide open in the unfinished butt of the Abbey; half the school coughing; fluttering linen; the glowing brazier and the priest with his hyssop, paradoxically blessing fire with water.

'It was never much of a club,' said Ian. 'My father belonged.'

He relit his cigar and immediately a voice near their knees exclaimed: 'Put that light out.'

'A preposterous suggestion,' said Ian.

They looked over the railings beside them and descried in the depths of the area a helmet, lettered ARP.

'Take cover,' said the voice.

A crescent scream immediately, it seemed, over their heads; a thud which raised the paving-stones under their feet; a tremendous incandescence just north of Piccadilly; a pentecostal wind; the remaining panes of glass above them scattered in lethal splinters about the street.

'You know, I think he's right. We had better leave this to the civilians.'

Soldier and airman trotted briskly to the steps of Bellamy's. As they reached the doors, the engines overhead faded and fell silent and only the crackling flames at Turtle's disturbed the midnight hush.

'Most exhilarating,' said Guy.

'Ah, you're new to it. The bore is that it goes on night after night. It can be pretty dangerous too with these fire-engines and ambulances driving all over the place. I wish I could have an African holiday. My awful Air Marshal won't let me go. He seems to have taken a fancy to me.'

'You can't blame yourself. It wasn't to be expected.'

'No indeed.'

In the front hall Job, the night-porter, greeted them with unnatural unction. He had had recourse to the bottle. His was a lonely and precarious post, hemmed in with plate glass. No one at that season grudged him his relaxation. Tonight he was acting – grossly over-acting – the part of a stage butler.

'Good evening, sir. Permit me to welcome you to England, home and safety. Good evening, my lord. Air Marshal Beech is in the billiard-room.'

'Oh, God.'

'I thought it right to apprise you, my lord.'

'*Quite* right.'

'The gutters outside are running with whisky and brandy.'

'No, Job.'

'So I was informed, sir, by Colonel Blackhouse. All the spirit store of Turtle's, gentlemen, running to waste in the streets.'

'We didn't see it.'

'Then we may be sure, my lord, the fire brigade have consumed it.'

Guy and Ian entered the back-hall.

'So your Air Marshal got into the club after all.'

'Yes, it was a shocking business. They held an election during what the papers call "the Battle of Britain", when the Air Force was for a moment almost respectable.'

'Well, it's worse for you than for me.'

'My dear fellow, it's a *nightmare* for *everyone*.'

The windows of the card-room had been blown out and bridge-players, clutching their score sheets, filled the hall. Brandy and whisky were flowing here, if not in the gutters outside.

'Hullo, Guy. Haven't seen you about lately.'

'I only got back from Africa this afternoon.'

'Odd time to choose. I'd have stayed put.'

'I've come home under a cloud.'

'In the last war we used to *send* fellows to Africa when they were under a cloud. What will you drink?'

Guy explained the circumstances of his recall.

More members came in from the street.

'All quiet outside.'

'Job tells me it's overrun with drunk firemen.'

'Job's drunk himself.'

'Yes, every night this week. Can't blame him.'

'Two glasses of wine, Parsons.'

'Some of the servants ought to be sober some of the time.'

'There's a fellow under the billiard-table now.'

'One of the servants?'

'Not one I've ever seen before.'

'Whisky, please, Parsons.'

'I say, I hope we don't have to take Turtle's in.'

'They come here sometimes when they're cleaning. Timid little fellows. Don't give any trouble.'

'Three whiskies and soda, please, Parsons.'

'Heard about Guy's balls-up at Dakar? Tell him, Guy. It's a good story.'

Guy told his good story again and many times that night.

Presently his brother-in-law, Arthur Box-Bender, appeared in shirt-sleeves from the billiard-room, accompanied by another Member of Parliament, a rather gruesome crony of his named Elderbury.

'D'you know what put me off that lost shot?' said Elderbury. 'I trod on someone.'

'Who!'

'No one I know. He was under the table and I trod on his hand.'

'Extraordinary thing. Passed out?'

'He said: "Damn".'

'I don't believe it. Parsons, is there anyone under the billiard-table?'

'Yes, sir, a new member.'

'What's he doing there?'

'Obeying orders, he says, sir.'

Two or three bridge-players went to investigate the phenomenon.

'Parsons, what's all this about the streets running with wine?'

'I haven't been out myself, sir. A lot of the members have been talking about it.'

The reconnaissance party returned from the billiard-room and reported:

'It's perfectly true. There *is* a fellow under the table.'

'I remember poor old Binkie Cavanagh used to sit there sometimes.'

'Binkie was mad.'

'Well, I daresay this fellow is too.'

'Hullo, Guy,' said Box-Bender, 'I thought you were in Africa.'

Guy told him his story.

'How very awkward,' said Box-Bender.

Tommy Blackhouse joined them.

'Tommy, what's all this you told Job about the streets running with wine?'

'*He* told *me*. Just been out to look. Not a drop in sight.'

'Have you been in to the billiard-room?'

'No.'

'Go and have a look. There's something worth seeing.'

Guy accompanied Tommy Blackhouse. The billiard-room was

full but no one was playing. In the shadows under the table lurked a human shape.

'Are you all right down there?' Tommy asked kindly. 'Want a drink or anything?'

'I am perfectly all right, thank you. I am merely obeying the regulations. In an air raid it is the duty of every officer and man not on duty to take the nearest and safest cover wherever he may be. As the senior officer present I thought I should set an example.'

'Well, there's not room for us all, is there?'

'You should go under the stairs or into the cellar.'

The figure now revealed itself as Air Marshal Beech. Tommy was a professional soldier with a career ahead. It was his instinct to be agreeable to the senior officers of all services.

'I think it's pretty well over now, sir.'

'I have not heard the All Clear.'

As he spoke the siren sounded and the sturdy grey figure scrambled to its feet.

'Good evening.'

'Ah, Crouchback, isn't it? We met at Lady Kilbannock's.'

The Air Marshal stretched and dusted himself.

'I want my car. You might just call Air Headquarters, Crouchback, and have it sent round.'

Guy rang the bell.

'Parsons, tell Job that Air Marshal Beech wants his car.'

'Very good, sir.'

The Air Marshal's small eyes looked suspicious. He began to say one thing, thought better of it, said 'Thanks,' and left.

'You never were a good mixer, were you, Guy?'

'Oh, dear. Was I beastly to that poor wretch?'

'He won't look on you as a friend in future.'

'I hope he never did.'

'Oh, he's not such a bad fellow. He's putting in a lot of useful work at the moment.'

'I can't imagine his ever being much use to me.'

'It's going to be a long war, Guy. One may need all the friends one can get before it's over. Sorry about your trouble at Dakar. I happened to see the file yesterday. But I don't think it will come to much. There were some damn silly minutes on it, though. You ought to see it gets to the top level at once before too many people commit themselves.'

'How on earth can I do that?'

'Talk about it.'

'I have.'

'Keep talking. There are ears everywhere.'

Then Guy asked: 'Is Virginia all right?'

'As far as I know. She's left Claridge's. Someone told me she'd moved out of London somewhere. Didn't care for the blitz.'

From the way Tommy spoke, Guy thought that, perhaps, Virginia was not entirely all right.

'You've come up in the world, Tommy.'

'Oh, I'm just messing round with HOO. As a matter of fact there's something rather attractive in the air I can't talk about. I'll know for certain in a day or two. I might be able to fit you in. Have you reported to your regiment yet?'

'Going tomorrow. I only landed today.'

'Well, be careful or you'll find yourself part of the general parcel-post. I should stick around Bellamy's as much as you can. This is where one gets the amusing jobs nowadays. That is, if you want an amusing job.'

'Of course.'

'Well, stick around.'

They returned to the hall. It was thinning out since the All Clear. Air Marshal Beech was on the fender talking to the two Members of Parliament.

'. . . You back-benchers, Elderbury, can do quite a lot if you set yourselves at it. Push the Ministries. Keep pushing . . .'

As in a stage farce Ian Kilbannock's head emerged cautiously from the wash-room, where he had taken refuge from his chief. He withdrew hastily but too late.

'Ian. Just the man I want. Tool off to Headquarters and get the gen about tonight's do and ring through to me at home.'

'The air raid, sir? I think it's over. They got Turtle's.'

'No, no. You must know what I mean. The subject I discussed yesterday with Air Marshal Dime.'

'I wasn't there when you discussed it, sir. You sent me out.'

'You should keep yourself in the picture . . .'

14

But the rebuke never took full shape; the strip, as he would have preferred it, was not torn off, for at that moment there appeared from the outer hall the figure of Job, strangely illuminated. In some strictly private mood of his high drama Job had possessed himself of one of the six-branched silver candelabra from the dining-room; this he bore aloft, rigid but out of the straight so that six little dribbles of wax bespattered his livery. All in the back-hall fell silent and watched fascinated as this fantastic figure advanced upon the Air Marshal. A pace distant he bowed; wax splashed on the carpet before him.

'Sir,' he announced sonorously, 'your carriage awaits you.' Then he turned, and, moving with the confidence of a sleep-walker, retreated whence he had come.

The silence endured for a moment. Then: 'Really,' began the Air Marshal, 'that man – ' but his voice was lost in the laughter. Elderbury was constitutionally a serious man, but when he did see a joke he enjoyed it extravagantly. He had felt resentful of Air Marshal Beech since missing an easy cannon through stepping on him. Elderbury chortled.

'Good old Job.'

'One of his very best.'

'Thank heaven I stayed on long enough to see that.'

'What would Bellamy's be without him?'

'We must have a drink on that. Parsons, take an order all round.'

The Air Marshal looked from face to happy face. Even Box-Bender's was gleeful. Ian Kilbannock was laughing more uproariously than anyone. The Air Marshal rose.

'Anyone going my way want a lift?'

No one was going his way.

As the doors, which in the past two centuries had welcomed grandee and card sharper, duellist and statesman, closed behind Air Marshal Beech, he wondered, not for the first time in his brief membership, whether Bellamy's was all it was cracked up to be.

He sank into his motor-car; the sirens sounded another warning.

'Home,' he ordered. 'I think we can just make it.'

2

BOMBS were falling again by the time that Guy reached his hotel, but far away now, somewhere to the east among the docks. He slept fitfully and when the All Clear finally woke him the rising sun was disputing the sky with the sinking fires of the raid.

He was due in barracks that morning and he set out as uncertainly as on the day he first joined.

At Charing Cross trains were running almost to time. Every seat was taken. He jammed his valise across the corridor with his suitcase a few yards from him, making for himself a seat and a defence.

There were Halberdier badges in most of the carriages and the traffic at his destination was all for the barracks. The men hoisted their kit bags and climbed on board a waiting lorry. The handful of young officers squeezed together into two taxis. Guy took the third alone. As he passed the guard-room he had a brief, vague impression that there was something rather odd about the sentry. He drove to the Officers' House. No one was about. The preceding taxis disappeared in the direction of New Quarters. Guy left his luggage in the ante-room hall and crossed the square to the offices. A squad approached bearing buckets, their faces transformed as though by the hand of Circe from those of men to something less than the beasts. A muffled voice articulated: 'Eyes right.'

Ten pig-faces, visions of Jerome Bosch, swung towards him. Unnerved, automatically, Guy said: 'Eyes front, please, Corporal.'

He entered the adjutant's office, stood to attention and saluted. Two obscene fronts of canvas and rubber and talc were raised from the table. As though from beneath layers of bedclothes a voice said: 'Where's your gas-mask?'

'With the rest of my gear, sir, at the Officers' House.'

'Go and put it on.'

Guy saluted, turned about and marched off. He put on his gas-mask and straightened his cap before the looking-glass, which just a year ago had so often reflected his dress cap and high blue

16

collar and a face full of hope and purpose. He gazed at the gross snout, then returned to the Adjutant. A company had fallen-in on the square; normal, pink young faces. In the orderly-room the Adjutant and Sergeant-Major sat undisguised.

'Take that thing off,' said the Adjutant. 'It's past eleven.'

Guy removed his mask and let it hang, in correct form, across his chest to dry.

'Haven't you read the Standing Orders?'

'No, sir.'

'Why the hell not?'

'Reporting back today, sir, from overseas.'

'Well, remember in future that every Wednesday from 1000 to 1100 hours all ranks take anti-gas precautions. That's a Command Standing Order.'

'Very good, sir.'

'Now, who are you and what do you want?'

'Lieutenant Crouchback, sir. Second Battalion Royal Halberdiers Brigade.'

'Nonsense. The Second Battalion is abroad.'

'I landed yesterday, sir.'

And then slowly, after all the masquerade with the gas-masks, old memories revived.

'We've met before.'

It was the nameless major, reduced now to captain, who had appeared at Penkirk and vanished three days later at Brookwood.

'You had the company during the great flap.'

'Of course. I say, I'm awfully sorry for not recognizing you. There have been so many flaps since. So many chaps through my hands. How did you get here? Oughtn't you to be in Freetown?'

'You weren't expecting me?'

'Not a word. I dare say your papers have gone to the Training Depot. Or up to Penkirk to the Fifth Battalion. Or down to Brook Park to the Sixth. Or to HOO. We've been expanding like the devil in the last two months. Records can't keep up. Well, I've about finished here. Carry on, Sergeant-Major. I shall be at the Officers' House if you want me. Come along, Crouchback.'

He and Guy went to the ante-room. It was not the room Guy had known, where he had sprained his knee on Guest Night. A dark rectangle over the fireplace marked the spot where 'The Un-broken Square' had hung; the bell from the Dutch frigate, the Afridi banner, the gilt idol from Burma, the Napoleonic cuirasses, the Ashanti drum, the loving-cup from Barbados, Tipu Sultan's musket, all were gone.

The Adjutant observed Guy's roving, lamenting eyes.

'Pretty bloody, isn't it? Everything has been stored away under-ground since the blitz.' Then from the bleakest spot in the univer-sal desolation: 'I've lost a pip, too.'

'So I saw. Bad luck.'

'I expected it,' said the Adjutant. 'I wasn't due for promotion for another two years in the regular way. I thought the war might hurry things along a bit. It has for most chaps. It did for me for a month or two. But it didn't last.'

There was no fire.

'It's cold in here,' said Guy.

'Yes. No fires until evening. No drinks either.'

'I suppose it's the same everywhere?'

'No, it's *not*,' said the Adjutant crossly. 'Other regiments still manage to live quite decently. The Captain-Commandant is a changed character. Austerity is the order now. Trust the Corps to do it in a big way. We're sleeping four in a room and the mess sub-scription has been halved. We practically live on rations – like wild beasts,' he specified woefully but inaptly. 'I wouldn't stay here long if I were you. By the way, why *are* you here?'

'I came home with the Brigadier.' That seemed at the moment the most convenient explanation. 'You know he's back, of course?'

'First I've heard of it.'

'You know he got wounded?'

'No. Nothing ever seems to come to us here. Perhaps they've lost our address. The Corps got on very nicely the size it was. All this expansion has been the devil. They've taken my servant away – a man I'd had eight years. I have to share an old sweat with the Regimental Surgeon. That's what we've come to. They've even taken the band.'

'It's too cold to sit here,' said Guy.

'There's a stove in my office but the telephone keeps ringing. Take your choice.'

'What am I to do now?'

'My dear chap, as far as I'm concerned you're still in Africa. I'd send you on leave but you aren't on our strength. D'you want to see the Captain-Commandant? That could be arranged.'

'A changed character?'

'Horribly.'

'I don't see any reason to bother him.'

'No.'

'Well, then?'

They gazed hopelessly at one another across the empty grate.

'You must have had a move order.'

'No. I was just packed off like a parcel. The Brigadier left me at the aerodrome saying I'd be hearing from him.'

The Adjutant had exhausted all his meagre official repertoire.

'It couldn't have happened in peacetime,' he said.

'That is certainly true.'

Guy observed that this unknown soldier was collecting all his resolution for a desperate decision; at length: 'All right, I'll take a chance on it. You can use some leave, I suppose?'

'I promised to do something for Apthorpe – you remember him at Penkirk?'

'Yes, I do. Very well.' Exhilarated to find at last a firm mental foothold: 'Apthorpe. Temporary officer who somehow got made second-in-command of the Battalion. I thought him a bit mad.'

'He's dead now. I promised I'd collect his possessions and hand them over to his heir. I could do that in the next few days.'

'Excellent. If there's any bloodiness, that catches them two ways. We can call it compassionate or disembarkation leave, just as the cat jumps. Staying to lunch in the mess? I shouldn't.'

'I won't,' said Guy.

'If you hang about, there may be some transport going to the station. Two months ago I could have laid it on. That's all been stopped.'

'I'll get a taxi.'

'You know where to find the telephone? Don't forget to leave twopence in the box. I think I'll get back to my office. As you say, it's too cold here.'

Guy lingered. He entered the mess under the gallery which had

19

lately resounded with 'The Roast Beef of Old England'. The portraits were gone from the walls, the silver from the side tables. There was little now to distinguish it from the dining-hall of Kut-al-Imara House. An AT came in from the serving door whistling; she saw Guy and continued to whistle as she rubbed a cloth over the bare boards of a table.

There was a click of balls from the billiard-room. Guy looked in and saw chiefly a large khaki behind. The player struck and widely missed an easy cannon. He stood up and turned.

'Wait for the shot,' he said with a stern but paternal air which purged the rebuke of all offence.

He was in his shirt-sleeves, revealing braces striped with the Halberdier colours. A red-tabbed tunic hung on the wall. Guy recognized him as an elderly colonel who had pottered about the mess a year ago. 'Care for a hundred up?' and 'Not much news in the papers today,' had been his constant refrain.

'I'm very sorry, sir,' said Guy.

'Puts a fellow off, you see,' said the Colonel. 'Care for a hundred up?'

'I'm afraid I am just going.'

'Everyone here is always going,' said the Colonel.

He padded round to his ball and studied the position. It seemed hopeless to Guy.

The Colonel struck with great force. All three balls sped and clicked and rebounded and clicked until finally the red trickled slower and slower towards a corner, seemed to come to a dead stop at the edge of the pocket, mysteriously regained momentum and fell in.

'Frankly,' said the Colonel, 'that was something of a fluke.'

Guy slipped away and gently closed the door. Glancing back through the glazed aperture he observed the next stroke. The Colonel put the red on its spot, studied the uncongenial arrangement and then with plump finger and thumb nonchalantly moved his ball three inches to the left. Guy left him to his solitary delinquency. What used the regulars to call him? Ox? Tiny? Hippo? The nickname escaped him.

With sterner thoughts he turned to the telephone and called for his taxi.

So Guy set out on the second stage of his pilgrimage, which had begun at the tomb of Sir Roger. Now, as then, an act of *pietas* was required of him; a spirit was to be placated. Apthorpe's gear must be retrieved and delivered before Guy was free to follow his fortunes in the King's service. His road lay backward for the next few days, to Southsand and Cornwall. 'Chatty' Corner, man of the trees, must be found, somewhere in the trackless forests of wartime England.

He paused in the ante-room and turned back the pages of the Visitors' Book to the record of that Guest Night last December. There, immediately below Tony Box-Bender's name, he found 'James Pendennis Corner'. But the column where his address or regiment should have stood, lay empty.

3

THE last hour of the day at Our Lady of Victory's Preparatory School, temporarily accommodated at Matchet. Selections from Livy in Mr Crouchback's form-room. Black-out curtains drawn. Gas fire hissing. The customary smell of chalk and ink. The Fifth Form drowsy from the football field, hungry for high tea. Twenty minutes to go and the construe approaching unprepared passages.

'Please, sir, it is true, isn't it, that the Blessed Gervase Crouchback was an ancestor of yours?'

'Hardly an ancestor, Greswold. He was a priest. His brother, from whom I am descended, didn't behave quite so bravely, I'm sorry to say.'

'He didn't *conform*, sir?'

'No, but he kept very quiet – he and his son after him.'

'Do tell us how the Blessed Gervase was caught, sir.'

'I'm sure I've told you before.'

'A lot of us were absent that day, sir, and I've never quite understood what happened. The steward gave him away, didn't he?'

'Certainly not. Challoner misread a transcript from the St Omers records and the mistake has been copied from book to book.

All our own people were true. It was a spy from Exeter who came to Broome asking for shelter, pretending to be a Catholic.'

The Fifth Form sat back contentedly. Old Crouchers was off. No more Livy.

'Father Gervase was lodged in the North turret of the forecourt. You have to know Broome to understand how it happened. There is only the forecourt, you see, between the house and the main road. Every good house stands on a road or a river or a rock. Always remember that. Only hunting-lodges belong in a park. It was after the Reformation that the new rich men began hiding away from the people. . . .'

It was not difficult to get old Crouchers talking. Greswold major, whose grandfather he had known, was adept at it. Twenty minutes passed.

' . . . When he was examined by the Council the second time he was so weak that they gave him a stool to sit on.'

'Please, sir, that's the bell.'

'Time? Oh, dear, I'm afraid I've let myself run on, wasting your time. You ought to stop me, Greswold. Well, we'll start tomorrow where we left off. I shall expect a long, thorough construe.'

'Thank you, sir; good night. It was jolly interesting about the Blessed Gervase.'

'Good night, sir.'

The boys clattered away. Mr Crouchback buttoned his great-coat, slung his gas-mask across his shoulder and, torch in hand, walked downhill towards the lightless sea.

The Marine Hotel which had been Mr Crouchback's home for nine years was as full now as though in the height of summer. Every chair in the Residents' Lounge was held prescriptively. Novels and knitting were left to mark the squatters' rights when they ventured out into the mist.

Mr Crouchback made straight for his own rooms, but, encountering Miss Vavasour at the turn of the stairs, he paused, pressing himself into the corner to let her pass.

'Good evening, Miss Vavasour.'

'Oh, Mr Crouchback, I have been waiting for you. May I speak to you for a moment?'

'Of course, Miss Vavasour.'

'It's about something that happened today.' She spoke in a whisper. 'I don't want Mr Cuthbert to overhear me.'

'How very mysterious! I'm sure I have no secrets from the Cuthberts.'

'They have from you. There is a plot, Mr Crouchback, which you should know about.'

Miss Vavasour had turned about and was now making for Mr Crouchback's sitting-room. He opened the door and stood back to admit her. A strong smell of dog met their nostrils.

'Such a nice manly smell,' said Miss Vavasour.

Felix, his golden retriever, rose to meet Mr Crouchback, stood on his hind legs and pawed Mr Crouchback's chest.

'Down, Felix, down, boy. I hope he's been out.'

'Mrs Tickeridge and Jenifer took him for a long walk this afternoon.'

'Charming people. Do sit down while I get rid of this absurd gasbag.'

Mr Crouchback went into his bedroom, hung up his coat and haversack, peered at his old face in the looking-glass and returned to Miss Vavasour.

'Well, what is this sinister plot?'

'They want to turn you out,' said Miss Vavasour.

Mr Crouchback looked round the shabby little room, full of his furniture and books and photographs. 'I don't think that's possible,' he said; 'the Cuthberts would never do a thing like that – after all these years. You must have misunderstood them. Anyway, they can't.'

'They can, Mr Crouchback. It's one of these new laws. There was an officer here today – at least he was dressed as an officer – a dreadful sort of person. He was counting all the rooms and looking at the register. He talked of taking over the whole place. Mr Cuthbert explained that several of us were permanent residents and that the others had come from bombed areas and were the wives of men at the front. Then the so-called officer said: "Who's this man occupying two rooms?" and do you know what Mr Cuthbert said? He said, "He works in the town. He's a school-teacher." *You*, Mr Crouchback, to be described like that!'

'Well, it's what I am, I suppose.'

'I very nearly interrupted them then and there, to tell them *who you are*, but of course I wasn't really part of the conversation. In fact I don't think they realized I was within hearing. But I *boiled*. Then this officer asked: "Secondary or Primary?" and Mr Cuthbert said: "Private" and then the officer laughed and said: "Priority nil." And after that I simply could not restrain myself any more so I simply got up and looked at them and left the room without a word.'

'I'm sure you did much the wisest thing.'

'But the impertinence of it!'

'I'm sure nothing will come of it. There are all sorts of people all over the place nowadays making inquiries. I suppose it's necessary. Depend upon it, it was just routine. The Cuthberts would never do a thing like that. Never. After all these years.'

'You are too trustful, Mr Crouchback. You treat everyone as if he were a gentleman. That officer definitely was *not*.'

'It was very kind of you to warn me, Miss Vavasour.'

'It makes me boil,' she said.

When Miss Vavasour had gone Mr Crouchback took off his boots and socks, his collar and his shirt and standing before the wash-hand-stand in trousers and vest washed thoroughly in cold water. He donned a clean shirt, collar and socks, shabby pumps and a slightly shabby suit made of the same cloth as he had worn throughout the day. He brushed his hair. And all the time he thought of other things than Miss Vavasour's disclosure. She had cherished a chivalrous devotion for him since she first settled at Matchet. His daughter Angela joked of it rather indelicately. For the six years of their acquaintance he had paid little heed to anything Miss Vavasour said. Now he dismissed the Cuthbert plot and considered two problems that had come to him with the morning's post. He was a man of regular habit and settled opinion. Doubt was a stranger to him. That morning, in the hour between Mass and school, he had been confronted with two intrusions from an unfamiliar world.

The more prominent was the parcel; bulky and ragged from the investigations of numberless clumsy departmental hands. It was covered with American stamps, customs declarations, and certificates of censorship.

'American parcel' was just beginning to find a place in the English vocabulary. This was plainly one of these novelties. His three Box-Bender granddaughters had been sent to a place of refuge in New England. Doubtless it came from them. 'How kind. How very extravagant,' he had thought and had borne it to his room for later study.

Now he cut the string with his nail scissors and spread the contents in order on his table.

First came six tins of 'Pullitzer's Soup'. They were variously, lusciously named but soup was one of the few articles of diet in which the Marine Hotel abounded. Moreover, he had an ancient conviction that all tinned foods were made of something nasty. 'Silly girls. Well, I daresay we shall be glad of it one day.' Next there was a transparent packet of prunes. Next a very heavy little tin labelled '*Brisko. A Must in every home.*' There was no indication of its function. Soap? Concentrated fuel? Rat poison? Boot polish? He would have to consult Mrs Tickeridge. Next a very light larger tin named 'Yumcrunch'. This must be edible for it bore the portrait of an obese and badly brought-up little girl waving a spoon and fairly bawling for the stuff. Last and oddest of all a bottle filled with what seemed to be damp artificial pearls, labelled 'Cocktail Onions'. Could it be that this remote and resourceful people who had so generously (and, he thought, so unnecessarily) sheltered his grandchildren; this people whose chief concern seemed to be the frustration of the processes of nature – could they have contrived an alcoholic onion?

Mr Crouchback's elation palled; he studied his gift rather fretfully. Where in all this exotic banquet was there anything for Felix? The choice seemed to lie between Brisko and Yumcrunch.

He shook Yumcrunch. It rattled. Broken biscuits? Felix stood and pointed his soft muzzle.

'Yumcrunch?' said Mr Crouchback seductively. Felix's tail thumped the carpet.

And then suspicion darkened Mr Crouchback's contentment: suppose this were one of those new patent foods he had heard described, something 'dehydrated' which, eaten without due preparation, swelled enormously and fatally in the stomach.

'No, Felix,' he said. 'No Yumcrunch. Not until I have asked

Mrs Tickeridge,' and at the same time he resolved to consult that lady about his other problem: the matter of Tony Box-Bender's odd postcard and Angela Box-Bender's odd letter.

The postcard had been enclosed in the letter. He had taken both to school with him and reread them often during the day. The letter read:

> Lower Chipping Manor,
> Nr Tetbury

Dearest Papa,

News at last from Tony. Nothing very personal poor boy but such a joy to know he is safe. Until this morning I didn't realize how anxious I have been. After all the man who got away and wrote to us that he had seen Tony in the POW column might have been mistaken. Now we know.

He seems to think we can send him anything he needs but Arthur has been into it and says no, that isn't the arrangement. Arthur says he can't approach neutral embassies and I mustn't write to America either. Only regular Red Cross parcels may be sent and they get those anyhow apparently whether we pay for them or not. Arthur says the parcels are scientifically chosen so as to have all the right calories and that there can't be one law for the rich and one for the poor when it comes to prison. I see he's quite right in a way.

The girls seem to be enjoying America tremendously.

How is Dotheboys Hall?

> Love,
> Angela.

Tony's card read:

Was not allowed to write before. Now in permanent camp. A lot of our chaps here. Can daddy arrange parcels through neutral embassies? This is most important and everyone says safest and quickest way. Please send cigarettes, chocolates, golden syrup, cocoa, tinned meat and fish (all kinds). Glucose 'D'. Hard biscuits (ships) cheese, toffee, condensed milk, camel hair sleeping bag, air-cushion, gloves, hair brush. Could girls in US help? Also Boulestin's Conduct of Kitchen. Trumper's Eucris. Woolly slippers.

There had been one other letter in Mr Crouchback's post, which saddened him though it presented no problem. His wine merchants wrote to say that their cellars had been partly destroyed by enemy action. They hoped to maintain diminished supplies to their regular customers but could no longer fulfil specific orders. Monthly parcels would be made up from whatever stock was available. Pilfering and breakages were becoming frequent on the railways. Customers were requested to report all losses immediately.

Parcels, thought Mr Crouchback. Everything that day seemed to be connected with parcels.

After dinner, according to the custom of more than a year, Mr Crouchback joined Mrs Tickeridge in the Residents' Lounge.

Their conversation began, as always, with the subject of Felix's afternoon exercise. Then:

'Guy's home. I hope we shall see him here soon. I don't know what he's up to. Something rather secret, I expect. He came back with his Brigadier – the man you call "Ben".'

Mrs Tickeridge had that day received a letter from her husband in which certain plain hints informed her that Brigadier Ritchie-Hook had got into another of his scrapes. Well trained in service propriety she changed the subject.

'And your grandson?'

'That's just what I wanted to ask about. My daughter has had this postcard. May I show it to you – and her letter? Aren't they puzzling?'

Mrs Tickeridge took the documents and perused them. At length she said: 'I don't think I ever read Trumper's *Eucris*.'

'No, no. It's not that I'm puzzled by. That's hair-stuff. Used to use it myself when I could afford it. But don't you think it very peculiar that in his first postcard home he should only be asking for things for himself? It's most unlike him.'

'I expect he's hungry, poor boy.'

'Surely not? Prisoners of war have full army rations. There's an international agreement about it, I know. You don't suppose it's a code. "Glucose D" – whoever heard of "Glucose D"? I'm sure Tony has never seen the stuff. Someone put him up to it. You would think that a boy writing to his mother for the first time, when he must know how anxious she has been, would have something better to say than "Glucose D".'

'Perhaps he's *really* hungry.'

'Even so, he ought to consider his mother's feelings. You've read her letter?'

'Yes.'

'I'm sure she's got quite the wrong end of the stick. My son-in-law is in the House of Commons and of course he picks up some rather peculiar ideas there.'

'No, it's been on the wireless.'

'*The wireless*,' said Mr Crouchback in a tone as near bitterness as he possessed. 'The wireless. Just the sort of thing they would put about. It seems to me the most improper idea. Why should we not send what we want to those we love – even "Glucose D"?'

'I suppose in wartime it's only fair to share things equally.'

'Why? Less in wartime than ever I should have thought. As you say, the boy may be really hungry. If he wants "Glucose D" why can't I send it to him? Why can't my son-in-law get foreigners to help? There's a man in Switzerland who used to come and stay at Broome year after year. I know he'd like to help Tony. Why shouldn't he? I don't understand.'

Mrs Tickeridge saw the gentle, bewildered old man gaze earnestly at her, seeking an answer she could not give. He continued:

'After all, *any* present means that you want someone to have something someone else hasn't got. I mean even if it's only a cream jug at a wedding. I shouldn't wonder if the Government didn't try and stop us praying for people next.' Mr Crouchback sadly considered this possibility and then added: 'Not that anyone really *needs* a cream-jug and apparently Tony needs these things he asks for. It's all *wrong*. I'm not much of a dab at explaining things, but I *know* it's all *wrong*.'

Mrs Tickeridge was mending Jenifer's jersey. She darned silently. She was not much of a dab herself at explaining things. Presently Mr Crouchback spoke again, from the tangle of his perplexities.

'And what is Brisko?'

'Brisko?'

'And Yumcrunch? Both these things are in my room at the moment and I don't for the life of me know what to do with them. They're American.'

28

'I know just what you mean. I've seen them advertised in a magazine. Yumcrunch is what they eat for breakfast instead of porridge.'

'Would it suit Felix? Wouldn't blow him up?'

'He'd love it. And the other thing is what they use instead of lard.'

'Pretty rich for a dog?'

'I'm afraid so. I expect Mrs Cuthbert will be very grateful for it in the kitchen.'

'There's nothing you don't know.'

'Except Trumper's whatever-it-was.'

Presently Mr Crouchback took his leave, fetched Felix and let him out into the darkness. He brought down with him the tin of Brisko and carried it to the proprietress of the hotel in her 'Private Parlour'.

'Mrs Cuthbert, I have been sent this from America. It is lard. Mrs Tickeridge seems to think you might find it useful in the kitchen.'

She took it and thanked him rather awkwardly.

'There was something Mr Cuthbert wanted to see you about.'

'I am here.'

'Everything is getting so difficult,' she said; 'I'll fetch Mr Cuthbert.'

Mr Crouchback stood in the Private Parlour and waited. Presently Mrs Cuthbert returned alone.

'He says, will I speak to you. I don't know quite how to begin. It's all because of the war and the regulations and the officer who came today. He was the Quartering Commandant. You know it's nothing personal, don't you, Mr Crouchback? I'm sure we've always done all we can to oblige, making all sorts of exceptions for you, not charging for the dog's meals and your having your own wine sent in. Some of the guests have mentioned it more than once how you were specially favoured.'

'I have never made any complaint,' said Mr Crouchback. 'I am satisfied that you do everything you can in the circumstances.'

'That's it,' said Mrs Cuthbert, 'circumstances.'

'I think I know what you wish to say to me, Mrs Cuthbert. It is really quite unnecessary. If you fear I'll desert you now when you are going through difficult times, after I have been so comfortable for so many years, you may put your mind quite at rest. I know you are both doing your best and I am sincerely grateful.'

'Thank you, sir. It wasn't quite that . . . I think Mr Cuthbert had better speak to you.'

'He may come to me whenever he likes. Not now. I am just going to take Felix off to bed. Good night, I hope that tin will be of help.'

'Good night and thank you, sir.'

Miss Vavasour met him on the stairs.

'Oh, Mr Crouchback, I couldn't help seeing you go into the Private Parlour. Is everything all right?'

'Yes, I think so. I had a tin of lard for Mrs Cuthbert.'

'They didn't say anything about what I told you about?'

'The Cuthberts seemed to be worried about the falling off of the service. I think I was able to reassure them. It is a difficult time for both of them – for all of us. Good night, Miss Vavasour.'

4

MEANWHILE the talk in Bellamy's had drifted irresistibly upward. That very morning in a deep bed in a deep shelter a buoyant busy personage had lain, apportioning the day's work of an embattled Empire in a series of minutes.

'Pray inform me today on one half sheet of paper why Brig. Ritchie-Hook has been relieved of the command of his Brigade.'

And twenty-four hours later, almost to the minute, while Mr Crouchback's form was beginning to construe the neglected passage of Livy, from the same heap of pillows the ukase went out:

P.M. to Secretary of State for War.

I have directed that no commander be penalized for errors in discretion *towards the enemy*. This directive has been flouted in a grievous and vexatious manner in the case of Col. late Brig. Ritchie-Hook, Royal Corps of Halberdiers. Pray assure me that suitable employment has been found for this gallant and resourceful officer as soon as he is passed fit for active service.

Telephones and typewriters relayed the trumpet note. Great men called to lesser men, and they to men of no consequence at all. Somewhere on the downward official slope Guy's name too appeared, for Ritchie-Hook, in his room at Millbank Hospital, had not forgotten his companion in guilt. Papers marked '*Passed to you for immediate action*' went from 'In' tray to 'Out' tray, until at length they found sea level with the Adjutant of the Halberdier Barracks.

'Sergeant-Major, we have Mr Crouchback's leave address?'

'Marine Hotel, Matchet, sir.'

'Then make out a move order for him to report forthwith to HOO HQ.'

'Am I to give the address, sir?'

'That wouldn't do. It's on the Most Secret list.'

'Sir.'

Ten minutes later the Adjutant remarked: 'Sergeant-Major, if we withhold the address, how will Mr Crouchback know where to report?'

'Sir.'

'We could refer it back to HOO HQ.'

'Sir.'

'But it is marked "Immediate Action".'

'Sir.'

These two men of no consequence at all sat silent and despairing.

'I take it, sir, the correct procedure would be to send it by hand of officer?'

'Can we spare anyone?'

'There's one, sir.'

'Colonel Trotter?'

'Sir.'

'Jumbo' Trotter, as his nickname suggested, was both ponderous and popular; he retired with the rank of full colonel in 1936. Within an hour of the declaration of war he was back in barracks and there he had sat ever since. No one had summoned him. No one cared to question his presence. His age and rank rendered him valueless for barrack duties. He dozed over the newspapers, lumbered round the billiard-table, beamed on his juniors' scrimmages on Guest Nights, and regularly attended Church Parade. Now and then he expressed a wish to 'have a go at the Jerries'. Mostly he slept. It was he whom Guy had disturbed in the billiard-room on his last visit to the barracks.

Once or twice a week the Captain-Commandant, in his new role of martinet, resolved to have a word with Jumbo, but the word was never spoken. He had served under Jumbo in Flanders and there learned to revere him for his sublime imperturbability in many dangerous and disgusting circumstances. He readily gave his approval to the old boy's outing and left him to make his own arrangements.

It was a hundred and fifty miles to Matchet. Jumbo's few indispensable possessions could be contained in one japanned-tin uniform case and a pig-skin Gladstone. But there was his bedding. Never move without your bed and your next meal; that was a rule, said Jumbo. Altogether his luggage comprised rather a handful for Halberdier Burns, his aged servant; too much to take by train, he explained to the Barrack Transport Officer. Besides, it was the duty of everyone to keep off the railways. The wireless had said so. Trains were needed for troop movements. The Transport Officer was a callow, amenable, regular subaltern. Jumbo got a car.

Early next day, in that epoch of mounting oppression, it stood at the steps of the Officers' House. The luggage was strapped behind. Driver and servant stood beside it. Presently Jumbo emerged, well buttoned up against the morning chill, smoking his after-breakfast pipe, carrying under his arm the ante-room's only copy of *The Times*. The men jumped to the salute. Jumbo beamed benignantly on them and raised a fur-lined glove to the peak of his red hat. He conferred briefly with the driver over the map, ordering a detour which would bring him at lunch-time to a friendly mess, then settled himself in the rear-seat. Burns tucked in the rug and leapt to his place beside the driver. Jumbo glanced at the Deaths in the paper before giving the order to move.

The Adjutant, watching these sedate proceedings from his office window, suddenly said: 'Sergeant-Major, couldn't we have recalled Mr Crouchback here and given him the address ourselves?'

'Sir.'

'Too late to change now. Order, counter order, disorder, eh?'

'Sir.'

The car moved across the gravel towards the guard-house. It might have been carrying an elderly magnate from a London square to a long week-end in the Home Counties, in years before the Total War.

Mrs Tickeridge knew Colonel Trotter of old. She found him dozing in the hall of the Marine Hotel when she and Jenifer returned from their walk with Felix. He opened his pouchy eyes and accepted their presence without surprise.

'Hullo, Vi. Hullo, shrimp. Nice to see you again.'

He began to raise himself from his chair.

'Sit down, Jumbo. What on earth are you doing here?'

'Waiting for my tea. Everyone seems half asleep here; said tea was "off". Ridiculous expression. Had to send my man Burns into the kitchen to brew up. Met opposition from some civilian cook, I gather. Soon settled that. Had some opposition about quarters, too, from the woman in the office. Said she was full up. Soon settled that. Had my bed made up and my things laid out in a bathroom. Woman didn't seem too pleased about that either. Poor type. Had to remind her there was a war on.'

'Oh, Jumbo, there's only two baths between the whole lot of us.'

'Shan't be here long. All have to rough it a bit these days. Burns and the driver fixing themselves up in the town. Trust an old Halberdier to make himself comfortable. No camp-bed in a bathroom for Burns.'

Burns appeared at that moment with a laden tray and put it beside the colonel.

'Jumbo, what a tea! We never get anything like that. Hot buttered toast, sandwiches, an egg, cherry cake.'

'Felt a bit peckish. Told Burns to scrounge round.'

'Poor Mrs Cuthbert. Poor us. No butter for a week.'

'I'm looking for a fellow called Crouchback. Woman in the office said he was out. Know him?'

'He's a heavenly old man.'

'No. Young Halberdier officer.'

'That's his son, Guy. What d'you want with him? You're not taking him under arrest?'

'Lord, no.'

A look of elephantine cunning came into his eyes. He had no idea of the contents of the sealed envelope buttoned up below his medals.

'Nothing like that. Just a friendly call.'

Felix sat with his muzzle on Jumbo's knee gazing at him with devotion. Jumbo cut a corner of toast, dipped it in jam and placed it in the gentle mouth.

'Take him away, Jenifer, there's a good girl, or he'll have all my tea off me.'

Presently Jumbo fell into a doze.

He woke to the sound of voices near him. The woman from the office, the poor type, was in converse with a stout, upright Major wearing RASC badges.

'I've hinted,' the woman was saying. 'Mr Cuthbert as good as told him outright. He won't seem to understand.'

'He'll understand all right when he finds his furniture on the doorstep. If you can't move him quietly, I shall use my powers.'

'It does seem a shame rather.'

'You should be grateful, Mrs Cuthbert. I could have taken the whole hotel if I'd cared, and I would have but for Mr Cuthbert being on the square. I've taken over the Monte Rosa boarding house instead. The people from there have to sleep somewhere, don't they?'

'Well, it's your responsibility. He'll be very upset, poor old gentleman.'

Jumbo studied the man carefully and suddenly said very loudly: 'Grigshawe.'

The effect was immediate. The Major swung round, stamped, stood to attention and roared back: 'Sir.'

'Bless my soul, Grigshawe, it *is* you. Wasn't sure. I'm very pleased to see you. Shake hands.'

'You're looking very well, sir.'

'You've had quick promotion, eh?'

'Acting-rank, sir.'

'We missed you when you put in for a commission. You shouldn't have left the Halberdiers, you know.'

'I wouldn't have but for the missus and it being peacetime.'

'What are you up to now?'

'Quartering Commandant, sir. Just clearing a little room here.'

'Excellent. Well, carry on. Carry on.'

'I've about finished, sir.' He stood to attention, nodded to Mrs Cuthbert and left, but there was no peace for Jumbo that afternoon. The room was hardly empty of Mrs Cuthbert before an elderly lady raised her head from a neighbouring chair and coughed. Jumbo regarded her sadly.

'Excuse me,' she said, 'I couldn't help overhearing. You know that officer?'

'What, Grigshawe? One of the best drill-sergeants we had in the Corps. Extraordinary system taking first-rate NCOs and making second-rate officers of them.'

'That's dreadful. I had quite made up my mind he must be some sort of criminal, dressed up – a blackmailer or burglar or something. It was our last hope.'

Jumbo had little curiosity about the affairs of others. It seemed to him vaguely odd that this pleasant-looking lady should so ardently desire Grigshawe to be an impostor. From time to time in his slow passage through life Jumbo had come up against things that puzzled him and had learned to ignore them. Now he merely remarked: 'Known him twenty years' and was preparing to leave his seat for a sniff of fresh air, when Miss Vavasour said: 'You see, he is trying to take Mr Crouchback's sitting-room.'

The name gave Jumbo pause and before he could disengage himself Miss Vavasour had begun her recital.

She spoke vehemently but furtively. In the Marine Hotel, scorn of the Quartering Commandant had quickly given place to dread. He came none knew whence, armed with unknown powers, malevolent, unpredictable, implacable. Miss Vavasour would with relish have thrown herself on any German paratrooper and made short work of him with poker or bread-knife. Grigshawe was a projection of the Gestapo. For two weeks now the permanent residents had lived in a state of whispering agitation. Mr Crouchback followed his routine, calmly refusing to share their alarm. He was the symbol of their security. If he fell, what hope was there for them? And his fall, it seemed, was now encompassed.

Jumbo listened restively. It was not for this he had driven all day with his Most Secret missive. He was out for a treat. There had been a number of jokes lately in the papers about selfish old women in safe hotels. He had chuckled over them often. He was on the point of reminding Miss Vavasour that there was a war on, when Mr Crouchback himself appeared before them, back from school with a pile of uncorrected exercise books, and suddenly the whole evening was changed and became a treat again.

Miss Vavasour introduced them. Jumbo, slow in some of his perceptions, was quick to recognize 'a good type'; not only the father of a Halberdier but a man fit to be a Halberdier himself.

Mr Crouchback explained that Guy was at Southsand, many miles away, collecting the possessions of a brother-officer who had died on active service. These were unexpectedly good tidings. Jumbo saw days, perhaps weeks, of pleasant adventure ahead. He had no objection to prolonging his tour of the seaside resorts indefinitely.

'No, no. Don't telephone him. I'll go there tomorrow myself.'

Then Mr Crouchback showed immediate solicitude for Jumbo's comfort. He must not think of sleeping in a bathroom. Mr Crouchback's sitting-room was at his disposal. Then Mr Crouchback gave him some excellent sherry and later, at dinner, burgundy and port. He did not mention that this was the last bottle of a little store which he could never hope to replenish.

They touched lightly on public affairs and found themselves in close agreement. Jumbo mentioned that in his latter years he had made a modest collection of old silver. Mr Crouchback knew a lot about that. They talked of fishing and pheasant-shooting, not competitively but in placid accord.

Mrs Tickeridge joined them later and gossiped about the Halberdiers. They did two-thirds of the crossword together. It was exactly Jumbo's idea of a pleasant evening. Nothing was said of Grigshawe and grievances, and in the end it was he who brought the matter up.

'Sorry to hear there's been trouble about your room here.'

'Oh, no trouble really. I've never even seen this Major Grigshawe they all talk about. I think he must rather have muddled the Cuthberts, and you know how rumours spread and get exaggerated in a little place like this. Poor Miss Vavasour seems to think we shall all be put into the street. I don't believe a word of it myself.'

'I've known Grigshawe for twenty years. Dare say he's got a bit too big for his boots. I'll have a word with him in the morning.'

'Not on *my* account, please. But it would be kind to put Miss Vavasour's mind at rest.'

'Perfectly simple matter if he handles it in the proper service way. All he has to do is put in a report that on the relevant date the room was occupied by a senior officer. You won't have any more trouble with Grigshawe, I can promise.'

'He's been no trouble to me, I assure you. He seems to have been a little brusque with the Cuthberts. I expect he thought he was only doing his duty.'

'I'll show him his duty.'

Mr Crouchback had already left the hotel when Jumbo came down next morning, but Jumbo did not forget. Before his leisurely departure he had a few words with Major Grigshawe.

Two days later Mr and Mrs Cuthbert sat in their Private Parlour. Major Grigshawe had just left them with the assurance that their pensionnaires would be left undisturbed. The news was not welcome.

'We could have let that room of old Crouchback's for eight guineas a week,' said Mr Cuthbert.

'We could let every room in the house twice over.'

'Permanent residents were all very well before the war. They kept us going nicely in the winter months.'

'But there's a war on now. We can put the rates up again, I suppose.'

'We ought to make a clean sweep and take people only by the week. That's where the money comes. Keep people moving. Keep them anxious where they're going next. Some of these people with their houses blitzed are grateful for anything. Grigshawe's let us down, that's the truth of the matter.'

'Funny his giving up like that just when everything seemed so friendly.'

'You can't trust the army, not in business.'

'It was old Crouchback did it. I don't know how, but he did.

He's an artful old bird if you ask me. Talks so that butter wouldn't melt in his mouth. "I do appreciate your difficulties, Mrs Cuthbert." "So grateful for all your trouble, Mrs Cuthbert."'

'He's seen better days. We all know that. There's something about people like him. They were brought up to expect things to be easy for them and somehow or other things always *are* easy. Damned if I know how they manage it.'

There was a knock at the door and Mr Crouchback entered. His hair was rough from the wind and his eyes watery, for he had been sitting outside in the dark.

'Good evening. Good evening. Please don't get up, Mr Cuthbert. I just wanted to tell you something I've just decided. A week or so ago you said there was someone in need of a room here. I dare say you've forgotten, but I hadn't. Well, you know, thinking it over it seems to me that it's rather selfish keeping on both my rooms at a time like this. There's my grandson in a prison camp, people homeless from the towns, all those residents from Monte Rosa turned out with nowhere to go. It's all wrong for one old man like myself to take up so much space. I asked at the school and they're able to store my few sticks of furniture. So I came to give a week's notice that I shan't need the sitting-room in future, not in the immediate future, that is. After the war I shall be very pleased to take it on again, you know. I hope this isn't inconvenient. I'll stay, of course, until you find a suitable tenant.'

'We'll do that easy enough. Much obliged to you, Mr Crouchback.'

'That's settled then. Good night to you both.'

'Talk of the devil,' said Mrs Cuthbert, when Mr Crouchback had left. 'What d'you make of that?'

'Maybe he's feeling the pinch.'

'Not him. He's worth much more than you'd think. Why, he *gives* it away, right and left. I know because I've done his room sometimes. Letters of thanks from all over the shop.'

'He's a deep one and no mistake. I never have understood him, not properly. Somehow his mind seems to work different than yours and mine.'

5

The Times. 2 November 1940
  Personal.
In the breakfast room of the Grand Hotel, Southsand, Guy
sought his advertisement in the Agony Column, and at length
found it.

CORNER, James Pendennis, popularly known as 'CHATTY', late of
Bechuanaland or similar territory, please communicate with Box 108
when he will learn something to his advantage.

The grammar, he noted with chagrin, was defective but the call
was as unambiguous as the Last Trump. It sounded a despairing
note, as though from the gorge of Roncesvalles, for he had done
his utmost in the matter of Apthorpe's gear and could now merely
wait.

It was the sixteenth day since he had left barracks, his eleventh
at Southsand. The early stages of his quest had been easy. Brook
Park, where Apthorpe had jettisoned all that final residuum of the
possessions which he regarded as the bare necessaries of life, was
still in Halberdier hands. The stores left there were intact and
accessible. An amiable Quartermaster was ready to part with anything that was 'signed for' in triplicate. Guy signed. He was
received at the strange mess with fraternal warmth; with curiosity
also for he was the first Halberdier to bring news from Dakar.
They induced him to lecture the battalion on 'the lessons of an
opposed landing'. He stayed mum on the subject of Ritchie-
Hook's wound. They gave him transport and he was sent on his
way with honour.

At Southsand he found the Commodore of the Yacht Club
eager to disencumber himself. In his small spare bedroom Apthorpe had left what, at a pinch, might be regarded as superfluities.
Three journeys by taxi were required to move them. The Commodore helped with his own hands to carry them downstairs and
load them. When it was accomplished and the hotel porter had

wheeled everything into the vaults, the Commodore asked: 'Staying here long?' and Guy had been obliged to answer: 'I really don't know.'

And still he did not know. Suddenly he found himself alone. The energizing wire between him and the army was cut. He was as immobile as Apthorpe's gear. Various cryptic prohibitions had lately been proclaimed on the movement of goods. Guy sought aid of the RTO and was rebuffed.

'No can do, old boy. Read the regulations. Officers proceeding on, or returning from, leave may take only a haversack and one suitcase. You'll have to get a special move order for that stuff.'

Guy telegraphed to the Adjutant in barracks and after two days received in reply, merely: *Extension of leave granted.*

Here he was still, all animation suspended, while autumn turned sharply to winter, and gales shook the double windows of the hotel and great waves broke over the pill-boxes and barbed wire on the promenade.

Here it seemed he was doomed to remain forever, standing guard over a heap of tropical gadgets, like the Russian sentry he had once been told of, the Guardsman who was posted daily year in, year out, until the revolution, in the grounds of Tsarskoe Selo on the spot where Catherine the Great had once wished to preserve a wild-flower.

Southsand, though unbombed, was thought to be dangerous and had attracted no refugees of the kind who filled other resorts. It was just as he had known it nine months earlier, spacious and desolate and windy and shabby. One change only was apparent; the Ristorante Garibaldi was closed. Mr Pelecci, he learned, had been 'taken away' on the day Italy declared war, consigned in a ship to Canada and drowned in mid-Atlantic, sole spy among a host of innocents. Guy visited Mr Goodall and found him elated by the belief that a great rising was imminent throughout Christian Europe; led by the priests and squires, with blessed banners, and the relics of the saints borne ahead, Poles, Hungarians, Austrians, Bavarians, Italians and plucky little contingents from the Catholic cantons of Switzerland would soon be on the march to redeem the times. Even a few Frenchmen, Mr Goodall conceded, might join this Pilgrimage of Grace but he could promise no part in it for Guy.

The days passed. Ever prone to despond, Guy became sure that his brief adventure was over. He had his pistol. Perhaps, finally, he would get a shot at an invading Storm Trooper and die unrecognized, but sweetly and decorously. More probably he would still be sitting years hence in the Yacht Club and hear on the wireless that the war was won. Ever prone to elaborate his predicament rather fancifully, Guy saw himself make a hermitage of Apthorpe's tent and end his days encamped on the hills above Southsand, painfully acquiring the skills of 'Chatty' Corner, charitably visited once a week by Mr Goodall, a gentler version of poor mad Ivo, who had starved to death in the slums of North-West London.

So Guy mused while even at that moment, in the fullness of his time, 'Jumbo' Trotter was on the move to draw him back into the life of action.

It was All Souls' Day. Guy walked to church to pray for his brothers' souls – for Ivo especially; Gervase seemed far off that year, in Paradise perhaps, in the company of other good soldiers. Mr Goodall was there, popping in and down and up and out and in again assiduously, releasing *toties quoties* soul after soul from Purgatory.

'Twenty-eight so far,' he said. 'I always try and do fifty.'

The wings of the ransomed beat all about Mr Goodall, but as Guy left church he was alone in the comfortless wind.

'Jumbo' arrived after luncheon and found Guy rereading *Vice Versa* in the winter garden. Guy recognized him at once and jumped to his feet.

'Sit down, my dear boy. I've just been making friends with your father.' He unbuttoned himself and took the letter from his breast pocket.

'Something important for you,' he said. 'I don't know what you're up to and I won't ask. I am a mere messenger. Better take it up to your room and read it there. Then burn it. Crumple the ash. Well, I expect in your job, whatever it is, you know more than I do about that sort of thing.'

Guy did as he was told. There was an outer envelope marked in red *By hand of officer* and an inner one marked *Most Secret*. He drew out a simple orderly-room chit on which was typed:

T/y Lt Crouchback, G. Royal Corps of Halberdiers

The above named officer will report forthwith to Flat 211 Marchmain House, St James's, s w 1.

Capt. for Captain-Commandant Royal Corps of Halberdiers.

An undecipherable trail of ink preceded the last line. Even in the innermost depths of military secrecy the Adjutant continued to maintain his anonymity.

The ashes needed no crumbling; they fell in dust from Guy's fingers.

He returned to Jumbo.

'I've just had orders to report in London.'

'Tomorrow will do, I suppose?'

'It says "forthwith".'

'We couldn't get there before dark. Everyone packs up when the sirens go. I can run you up to London tomorrow morning.'

'That's very good of you, sir.'

'It's a pleasure. I like to look in at "the Senior" every so often to hear how the war's going. Plenty of room for you. Have you much luggage?'

'About a ton, sir.'

'Have you, by God? Let's have a look at it.'

Together they visited the baggage store and stood in silence before the heap of steel trunks, leather cases, brass-bound chests, shapeless canvas sacks, buffalo-hide bags. Jumbo was visibly awed. He himself believed in ample provision for the emergencies of travel. Here was something quite beyond his ambition.

'Nearer two tons than one,' he said at length. 'I say, you *must* be up to something? This needs organization. Where are Area Head-quarters?'

'I'm afraid I don't know, sir.'

Such an admission would have earned any other subaltern a rebuke from 'Jumbo', but Guy was now enveloped in an aura of secrecy and importance.

'Lone wolf, eh?' he said. 'I'd better get to work on the blower.'

By this expression Jumbo and many others meant the telephone. He telephoned and presently reported that a lorry would call for them next morning.

'It's a small world,' he said. 'I found the fellow I was talking to at Area was a fellow I used to know well. Junior to me, of course. On old Hamilton-Brand's staff at Gib. Said I'd go along and look him up. Probably dine there. See you in the morning. No point in getting away too early. I told them to have our lorry loaded by ten. All right?'

'Very good, sir.'

'Lucky I knew the fellow at Area. Didn't have to tell him anything about you and your affairs. I just said "Mum's the word" and he twigged.'

All went smoothly next day; they drove to London with the lorry behind them and reached the Duke of York's Steps at one o'clock.

'No use your going to see your fellow now,' said Jumbo. 'Bound to be out. We can lunch here. Must see the men fed too. Problem is to find a place for your gear.'

At this moment a Major-General appeared up the steps, clearly bound for the club. Guy saluted him. Jumbo embraced him by both elbows.

'Beano.'

'Jumbo. What are you up to, old boy?'

'Looking for lunch.'

'Better hurry. Everything decent is off the table by one. Awful greedy lot, the young members.'

'Can you find me a guard, Beano?'

'Impossible, old boy. War House these days. Can't even find a batman.'

'Got a lot of hush-hush stuff here.'

'Tell you what,' said Beano after a pause for thought. 'There's a parking place at the War House, CIGS only. He's away today. I should put your stuff there. No one will touch it. Say it's the CIGS's personal baggage. I'll give your driver a chit. Then he and your other fellow can use the canteen.'

'Good for you, Beano.'

'Not at all, Jumbo.'

Guy accompanied these two senior officers into the club and found himself swept into the dining-room in a surge of naval and military might. Bellamy's had its sprinkling of distinguished officers but here everyone in sight was aflame with red tabs, gold braid, medal ribbons, and undisguised hunger. Guy diffidently stood back from the central table round which, as though at a hunt ball, they were struggling for food.

'Go in and fight for it,' said Beano. 'Every man for himself.'

Guy got the last leg of chicken but a Rear-Admiral deftly whisked it off his plate. Presently he emerged victualled in accordance with his rank with bully beef and beetroot.

'Sure that's all you want?' asked Jumbo hospitably. 'Doesn't look much to me.'

He himself had half a steak pie before him.

Throughout the meal Beano talked of a bomb which had narrowly missed him an evening or two earlier.

'I went down flat on my face, old boy, and got up covered in plaster. A narrow squeak, I can tell you.'

Eventually they left the table.

'Back to the grindstone,' Beano said.

'I'll wait here,' said Jumbo. 'I shan't desert you till I've seen my mission safely accomplished.'

On the steps of the club Guy turned aside from the main stream of members who were making for Whitehall, and walked the quarter-mile to Marchmain House, a block of flats in St James's, where his appointment lay.

Hazardous Offensive Operations Headquarters, that bizarre product of total war which later was to proliferate through five acres of valuable London property, engrossing the simple high staff officers of all the Services with experts, charlatans, plain lunatics and every unemployed member of the British Communist Party – HOO HQ, at this stage of its history, occupied three flats in a supposedly luxurious modern block.

Guy, reporting there, found a Major of about his own age, with the D.S.O., M.C. and a slight stammer. The interview lasted a bare five minutes.

'Crouchback, Crouchback, Crouchback, Crouchback,' he

said, turning over a sheaf of papers on his table. 'Sergeant, what do we know of Mr Crouchback?'

The Sergeant was female and matronly.

'Ritchie-Hook file,' she said. 'General Whale had it last.'

'Go and get it, there's a good girl.'

'I daren't.'

'Well, it doesn't matter. I remember all about it now. You've been wished on us with your former Brigadier for "special duties". What are your "special duties"?'

'I don't know, sir.'

'Nor does anyone. You've come whistling down from a very high level. Do you know all about Commandos?'

'Not much.'

'You shouldn't know anything. They're supposed to be a secret, though from the security reports we get from Mugg, they've made themselves pretty conspicuous there. I've had a letter from someone whose signature I can't read, complaining in strong terms that they've been shooting his deer with tommy-guns. Don't see how they get near enough. Remarkably fine stalking if true. Anyway that's where you're going – temporary attachment for training purposes X Commando, Isle of Mugg. All right?'

'Very good, sir.'

'Sergeant Trenchard here will make out your travel warrant. Have you got a batman with you?'

'At the moment,' said Guy, 'I have a service car, a three-ton lorry, an RASC driver, a Halberdier servant and a full Colonel.'

'Ah,' said the Major who was fast founding the HOO HQ tradition of being surprised at nothing. 'You ought to be all right, then. Report to Colonel Blackhouse at Mugg.'

'Tommy Blackhouse?'

'Friend of yours?'

'Yes. He married my wife.'

'Did he? *Did* he? I thought he was a bachelor.'

'He is, now.'

'Yes, I thought so. I was at the Staff College with him. Good chap; got some good chaps in his Commando too. Glad he's a friend of yours.'

Guy saluted, turned about and departed only very slightly

disconcerted. This was the classic pattern of army life as he had learned it, the vacuum, the spasm, the precipitation, and with it all the peculiar, impersonal, barely human geniality.

Jumbo was asleep in the morning-room when Guy reached him.

'To horse, to horse,' he said, when fully awake and aware of the long road ahead. 'We ought to get clear of London before those bombs begin. Anything that puts the wind up Beano, is better avoided. Besides, we've got your stores to think of.'

Their lorry when they reached it bore marks of promotion. An efficient guard had plastered it with printed notices: *CIGS*.

'Shall I remove those, sir, before starting?'

'Certainly not. They can do no harm and may do a lot of good.'

'Shall I get one for the car too, sir?'

Jumbo paused. He was rather light-headed from his outing, breathing once more the bracing air of his youth when as an irresponsible subaltern he had participated in many wild extravagancies.

'Why not?' he said.

But he thought again. Reason regained its sway. He drew from the deep source of his military experience and knew to a finger's breadth how far one could go.

'No,' he said regretfully. 'That wouldn't do.'

They drove away from the stricken city. At St Albans they turned on the dim little headlights and almost immediately the first sirens wailed around them.

'No point in going much farther tonight,' said Jumbo. 'I know a place where we can put up about thirty miles north.'

6

THE Isle of Mugg has no fame in song or story. Perhaps because whenever they sought a rhyme for the place, they struck absurdity, it was neglected by those romantic early-Victorian English ladies who so prodigally enriched the balladry, folk-lore and costume of the Scottish Highlands. It has a laird, a fishing fleet, an hotel (erected just before the First World War in the unfulfilled hope of attracting tourists) and nothing more. It lies among other monosyllabic protuberances. There is seldom clear weather in those waters, but on certain rare occasions Mugg has been descried from the island of Rum in the form of two cones. The crofters of Muck know it as a single misty lump on their horizon. It has never been seen from Eigg.

It is served twice weekly by steamer from the mainland of Inverness. The passenger rash enough to stay on deck may watch it gradually take shape, first as two steep hills; later he can recognize the castle – granite 1860, indestructible and uninhabitable by anyone but a Scottish laird, the quay, cottages and cliffs, all of granite, and the unmellowed brick of the hotel.

Guy and his entourage arrived at the little port a few hours before this steamer was due to sail. The sky was dark and the wind blowing hard. Jumbo made a snap decision.

'I shall remain here,' he said. 'Mustn't on any account hazard our stores. You go ahead and make your number with your CO. I will follow when the weather clears.'

Guy set out alone to find X Commando.

When the exotic name, 'Commando', was at length made free to the press it rapidly extended its meaning to include curates on motor bicycles. In 1940 a Commando was a military unit, about the size of a battalion, composed of volunteers for special service. They kept the badges of their regiments; no flashes or green berets then, nothing to display in inns. They were a secret force whose only privilege was to find their own billets and victuals. Each unit took its character from its commander.

Tommy Blackhouse declared: 'It's going to be a long war. The great thing is to spend it among friends.'

Tommy's friends inhabited his own ample world. Some were regular soldiers; others had spent a year or two of adolescence in the Brigade of Guards, to satisfy the whim of parents and trustees, before taking to other activities or to inactivity. To these he turned when at last his patiently awaited appointment was confirmed. Bellamy's rallied to him. He sent his troop leaders on a recruiting tour of their regiments. Too soon for some the Commando came into existence and was dispatched to train at Mugg. There Guy found them. He was directed from the quay to the hotel.

At three o'clock he found it empty except for a Captain of the Blues who reclined upon a sofa, his head enveloped in a turban of lint, his feet shod in narrow velvet slippers embroidered in gold thread with his monogram. He was nursing a white pekinese; beside him stood a glass of white liqueur.

The sofa was upholstered in Turkey carpet. The table which held the glass and bottle was octagonal, inlaid with mother-of-pearl. The pictorial effect was of a young prince of the Near East in his grand divan in the early years of the century.

He did not look up on Guy's entry.

Guy recognized Ivor Claire, a young show-jumper of repute, the owner of a clever and beautiful horse named Thimble. Guy had seen them in Rome at the Concorso Ippico; Claire leaning slightly forward in the saddle with the intent face of a pianist, the horse precisely placing his feet in the tan, leaping easily, without scuffle or hesitation, completing a swift, faultless round, in dead silence which broke at last into a tumult of appreciation. Guy knew him, too, as a member of Bellamy's. He should have known Guy for they had often sat opposite one another in the listless days of the preceding year and had stood together in the same group at the bar.

'Good afternoon,' said Guy.

Claire looked up, said, 'Good afternoon,' and wiped his dog's face with a silk handkerchief. 'The snow is very bad for Freda's eyes. Perhaps you want Colonel Tommy. He's out climbing.' Then, after a pause, politely: 'Have you seen last week's paper?'

And he held out the *Rum, Muck, Mugg and Eigg Times*.

Guy gazed about him at the heads of deer, the fumed oak staircase, the vast extent of carpet woven in the local hunting tartan.

'I think I've seen you about in Bellamy's.'

'How one longs for it.'

'My name is Crouchback.'

'Ah.' Claire had the air of having very shrewdly elicited this piece of information, of having made a move, early in a game of chess, which would later develop into mate. 'I should have some Kümmel if I were you. We've unearthed a cache of Wolfschmidt. You just score it up on that piece of paper over there.'

There were glasses on the central table and bottles and a list of names, marked with their potations.

'I'm here for training,' Guy volunteered.

'It's a death-trap.'

'Have you any idea where my quarters will be?'

'Colonel Tommy lives here. So do most of us. But it's full up now. Recent arrivals are at the coastguard station, I believe. I looked in once. It smells awfully of fish. I say, do you mind much if we don't talk? I fell fifty feet on the ice the other morning.'

Guy studied last week's *Rum, Muck, Mugg and Eigg Times*. Claire plucked Freda's eyebrows.

Soon, as in an old-fashioned, well-constructed comedy, other characters began to enter Left: first a medical officer.

'Is the boat in?' he asked of both indiscriminately.

Claire shut his eyes, so Guy answered: 'I came in her a few minutes ago.'

'I must telephone the harbour-master and have her held. Anstruther-Kerr has had a fall. They're bringing him down as fast as they can.'

Claire opened his eyes.

'Poor Angus. Dead?'

'Certainly not. But I must get him to the mainland at once.'

'That is your opportunity,' Claire said to Guy. 'Angus had a room here.'

The doctor went to the telephone, Guy to the reception office.

The manageress said: 'Poor Sir Angus, and he a Scot too. He should know better than to go scrambling about the rocks at his age.'

As Guy returned, an enormous Grenadier Captain in the tradition of comedy hustled into the hall. He was dressed in damp dungarees and panting heavily.

'Thank God,' he said. 'Just made it. Angus's fall has started a stampede. I was half-way up the cliff when we got the news and slid down fast.'

The medical officer returned.

'They'll hold the steamer another fifteen minutes. They say they can't make port in the dark.'

'Well,' said the breathless Captain, 'I'll cut along and get his room.'

'Too late, Bertie,' said Claire. 'It's gone.'

'Not possible.' Then he noticed Guy. 'Oh,' he said. 'Damn.'

The stretcher party arrived and a comatose figure, covered in great-coats, was gently laid on the tartan floor while the stretcher-bearers went up to pack his belongings.

Another gasping officer arrived.

'Oh, God, Bertie,' he said, seeing the Grenadier, 'have you got his room?'

'I have not, Eddie. You should be out with your troop.'

'I just thought I should come and make arrangements for Angus.'

'Don't make such a noise,' said the doctor. 'Can't you see there's a sick man here?'

'Two sick men,' said Claire.

'Isn't he dead?'

'They say not.'

'*I* was told he was.'

'Perhaps you will allow me to know better,' said the doctor.

As though to resolve the argument, a muffled voice from the stretcher said: 'Itching, Eddie. Itching all over like hell.'

'Formication,' said the doctor. 'Morphia often has that effect.'

'How very odd,' said Claire, showing real interest for the first time. 'I've an aunt who takes quantities of it. I wonder if she itches.'

'Well, if you haven't got it, Bertie,' said Eddie, 'I think I'll just cut along and get that room fixed up for myself.'

'Too late. It's gone.'

Eddie looked incredulously around the hall, saw Guy for the first time and like Bertie said: 'Damn.'

It occurred to Guy that he had better make sure of his claim. He carried his valise and suitcase upstairs and before Anstruther-Kerr's hair brushes were off the dressing-table, his were on it. He unpacked fully, waited until the stretcher-bearers had finished their work, then followed them, locking the door behind him.

More damp and snowy officers were gathered below, among

them Tommy Blackhouse. No one took any notice of Guy, except Tommy, who said:

'Hullo, Guy. What on earth brings you here?'

There was a very slight difference between the Tommy whom he had known for twelve years and Tommy the commanding officer, which made Guy say: 'I've orders to report to you, Colonel.'

'Well, it's the first I've heard about it. I looked for you when we were forming, but that ass Job said you'd gone to Cornwall or somewhere. Anyway, we're losing chaps so fast that there's room for anyone. Bertie, have we had any bumf about this Applejack – Guy Crouchback?'

'May be in the last bag, Colonel. I haven't opened it yet.'

'Well, for Christ's sake do.'

He turned again to Guy. 'Any idea what you're supposed to be here for?'

'Attached for training.'

'For you to train us, or for us to train you?'

'Oh, for you to train me.'

'Thank God for that. The last little contribution from HOO HQ came to train us. And that reminds me, Bertie, Kong must go.'

'Very good, Colonel.'

'Can you get him on Angus's boat?'

'Too late.'

'Everything always seems to be too late in this bloody island. Keep him away from my men anyhow, until we find somewhere to hide him. I'll see you later, Guy, and sort you out. *Very* pleased you're here. Come on, Bertie. We've got to open that bag and get some signals off.'

The melting men in dungarees began to fill their glasses.

Guy said to Eddie: 'I take it Bertie is the Adjutant?'

'In a sort of way.'

'Who is Kong?'

'Difficult to say. He looks like a gorilla. They caught him somewhere in HOO HQ and sent him here to teach us to climb. We call him King Kong.'

Presently the medical officer returned.

Everyone except Guy, who felt that his acquaintance was too small to justify solicitude, asked news of Angus.

'Quite comfortable.'

'Not itching?' asked Claire.

'He's as comfortable as possible. I've arranged for his reception the other end.'

'Well, in that case, doc, will you come and have a look at that chap of mine, Cramp, who took a toss today?'

'And I wish you'd see Corporal Blake, the fellow you patched up yesterday.'

'I'll see them at sick parade tomorrow.'

'Blake doesn't look fit to walk. No, come on, doc, and I'll stand you a drink. I don't like the look of him.'

'And Trooper Eyre,' said another officer. 'He's either tight or delirius. He landed on his head yesterday.'

'Probably tight,' said Claire.

The doctor looked at him with loathing. 'Rightho. You'll have to show me their billets.'

Soon Guy and Claire were left alone once more.

'I'm glad you beat Bertie and the rest to that room,' said Claire. 'Of course you can't expect it to make you popular. But perhaps you won't be here very long.' He shut his eyes and for some minutes there was silence.

The final entry was a man in the kilt and uniform of a highland regiment. He carried a tall shepherd's staff and said in a voice that had more of the Great West Road in it than of the Pass of Glencoe, 'Sorry to hear about Angus.'

Claire looked at him. 'Angus who?' he asked with distaste that was near malevolence.

'Kerr, of course.'

'You are referring to Captain Sir Angus Anstruther-Kerr?'

'Who do you think?'

'I did not speculate.'

'Well, how is he?'

'He is said to be comfortable. If so, it must be the first occasion for weeks.'

During this conversation Guy had been studying the newcomer with growing wonder. At length he said:

'Trimmer.'

The figure, bonnet, sporran, staff and all, swung round.

'Why, if it isn't my old uncle!'

Claire said to Guy, 'Are you in fact related to this officer?'

'No.'

'On the occasions he has been here, we have known him as McTavish.'

'Trimmer is a sort of nickname,' said Trimmer.

'Curious. I remember your lately asking me to call you "Ali".'

'That's another nickname – short for Alistair, you know.'

'So I supposed. I won't ask you what "Trimmer" is short for. "Trimlestown" hardly seems probable. Well, I will leave you two old friends together. Good-bye, *Trimmer*.'

'So long, Ivor,' said Trimmer unabashed.

When they were alone, Trimmer said:

'You musn't mind old Ivor. He and I are great pals and chaff each other a bit. Did you spot his M.C.? Do you know how he got it? At Dunkirk, for shooting three territorials who were trying to swamp his boat. Great chap old Ivor. Care to give me a drink, uncle? That was the object of the exercise.'

'Why are you called McTavish?'

'That's rather a long story. My mother is a McTavish. Chaps often sign on under assumed names, you know. After I left the Halberdiers I didn't want to hang about waiting to be called up. My firm had been bombed out and I was rather at a loose end. So I went to Glasgow and joined up, no questions asked. McTavish seemed the right sort of name. I fairly whizzed through OCTU. None of that pomp and ceremony of the Halberdiers. I get a good laugh when I remember those guest nights and the snuff and all that rot. So here I am with the Jocks.' He had already helped himself to whisky. 'One for you? I'll sign Angus's name for both. It is a good system they have here. I often drop in and if there isn't a pal about, I sign another bloke's name. Only chaps I know would give me a drink if they were in, of course. Chaps like Angus, who's a Scot too.'

'You can sign my name,' said Guy. 'I belong here.'

'Good for you, uncle. Cheers. I've sometimes thought of joining the Commando myself, but I am sitting pretty snug at the moment. The rest of my battalion went off to Iceland. We had a roughish farewell party and I got a wrist sprained, so they left me behind with the other odds and sods and then we got sent here on defence duties.'

'Bad luck.'

'I don't imagine I'm missing much fun in Iceland. I say, talking of roughish parties, do you remember how you sprained a knee at that guest night with the Halberdiers?'

'I do.'

'Well, the chap they call King Kong was there.'

'Chatty Corner?'

'Never heard the name. Bloke who passed out.'

'The very man I am looking for.'

'No accounting for tastes. He's got himself quite a reputation in these parts as a killer. He lives round the point near our gun. A mean sort of billet. Never been inside. I'll take you there now if you like.'

It was deadly cold out of doors and the light fading. Beyond the quays lay a stone track, iced over now, in the shadows of the cliff. Guy envied Trimmer his shepherd's staff. They made slow time towards the point.

Trimmer pointed out local places of interest.

'That's where Angus came down.'

They paused, then made slowly forward until, rounding the cape, they met the biting wind.

'There's my gun,' said Trimmer.

Through tear-filled eyes Guy saw something sheeted, pointing out to sea.

'Salvage, off an armed trawler that got sunk near shore. We've got twenty rounds with her too.'

'I'll see it another day.'

'At the moment one of the twenty rounds is stuck half in and half out of the breech. Can't move it one way or the other. Tried everything. My men aren't used to artillery. Why should they be?'

Presently they came to a cluster of huts with some dim, golden windows.

'That's where the natives hang out. One can't make them understand black-out. Got Mugg to lecture them. No good.'

'Mugg?'

54

'That's what he calls himself. Stuffy old goat but he seems to be God almighty in these parts. Lives in the Castle.'

At last they reached a high, solitary building. What few and small windows it had were deep shadows. Not a chink showed.

'They call that the Old Castle. The factor lives there and Kong with him. I'll leave you here, if you don't mind. Kong and I don't hit it off and the factor's always making dirty cracks about my being Scotch.'

They parted with words of friendliness which froze like their breath in the wind and Guy approached the unfriendly place alone – *Child Roland to the dark tower*, he thought.

Whatever the age of the building – its outline seemed medieval – the entrance was Victorian and prosaic; a small granite porch, with brass on the door, which was embellished with small stained-glass panels. Guy, in obedience to the instructions dimly legible by torch light on the brass plate, knocked and rang. Soon there was a glimmer of light, footsteps, the turning of a lock and the door stood three inches open on its chain. A female voice challenged him, as plain in meaning and as obscure in vocabulary as the bark of a dog. Guy answered firmly: 'Captain James Pendennis Corner.'

'The Captain?'

'Corner,' said Guy.

The door shut and firm feet in loose slippers wandered away and the light in the glass panels with them.

Guy huddled in the lee of the little granite column. The wind blew harder, deafening him to the sounds of lock and chain within, so that when the door suddenly opened, he stumbled and nearly fell into the lightless hall. He was aware of the door being banged to and of the presence of another human being, first quite near him, then retreating and mounting. He stood where he was until a door above him opened and cast a golden light over the hall and a stone spiral staircase which rose immediately in front of him. A female figure stood black in the doorway. The structure no doubt was medieval but the scene might have been a set by Gordon Craig for a play of Maeterlinck's.

'Who the devil is it?' said a deep voice from within.

Guy climbed as cautiously as he had walked the track. The

granite steps were smoother and harder than the ice outside. The female withdrew upwards into the shadows as he approached.

'Come in, whoever you are,' said the voice within.

Guy entered.

Thus he attained Chatty Corner's lair.

It had been a day of diverse happenings; the warm breakfast with Jumbo, the long drive over the frozen moorland, the sea-crossing during which Guy had sat below, gripping the corner of the teak table – receiving whenever he relaxed his hold a tremendous buffet backward and forward into one corner or other of the little saloon; the Kümmel at tea time, the drugged, sheeted figure of Anstruther-Kerr, whisky with Trimmer, the agonizing stumbling march against the wind, the villa door which opened into the dark tower – it had been an unnerving day and its climax found Guy so confounded between truth and fantasy that he was prepared, as he entered the room, to find a *tableau* from some ethnographic museum, some shaggy, prognathous hypothetical ancestor, sharpening a flint spear-head among a heap of gnawed bones between walls scrawled with imitation Picassos. Instead he found a man, bulky and hirsute indeed, but a man made in the same image as himself, and plainly far from well, wrapped in army blankets, seated before a peat fire on a commonplace upright chair, with his feet in a steaming bucket of mustard and water. At his hand stood a whisky bottle and on the hob a kettle of water.

'Chatty,' said Guy; tears of emotion filled his eyes (the lachrymatory glands being already over-stimulated by the cold wind). 'Chatty, is it really you?'

Chatty stared under his lowering brow, sneezed and drank hot whisky. Plainly his memories of the night with the Halberdiers were less vivid than Guy's.

'They called me that in Africa,' he said at last. 'Here they call me "Kong". Can't think why.'

He stared and sipped and sneezed. 'Can't think why they called me "Chatty" in Africa. My names are James Pendennis.'

'I know. I have been advertising for you in *The Times*.'

'*Rum, Muck, Mugg and Eigg Times*?'

'No, the London *Times*.'

'Well, that wouldn't be much good, would it? Not,' he added in fairness, 'that I often read the *Rum, Muck, Mugg and Eigg Times*, either. I'm not much of a reading man.'

Guy saw that the conversation must be brought sharply to its point.

'Apthorpe,' he said.

'Yes,' said Chatty. 'He's one for reading papers. Reads anything he picks up. He's a very well-informed man, Apthorpe. There's nothing he doesn't know about. He's told me a lot of things you'd never believe, Apthorpe has. Do you know him?'

'He's dead.'

'No, no. I dined with him less than a year ago in his mess. I'm afraid I got a bit tight that evening. Apthorpe used to hit the bottle a bit, you know.'

'Yes, I know. And now he's dead.'

'I'm very sorry to hear it.' He sneezed, drank and silently pondered the news. 'A man who knew everything. No age either. Years younger than me. What did he die of?'

'I suppose you might call it Bechuana tummy.'

'Beastly complaint. Never heard of anyone dying of it before. Very well off, too.'

'Not *very*, surely?'

'Private means. *Everyone* with *any* private means is well off. That's what has always held *me* back. Parson's son. No private means.'

It was like the game Guy used to play when he was an undergraduate and stayed at country houses – the game in which two contestants strove to introduce a particular sentence into their conversation in a natural manner. This was Guy's opening.

'Whatever money he had, he left to his aunt.'

'He used to talk a lot about his aunts. One lived . . .'

'But,' said Guy inexorably, 'he left all his tropical gear to you. I've got it here – on the mainland, at least – to hand over.'

Chatty refilled his glass. 'Decent of him,' said Chatty. 'Decent of you.'

'There's an awful lot of it.'

'Yes. He was always collecting more and more. He used to show it to me whenever I dropped in. He was the soul of hospitality, Apthorpe. He used to put me up, you know, when I was in from the bush. We used to drink a lot at the club and then he'd show me his latest purchases. It was quite a routine.'

'But wasn't he in the bush, too?'

'Apthorpe! No, he had his job to look after in town. I took him for a day or two's shooting now and then – repaying hospitality, you know. But he was such an awful bad shot and got in the way, poor chap, and he never had long enough leave to travel any distance. They work them jolly hard in the tobacco company.'

Chatty sneezed.

'This is the hell of a place to send a man like me,' he continued. 'I offered my services as a tropical expert when the war began. They put me in charge of a jungle warfare school. Then, after Dunkirk, that was abolished and they somehow got my name on a list of mountaineers. Never been out of the bush in my life. I don't know a thing about rocks, still less ice. No wonder we get casualties.'

'About your gear,' said Guy firmly.

'Oh, don't worry about that. There's nothing I should need here, I don't suppose. I'll look it over some time. There's a perfectly awful fellow called McTavish lives next door. He goes across to the mainland now and then. I'll go with him, one of these days.'

'Chatty, you don't understand. I've legal obligations. I *must* hand over your legacy to you.'

'My dear chap, I shan't sue you.'

'There are moral obligations, too. Please. I can't explain, but it's most important to me.'

The wind howled and Chatty began:

'Queer old place this. Used to be the laird's castle before they built the present edifice. His agent lives here now.'

'Chatty, I think I can get your stuff over. I have connexions on the mainland.'

'They say it's haunted. I suppose it is in a way, but I tell them if they'd seen a few of the things I've seen in Africa . . .'

'Plenty of storage here. I expect there's a cellar. All the gear will fit in without being in the way of anyone . . .'

'There was a village just north of Tambago . . .'

'Chatty,' said Guy. 'Will you do this? Will you sign for it?'

'Unseen?'

'Unseen and in triplicate.'

'I don't know much about the law.'

Guy folded the carbon paper in his field notebook and wrote: *Received 7 November 1940 Apthorpe's gear.*

'Sign here,' he said.

Chatty took the book and studied it with his head first on one side and then on the other. Till the final moment Guy feared he would refuse. Then Chatty wrote, large and irregularly, *J. P. Corner.*

Suddenly the wind dropped. It was a holy moment. Guy rose in silence and ritually received the book.

'Come back when you've time for a pow-wow,' said Chatty. 'I'd like to tell you about that village near Tambago.'

Guy descended and let himself out. It was cold but the wind had lost all its hostility. The sky was clear. There was even a moon. He calmly made his way back to the hotel which was full of the Commando.

Tommy greeted him.

'Guy, I've bad news. You've got to dine out tonight at the Castle. The old boy had been making a lot of complaints so I sent Angus round to make peace. He couldn't see the laird but it turned out he was some kind of cousin, so next day I got a formal invitation to dine there with Angus. I can't chuck now. No one else wants to come. You're the last to join, so go and change quick. We're off in five minutes.'

In his room Guy superstitiously deposited each copy of Chatty's acquittal in a separate hiding-place.

7

THE seat of Colonel Hector Campbell of Mugg was known locally as 'the New Castle', to distinguish it from the ancient and more picturesque edifice occupied by the factor and Chatty Corner. The Campbells of Mugg had never been rich but at some moment in the middle of the nineteenth century a marriage, or the sale of property on the mainland which was being transformed from

moorland to town, or a legacy from emigrant kinsmen in Canada
or Australia – by an accession of fortune of some kind common
among lairds, the Mugg of the time got money in his hands and
proceeded to build. The fortune melted, but the new castle stood.
The exterior was German in character, Bismarckian rather than
Wagnerian, of moderate size but designed to withstand assault
from all but the most modern weapons. The interior was pitch-
pine throughout and owed its decoration more to the taxidermist
than to sculptor or painter.

Before Guy and Tommy had left their car, the double doors of
the New Castle were thrown open. A large young butler, kilted
and heavily bearded, seemed to speak some words of welcome but
they were lost in a gale of music. A piper stood beside him, more
ornately clothed, older and shorter; a square man, red bearded.
If it had come to a fight between them the money would have been
on the piper. He was in fact the butler's father. The four of them
marched forward and upward to the great hall.

A candelabrum, consisting of concentric and diminishing circles
of tarnished brass, hung from the rafters. A dozen or so of the
numberless cluster of electric bulbs were alight, disclosing the dim
presence of a large circular dinner table. Round the chimney-
piece, whose armorial decorations were obscured by smoke, the
baronial severity of the rest of the furniture was mitigated by a
group of chairs clothed in stained and faded chintz. Everywhere
else were granite, pitch-pine, tartan and objects of furniture con-
structed of antlers. Six dogs, ranging in size from a couple of deer-
hounds to an almost hairless pomeranian, gave tongue in inverse
proportion to their size. Above all from the depths of the smoke
cloud a voice roared.

'Silence, you infernal brutes. Down, Hercules. Back, Jason.
Silence, sir.'

There were shadowy, violent actions and sounds of whacking,
kicking, snarling and whining. Then the piper had it all to himself
again. It was intensely cold in the hall and Guy's eyes wept anew
in the peat fumes. Presently the piper, too, was hushed and in the
stunning silence an aged lady and gentleman emerged through the
smoke. Colonel Campbell was much bedizened with horn and
cairngorms. He wore a velvet doublet above his kilt, high stiff

collar and a black bow tie. Mrs Campbell wore nothing memorable.

The dogs fanned out beside them and advanced at the same slow pace, silent but menacing. His probable destiny seemed manifest to Guy, to be blinded by smoke among the armchairs, to be frozen to death in the wider spaces, or to be devoured by the dogs where he stood. Tommy, the perfect soldier, appreciated the situation and acted promptly. He advanced on the nearest deerhound, grasped its muzzle and proceeded to rotate its head in a manner which the animal appeared to find reassuring. The great tail began to wave in the fumes. The hushed dogs covered their fangs and advanced to sniff first at his trousers, then at Guy's. Meanwhile Tommy said:

'I'm awfully sorry we couldn't let you know in time. Angus Anstruther-Kerr had an accident today on the rocks. I didn't want to leave you a man short, so I've brought Mr Crouchback instead.'

Guy had already observed the vast distances that separated the few places at table and thought this explanation of his presence less than adequate to the laird's style of living. Mrs Campbell took his hand gently.

'Mugg will be disappointed. We make more of kinship here than you do in the south, you know. He's a little deaf, by the way.'

But Mugg had firmly taken his hand.

'I never met your father,' he said. 'But I knew his uncle, Kerr of Gellioch, before his father married Jean Anstruther of Glenaldy. You resemble neither the one nor the other. Glenaldy was a fine man, though he was old when I knew him, and it was a sorrow having no son, to pass the place of Gellioch to.'

'This is Mr Crouchback, dear.'

'Maybe, maybe, I don't recollect. Where's dinner?'

'Katie's not here yet.'

'Is she dining down tonight?'

'You know she is, dear. We discussed it. Katie is Mugg's great-niece from Edinburgh, who's paying us a visit.'

'Visit? She's been here three years.'

'She worked too hard at her exams,' said Mrs Campbell.

'We'll not wait for her,' said Mugg.

As they sat at the round table the gulf that should have been filled by Katie, lay between Guy and his host. Tommy had at once begun a brisk conversation about local tides and beaches with Mrs Campbell. The laird looked at Guy, decided the distance between them was insurmountable and contentedly splashed about in his soup.

Presently he looked up again and said:

'Got any gun-cotton?'

'I'm afraid not.'

'Halberdier?'

'Yes.'

He nodded towards Tommy.

'Coldstreamer?'

'Yes.'

'Same outfit?'

'Yes.'

'Extraordinary thing.'

'We're rather a mixed unit.'

'Argyll myself, of course. No mixture there. They tried cross-posting at the end of the last war. Never worked.'

Fish appeared. Colonel Campbell was silent while he ate, got into trouble with some bones, buried his head in his napkin, took out his teeth and at last got himself to rights.

'Mugg finds fish very difficult nowadays,' said Mrs Campbell during this process.

The host looked at Tommy with a distinctly crafty air now and said:

'Saw some sappers the day before yesterday.'

'They must have been ours.'

'They got gun-cotton?'

'Yes, I think so. They've got a lot of stores marked "Danger".'

The laird now looked sternly at Guy.

'Don't you think it would have been a more honest answer to admit it in the first place?'

Tommy and Mrs Campbell stopped talking of landing-places and listened.

'When I asked you if you had gun-cotton, do you suppose I imagined you were carrying it on your person now? I meant, have you brought any gun-cotton on to my island?'

Here Tommy intervened. 'I hope you've no complaint about it being misused, sir?'

'Or dynamite?' continued the laird disregarding. 'Any explosive would do.'

At this moment the piper put an end to the conversation. He was followed by the butler bearing a huge joint which he set before the host. Round and round went the skirl. Colonel Campbell hacked away at the haunch of venison. The butler followed his own devious course with a tray of red-currant jelly and unpeeled potatoes. Not before the din was over and a full plate before him did Guy realize that a young lady had unobtrusively slipped into the chair beside him. He bowed as best he could from the intricate framework of antlers which constituted his chair. She returned his smile of greeting liberally.

She was, he judged, ten or twelve years younger than himself. Either she was freckled, which seemed unlikely at this place and season, or else she had been splashed with peaty water and had neglected to wash, which seemed still less likely in view of the obvious care she had taken with the rest of her toilet. An hereditary stain perhaps, Guy thought, suddenly appearing in Mugg to bear evidence of an ancestral seafaring adventure long ago among the Spice Islands. Over the brown blotches she was richly rouged, her short black curls were bound with a tartan ribbon, held together by a brooch of the kind Guy had supposed were made only for tourists, and she wore a dress which in that hall must have exposed her to an extremity of frigeration. Her features were regular as marble and her eyes wide and splendid and mad.

'You aren't doing very well, are you?' she remarked suddenly on a note of triumph.

'This is Mr Crouchback, dear,' said Mrs Campbell, frowning fiercely at her husband's great-niece. 'Miss Carmichael. She comes from Edinburgh.'

'And a true Scot,' said Miss Carmichael.

'Yes, of course, Kate. We all know that.'

'Her grandmother was a Campbell,' said the laird, in a tone of deepest melancholy, 'my own mother's sister.'

'My mother was a Meiklejohn and her mother a Dundas.'

'No one is questioning your being a true Scot, Katie,' said the great-aunt; 'eat your dinner.'

During this exchange of genealogical information, Guy had pondered on Miss Carmichael's strange preliminary challenge. He had not distinguished himself, he fully realized, in the preceding conversation, though it would have taken a master, he thought, to go right. And, anyway, how did this beastly girl know? Had she been hiding her freckles in the smoke, or, more likely, was she that phenomenon, quite common, he believed, in these parts – the seventh child of a seventh child? He had had a hard day. He was numb and choked and under-nourished. An endless procession marched across his mind, Carmichaels, Campbells, Meiklejohns, Dundases, in columns of seven, some kilted and bonneted, others in the sober, durable garb of the Edinburgh professions, all dead.

He steadied himself with wine, which in contrast to soup or fish was excellent. 'Doing well', of course, was an expression of the nursery. It meant eating heavily. Hitherto instinct and experience alike had held him back from the venison. Now, openly rebuked, he put a fibrous, rank lump of the stuff into his mouth and began desperately chewing. Miss Carmichael turned back to him.

'Six ships last week,' she said. 'We can't get Berlin, so we have to go by your wireless. I expect it's a lot more really, ten, twenty, thirty, forty . . .'

The laird cut across this speculation by saying to Tommy, 'That's what sappers are for, aren't they? – blowing things up.'

'They built the Anglican Cathedral in Gibraltar,' said Guy, in a stern effort to 'do better' but rather indistinctly, for the venison seemed totally unassimilable.

'No,' said the laird. 'I went to a wedding there. They didn't blow that up. Not at the time of the wedding anyhow. But rocks, now.' (He looked craftily at Tommy.) 'They could blow rocks up, I dare say, just as easily as you and I would blow up a wasps' nest.'

'I should keep a long way off if they tried,' said Tommy.

'I always told my men that the nearer you are to the point of an explosion, the safer you are.'

'That's not the orthodox teaching nowadays, I'm afraid.'

Miss Carmichael had stopped counting and said:

'We have quite grown out of the Bonnie Prince Charlie phase, you know. Edinburgh is the heart of Scotland now.'

'A magnificent city,' said Guy.

'It's *seething*.'

'Really?'

'Absolutely seething. It is time I went back there. But I'm not allowed to talk about it, of course.'

She produced from her bag a gold pencil and wrote on the table-cloth, guarding her message with her forearm.

'Look.'

Guy read: 'POLLITICAL PRISNER' and asked with genuine curiosity:

'Did you *pass* your exams at Edinburgh, Miss Carmichael?'

'Never. I was far too busy with more important things.'

She began vigorously rubbing the cloth with breadcrumbs and suddenly, disconcertingly, assumed party manners saying:

'I miss the music so. All the greatest masters come to Edinburgh, you know.'

While she wrote, Guy had managed to remove the venison from his mouth to his plate. He took a draft of claret and said clearly:

'I wonder if you came across a friend of mine at the University. Peter Ellis – he teaches Egyptology or something like that. He used to seethe awfully when I knew him.'

'He did not seethe *with us*.'

The laird had finished his plateful and was ready to resume the subject of explosives.

'They need practice,' he roared, interrupting his wife and Tommy who were discussing submarines.

'We all do, I expect,' said Tommy.

'I will show them just the place. I *own* the hotel, of course,' he added without apparent relevance.

'You think it spoils the view? I'm inclined to agree with you.'

'Only one thing wrong with the hotel. Do you know what?'

'The heating?'

'It doesn't pay. And d'you know why not? No bathing beach. Send those sappers of yours up to me and I can show them the very place for their explosion. Shift a few tons of rock and what do you find? Sand. There was sand there in my father's time. It's marked as sand on the Survey and the Admiralty chart. Bit of the cliff came down; all it needs is just lifting up again.'

The laird scooped the air as though building an imaginary sand-castle.

With the pudding came the nine-o'clock news. A wireless-set was carried to the centre of the table, and the butler tried to adjust it.

'Lies,' said Miss Carmichael. 'All lies.'

There was a brief knock-about turn such as Scots often provide for their English guests, between the laird and his butler, each displaying feudal loyalty, independence, pure uncontrolled crossness and ignorance of the workings of modern science.

Sounds emerged but nothing which Guy could identify as human speech.

'Lies,' repeated Miss Carmichael. 'All lies.'

Presently the machine was removed and replaced with apples.

'Something about Khartoum, wasn't it?' said Tommy.

'It will be retaken,' announced Miss Carmichael.

'But it was never lost,' said Guy.

'It was lost to Kitchener and the Gatling-gun,' said Miss Carmichael.

'Mugg served under Kitchener,' said Mrs Campbell.

'There was something I never liked about the fellow. Something fishy, if you know what I mean.'

'It is a terrible thing,' said Miss Carmichael, 'to see the best of our lads marched off, generation after generation, to fight the battles of the English for them. But the end is upon them. When the Germans land in Scotland, the glens will be full of marching men come to greet them, and the professors themselves at the universities will seize the towns. Mark my words, don't be caught on Scottish soil on that day.'

'Katie, go to bed,' said Colonel Campbell.

'Have I gone too far again?'

'You have.'

'May I take some apples with me?'

'Two.'

She took them and rose from her chair.

'Good night, all,' she said jauntily.

'It was those exams,' said Mrs Campbell. 'Far too advanced for

a girl. I will leave you to your port,' and she followed Miss Carmichael out, perhaps to chide her, perhaps to calm her with a glass
of whisky.

Colonel Campbell was not by habit a drinker of port. The glasses
were very small indeed and it did not need the seventh child of a
seventh child to detect that the wine had been decanted for some
time. Two wasps floated there. The laird, filling his own glass first,
neatly caught one of them. He held it up to his eye and studied it
with pride.

'It was there when the war began,' he said solemnly. 'And I was
hoping it could lie there until we pledged our victory. Port, you
understand, being more a matter of ceremony here than of enjoy-
ment. Gentlemen, the King.'

They swallowed the noxious wine. At once Mugg said:

'Campbell, the decanter!'

Heavy cut-glass goblets were set before the three men; a trumpery little china jug of water and a noble decanter of almost colourless, slightly clouded liquid.

'Whisky,' said Mugg with satisfaction. 'Let me propose a toast.
The Coldstream, the Halberdiers *and* the Sappers.'

They sat round the table for an hour or more. They talked of
military matters with as much accord as was possible between a
veteran of Spion Cop and tyros of 1940. They reverted in their
talk, every few minutes, to the subject of high explosive. Then Mrs
Campbell returned to them. They stood up. She said:

'Oh dear, how quickly the evening goes. I've barely seen anything of you. But I suppose you have to get up so early in the
mornings.'

Mugg put the stopper in the whisky decanter.

Before Tommy or Guy could speak, the piper was among them.
They mouthed their farewells and followed him to the front door.
As they got into their car they saw a storm-lantern waving wildly
from an upper window. Tommy made the gesture of taking a
salute, the piper turned about and blew away up the corridor. The
great doors shut. The lantern continued to wave and in the silence
came the full and friendly challenge: 'Heil Hitler.'

Tommy and Guy did not exchange a word on the road home.
Instead they laughed, silently at first, then loud and louder. Their

driver later reported that he had never seen the Colonel like it, and as for the new Copper Heel, he was 'well away'. He added that his own entertainment below stairs had been 'quite all right too'.

Tommy and Guy were indeed inebriated, not solely, nor in the main, by what they had drunk. They were caught up and bowled over together by that sacred wind which once blew freely over the young world. Cymbals and flutes rang in their ears. The grim isle of Mugg was full of scented breezes, momentarily uplifted, swept away and set down under the stars of the Aegean.

Men who have endured danger and privation together often separate and forget one another when their ordeal is ended. Men who have loved the same woman are blood brothers even in enmity; if they laugh together, as Tommy and Guy laughed that night, orgiastically, they seal their friendship on a plane rarer and loftier than normal human intercourse.

When they reached the hotel Tommy said:

'Thank God you were there, Guy.'

They moved from the heights of fantasy into an unusual but essentially prosaic scene.

The hall had become a gaming-house. On the second day of the Commando's arrival Ivor Claire had ordered the local carpenter, a grim Calvinist with an abhorrence of cards, to make a baccarat shoe on the pretext that it was an implement of war. He now sat at the central table, which was now neatly chalked into sections, paying out a bank. At other tables there was a game of poker and two couples of backgammon. Tommy and Guy made for the table of drinks.

'Twenty pounds in the bank!'

Without turning round Tommy called 'Banco', filled his glass and joined the large table.

Bertie from the poker table asked Guy:

'Want a hand? Half-crown ante and five-bob raise.'

But the cymbals and flutes were still sounding faintly in Guy's ears. He shook his head and wandered dreamily upstairs to a dreamless sleep.

'Tight,' said Bertie. 'Tight as a drum.'

'Good luck to him.'

Next morning at breakfast Guy was told: 'Ivor cleaned up more than £150 last night.'

'They weren't playing a big game when I saw them.'

'Things always tend to get bigger when Colonel Tommy is about.'

It was still dark outside at breakfast-time. The heating apparatus was not working yet; the newly rekindled peat fire sent a trickle of smoke into the dining-room. It was intensely cold.

Civilian waitresses attended them. Presently one of them approached Guy.

'Lieutenant Crouchback?'

'Yes.'

'There's a soldier outside asking for you.'

Guy went to the door and found the driver from last night. There was something indefinably cheeky about the man's greeting.

'I found these in the car, sir. I don't know whether they are the Colonel's or yours.'

He handed Guy a bundle of printed papers. Guy examined the top sheet and read, in large letters:

CALL TO SCOTLAND.
ENGLANDS PERIL IS SCOTLANDS HOPE.
WHY HITLER MUST WIN.

This, he realized, was Katie's doing.

'Have you ever seen anything like these before?'

'Oh, yes, sir. All the billets are full of them.'

'Thank you,' Guy said: 'I'll take charge.'

The driver saluted. Guy turned about and his feet slipped on the frozen surface of the steps. He dropped the papers, breaking the frail bond of knitting-wool which held them together and saved himself from falling only by clutching at the departing driver. A great gust of wind came as they stood embracing and bore away the treasonable documents, scattering them high in the darkness.

'Thank you,' said Guy again and returned more cautiously indoors.

The Regimental orderly room was upstairs, two communicating bedrooms. Grey dawn had broken when Guy went to report officially to his Commanding Officer.

Bertie, the large Grenadier whom Eddie had described as being 'in a sort of way' the Adjutant, was in the outer room smoking a pipe. Guy saluted. Bertie said:

'Oh, hullo. D'you want to see Colonel Tommy? I'll see if he's busy.'

He put down his pipe on an ash tray which advertised a sort of soda-water and went next door. Presently his head appeared.

'Come in.'

Guy saluted at the door, as he had been taught in the Halberdiers, marched to the centre of Tommy's table and stood to attention until Tommy said: 'Good morning, Guy.'

'That was a surprisingly funny evening we had last night,' Tommy said, and then to Bertie: 'Have you found out anything about this officer, Bertie?'

'Yes, Colonel.'

Tommy took a paper from his Adjutant.

'Where was it?'

'On my table, Colonel.'

Tommy read the letter carefully. 'See the reference CP oblique RX? That's the same reference as they used when they sent Kong here if I'm not mistaken. It looks as though HOO HQ have got into a muddle with their filing system. We at least leave our bumf handy on the table.' He flicked the paper into a wire tray.

'Well, Guy, you aren't to be one of us, I'm afraid. You're the personal property of Colonel Ritchie-Hook, Royal Halberdiers, sent here until he's passed fit. I'm sorry. I could have used you to take over Ian's section. But it's not fair on the men to keep switching officers about. We'll have to get a proper replacement for Ian. The question now is, what's to be done with you?'

In all his military service Guy never ceased to marvel at the effortless transitions of intercourse between equality and superiority. It was a figure which no temporary officer ever learned to cut. Some of them were better than the regulars with their men. None ever achieved the art of displaying authority over junior officers without self-consciousness and consequent offence. Regular soldiers were survivals of a happy civilization where differences of rank were exactly defined and frankly accepted.

In the thirteen years of Guy's acquaintance with Tommy he had spent few hours in his company, yet their relationship was peculiar. He had known him first as an agreeable friend of his wife's; then, when momentarily she took him as her lover, as some kind of elemental which had mindlessly sent all Guy's world spinning in fragments; later, without bitterness, as an odd uncomfortable memory, someone to be avoided for fear of embarrassment; Tommy had lost as much as he by his adventure.

Then the war came, collecting, as it seemed, the scattered jig-saw of the past and setting each piece back into its proper place. At Bellamy's he and Tommy were amiable acquaintances, as they had been years before. Last night they had been close friends. Today they were Colonel and Subaltern.

'Is there no chance of the Halberdiers seconding me to you?'

'None by the look of this letter. Besides, you're getting a bit long in the tooth for the kind of job we're going to do. Do you think you could climb those cliffs?'

'I could try.'

'Any damn fool can try. That's why I'm five officers short. Do you think you could handle the office bumf better than Bertie?'

'I am sure he could, Colonel,' said Bertie.

Tommy looked at them both sadly. 'What I want is an administrative officer. An elderly fellow who knows all the ropes and can get round the staff. Bertie doesn't fit; I'm afraid you don't either.'

Suddenly Guy remembered Jumbo.

'I think I've got the very thing for you, Colonel,' he said, and described Jumbo in detail.

When he finished Tommy said: 'Bertie, go and get him. People like that are joining the Home Guard in hundreds. Catch him before they do. He'll have to come down in rank, of course. If he's all you say he is, he'll know how to do it. He can transfer to the navy or something and come here as an RNVR Lieutenant. For Christ's sake, Bertie, why are you standing there?'

'I don't know how to fetch him, Colonel.'

'All right, go out to C troop and take over Ian's section. Guy, you're assistant adjutant. Go and get your man. Don't stand there like Bertie. See the harbour-master, get a lifeboat, get moving.'

'I've also got a three-ton lorry, shall I bring that?'

'Yes, of course. Wait.'

Guy recognized the look of the professional soldier, as he had seen it in Jumbo, overclouding Tommy's face. The daemon of caution by which the successful are led, was whispering: 'Don't go too far. You won't get away with a lorry.'

'No,' he said. 'Leave the lorry and bring the naval candidate.'

8

NEITHER character nor custom had fitted Trimmer to the life of a recluse. For a long time now he had been lying low doing nothing to call himself to the notice of his superiors. He had not reported the condition of his piece of artillery. So far there had been no complaints. His little detachment were well content; Trimmer alone repined as every day his need for feminine society became keener. He was in funds, for he was not admitted to the gambling sessions at the hotel. He was due for leave and at last he took it, seeking what he called 'the lights'.

Glasgow in November 1940 was not literally a *ville lumière*. Fog and crowds gave the black-out a peculiar density. Trimmer, on the afternoon of his arrival, went straight from the train to the station hotel. Here too were fog and crowds. All its lofty halls and corridors were heaped with luggage and thronged by transitory soldiers and sailors. There was a thick, shifting mob at the reception office. To everybody the girl at the counter replied: 'Reserved rooms only. If you come back after eight there may be some cancellations.'

Trimmer struggled to the front, leered and asked: 'Have ye no a wee room for a Scottish laddie?'

'Come back after eight. There may be a cancellation.'

Trimmer gave her a wink and she seemed just perceptibly responsive, but the thrust of other desperate and homeless men made further flirtation impossible.

With his bonnet on the side of his head, his shepherd's crook in his hand and a pair of major's crowns on his shoulders (he had changed them for his lieutenant's stars in the train lavatory), Trimmer began to saunter through the ground floor. There were men everywhere. Of the few women each was the centre of a noisy little circle of festivity, or else huddled with her man in a gloom of leave-taking. Waiters were few. Everywhere he saw heads turned and faces of anxious entreaty. Here and there a more hopeful party banged the table and impolitely shouted: 'We want service.'

But Trimmer was undismayed. He found it all very jolly after his billet on Mugg and experience had taught him that anyone who really wants a woman, finds one in the end.

He passed on with all the panache of a mongrel among the dustbins, tail waving, ears cocked, nose a-quiver. Here and there in his passage he attempted to insinuate himself into one or other of the heartier groups, but without success. At length he came to some steps and the notice: *CHÂTEAU de MADRID. Restaurant de grand luxe.*

Trimmer had been to this hotel once or twice before but he had never penetrated into what he knew was the expensive quarter. He took his fun where he found it, preferably in crowded places. To-night would be different. He strolled down rubber-lined carpet and was at once greeted at the foot of the stairs by a head waiter.

'*Bon soir, monsieur.* Monsieur has engaged his table?'

'I was looking for a friend.'

'How large will monsieur's party be?'

'Two, if there is a party. I'll just sit here a while and have a drink.'

'*Pardon, monsieur.* It is not allowed to serve drinks here except to those who are dining. Upstairs . . .'

The two men looked at one another, fraud to fraud. They had both knocked about a little. Neither was taken in by the other. For a moment Trimmer was tempted to say: 'Come off it. Where did you get that French accent? The Mile End Road or the Gorbals?'

The waiter was tempted to say: 'This isn't your sort of place, chum. Hop it.'

In the event Trimmer said: 'I shall certainly dine here if my friend

73

turns up. You might give me a look at the menu while I have my cocktail.'

And the head waiter said: '*Tout suite, monsieur.*'

Another man deprived Trimmer of his bonnet and staff.

He sat at the cocktail bar. The decoration here was more trumpery than in the marble and mahogany halls above. It should have been repainted and re-upholstered that summer, but war had intervened. It wore the air of a fashion magazine, once stiff and shiny, which too many people had handled. But Trimmer did not mind. His acquaintance with fashion magazines had mostly been in tattered copies.

Trimmer looked about and saw that one chair only was occupied. Here in the corner was what he sought, a lonely woman. She did not look up and Trimmer examined her boldly. He saw a woman equipped with all the requisites for attention, who was not trying to attract. She was sitting still and looking at the half-empty glass on her table and she was quite unaware of Trimmer's brave bare knees and swinging sporran. She was, Trimmer judged, in her early thirties; her clothes – and Trimmer was something of a judge – were unlike anything worn by the ladies of Glasgow. Less than two years ago they had come from a *grand couturier*. She was not exactly Trimmer's type but he was ready to try anything that evening. He was inured to rebuffs.

A sharper eye might have noted that she fitted a little too well into her surroundings – the empty tank which had lately been lit up and brilliant with angel fish; the white cordings on the crimson draperies, now a little grimy, the white plaster sea-horses, less gay than heretofore – the lonely woman did not stand out distinctly from these. She sat, as it were, in a faint corroding mist – the exhalation perhaps of unhappiness or ill health, or of mere weariness. She drained her glass and looked past Trimmer to the barman who said: 'Coming up right away, madam,' and began splashing gin of a previously unknown brand into his shaker.

When Trimmer saw her face he was struck by a sense of familiarity; somewhere, perhaps in those shabby fashion-magazines, he had seen it before.

'I'll take it over,' he said to the barman, quickly lifting the tray with the new cocktail on it.

74

'Excuse me, sir, *if* you please.'

Trimmer retained his hold. The barman let go. Trimmer carried the tray to the corner.

'Your cocktail, madam,' he said jauntily.

The woman took the glass, said 'Thank you' and looked beyond him. Trimmer then remembered her name.

'You've forgotten me, Mrs Troy?'

She looked at him slowly, without interest.

'Have we met before?'

'Often. In the *Aquitania*.'

'I'm sorry,' she said. 'I'm afraid I don't remember. One meets so many people.'

'Mind if I join you?'

'I am just leaving.'

'You could do with a rinse and set,' said Trimmer, adding in the tones of the *maître d'hôtel*, 'Madam's hair is *un peu fatigué*, *n'est ce-pas*? It is the sea-air.'

Her face showed sudden interest, incredulity, welcome.

'Gustave! It can't be you?'

'Remember how I used to come to your cabin in the mornings? As soon as I saw your name on the passenger list I'd draw a line through all my eleven-thirty appointments. The old trouts used to come and offer ten-dollar tips but I always kept eleven-thirty free in case you wanted me.'

'Gustave, how awful of me! How could I have forgotten? Sit down. You must admit you've changed a lot.'

'You haven't,' said Trimmer. 'Remember that little bit of massage I used to give you at the back of the neck. You said it cured your hangovers.'

'It did.'

They revived many fond memories of the Atlantic.

'Dear Gustave, how you bring it all back. I always loved the *Aquitania*.'

'Mr Troy about?'

'He's in America.'

'Alone here?'

'I came to see a friend off.'

'Boy friend?'

75

'You always were too damned fresh.'

'You never kept any secrets from me.'

'No great secret. He's a sailor. I haven't known him long but I liked him. He went off quite suddenly. People are always going off suddenly nowadays, not saying where.'

'You've got me for a week if you're staying on.'

'I've no plans.'

'Nor me. Dining here?'

'It's very expensive.'

'My treat, of course.'

'My dear boy, I couldn't possibly let you spend your money on me. I was just wondering whether I could afford to stand you dinner. I don't think I can.'

'Hard up?'

'Very. I don't quite know why. Something to do with Mr Troy and the war and foreign investments and exchange control. Anyway, my London bank manager has suddenly become very shifty.'

Trimmer was both shocked and slightly exhilarated by this news. The barrier between hairdresser and first-class passenger was down. It was important to start the new relationship on the proper level – a low one. He did not fancy the idea of often acting as host at the Château de Madrid.

'Anyway, Virginia, let's have another drink here?'

Virginia lived among people who used Christian names indiscriminately. It was Trimmer's self-consciousness which called attention to his familiarity.

'Virginia?' she said, teasing.

'And I, by the way, am Major McTavish. My friends call me "Ali" or "Trimmer".'

'They know about your being a barber, then?'

'As a matter of fact they don't. The name Trimmer has nothing to do with that. Not that I'm ashamed of it. I got plenty of fun on the *Aquitania*, I can tell you – with the passengers. You'd be surprised, if I told you some of the names. Lots of your own set.'

'Tell me, Trimmer.'

For half an hour he kept her enthralled by his revelations, some of which had a basis of truth. The restaurant and foyer began to fill up with stout, elderly civilians, airmen with showy local girls, an admiral with his wife and daughter. The head waiter approached Trimmer for the third time with the menu.

'How about it, Trimmer?'

'I wish you'd call me "Ali".'

'Trimmer to me, every time,' said Virginia.

'How about a Dutch treat as we're both in the same boat?'

'That suits me.'

'Tomorrow we may find something cheaper.'

Virginia raised her eyebrows at the word 'tomorrow', but said nothing. Instead she took the menu card and without consultation ordered a nourishing but economical meal.

'*Et pour commencer*, some oysters? A little *saumon fumé*?'

'No,' she said firmly.

'Not keen on them myself,' said Trimmer.

'I am, but we're not having any tonight. Always read the menu from right to left.'

'I don't get you.'

'Never mind. I expect there are all sorts of things we don't "get" about one another.'

Virginia was looking her old self when she entered the restaurant; 'class written all over her' as Trimmer inwardly expressed it, and, besides, she gleamed with happy mischief.

At dinner Trimmer began to boast a little about his military eminence.

'How lovely,' said Virginia; 'all alone on an island.'

'There are some other troops there in training,' he conceded, 'but I don't have much to do with them. I command the defence.'

'Oh, damn the war,' said Virginia. 'Tell me more about the *Aquitania*.'

She was not a woman who indulged much in reminiscence or speculation. Weeks passed without her giving thought to the past fifteen years of her life – her seduction by a friend of her father's, who had looked her up, looked her over, taken her out, taken her in, from her finishing-school in Paris; her marriage to Guy, the Castello Crouchback and the endless cloudy terraces of the Rift Valley; her marriage to Tommy, London hotels, fast cars, regimental point-to-points, the looming horror of an Indian cantonment; fat Augustus with his cheque book always handy; Mr Troy and his taste for 'significant people' – none of this, as Mr Troy would say, 'added up' to anything. Nor did age or death. It was the present moment and the next five minutes which counted with Virginia. But just now in this shuttered fog-bound place, surrounded by strangers in the bright little room, surrounded by strangers in the blackness outside, miles of them, millions of them, all blind and deaf, not 'significant people'; now while the sirens sounded and bombs began to fall and guns to fire far away among the dockyards – now, briefly, Virginia was happy to relive, to see again from the farther side of the looking-glass, the ordered airy life aboard the great liner. And faithful Gustave who always kept his crowded hour for her, with his false French and his soothing thumb on the neck and shoulders and the top of the spine, suddenly metamorphosed beside her into a bare-kneed major with a cockney accent, preposterously renamed – Gustave was the guide providentially sent on a gloomy evening to lead her back to the days of sun and sea-spray and wallowing dolphins.

At that moment in London Colonel Grace-Groundling-Marchpole, lately promoted head of his most secret department, was filing the latest counter-intelligence:

Crouchback, Guy, temporary Lieutenant Royal Corps of Halberdiers, now stationed with undefined duties at Mugg at HQ X Commando. This suspect has been distributing subversive matter at night. Copy attached.

He glanced at *Why Hitler must win.*

'Yes, we've seen this before. Ten copies have been found in the Edinburgh area. This is the first from the islands. Very interesting. It links up the Box case with the Scottish Nationalists – a direct connexion from Salzburg to Mugg. What we need now is to connect Cardiff University with Santa Dulcina. We shall do it in time, I've no doubt.'

Colonel Marchpole's department was so secret that it communicated only with the War Cabinet and the Chiefs of Staff. Colonel Marchpole kept his information until it was asked for. To date that had not occurred and he rejoiced under neglect. Premature examination of his files might ruin his private, undefined Plan. Somewhere in the ultimate curlicues of his mind, there was a Plan. Given time, given enough confidential material, he would succeed in knitting the entire quarrelsome world into a single net of conspiracy in which there were no antagonists, merely millions of men working, unknown to one another, for the same end; and there would be no more war.

Full, Dickensian fog enveloped the city. Day and night the streets were full of slow-moving, lighted trams and lorries and hustling coughing people. Sea-gulls emerged and suddenly vanished overhead. The rattle and shuffle and the hooting of motor-horns drowned the warnings of distant ships. Now and then the air-raid sirens rose above all. The hotel was always crowded. Between drinking hours soldiers and sailors slept in the lounges. When the bars opened they awoke to call plaintively for a drink. The mêlée at the reception counter never diminished. Upstairs the yellow lights burned by day against the whitish-yellow lace which shut out half the yellow-brown obscurity beyond; by night against a frame of black. This was the scene in which Trimmer's idyll was laid.

It ended abruptly on the fourth day.

Trimmer had ventured down about midday into the murky hall to engage tickets for the theatre that evening. One of the suppliant figures at the reception-counter disengaged himself and jostled him.

'Sorry. Why, hullo, McTavish. What are you doing here?'

It was the second-in-command of his battalion, a man Trimmer believed to be far away in Iceland.

'On leave, sir.'

'Well, it's lucky running into you. I'm looking for bodies to take up north. Just landed at Greenock this morning.'

The Major looked at him more closely and fixed his attention on the badges of rank.

'Why the devil are you dressed like that?' he asked.

Trimmer thought quickly.

'I was promoted the other day, sir. I'm not with the regiment any more. I'm on special service.'

'First I've heard of it.'

'I was seconded some time ago to the Commandos.'

'By whose orders?'

'HOO HQ.'

The Major looked doubtful.

'Where are your men?'

'Isle of Mugg.'

'And where are you when you're not on leave?'

'Isle of Mugg, too, sir. But I'm nothing to do with the men now. I think they are expecting an officer to take over any day. I am under Colonel Blackhouse.'

'Well, I suppose it's all right. When is your leave up?'

'This afternoon, as a matter of fact.'

'I hope you've enjoyed it.'

'Thoroughly, thank you.'

'It's all very rum,' said the Major. 'Congratulations on your promotion, by the way.'

Trimmer turned to go. The Major called him back. Trimmer broke into a sweat.

'You're leaving your room here? I wonder if anyone else has got it.'

'I'm rather afraid they have.'

'Damn.'

Trimmer pushed his way forward to the hall porter. Instead of theatre tickets, it was train and ship he wanted now.

'Mugg? Yes, sir. You can just do it. Train leaves at 12.45.'

Virginia was sitting at the dressing-table. Trimmer seized his hair-brushes from under her hands and began filling his sponge-bag at the wash-hand-stand.

'What are you doing? Did you get the tickets all right?'

'I'm sorry, it's off.'

'Gustave!'

'Recalled for immediate service, my dear. I can't explain. War on, you know.'

'Oh God!' she said. 'Another of them.'

Slowly she took off her dressing-gown and returned to bed.

'Aren't you coming to see me off?'

'Not on your life, Trimmer.'

'What are you going to do?'

'I'll be all right. I'm going to sleep again. Good-bye.'

So Trimmer returned to Mugg. He had enjoyed his leave beyond all expectation, but it had left him with a problem of which he could see only one solution, and that a most unwelcome one.

While Trimmer was in Glasgow Tommy Blackhouse had been called to London. In his absence a lassitude fell on the Commando. In the brief hours of daylight the troops marched out to uninhabited areas and blazed away their ammunition into the snowy hillside and the dark sea. One of them killed a seal. Card playing languished and in the evenings the hotel lounge was full of silent figures reading novels – *No Orchids for Miss Blandish*, *Don't, Mr Disraeli*, the *Chartreuse de Parme* and other oddly assorted works of fiction passed from hand to hand.

Jumbo Trotter completed his work of filing and indexing the waste paper in the orderly-room. He had transformed himself for the time being into a Captain of the Home Guard, pending 'posting' to RNVR.

He and Guy sat in the orderly-room on the morning after Trimmer's return. They both wore their greatcoats and gloves. Jumbo was further muffled in a balaclava helmet. He had *Don't, Mr Disraeli* that morning and was visibly puzzled by it.

Presently he said:

'Did you see the letter from the laird?'

'Yes.'

'He seems to think the Colonel promised to give him some explosives. Doesn't sound likely.'

'I was there. Nothing was promised.'

'I rather like a bit of an explosion myself.'

He resumed his reading.

After a few minutes Guy shut *No Orchids for Miss Blandish*.

'Unreadable,' he said.

'Other fellows seemed to enjoy it. Claire recommended this book. Can't make it out at all. Is it a sort of skit on something?'

Guy turned over the papers in the 'pending' tray.

'What about Dr Glendening-Rees?' he asked. 'I don't think Colonel Tommy is going to be much interested in him.'

Jumbo took the letter and re-read it.

'Can't do anything until he comes back. Can't do very much then. This reads like an order to me. HOO HQ seem to send us every crank in the country. First Chatty Corner, now Dr Glendening-Rees. "Eminent authority on dietetics" . . . "original and possibly valuable proposal concerning emergency food supplies in the field" . . . "afford every facility for research under active service conditions". Can't we put him off?'

'He seems to have started. I dare say he'll liven things up a bit.'

A letter had lain on the table all the morning addressed in sprawling unofficial writing. The envelope was pale violet in colour and flimsy in texture.

'Do you think this is private?'

'It's addressed "OC X Commando", not to the Colonel by name. Better open it.'

It was from Trimmer.

'McTavish has put in an application to see Colonel Tommy.'

'The fellow who was chucked out of the Halberdiers? What does he want?'

'To join the Commando apparently. He seems very eager about it suddenly.'

'Of course,' said Jumbo tolerantly, 'there are lots of fellows who aren't quite up to the mark for *us*, who are quite decent fellows all the same. If you ask me, there are several fellows here already who wouldn't quite do in the Corps. Decent fellows, mind you, but not up to the mark.' Jumbo gazed before him, sadly, tolerantly, considering the inadequacy of No. X Commando.

'You know,' he said, 'they've issued NCOs with binoculars.'

'Yes.'

'I call that unnecessary. And I'll tell you something. There's one of them – Claire's CSM – queer looking fellow with pink eyes – they call him a "Corporal-Major" I believe. I overheard him the other day refer to these binoculars of his as his "opera glasses". Well, I mean to say – ' He paused for effect and continued on the original topic.

'I gather McTavish wasn't a great success in his own regiment. Sergeant Bane got it from his Sergeant that they threw him out of a window the day before embarking for Iceland.'

'I heard it was a horse-trough. Anyway, they knocked him

about a bit. There was a lot of that sort of thing when I joined. Ink baths and so forth. No sense in it. Only made bad fellows worse.'

'Colonel Tommy's coming back tonight. He'll know what to do with him.'

Tommy Blackhouse returned as expected. He immediately called for the troop-leaders and said:

'Things are beginning to move. There's a ship coming for us tomorrow or the day after. Be ready to embark at once. She's fitted with ALCs. What are they, Eddie?'

'I don't know, Colonel.'

'Assault landing craft. These are the first lot made. You may have seen some of them on your Dakar jaunt, Guy. We start full-scale landing exercises at once. HOO HQ are sending observers so they had better be good. Issue maps to everyone down to Corporals. I'll give details of the scheme tomorrow.

'I haven't been so lucky with replacements. OCs don't seem as ready to play now as they were six weeks ago, but HOO have promised to bring us up to strength somehow. That's all. Guy, I shall want you.'

When the troop leaders had left, Tommy said:

'Guy, have you ever wondered why we are here?'

'No. I can't say I have.'

'I dare say nobody has. This place wasn't chosen simply for its bloodiness. You'll all know in good time. If you'd ever studied *Admiralty Sailing Directions* it might occur to you that there is another island with two hills, steep shingle beaches and cliffs. Somewhere rather warmer than this. The name doesn't matter now. The point is that these exercises aren't just a staff college scheme for Northland against Southland. They're the dress rehearsal for an operation. It won't do any harm if you pass that on. We've been playing about too long. Anything happen while I was away?'

'McTavish is very anxious to see you. He wants to join.'

'The wet highlander who jammed his gun?'

'Yes, Colonel.'

'Right. I'll see him tomorrow.'

'He's no good, you know.'

'I can use anyone who's really keen.'

'He's keen all right. I don't quite know why.'

Ivor Claire occupied himself during the 'flap' in making elaborate arrangements for the safe-conduct of his pekinese, Freda, to his mother's care.

9

THE promised ship did not come next day or the day after or for many days, while the nights lengthened until they seemed continuous. Often the sun never appeared and drab twilight covered the island. The fishermen sat at home over the peat and the streets of the little town were as empty at noon as at midnight. Once or twice the mist lifted, the two hills appeared and a cold glare on the horizon cast long shadows across the snow. No one looked for the ship. Officers and men began to wish themselves back with their regiments.

There should be a drug for soldiers, Guy thought, to put them to sleep until they were needed. They should repose among the briar like the knights of the Sleeping Beauty; they should be laid away in their boxes in the nursery cupboard. This unvarying cycle of excitement and disappointment rubbed them bare of paint and exposed the lead beneath.

Now that Jumbo was installed in the orderly-room, Guy's position became that of an ADC. Tommy kept him busy. He acquired a certain status in the unit as someone likely to be in the know about Christmas leave, as a mediator for the troop-leaders in their troubles and squabbles. His age was unremarkable here. Jumbo set a high standard of antiquity. Half a dozen of the troop-leaders were also in their middle thirties. No one called him 'Uncle'. Indeed, he was not one of the family at all, merely a passing guest. He knew, now, the name of the Mediterranean island they were planning to take, but he would not be with them on the night. There was here none of the exhilaration of a year ago, of Brigadier Ritchie-Hook's: 'These are the men you will lead in battle.' His work was solely among the officers; notoriously a deleterious form of soldiering. For relaxation he collected the poorest men in the mess and played poker with them for low stakes. He was slightly better off than they and he played a reasonably good game. Whenever one of his party showed too much confidence, Guy advised him to join the big game. After a night with the rich, he invariably returned crestfallen and cautious. Thus Guy made a regular five or six pounds a week.

The assault of the island was rehearsed, first by day, the troops marching to their beaches and from there scrambling inland to objectives which in Mugg was merely map-references, but, in the Mediterranean, were gun-emplacements and signal-posts. Guy acted as intelligence officer and observer and umpire. All went well.

They tried it again on a night of absolute blackness. Tommy and Guy stood by their car on the road near the old Castle. The RSM sent up the rocket which announced the start of the exercise. Bertie's troop stumbled through the glow of the dimmed motor lamps and disappeared noisily into the blackness beyond. A civilian bus passed them. All was silent. Tommy and Guy sat in the car waiting while the headquarters signallers huddled in blankets at the road-side like a group of Bedouin. Wireless silence was being observed until the objectives were gained.

'We might as well be in bed,' said Tommy. 'Nothing can happen for two hours or more and then we can't do anything about it.'

But within twenty minutes of the start there was a twinkle in the sky.

'Verey light, sir,' reported the RSM.

'Can't be.'

Another tiny spark appeared from the same direction. Guy consulted the map.

'Looks like D Troop.'

'Dammit, they've got the farthest to go of anyone. I specially gave it to them to make Ivor do some work for a change.'

There was a mutter from the signallers and presently one of them reported.

'D Troop in position, sir.'

'Give me the damn thing,' said Tommy. He took the instrument.

'Headquarters to D Troop. Where are you? Over . . . I can't hear you. Speak up. Over . . . Colonel Blackhouse here. Give me Captain Claire. Over . . . Ivor, where are you? . . . You can't be . . . Damn. Out.' He turned to Guy. 'All I can get is a request to return. Go and see them, Guy.'

On the island of Mugg there were two routes to the site of D Troop's objective. Their orders sent them across four miles of moorland to a spot twelve miles distant by the main coast-road and just off it. In the future operation this road led through a populous and heavily garrisoned village. Guy, in the car, now took this route. He followed the track on foot where it diverged.

He was soon challenged by a sentry.

Claire's voice came from nearby. 'Hullo. Who's that?'

'Colonel Tommy sent me.'

'You're very welcome, we're getting frozen. Position occupied and defence consolidated. That I think was the object of the exercise.'

The troop were established in the comparative comfort of a sheep-pen. There was a perceptible smell of rum all about them. Claire held a mug.

'How the hell did you get here, Ivor?'

'I hired a bus. You might call it "captured transport". Can I take the troop back and dismiss? They're getting cold.'

'Not as cold as most.'

'I make their comfort my first concern. Well, can we go?'

'I suppose so. Colonel Tommy will want to talk about this.'

'I am expecting congratulations.'

'Congratulations, Ivor, from myself. I don't know what anyone else is going to say about it.'

Every other troop lost itself that night. After three hours Tommy ordered rockets to be fired, ending the exercise, and sections appeared out of the darkness until dawn, shuffling, soaked and spiritless as stragglers on the road from Moscow.

'I'll see Ivor first thing tomorrow,' said Tommy grimly as he and Guy finally separated.

But Claire's case was unanswerable. The Commandos were expressly raised for irregular action, for seizing tactical advantages on their own initiative. In the operation, Claire explained, there would probably be a bus lying about somewhere.

'In the operation that road leads through a battalion of light infantry.'

'Nothing about that in orders, Colonel.'

Tommy sat silent for some time. At last he said: 'All right, Ivor, you win.'

'Thank you, Colonel.'

The episode greatly endeared Claire to his own troop. The rest of the Commando were very angry about it indeed. Among the men it led to a feud; among the officers to marked coldness. And thus unexpectedly it drew Claire and Guy closer together. Claire required someone to talk to, and was limited in his choice by his sudden unpopularity. Moreover, he had observed with respect Guy's conduct of his poker table. As for Guy, he had recognized from the first a certain remote kinship with this most dissimilar man, a common aloofness, differently manifested – a common melancholy sense of humour; each in his way saw life *sub specie aeternitatis*; thus with numberless reservations they became friends, as had Guy and Apthorpe.

One man who remained in nervous expectation of the ship's arrival was Trimmer. Nemesis, in the shape of 'a spot of awkwardness', seemed very near. Once on the high seas, bound for a secret destination; better still torpedoed and cast up on a neutral shore, Trimmer would be all right. Meanwhile there was the danger that the second-in-command of his battalion had made inquiries about his rank and posting and that somewhere between the Headquarters of Scottish Command and the Adjutant-General's Office in London papers were slowly passing from tray to tray which might at any moment bring his doom.

There was also the danger that his detachment might become restive, but this he solved by sending them all on fourteen days' leave. The men looked doubtful. Trimmer looked confident. He emptied his book of travel-vouchers, giving each man of his plenty. In the case of his Sergeant-Major he added five one-pound notes.

'Where do we report back after leave, sir?'

Trimmer considered this. Then an inspiring thought came to him.

'India,' he said; 'report to the Fourth Battalion.'

'Sir?'

'Climate a great change from Mugg. I leave the detachment in your charge, Sergeant-Major. Enjoy your leave. Then report to Sea Transport. They'll find you a ship.'

'What, without a move order, sir?'

'But you see I am no longer in command. I've been seconded. I can't sign a move order in any case.'

'Should we go back to regimental headquarters, sir?'

'Perhaps that might be more strictly correct. But I should mess about at the docks first a bit. We must try and cut red-tape where we can.'

'Which docks, sir?'

That was easy. 'Portsmouth,' said Trimmer with decision.

'Must have something in writing, sir.'

'I've just explained to you, I'm not in a position to give any orders. All I know is that the Fourth Battalion want you in India. I saw our battalion second-in-command in Glasgow and he gave me the order verbally.' He looked in his note-case and reluctantly produced another two pounds. 'That's all I have,' he said.

'Very good, sir,' said the Sergeant-Major.

He was not the best of soldiers nor the brightest but there was a look in his eyes which made Trimmer fear that seven pounds had been wasted. That man would make for the depot like a homing pigeon, the day his leave expired.

It fell to Guy to find employment for Trimmer himself. It was easy for Tommy in the exhilarating prospect of immediate embarkation to take Trimmer on; it was a different matter to impose him on a disillusioned troop-leader.

The trouble was that three of the four troops who were short of officers, were volunteers from the Household Brigade. Their commanders protested that it was impossible for guardsmen to serve under an officer from a line regiment, and Tommy, a Coldstreamer, agreed. There was a Scottish Troop to which Trimmer should properly go, but that was up to strength. The composite troop of Rifle Brigade and 60th needed an officer, but here the huge hos-

tility that had subsisted underground between them and the Foot
Guards came at once to the surface. Why should a rifleman accept
Trimmer, when a guardsman would not? It had not occurred to
Tommy that he could be suspected of personal bias in the matter;
he had merely followed what seemed to him the natural order of
things. His own brief service in a line regiment he regarded as a
period of detention, seldom remembered. For the first and last
time in his career he had made a minute military *gaffe*.

'If they don't want McTavish, I can give them Duncan. He's
H L I. Dammit, all light infantry drill is much the same, isn't it?'

But Duncan would not do, nor would the leader of the Scottish
troop surrender him. Generations of military history, the smoke
of a hundred battlefields darkened the issue.

Guy and Jumbo, Halberdiers, serenely superior to such
squabbles, solved the problem.

There existed in a somewhat shadowy form a sixth troop,
named 'Specialists'. It comprised a section of Marines skilled with
boats and ropes and beaches, two interpreters, a field-security
policeman, heavy machine gunners, and a demolition squad. The
commander was an Indian cavalryman chosen for his experience
in mountain warfare. This officer, Major Graves, had been playing
Achilles from days before Guy landed on Mugg. He had taken
Chatty Corner's arrival as a deliberate slight on his own hardily-
acquired skills. He made no protest but he brooded. The dark
mood was only lighted by the tale of Chatty's casualties, one of
the first of whom was his sapper Subaltern who commanded the
demolition squad.

Guy had warmed to this disgruntled, sandy little man whose
heart was in the North-West Frontier and he had more than once
cajoled him to the poker table. He found him, now, at the time of
crisis, playing patience in his troop office.

'I wonder if you've met McTavish, who's just joined us?'

'No.'

'You're short of an officer, aren't you?'

'I'm short of a bloody lot of things.'

'Colonel Tommy wants to send McTavish to you.'

'What's his particular line?'

'Well, nothing *particular*, I think.'

'A specialist in damn-all?'

'He seems a fairly adaptable chap. He might make himself generally helpful, Colonel Tommy thought.'

'He can have the sappers if he wants them.'

'Do you think that's a good thing?'

'I think it's a bloody silly thing. I had a perfectly good chap. Then the CO sent a sort of human ape with orders to break his neck. Since then I've barely seen the sappers. I don't know what they do. I'm sick of them. McTavish can have them.'

Thus, Trimmer first set foot upon the path to glory, little knowing his destination.

That afternoon Tommy left the island once more on a summons from London.

A few days later Jumbo said to Guy: 'Busy?'

'No.'

'It wouldn't be a bad thing if you went up to the Castle. Colonel Campbell has been writing again. Always keep in with the civilian population if you can.'

Guy found the laird at home, indeed in carpet slippers, and in a genial mood. They sat in a circular turret room full of maps and the weapons of sport. He maundered pleasantly for some minutes about 'a ranker fellow! . . . Not a Scot at all . . . Nothing against rankers except they will stick by the book . . . Nothing against English regiments. A bit slow to get moving, that was all . . . Have to give commissions to all sorts now of course . . . Same in the last war . . . Met him when he first came to the island. . . . Didn't think much of him . . . Didn't know he was one of yours. Not a bad fellow when you got to know him . . .' Until gradually Guy realized that the laird was talking of Trimmer.

'Had him up after lunch yesterday.'

To bring matters to the point Guy said: 'McTavish now commands the demolition squad.'

'*Exactly.*'

Mugg rose and began fumbling under his writing-table. At length he produced a pair of boots.

'You know what we were talking about the other evening. I'd like you to come and see.'

He donned his boots and an inverness cape and selected a tall stick from the clutter of rods, gaffs and other tall sticks. Together he and Guy walked into the wind until they stood on the cliff half a mile from the house, overlooking a rough shore of rocks and breakers.

'There,' Mugg said. 'The bathing beach. McTavish says it may be a long job.'

'I'm no expert but I should rather think he is right.'

'We have a proverb here, "What's gone down has to come up."'

'In England we have one like that only the other way round.'

'*Not* quite the same thing,' said Mugg severely.

They looked down on the immense heap of granite.

'It came down all right,' said Mugg.

'Evidently.'

'It was rather a mistake.'

An odd look, a Mona Lisa smirk under the moustache, came into the laird's weather-beaten face.

'I blew it down,' said the laird at length.

'You, sir?'

'I used to do a lot of blowing,' said the laird, 'up and down. Come over here.'

They walked back a quarter of a mile along the headland in the direction of the castle and looked inland.

'Over there,' said the laird. 'It's hard to see in the snow. Where there's that hollow. You can see thistle tops round the edge. You'd not think there had been a stable there, would you?'

'No, sir.'

'Stabling for ten, a coach-house, harness-rooms?'

'No.'

'There *was*. Place wasn't safe, woodwork all rotten, half the tiles gone. Couldn't afford to repair it and no reason to. I hadn't any horses. *So up it went*. They heard the bang at Muck. It was a wonderful sight. Great lumps of granite pitching into the sea and all the cattle and sheep on the island stampeding in every direction. That was on 15 June 1923. I don't suppose anyone on the island has forgotten that day. I certainly haven't.' The laird sighed. 'And now I haven't a stick of gelignite on the place. I'll show you what I have got.'

He led Guy into the crater to a little hut, hitherto invisible. It was massively built of granite.

'We made that from part of the stable which didn't go up for some reason or other. The rest of the stone went on the roads. I sold it to the government. It's my only explosion so far that has shown a profit. Something very near £18 after everything was paid, including the labour on the magazine. This is the magazine.'

The snow, which had drifted high round the hut, had been dug clear to make a narrow passage to the door.

'Must have ready access. You never know when you'll need a bit of gun-cotton, do you? But I don't bring many people here. There was a sort of inspector from the mainland came last summer. Said there had been a report that I was storing explosives. I showed him a few boxes of cartridges. Told him to look anywhere. He never found the magazine. You know how reports get about in a small place like this. Everyone knows everyone and then you get grudges. My factor has grudges with almost everyone on the island, so they try and take it out of him by making reports. Let me lead the way.'

The laird took a key from his pocket and opened the door on a single, lightless chamber. He lit an end of candle and held it high with the air of an oenophilist revealing his most recondite treasure. There was in fact a strong resemblance to a wine-cellar in the series of stone bins which lined the walls – a cellar sadly depleted.

'My gelignite once,' said the laird, 'from here to here. . . . Now this is gun-cotton. I'm still fairly well-off for that, as you can see. That's all that's left of the nitro-glycerine. I haven't used any for fifteen years. It may have deteriorated. I'll get some up soon and try it out. . . . This is all empty, you see. In fact, you might say there's nothing much worth having now. You have to keep filling up, you know, or you soon find yourself with nothing. My main shortages are fuses and detonators. . . . Hullo, here's a bit of luck.' He put his candle down so that huge shadows filled the magazine. 'Catch.'

He tossed something out of the farther darkness into the darkness where Guy stood. It passed for a moment through the candle light, hit Guy on the chest and fell to the ground.

'Butter fingers,' said the laird. 'That's dynamite. Didn't know I had any left. Throw it back, there's a good fellow.'

Guy groped and at last found the damp paper-wrapped cylinder. He held it out cautiously.

'That won't hurt you. Thousand-to-one chance of trouble with dynamite. Not like some things I've had in my time.'

They turned to the door. Guy was sweating in the bitter cold. At last they were in the open air, between the walls of snow. The door was locked.

'Well,' said the laird, 'I've let you spy out the poverty of the land. You understand now why I'm appealing for help. Now let me show you some of the things that need doing.'

They walked for two hours, examining falls of rock, derelict buildings, blocked drains, tree stumps and streams which needed damming.

'I couldn't get the ranker fellow really interested. I don't suppose he ever caught a fish in his life.'

For every problem the laird had a specific, drawn from a simple range of high or slow explosive.

When they parted the laird seemed to wait for thanks, as might an uncle who has been round Madame Tussaud's with a nephew and put himself out to make the tour amusing.

'Thank you,' said Guy.

'Glad you enjoyed it. I shall expect to hear from your Colonel.'

They were standing at the Castle gates.

'By the way,' said the laird. 'My niece, whom you met the other evening. She doesn't know about the magazine. It's not really any business of hers. She's just here on a visit.' He paused and regarded Guy with his fine old blue, blank eyes and then added, 'Besides, she might waste it, you know.'

But the prodigies of the island were not yet exhausted.

As Guy returned to the hotel, he paused to observe a man with a heavy load on his back who stood on the edge of the sea, bent double among the rocks and clawing at them, it appeared, with both hands. He rose when he saw Guy, and advanced towards him carrying a dripping mass of weed; a tall wild man, hatless and clothed in a suit of roughly dressed leather; his grey beard spread in the wind like a baroque prophet's; the few exposed portions of skin were as worn and leathery as his trousers; he wore gold-rimmed pince-nez and spoke not in the accents of Mugg but in precise academic tones.

'Do I, perhaps, address Colonel Blackhouse?'

'No,' said Guy. 'No, not at all. Colonel Blackhouse is in London.'

'He is expecting me. I arrived this morning. The journey took me longer than I expected. I came North on my bicycle and ran into some very rough weather. I was just getting my lunch before making myself known. Can I offer you some?'

He held out the seaweed.

'Thank you,' said Guy. 'No, I am just going to the hotel. You must be Dr Glendening-Rees!'

'Of course.' He filled his mouth with weed and chewed happily, regarding Guy with fatherly interest. 'Lunch at the hotel?' he said. 'You won't find hotels on the battle-field, you know.'

'I suppose not.'

'Bully beef,' said the doctor. 'Biscuit, stewed tea. Poison. I was in the first war. I know. Nearly ruined my digestion for life. That's why I've devoted myself to my subject.' He reached into his pocket and produced a handful of large limpets. 'Try these. Just picked them. Every bit as agreeable as oysters and *much* safer. There's everything a man can want here,' he said, gazing fondly at the desolate fore-shore. 'A rare banquet. I can warrant your men will miss it when they get inland. Things aren't made quite so easy for them there, particularly at this time of year. Not much showing above ground. You have to grub for it and know what you're looking for. It's all a matter of having a *flair*. The young roots of the heather, for instance, are excellent with a little oil and salt, but get a bit of bog myrtle mixed with them and you're done. I don't doubt we can train them.'

He sucked greedily at the limpets.

'I'm attached to headquarters. We heard you were coming. The Colonel will be very sorry to miss you.'

'Oh, I can start without him. I have a schedule prepared. Now don't let me keep you. Go along to your hotel lunch. I shall be a little time here. One of the lessons you will have to learn is to eat slowly in the natural, rational way. Where shall I find someone in authority?'

'At the hotel' – it was not a word to placate Dr Glendening-Rees – 'I'm afraid.'

'There were no hotels in Gallipoli.'

Some two hours later, when he had completed his natural and rational luncheon, Dr Glendening-Rees sat opposite Jumbo and Guy in the regimental office, explaining his plan of action.

'I shall want a demonstration squad from you. Half a dozen men will be enough at this stage. Pick them at random. I don't want the strongest or the youngest or the fittest – just a cross-section. We will be out five days. The essential thing is to make a thorough inspection first. My last experiment was ruined by bad discipline. The men were loaded with concealed food. Their officer even had a bottle of whisky. As a result their whole diet was unbalanced and instead of slowly learning to enjoy natural foods, they broke camp at night, killed a sheep and made themselves thoroughly sick. The only supplement they can possibly need is a little olive oil and barley sugar. I shall keep that and dole it out if I detect any deficiency in the roots. At the end of five days I suggest we hold a little tug-of-war between my squad and six men who have been normally victualled and I'll guarantee my men give a good account of themselves.'

'Yes,' said Jumbo. 'Yes. That should be most interesting. A pity the CO isn't here.'

'No doubt he will be here to see the tug-of-war. I've been studying the map of Mugg. It is ideal for our purpose. On the west coast there is a large tract that seems quite uninhabited. There will be no temptation for them to pilfer from farms. Eggs, for instance, would be fatal to the whole conception. I have a full training routine worked out for them – marching, PT, digging. They will get invaluable experience in making a snow bivouac. Nothing more snug if you go the right way about it.'

'Well,' said Jumbo. 'The thing to do is just to stand by, eh? The CO will be back tomorrow or the next day.'

'Oh, but I've got my orders, direct from HOO HQ. I'm to start "forthwith". Didn't they notify you?'

'We had a chit to say you were coming.'

'This, was it not?' The doctor produced from his fleecy bosom a carbon copy of the letter that lay in the pending tray. 'Correct me if I am wrong, but I read that as a direct order to give me every facility for my research.'

'Yes,' conceded Jumbo. 'It could be read in that sense. Why not go out and make a recce on your own? I've never been across to the west coast. Map may be out of date, you know. Often are. I daresay the whole place has been built over now. Why not take a few days off and make sure?'

Jumbo was replete with unnatural and irrational foods; he was drowsy and no match for an opponent exhilarated with rare marine salts and essences.

'That's not how I read my orders,' said the doctor, 'or yours.'

Jumbo looked anxiously at Guy. 'I can't see any of the troop leaders playing on this one.'

'Except Major Graves.'

'Yes, it's a case for the Specialists, plainly.'

'For Trimmer and the sappers.'

'They constitute a cross-section?'

'Yes, Dr Glendening-Rees. I think that would be a very fair description.'

Major Graves seemed to take a fierce relish in relaying these instructions.

'From tomorrow you cease to be under my command. Your section will report in full marching order to a civilian medico, under whose orders you will remain until further notice. You will live in the open on heather and seaweed. I can tell you no more than that. HOO HQ has spoken.'

'I take it, sir, that I shall not be required to go with them?'

'Oh yes, McTavish. There's a job of work for you, quite a job. You have to see that your men get nothing to eat, and of course set them an example yourself.'

'Why us, sir?'

'Why, McTavish? Because we aren't the Guards or the Green Jackets, that's why. Because we're a troop of odds and sods, McTavish. That's why *you* are here.'

Thus with no kind word to speed him Trimmer led his detachment into the unknown.

10

'A FAMILIAR sight surely?' said Ivor Claire.

Guy examined the yacht through his field-glasses.

'*Cleopatra*,' he read.

'Julia Stitch,' said Claire. 'Too good to be true.'

Guy also remembered the ship. She had put into Santa Dulcina not many summers ago. It was a tradition of the Castello, which Guy rather reluctantly observed, to call on English yachts. He dined on board. Next day the yacht-party, six of them, had climbed up to lunch with him, lightly, hyperbolically, praising everything.

A large dish of spaghetti had been fomented. A number of flesh-less fowls had been dismembered and charred; some limp lettuces drenched in oil and sprinkled with chopped garlic. It was a depressing luncheon which even Mrs Stitch's beauty and gaiety could barely enliven. Guy told the story of the romantic origin of the 'Castello Crauccibac'. The *vino scelto* began its soporific work. Conversation lapsed. Then as they sat rather gloomily in the loggia, while Josepina and Bianca were removing the meat-plates, there rose from above them the wild tocsin: '*C'e scappata la mucca.*'* It was the recurring drama of Santa Dulcinese life, the escape of the cow, more pit-pony than minotaur, from her cellar under the farm-house.

Josepina and Bianca took up the cry: '*Accidente!*' '*Porca miseria. C'e scappata la mucca,*' dropped everything and bounded over the parapet.

'*C'e scappata la mucca,*' cried Mrs Stitch, precipitately following.

The dazed animal tumbled from low terrace to terrace among the vines. Mrs Stitch was up with her first. Mrs Stitch was the one to grasp the halter and lead her back with soothing words to her subterranean stall.

* 'The cow has got out.'

97

'I was on board once,' Guy said.

'I sailed in her. Three weeks of excruciating discomfort. The things one did in peace-time!'

'It seemed a lap of luxury to me.'

'Not the bachelors' cabins, Guy. Julia was brought up in the old tradition of giving hell to bachelors. There was mutiny brewing all the time. She used to drag one out of the casino like a naval picket rounding up a red-light quarter. But there's no one, no one in the world I'd sooner see at the moment.' In the weeks of their acquaintance Guy had never seen Claire so moved with enthusiasm. 'Let's go down to the quay.'

'Can she know you're here?'

'Trust Julia to keep in touch with chums.'

'No chum of mine, alas.'

'Everyone is a chum of Julia's.'

But as the *Cleopatra* drew alongside, a chill struck the two watchers.

'Oh God,' said Claire, '*uniforms*.'

Half a dozen male figures stood at the rail. Tommy Blackhouse was there beside a sailor deeply laced with gold; General Whale was there; Brigadier Ritchie-Hook was there. Even, preposterously, Ian Kilbannock was there. But not Mrs Stitch.

The newcomers, even the Admiral, looked unwell. Guy and Claire stood to attention and saluted. The Admiral raised a feeble hand. Ritchie-Hook bared his teeth. Then, as if by previous arrangement, the senior officers went below to seek the repose which had been denied them on their voyage. The *Cleopatra* rudely commandeered, had taken her revenge; she had been built for more friendly waters.

Tommy Blackhouse and Ian Kilbannock came ashore. Tommy's servant, grey ghost of a guardsman, followed with luggage.

'Is Jumbo in the office?'

'Yes, Colonel.'

'We've got to lay on that exercise for tomorrow night.'

'Shall I come too?'

'This is where we part company, Guy. Your Brigadier is taking you over now. Our Brigadier. For your information we are now part of "Hookforce", Brigadier Ritchie-Hook commanding. Why the hell aren't you with your troop, Ivor?'

'We're training by sections today,' said Claire.

'Well, you can come and help get out tomorrow's orders.'

Ian said: 'I think Tommy might have done something about my suitcase. The RAF does not understand about servants.'

'What have you done with your Air Marshal?'

'I got him down,' said Ian. 'I got him right down in the end. All the preliminary symptoms of persecution mania. He had to let me go – like Pharaoh and Moses if you appreciate the allusion. I didn't actually have to slay his first-born, but I made him break out in boils and blains from social inferiority – literally. A dreadful sight. So now I'm at Hostile Offensive Operations, appropriately enough. Have you got a man you can send for my luggage?'

'No.'

'You may have noticed I've gone up in rank.' He showed his cuff.

'I'm afraid I don't know what that means.'

'But surely you can count? I don't expect people to know the names of RAF ranks, but you must notice there is one more of these things. It looks newer than the others. I rather think I equal a Major. It's monstrous I should have to carry my own bag.'

'You won't need your bag. There's nowhere to sleep on the island. What are you doing here, anyway?'

'There was to have been a conference on board – most secret operational planning. Sea-sickness intervened. Like a lunatic,' said Ian, 'I came for the trip. I thought it would be a nice change from the blitz, God help me. I've had no sleep or food. An awful inside cabin over the screw.'

'The bachelors' quarters?'

'Slave quarters, I should think. I had to share with Tommy. He was disgustingly sick. As a matter of fact I think I might be able to eat something now.'

Guy took him to the hotel. Food was found, and while Ian ate he explained his new appointment.

'It might have been made for me. In fact, I rather think it *was* made for me, on Air Marshal Beech's entreaty. I liaise with the Press.'

'You haven't come to write *us* up?'

'Good God, no. You're a deadly secret still. That's the beauty of my job. Everything at HOO is secret, so all I have to do is drink with the American journalists at the Savoy from time to time and refuse information. I tell them I'm a newspaper-man myself and know how they feel. They say I'm a regular guy. And so I am, dammit.'

'Are you, Ian?'

'You've never seen me with my fellow journalists. I show them the democratic side of my character – not what Air Marshal Beech saw.'

'I should awfully like to see it too.'

'You wouldn't understand.' He paused, drank deeply and then added: 'I've been pretty red ever since the Spanish war.'

Guy had nothing to do that morning. He watched Ian eat and drink and smoke. As an illusion of well-being returned, Ian became confidential.

'There's a ship coming for you today.'

'We've heard that before.'

'My dear fellow, I *know*. Hookforce sails in the next convoy. The three other Commandos are on board their ships already. You'll be quite an army if you aren't sunk on the way out.' He progressed from confidence to indiscretion. 'This exercise is all a blind. Tommy doesn't know, of course, but the moment you're all safely below the hatches, you up stick and away.'

'There was some loose talk about an island.'

'Operation Bottleneck? That was off weeks ago. Since then there's been Operation Quicksand and Operation Mousetrap. They're both off. It's Operation Badger now, of course.'

'And what is that?'

'If you don't know, I oughtn't to tell you.'

'Too late to go back now.'

'Well, frankly it's simply Quicksand under another name.'

'And they tell you all this, Ian, at HOO HQ?'

'I pick things up. Journalist's training.'

That afternoon, as on every preceding afternoon, the troopship failed. Tommy devised his orders for the exercise and issued them to the troop-leaders; troop-leaders relayed them to section commanders. The *Cleopatra* held her own secrets of recuperation and planning. At evening the hotel filled. X Commando was always the gayer for Tommy's presence. Most of the mess were old acquaintances of Ian's. They welcomed him with profusion until at length after midnight he sought assistance in finding his way back to the yacht. Guy led him.

'Delightful evening,' he said. 'Delightful fellows.' His voice was always slower and higher when he was in liquor. 'Just like Bellamy's without the bombing. How right you were, Guy, to fix yourself up with this racket. I've been round the other Commandos. Not at all the same sort of fellows. I should like to write a piece about you all. But it wouldn't do.'

'No, it would not. Not at all.'

'Don't misunderstand me,' – the night air was taxing his residue of self-command – 'I don't refer to security. There's an agitation now from the Mystery of Information to take you off the secret list. Heroes are in strong demand. Heroes are urgently required to boost civilian morale. You'll see pages about the Commandos in the papers soon. But not about your racket, Guy. They just won't do, you know. Delightful fellows, heroes too, I dare say, but the Wrong Period. Last-war stuff, Guy. Went out with Rupert Brooke.'

'You find us poetic?'

'No,' said Ian, stopping in his path and turning to face Guy in the darkness. 'Perhaps not poetic, exactly, but Upper Class. Hopelessly upper class. You're the "Fine Flower of the Nation". You can't deny it and *it won't do*.'

In the various stages of inebriation, facetiously itemized for centuries, the category, 'prophetically drunk', deserves a place.

'This is a People's War,' said Ian prophetically, 'and the People won't have poetry and they won't have flowers. Flowers stink. The upper classes are on the secret list. We want heroes of the people, to or for the people, by, with and from the people.'

The chill air of Mugg completed its work of detriment. Ian broke into song:

> 'When wilt thou save the people?
> Oh, God of Mercy! When?
> The People, Lord, the People!
> Not thrones and crowns, but men!'

He broke into a trot and breathlessly repeating the lines in a loud tuneless chant, reached the gangway.

Out of the night the voice of Ritchie-Hook rang terribly: 'Stop making that infernal noise, whoever you are, and go to bed.'

Guy left Ian cowering among the quayside litter, waiting a suitable moment to slip on board.

Next morning at first light to Guy's surprise the troopship at last emerged from the haze of myth and was seen to be solidly at anchor beyond the mouth of the harbour.

'Guy, if the Brigadier doesn't want you, you can make yourself useful to me. Jumbo and I have got to get out embarkation orders. You might go on board and fix up accommodation with the navy. It'll be the hell of a business getting everything on board. I hope to God they'll give us another day before the exercise.'

'According to Ian there isn't going to be an exercise.'

'Oh, rot. They've sent half HOO HQ down to watch it.'

'Ian says it's a blind.'

'Ian doesn't know what he's talking about.'

'There's that section of McTavish's I mentioned,' said Jumbo, 'out in the wilds.'

'Call them in.'

'No signal link.'

'Hell. Where are they?'

'No information. They're due back the day after tomorrow.'

'They'll have to miss the exercise, that's all.'

This was not Guy's first embarkation. He had been through it all before at Liverpool with the Halberdiers. This ship was not 'hired transport'. She was manned by a new naval crew. Guy conscientiously inspected mess decks and cabins. After two hours he said: 'There simply isn't room, sir.'

'There must be,' said the First Officer. 'We're fitted out to army specifications to carry one infantry battalion. That's all I know about it.'

'We aren't quite a normal battalion.'

'That's your pigeon,' said the First Officer.

Guy returned to report. He found Jumbo alone.

'Well, you and the Brigadier and whatever other headquarters he's taking had better go in another ship,' said Jumbo. 'I think everyone would have a happier voyage without the Brigadier.'

'That doesn't solve the problem of the Sergeants. Can't they muck in with the men for once?'

'Impossible. Trouble's begun already with the Sergeants. The Grenadiers formed up to Colonel Tommy. All their NCOs carry three stripes and claim to mess apart. Then the Green Jackets formed up to say that in that case their Corporals must too. By the way, I hope you've got me a decent cabin?'

'Sharing with Major Graves and the doctor.'

'I expected something rather better than that, you know.'

At luncheon Guy found himself the object of persecution.

'You've got to realize,' said Bertie with unusual severity, 'that my men are big men. They need space.'

'My servant must have quarters next door to me,' said Eddie. 'I can't go shouting down to the troop deck every time I want anything.'

'But, Guy, we *can't* sleep with the Coldstream.'

'I won't be responsible for the heavy machine-guns, Crouchback, unless I have a lock-up,' said Major Graves. 'And what's this about doubling up with the MO? I mean to say, that's a bit thick.'

'I can't possibly share the sick-bay with the ship's surgeon,' said the doctor. 'I'm entitled to a cabin of my own.'

'It doesn't seem to me you've done *anything* for us.'

'What they need is Julia Stitch to keep them in order,' said Claire sympathetically.

Tommy Blackhouse meanwhile was preparing himself for a disagreeable interview which he could no longer postpone. Tommy, like most soldiers, sought when possible to delegate unkindness. He now realized that he and only he must break bad news to Jumbo.

'Jumbo,' he said when they were alone in the office, 'I shouldn't bother to come on board tonight. We don't really need you for the exercise and there's a lot of stuff here to clear up.'

'Everything in the office is clear up to date, Colonel.'

'The ship's cram-full. You'll be more comfortable on shore.'

'I'd like to get settled in for the voyage.'

'The trouble is, Jumbo, that there's not going to be room for you.'

'Crouchback has found me a berth. Tight quarters, but I shall manage.'

'You see, you aren't really part of operational headquarters.'

'Not really part of the Commando?'

'You know our establishment. No administration officer. Supernumerary.'

'As far as that goes,' said Jumbo, 'I think it can be regularized.'

'It isn't only that, I'm afraid. I want to take you, of course. I don't know what I shall do without you. But the Brigadier's orders are that we only take combatant soldiers.'

'Ben Ritchie-Hook? I've known him for more than twenty years.'

'That's the trouble. The Brigadier thinks you're a bit senior for our sort of show.'

'Ben thinks that?'

'I'm afraid so. Of course I dare say if we set up a permanent headquarters in the Middle East you could come out and join us later. Meanwhile they want you at HOO HQ.'

Jumbo was a Halberdier, trained from first manhood in the giving and taking of orders. He was hard hit, but he excluded all personal feelings.

'I shall have to adjust my posting,' he said. 'It will be rather complicated. Back to barracks.'

'They can use you at HOO HQ.'

'They must apply in the proper quarter, in the proper form. My place is in barracks.' He sat among his files before his empty trays, his old heart empty of hope. 'You don't think it might help if I saw Ben Ritchie-Hook?'

'Yes,' said Tommy, rather eagerly. 'I should do that. You'll have plenty of time. He'll be in London for at least three weeks. They're flying him out to join us in Egypt. I dare say you can get him to take you with him.'

'Not if he doesn't want me. I've never known Ben do anything he doesn't want to do. You're taking Crouchback?'

'He's going to be Brigade Intelligence Officer.'

'I'm glad you'll have at least one Halberdier. He'll make a useful officer. A lot to learn, of course, but the right stuff in him.'

'I don't know when we sail. You'll stay here until then, of course.'

'Of course.'

It was a relief to both of them when Major Graves came to complain about the sappers' stores. None of his troop could be trusted to handle explosives. Was there a suitable magazine on board?

'Oh, leave them where they are until the sappers get back.'

'Unguarded?'

'They'll be safe enough.'

'Very good, sir.'

When Major Graves left, Tommy communed further with his orders for the exercise. The secret of their futility was kept from him until all were embarked. Then the party from the *Cleopatra* came aboard and it was announced that there was to be no exercise. Major-General Whale from HOO HQ had intended to address a full parade of all ranks but deck-space was lacking. Instead he told the officers. No embarkation leave. No last letters. The ship would join others carrying other Commandos under escort at a rendezvous on the high seas.

'Shanghaied, by God,' said Claire.

Jumbo could not know that Tommy had been kept in the dark too. To his sad old sense of honour it was the final betrayal. He watched from the icy fore-shore as the troopship and the yacht sailed away; then heavily returned to the empty hotel. His jaunt was over.

On his desert island Mugg crept out to pilfer the sapper stores, and the sappers themselves, emaciated and unshaven, presently lurched in carrying Dr Glendening-Rees on a wattle hurdle.

'I MUST say,' said Ivor Claire, 'the local inhabitants are uncommonly civil.'

He and Guy sat at sundown in the bar of the hotel. Light shone out into the dusk unscreened to join the headlamps of the cars, passing, turning and stopping on the gravel, and the bright shop windows in the streets beyond. Cape Town at the extremity of two dark continents was a *ville lumière* such as Trimmer had sought in vain.

'Three ships in and a reception committee for each. Something laid on for everybody.'

'It's partly to tease the Dutch, partly to keep the soldiery out of mischief. I gather they had trouble with the last Trooper.'

'Partly good nature too, I fancy.'

'Oh, yes, partly that, I've no doubt.'

'It didn't do B Commando much good. They've been taken on a route march, poor devils.'

'Probably the best thing for them.'

An upright elderly man came across the room. 'Good evening, gentlemen,' he said. 'Forgive my butting in. I'm secretary of the club here. I don't know whether you've been there yet.'

'Yes, indeed,' said Guy, 'thank you very much. I was taken to luncheon there today.'

'Ah, good. Do use it as your own if you want a game of billiards or bridge or anything. Remember the way? Next door to the post office.'

'Thank you very much.'

'There's usually a small gathering about this time. I'll look out for you if you drop in, and introduce you to some fellows.'

'Thanks awfully.'

'You've set us wondering, you know – the different regimental badges. Are you all replacements?'

'We're a mixed lot,' said Claire.

'Well, I know we mustn't ask questions. Are you both fixed up for dinner?'

'Yes, thank you very much.'

'Uncommonly civil fellows,' said Claire when they were again alone. 'Anyway, I've had the most satisfactory day.'

'I too.'

'I took my time going ashore but there were still friendly natives hanging about. A nice ass of a woman came up and said: "Is there anything special you'd like to do or see?" and I said: "Horses." I haven't thought of anything much except horses – and of course Freda – for the last six weeks, as you may imagine. "That may be a bit difficult," she said. "Are you safe on one?" So I pointed out I was in a cavalry regiment. "But aren't you all mechanized now?" I said I thought I could still keep up and she said: "There's Mr Somebody, but he's rather special. I'll see." So she got hold of Mr Somebody and as luck would have it, he'd seen Thimble win at Dublin and was all over me. He had a very decent stable indeed somewhere down the coast and let me pick my horse and we spent the morning hacking. After luncheon I took a jumper he's schooling over the fences. I feel a different and a better man. What happened to you?'

'Eddie and Bertie and I went to the Zoo. We persecuted the ostriches, tried to make them put their heads in the sand, but they wouldn't. Eddie got into the cage and chased them all over the place with a black keeper pleading through the wire. Bertie said one kick of an ostrich can kill three horses. Then we got picked up by a sugar-daddy who took us to the club. Excellent food and you know there's nothing really much the matter with South African wine.'

'I know nothing of wine.'

'The sugar-daddy explained they only send their bad vintages abroad and keep all the good to drink themselves. Bertie and Eddie went off with him afterwards to see vineyards. I went to the Art Gallery. They've two remarkable Noel Patons.'

'I know nothing of art.'

'Nor did Noel Paton. That's the beauty of him.'

Bertie and Eddie came into the bar, huge, unsteady, rosy and smiling.

'We've been sampling wine all the afternoon.'

'Eddie's tight.'

'We're both tight as owls.'

'We've got to take some girls dancing, but we're too tight.'

'Why not lie down for a bit?' said Claire.

'Exactly what I thought. That's why I brought Eddie here – to have a bath.'

'Might drown,' said Eddie.

'Charming girls,' said Bertie. 'Husbands away at the war. Must sober up.'

'Sleep would be the thing.'

'Sleep and bath and then dance with the girls. I'll get some rooms.'

'It's odd,' said Ivor Claire, 'I feel absolutely no urge to get tight now I'm allowed to. In that ship I hardly drew a sober breath.'

'Let's walk.'

They sauntered out into the town.

'I suppose one or more of those absurd stars is called the Southern Cross,' said Claire, gazing up into the warm and brilliant night.

'It's the kind of thing one ought to know, I suppose, for finding one's way in the dark.'

'The dark,' said Claire, 'the black-out. That's the worst thing about the ship. It's the worst thing about the whole war.'

Here everything was ablaze. Merchandise quite devoid of use or beauty shone alluringly in the shop windows. The streets were fun of Hookforce. Car-loads of soldiers drove slowly past laden with the spoils of farms and gardens, baskets of oranges and biblical bunches of grapes.

'Fair-day,' said Guy.

Then there was a sterner sound. The soldiers on the pavement, reluctant to lose their holiday mood, edged into doorways and slipped down side turnings. A column of threes in full marching order, arms swinging high, eyes grimly fixed to the front, tramped down the main street towards the docks. Guy and Claire saluted the leading officer, a glaring, fleshless figure.

'B Commando,' said Guy. 'Colonel Prentice.'

'Awfully mad.'

'I was told that he always wears the stockings his great-great-grandfather had at Inkermann. Can that be true?'

'I heard it. I think so.'

'Enclosing every thin man, there's a fat man demanding elbow-room.'

'No doubt he's enjoying himself in his own fashion. One way and another, Guy, Cape Town seems to have provided each of us with whatever we wanted.'

'Ali Baba's lamp.'

'We needed it. Where to now?'

'The club?'

'Too matey. Back to the hotel.'

But when they got there Claire said: 'Too many soldiers.'

'Perhaps there's a garden.'

There was. Guy and Claire sat on a wicker seat looking across an empty illumined tennis lawn. Claire lit a cigarette. He smoked rather seldom. When he did so, it was with an air of conscious luxury.

'What a voyage,' he said. 'Nearly over now. How one longed for a torpedo at times. I used to stand on deck at night and imagine one, a beautiful streak of foam, a bang, and then the heads all round bobbing up for the third time and myself, the sole survivor, floating gently away to some nearby island.'

'Wishful thinking. They cram you into open boats, you go mad from drinking sea-water.'

'What a voyage,' said Claire again. 'We're told, and we tell our men, that we have to hold Egypt so as to protect the Suez Canal. And to reach Suez we go half-way to Canada and Trinidad. And when we do get there we shall find the war's over. According to the chap I had lunch with, they can't build cages quick enough to hold the Italian prisoners coming in. I dare say we shall be turned on to guard duties.'

This was February 1941. English tanks were cruising far west of Benghazi; bankers, labelled 'AMGOT', were dining nightly at the Mohamed Ali Club in Cairo, and Rommel, all unknown, was even then setting up his first headquarters in Africa.

Of the nine weeks which had passed since X Commando sailed

from Mugg, five only had been spent on the high seas. In the war of attrition which raged ceaselessly against the human spirit, anti-climax was a heavy weapon. The Commando, for all the rude haste and trickery of departure, sailed exultingly. By noon on the second day rumour had it that the rendezvous with the navy was off. Rumour was right. At the second dawn they sailed into Scapa Flow and lay-to beside the sister ships which carried their fellow Commandos. There had been sinkings and diversions and counter-orders; a German capital ship was haunting the Western Approaches. Brigadier Ritchie-Hook appeared and for a month his force relentlessly 'biffed' the encircling hills, night after long night. He brought with him a Halberdier Brigade Major who instructed Guy in the otiose duties of Intelligence Officer. Guy chalked the nightly wanderings of the Commandos on the talc face of his map and recorded them next day in the War Diary. On these exercises the Brigadier seldom spent long at his 'battle headquarters'. Guy and the Brigade Major shivered alone on the beaches, while Ritchie-Hook roamed the moors alone with a haversack full of 'thunder-flashes'.

Guy was sorrowfully conscious that his old hero cut a slightly absurd figure in the eyes of X Commando. They were quick with injurious nicknames in that group. Someone dubbed Ritchie-Hook 'the Widow Twankey' and the preposterous name stuck.

Trimmer and his section were absent. They had momentarily slipped through one of the cracks in the military floor.

Hookforce remained at twelve hours' notice for service overseas. There was no leave; no private communication with the shore. Christmas and New Year passed in dire gloom. The RN officers stood aloof from the RNVR, touchy young men in beards. The bar, which might have been a place of sympathy, proved the centre of contention, for the navy were limited by rank in their wine bills, while the army were not. Below decks there was no wet canteen and gross rumours circulated there of orgies among the officers. It was not a happy ship. At length they sailed on their huge detour. Brigadier and Brigade Major returned for further conferences in London, to join them by air in the Middle East. Trimmer and his sappers arrived at Hoy two days later.

'I wonder,' said Guy, 'were we rather bloody to the navy?'

'They are such awful pip-squeaks,' said Claire without animosity. 'The little ones with beards particularly.'

'It didn't help when Bertie referred to the Captain as "that booby on the roof".'

'The name stuck. It didn't help, of course, when the Pay-Master took Eddie's place in the ward-room and Eddie told him he didn't expect to find a ticket collector in a restaurant car.'

'Eddie was tight that evening.'

'Colonel Tommy messing with the Booby-on-the-Roof had no idea what we had to suffer.'

'He always took our side when there were complaints.'

'Well, naturally. We are his chaps. The pip-squeaks complained altogether too much.'

'The sergeants have been awful.'

'All successful mutinies have been led by NCOs.'

'I shouldn't be surprised if Corporal-Major Ludovic turned out to be a communist.'

'He's all right,' said Claire, automatically defending his own man.

'His eyes are horrible.'

'They're colourless, that's all.'

'Why does he wear bedroom slippers all day?'

'He says it's his feet.'

'Do you believe him?'

'Of course.'

'He's a man of mystery. Was he ever a trooper?'

'I suppose so, once.'

'He looks like a dishonest valet.'

'Yes, perhaps he was that too. He hung about Knightsbridge Barracks and no one knew what to make of him. He just reported at the beginning of the war as a reservist and claimed the rank of Corporal of Horse. His name was on the roll all right, but no one seemed to know anything about him, so naturally they wished him on me when the troop formed.'

'He was the *éminence grise* behind the complaint that "Captain's rounds" violated the sanctity of the sergeants' mess.'

'So they do. I wonder,' said Claire, changing the subject delicately, 'how the other Commandos got on with their sailors?'

'Quite well, I believe. Prentice makes his officers keep to the same drink ration as the navy.'

'I bet that's against King's Regulations.' Then he added: 'I shouldn't be surprised if I didn't get rid of Ludovic when we reach Egypt.'

They sat in silence for some time. Then Guy said:

'It's getting cold. Let's go inside and forget the ship for one evening.'

They found Bertie and Eddie in the bar.

'We're quite sober now,' said Eddie.

'So we're just having one drink before joining the girls. Good evening, Colonel.'

Tommy had entered behind them.

'Well,' he said, 'well. I thought I'd find some of my officers here.'

'A drink, Colonel?'

'Yes, indeed. I've had the hell of a day at Simonstown and I've got some rather disturbing news.'

'I suppose,' said Claire, 'we're going to turn round now and sail back.'

'Not that, but about our Brigadier.'

'*La veuve?*'

'He and the Brigade Major. Their aeroplane left Brazzaville last week and hasn't been heard of since. It seems Hookforce may have to change its name.'

'Your friend, Guy,' said Eddie.

'I love him. He'll turn up.'

'He'd better hurry if he's going to command our operation.'

'Who's in charge now?'

'It seems I am, at the moment.'

'Ali Baba's lamp,' said Claire.

'Eh?'

'Nothing.'

Later that night Guy and Tommy and Claire returned to the ship. Eddie and Bertie were walking the decks; 'walking ourselves sober,' they explained. They carried a bottle and refreshed themselves every second circuit.

'Look,' Eddie said. 'We had to buy it. It's called "Kommando".'

'It's brandy,' said Bertie. 'Rather horrible. Do you think, Colonel, we might send it up to the Booby?'

'No.'

'The only other thing I can think of is to throw it overboard before it makes us sick.'

'Yes, I should do that.'

'No lack of *esprit de corps*? It's called Kommando.'

Eddie dropped the bottle over the rail and leant gazing after it.

'I think I'm going to be sick, all the same,' he said.

Later, in the tiny cabin he shared with the two deeply sleeping companions, Guy lay awake. He could not yet mourn Ritchie-Hook. That ferocious Halberdier, he was sure, was even then biffing his way through the jungle on a line dead straight for the enemy. Guy thought instead with deep affection of X Commando. 'The Flower of the Nation', Ian Kilbannock had ironically called them. He was not far wrong. There was heroic simplicity in Eddie and Bertie. Ivor Claire was another pair of boots entirely, salty, withdrawn, incorrigible. Guy remembered Claire as he first saw him in the Roman spring in the afternoon sunlight amid the embosoming cypresses of the Borghese Gardens, putting his horse faultlessly over the jumps, concentrated as a man in prayer. Ivor Claire, Guy thought, was the fine flower of them all. He was quintessential England, the man Hitler had not taken into account, Guy thought.

BOOK TWO

In the Picture

1

MAJOR-GENERAL WHALE held the appointment of Director of Land Forces in Hazardous Offensive Operations. He was known in countless minutes as the DLFHOO and to a few old friends as 'Sprat'. On Holy Saturday 1941 he was summoned to attend the ACIG's weekly meeting at the War Office. He went with foreboding. He was not fully informed of the recent disasters in the Middle East but he knew things were going badly. Benghazi had fallen the week before. It did not seem clear where the retreating army intended to make its stand. On Maundy Thursday the Australians in Greece had been attacked on their open flank. It was not clear where they would stand. Belgrade had been bombed on Palm Sunday. But these tidings were not Sprat's first concern that morning. The matter on the ACIG's agenda which accounted for Sprat's presence was '*Future of Special Service Forces in UK*'.

The men round the table represented a galaxy of potent initials, DSD, AG, QMG, DPS, and more besides. These were no snowy-headed, muddled veterans of English tradition but lean, middle-aged men who kept themselves fit; men on the make; a hanging jury, thought Sprat, greeting them heartily.

The Lieutenant-General in the chair said:

'Just remind us – will you, Sprat? – what precisely is your present strength?'

'Well, sir, there *were* the Halberdiers.'

'Not since last week.'

'And Hookforce.'

'Yes, Hookforce. What's the latest from them?' He turned to a Major-General who sat in a cloud of pipe-smoke on his left.

'No one seems to have found any use for them in ME. "Badger", of course, was cancelled.'

'Of course.'

115

'Of course.'

'Of course.'

'That is hardly their fault, sir,' said Sprat. 'First they lost their commander. Then they lost their assault ships. The canal was closed when they reached Suez, you remember. They were put into temporary camps in Canal Area. Then when the canal was cleared the ships were needed to take the Australians to Greece. They moved by train to Alex.'

'Yes, Sprat, we know. Of course it's not their fault. All I mean is, they don't seem to be exactly pulling their weight.'

'I rather think, sir,' said a foxy Brigadier, 'that we shall soon hear they've been broken up and used as replacements.'

'Exactly. Anyway, they are MEF now. What I want to get at is: what land forces do you command at this moment in UK?'

'Well, sir, as you know, recruiting was suspended after Hook-force sailed. That left us rather thin on the ground.'

'Yes?'

Hands doodled on the agenda papers.

'At the moment, sir, I have one officer and twelve men, four of whom are in hospital with frost-bite and unlikely to be passed fit for active service.'

'Exactly. I merely wanted your confirmation.'

Outside, in the cathedral, whose tower could be seen from the War Office windows; far beyond in the lands of enemy and ally, the Easter fire was freshly burning. Here for Sprat all was cold and dark. The gangmen of the departments closed in for the kill. The representative of the DPS drew a series of little gallows on his agenda.

'Frankly, sir, I don't think the DPS has even quite understood what function the Commandos have which could not be performed by ordinary regimental soldiers or the Royal Marines. The DPS does not like the volunteer system. Every fighting man shall be prepared to undertake any task assigned him, however hazardous.'

'Exactly.'

The staff officers pronounced judgement by turn.

'. . . I can only say, sir, that the special postings have put a considerable extra strain on our department. . . .'

'. . . As we see it, sir, either the Commandos become a *corps d'élite*, in which case they seriously weaken the other arms of the service, or they become a sort of Foreign Legion of throw-outs, in which case we can hardly see them making very much contribution to the war effort. . . .'

'I don't want to say anything against your chaps, Sprat. Excellent raw material, no doubt. But I think you must agree that the experiment of relaxing barrack discipline hasn't quite worked out. That explosion at Mugg . . .'

'I think, if you'll allow me, I can explain . . .'

'Yes, yes, no doubt. It's really quite beside the point. I'm sorry it was brought up.'

'The security precautions at the embarkation . . .'

'Yes, yes. Someone put a foot wrong. No blame attaches to HOO HQ.'

'If we could start another recruiting drive I am sure the response . . .'

'That is just what Home Forces do *not* want.'

'The Ministry of Information . . .' began Sprat desperately, most infelicitously. The doodling hands were still. Breaths were momentarily caught, then sharply, with clouds of smoke, expelled. 'The Ministry of Information,' said Sprat defiantly, 'have shown great interest. They are only waiting for a successful operation to release the whole story to the press. Civil morale,' he faltered, '. . . American opinion . . .'

'That, of course,' said the chairman, 'does not concern this committee.'

In the end a minute was drafted to the CIGS recommending that no steps were desirable with regard to Special Service Forces.

Sprat returned to his own office. All over the world, unheard by Sprat, the *Exultet* had been sung that morning. It found no echo in Sprat's hollow heart. He called his planners to him and his liaison officer.

'They're out to do us down,' he reported succinctly. He need not name the enemy. No one thought he meant the Germans. 'There's only one thing for it. We must mount an operation at once and call in the press. What have we got that's suitable for one rather moderate officer and eight men?'

The planners at HOO HQ were fertile. In their steel cupboards lay in various stages of elaboration and under a variety of sobriquets projects for the assault of almost every feature of the enemy's immense coast line.

A pause.

'There's "Popgun", sir.'

'"Popgun"? "Popgun"? That was one of yours, wasn't it, Charles?'

'No one was much interested. I always thought it had possibilities.'

'Remind me.'

'Popgun' was the least ambitious of all the plans. It concerned a tiny, uninhabited island near Jersey on which stood, or was believed to stand, a disused light-house. Someone on the naval side, idly scanning a chart, had suggested that supposing the enemy had tumbled to the tricks of RDF this island and this ruin might be a possible choice of station. Charles reminded Sprat of these particulars.

'Yes. Lay on "Popgun". Ian, you'll be up to the neck in this. You'd better get into touch with McTavish at once. You'll be going with him.'

'Where is he?' asked Ian Kilbannock.

'He must be somewhere. Someone must know. You and Charles find him while I collect a submarine.'

While the first bells of Easter rang throughout Christendom, the muezzin called his faithful to prayer from the shapeless white minaret beyond the barbed wire; South, West and North the faithful prostrated themselves towards the rising sun. His voice fell unheeded among the populous dunes of Sidi Bishr.

Already awake, Guy rose from his camp-bed and shouted for shaving-water. He was brigade duty-officer, nearing the end of his tour of duty beside the office telephone. During the night there had been one air-raid warning. GHQ Cairo had been silent.

The brigade, still named 'Hookforce', occupied a group of huts in the centre of the tented camp. Tommy Blackhouse was Deputy Commander with the acting rank of full colonel. He had returned from Cairo on the third day of their sojourn in Egypt with red tabs and a number of staff officers, chief among them a small, bald, youngish man named Hound. He was the Brigade Major. Neither in the Halberdiers nor in the Commandos had Guy met a soldier quite like Major Hound, nor had Major Hound met a force like Hookforce.

He had chosen a military career because he was not clever enough to pass into the civil service. At Sandhurst in 1925 the universal assumption was that the British army would never again be obliged to fight a European war. Young Hound had shown an aptitude for administration and his failures in the riding-school were compensated by prizes at Bisley. Later in the drift of war he was found in the pool of unattached staff officers in Cairo when Hookforce arrived leaderless at Suez. To them he came and he did not disguise his distaste for their anomalies. They had no transport, they had no cooks, they had far too many officers and sergeants, they wore a variety of uniforms and followed a multitude of conflicting regimental customs, they bore strange arms, daggers and toggle-ropes and tommy-guns. B Commando was ruled by a draconic private law and a code of punishment unauthorized by King's Regulations. X Commando might have seemed lawless but for the presence of fifty Free Spaniards who had drifted in from Syria and been inexplicably put under command; beside their anarchy all minor irregularities became unremarkable. The camp police were constantly flushing women in the Spanish lines. One morning they dug up the body of an Egyptian cab-driver, just beyond the perimeter, lightly buried in sand with his throat cut.

When Major Hound left Cairo he had been told:

'There's no place here for private armies. We've got to get these fellows, whoever they are, reorganized as a standard infantry brigade.'

Later a recommendation was made that Hookforce should be disbanded and distributed as replacements. An order followed from London to hold fast pending a decision at the highest level as to the whole future of Special Service Forces. Major Hound kept his own counsel about these matters. They were not communicated to him officially. He learned them in Cairo on his frequent trips to the Turf Club and to Shepheard's Hotel in conversation with cronies from G H Q. He mentioned the state of discipline in camp, also unofficially. And Hookforce remained at Sidi Bishr declining from boredom to disorder and daily growing more and more to justify the suspicions of GHQ.

Guy remained Intelligence Officer. Five spectacled men, throwouts from the Commandos, were attached to him as his section. In the employment of these men he waged a deadly private war with the Brigade Major. Lately he had shed them, attaching them to the Signals Officer for instruction in procedure.

Breakfast was brought him at the office table; a kind of rissole of bully beef gritty with sand, tea that tasted of chlorine. At eight the office clerks appeared; at a quarter past Corporal-Major Ludovic, whom Ivor Claire had succeeded in promoting to headquarters. He gazed about the hut with his pale eyes, observed Guy, saluted him in a style that was ecclesiastical rather than military, and began ponderously moving papers from tray to tray; not thus the Brigade Major, who arrived very briskly at twenty past.

'Morning, Crouchback,' said Major Hound. 'Nothing from GHQ? Then we can take it that the last cancellation stands. The units can get out into the country. How about your section? They've finished their signalling course, I think. How do you propose to exercise them today?'

'They're doing PT under Sergeant Smiley.'

'And after?'

'Infantry drill,' said Guy, crossly improvising, 'under me.'

'Good. Smarten 'em up.'

At nine Tommy arrived.

'More trouble with X Commando,' said Major Hound.

'Damn.'

'Graves is on his way to see you.'

'Damn. Guy, have you still got those obliques of "Badger"?'

'Yes, Colonel.'

'Bung 'em back to GHQ. They won't be wanted now.'

'You needn't stay in the office while Major Graves is here,' said the Brigade Major to Guy. 'Better get on with that drill parade.'

Guy went in search of his section. Sergeant Smiley called them hastily to their feet on his approach. Six cigarettes smouldered in the sand at their feet.

'Fall them in in a quarter of an hour with rifles and drill order, outside the brigade office,' he ordered.

For an hour he drilled them in the powdery sand. It all came back to him from the barrack square. He stood by the Brigade-Major's window, opened his mouth wide and roared like a Halberdier. Inside the hut Major Graves was telling his tale of injustice and neglect. Corporal-Major Ludovic was typing his journal.

'*Man is what he hates*,' he wrote. '*Yesterday I was Blackhouse. Today I am Crouchback. Tomorrow, merciful heaven, shall I be Hound?*'

'. . . The odd numbers of the front rank will seize the rifles of the even numbers of the rear rank with the left hand crossing the muzzles, magazines turned outward, at the same time raising the piling swivels with the fore-finger and thumb of both hands . . .'

He paused, aware of an obvious anomaly.

'In the present instance,' he continued, falling into a parody of his old drill-sergeant, 'number two being a blank file, there are no even numbers in the rear rank. Number three will therefore for the purpose of this exercise regard himself as even. . . .'

He concluded his exposition.

'Squad, pile arms. As you were. Listen to the detail. The odd numbers of the front rank – that's you, number one – will seize the rifles of even numbers of the rear rank – that's you, number three . . .'

The Brigade Major's head appeared at the window.

'I say, Crouchback, could you move your men a bit farther away?'

Guy spun on his heel and saluted.

'Sir.'

He spun back.

'Squad will retire. About turn. Quick march. Halt. About turn. As you were. About turn. As you were. About turn.' They were now fifty yards from him but his voice carried.

'I will give you the detail once more. The odd numbers of the front rank will seize the rifles of the even numbers of the rear rank . . .'

Behind their steamy goggles the men glimpsed that this performance was being played not solely for their own discomfort. Sergeant Smiley began to join his powerful tones to Guy's.

After half an hour Guy gave them a stand-easy. Tommy Black-house called him in.

'Most impressive, Guy,' he said. 'First rate. But I must ask you to dismiss now. I've got a job for you. Go into town and see Ivor and find out when he's coming back.'

For a fortnight Ivor Claire had been absent from duty. He had led a party armed with tent mallets in pursuit of Arab marauders, had tripped on a guy-rope and twisted his knee. Eschewing the services of the RAMC he had installed himself in a private nurs-ing-home.

Guy went to the car-park and found a lorry going in for rations. The road ran along the edge of the sea. The breeze was full of flying sand. On the beaches young civilians exposed hairy bodies and played ball with loud, excited cries. Army lorries passed in close procession, broken here and there by new, tight-shut limousines bearing purple-lipped ladies in black satin.

'Drop me at the Cecil,' said Guy, for he had other business in Alexandria besides Ivor Claire. He wished to make his Easter duties and preferred to do so in a city church, rather than in camp. Already, without deliberation, he had begun to dissociate himself from the army in matters of real concern.

Alexandria, ancient asparagus bed of theological absurdity, is now somewhat shabbily furnished with churches. Guy found what he sought in a side street, a large unobtrusive building attached to a school, it seemed, or a hospital. He entered into deep gloom.

A fat youth in shorts and vest was lethargically sweeping the aisle. Guy approached and addressed him in French. He seemed not to hear. A bearded, skirted figure scudded past in the darkness. Guy pursued and said awkwardly:

'*Excusez-moi, mon père. Y a-t-il un prêtre qui parle anglais ou italien?*'

The priest did not pause.

'*Français,*' he said.

'*Je veux me confesser, en français si c'est nécessaire. Mais je préfère beaucoup anglais ou italien, si c'est possible.*'

'*Anglais,*' said the hasty priest. '*Par-là.*'

He turned abruptly into the sacristy pointing as he went towards

122

a still darker chapel. Khaki stockings and army boots protruded from the penitents' side of the confessional. Guy knelt and waited. He knew what he had to say. The mutter of voices in the shadows seemed to be prolonged inordinately. At length a young soldier emerged and Guy took his place. A bearded face was just visible through the grille; a guttural voice blessed him. He made his confession and paused. The dark figure seemed to shrug off the triviality of what he had heard.

'You have a rosary? Say three decades.'

He gave the absolution.

'Thank you, father, and pray for me.' Guy made to go but the priest continued:

'You are here on leave?'

'No, father.'

'You have been here long?'

'A few weeks.'

'You have come from the desert?'

'No, father.'

'You have just come from England? You came with new tanks?'

Suddenly Guy was suspicious. He was shriven. The priest was no longer bound by the seal of confession. The grille still stood between them. Guy still knelt, but the business between them was over. They were man and man now in a country at war.

'When do you go to the desert?'

'Why do you ask?'

'To help you. There are special dispensations. If you are going at once into action I can give you communion.'

'I'm not.'

Guy rose and left the church. Beggars thronged him. He walked a few steps towards the main street where the trams ran, then turned back. The boy with the broom had gone. The confessional was empty. He knocked on the open door of the sacristy. No one came. He entered and found a clean tiled floor, cupboards, a sink, no priest. He left the church and stood once more among the beggars, undecided. The transition from the role of penitent to that of investigating officer was radical. He could not now remember verbatim what had occurred. The questions had been impertinent;

123

were they necessarily sinister? Could he identify the priest? Could he, if called to find a witness, identify the young soldier?

Two palm trees in a yard separated the church from the clergy-house. Guy rang the bell and presently the fat boy opened the door, disclosing a vista of high white corridor.

'I would like to know the name of one of your fathers.'

'The fathers have this moment gone to rest. They have had very long ceremonies this morning.'

'I don't want to disturb him – merely to know his name. He speaks English and was hearing confessions in the church two minutes ago.'

'No confessions now until three o'clock. The fathers are resting.'

'I have been to confession to this father. I want to know his name. He speaks English.'

'I speak English. I do not know what father you want.'

'I want his name.'

'You must come at three o'clock, please, when the fathers have rested.'

Guy turned away. The beggars settled on him. He strode into the busy street and the darkness of Egypt closed on him in the dazzling sunlight. Perhaps he had imagined the whole incident, and if he had not, what profit was there in pursuit? There were priests in France working for the allies. Why not a priest in Egypt, in exile, doing his humble bit for his own side? Egypt teemed with spies. Every troop movement was open to the scrutiny of a million ophthalmic eyes. The British order of battle must be known in minute detail from countless sources. What could that priest accomplish except perhaps gain kinder treatment for his community if Rommel reached Alexandria? Probably the only result, if Guy made a report, would be an order forbidding HM forces to frequent civilian churches.

Ivor Claire's nursing-home overlooked the Municipal Gardens. Guy walked there through the crowded streets so despondently that the touts looking at him despaired and let him pass unsolicited.

He found Claire in a wheeled-chair on his balcony.

'*Much* better,' he said in answer to Guy's inquiry. 'They are all very pleased with me. I may be able to get up to Cairo next week for the races.'

'Colonel Tommy is getting a little restive.'

'Who wouldn't be at Sidi Bishr? Well, he knows where to find me when he wants me.'

'He seems rather to want you now.'

'Oh, I don't think I'd be much use to him until I'm fit, you know. My troop is in good hands. When Tommy kindly relieved me of Corporal-Major Ludovic my anxieties came to an end. But we must keep touch. I can't have you doing a McTavish on me.'

'Two flaps since you went away. Once we were at two hours' notice for three days.'

'I know. Greek nonsense. When there's anything really up I shall hear from Julia Stitch before Tommy does. She is a mine of indiscretion. You know she's here?'

'Half X Commando spend their evenings with her.'

'Why don't you?'

'Oh, she wouldn't remember me.'

'My dear Guy, she remembers everyone. Algie has some sort of job keeping his eye on the King. They're very well installed. I thought of moving in on them but one can't be sure that Julia will give an invalid quite all he needs. There's rather too much coming and going, too – generals and people. Julia pops in most mornings and brings me the gossip.'

Then Guy recounted that morning's incident in the church.

'Not much to shoot a chap on,' said Claire. 'Even a clergyman.'

'Ought I to do anything about it?'

'Ask Tommy. It might prove a great bore, you know. Everyone is a spy in this country.'

'That's rather what I thought.'

'I'm sure the nurses here are. They walk out with the Vichy French from that ship in the harbour. What's the news from Sidi Bishr?'

'Worse. A little worse every day. B Commando are on the verge of mutiny. Prentice has confined them to camp until every man has swum a hundred yards in boots and equipment. They'll shoot him when they go into action. Major Graves still thinks he ought to command X Commando.'

'He must be insane to want to.'

'Yes. Tony is having a bad time. The Grenadiers are all down with Gyppy tummy. Five Coldstreamers put in to be returned to their regiment. Corporal-Major Ludovic is suspected of writing poetry.'

'More than probable.'

'Our Catalan refugees have even got Tommy worried. An Arab mess waiter went off with A Commando's medical stores. We've got four courts-martial pending and ten men adrift. God knows how many arms stolen. The NAAFI till has been burgled twice. Someone tried to set the camp cinema on fire. Nothing has been heard of the Brigadier.'

'That at least is good news.'

'Not to me, Ivor.'

They were interrupted by a shrill guttersnipe whistle from the street below.

'Julia,' said Claire.

'I'd better go.'

'Don't.'

A minute later Mrs Algernon Stitch was with them. She wore linen and a Mexican sombrero; a laden shopping basket hung over one white arm. She inclined the huge straw disc of her hat over Claire and kissed his forehead.

'Why are your nurses so disagreeable, Ivor?'

'Politics. They all claim to have lost brothers at Oran. You remember Guy?'

She turned her eyes, her true blue, portable and compendious oceans upon Guy, absorbed him and then very loudly, in rich Genoese accents, proclaimed:

'*C'e scappata la mucca.*'

'You see,' said Ivor, as though displaying a clever trick of Freda's, 'I told you she would remember.'

'Why wasn't I told you were here? Come to lunch?'

'Well, I don't know exactly. It's awfully kind of you . . .'

'Good. Are you coming, Ivor?'

'Is it a party?'

'I forget who.'

'Perhaps I'm best where I am.'

Mrs Stitch gazed over the balcony into the gardens.

'Forster says they ought to be "thoroughly explored",' she

said. 'Something for another day.' To Guy. 'You've got his *Guide*?'

'I've always wanted a copy. It's very scarce.'

'Just been reprinted. Here, take mine. I can always get another.'

She produced from her basket a copy of E. M. Forster's *Alexandria*.

'I didn't know. In that case I can get one for myself. Thanks awfully, though.'

'Take it, fool,' she said.

'Well, thanks awfully. I know his *Pharos and Pharillon*, of course.'

'Of course; the *Guide* is topping too.'

'Have you brought me anything, Julia?' Claire asked.

'Not today, unless you'd care for some Turkish delight.'

'Yes, please.'

'Here you are. I haven't finished shopping yet. In fact, I must go now.' To Guy. 'Come on.'

'Not much of a visit.'

'You should come to lunch when you're asked.'

'Well, thank you for the sweets.'

'I'll be back. Come on.'

She led Guy down and out. He tried to circumvent her at the door of her little open car but was peremptorily ordered away.

'Other side, fool. Jump in.'

Off she drove, darting between camels and trams and cabs and tanks, down the Rue Sultan, spinning left at the Nebi Daniel, stopping abruptly in the centre of the crossing and saying: 'Just look. The Soma. In the days of Cleopatra the streets ran from the Gate of the Moon to the Gate of the Sun and from the lake harbour to the sea harbour with colonnades all the way. White marble and green silk awnings. Perhaps you knew.'

'I didn't.'

She stood up in the car and pointed. 'Alexander's tomb,' she said. 'Somewhere under that monstrosity.'

Motor-horns competed with police whistles and loud human voices in half a dozen tongues. A uniformed Egyptian armed with a little trumpet performed a ritual dance of rage before her. A gallant RASC driver drew up beside her.

'Stalled has she, lady?'

Two guides attempted to enter the car beside them.

'I show you mosky. I show you all moskies.'

'Forster says the marble was so bright that you could thread a needle at midnight. Why are they making such a fuss? There is all the time in the world. No one here ever lunches before two.'

Mrs Stitch, Guy reflected, did not seem to require much conversation from him. He sat silent, quite soaked up by her.

'I'd never set foot in Egypt until now. It's been a great disappointment. I can't get to like the people,' she said sadly, drenching the rabble in her great eyes. 'Except the King – and it's not policy to like him much. Well, we must get on. I've got to find some shoes.'

She sat down, sounded her horn, and thrust the little car relentlessly forward.

Soon she turned off into a side street marked OUT OF BOUNDS TO ALL RANKS OF H.M. FORCES.

'Two Australians were picked up dead here the other morning,' Guy explained.

Mrs Stitch had many interests but only one interest at a time. That morning it was Alexandrian history.

'Hypatia,' she said, turning into an alley. 'I'll tell you an odd thing about Hypatia. I was brought up to believe she was murdered with oyster shells, weren't you? Forster says tiles.'

'Are you sure we can get down this street?'

'Not sure. I've never been here before. Someone told me about a little man.'

The way narrowed until both mudguards grated against the walls.

'We'll have to walk the last bit,' said Mrs Stitch, climbing over the windscreen and sliding down the hot bonnet.

Contrary to Guy's expectation they found the shop. The 'little man' was enormous, bulging over a small stool at his doorway, smoking a hubble-bubble. He rose affably and Mrs Stitch immediately sat in the place he vacated.

'Hot sit-upon,' she remarked.

Shoes of various shapes and colours hung on strings all about them. When Mrs Stitch did not see what she wanted, she took a pad and pencil from her basket and drew, while the shoemaker beamed and breathed down her neck. He bowed and nodded and produced a pair of crimson slippers which were both fine and funny, with high curling toes.

'Bang right,' said Mrs Stitch. 'Got it in one.'

She removed her white leather shoes and put them in her basket. Her toe nails were pale pink and brilliantly polished. She donned the slippers, paid and made off. Guy followed at her side. After three steps she stopped and leaned on him, light and balmy, while she again changed shoes.

'Not for street wear,' she said.

When they reached the car they found it covered with children who greeted them by sounding the horn.

'Can you drive?' asked Mrs Stitch.

'Not awfully well.'

'Can you back out from here?'

Guy gazed over the little car down the dusty populous ravine.

'No,' he said.

'Neither can I. We'll have to send someone to collect it. Algie doesn't like my driving myself anyhow. What's the time?'

'Quarter to two.'

'Damn. We'll have to take a taxi. A tram might have been fun. Something for another day.'

The villa provided for the Stitches lay beyond Ramleh, beyond Sidi Bishr, among stone-pine and bougainvillaea. The white-robed, red-sashed Berber servants alone were African. All else smacked of the Alpes Maritimes. The party assembled on the veranda was small but heterogeneous. Algernon Stitch lurked in the background; in front were two little local million-airesses, sisters, who darted towards Mrs Stitch a-tiptoe with adulation.

'*Ah, chère madame, ce que vous avez l'air* star, *aujourd'hui.*'

'Lady Steetch, Lady Steetch, your hat. *Je crois bien que vous n'avez pas trouvé cela en Egypte.*'

'*Chère madame, quel drôle de panier.* I find it original.'

'Lady Steetch, your shoes.'

'Five piastres in the bazaar,' said Mrs Stitch (she had changed again in the taxi), leading Guy on.

'*Ça, madame, c'est génial.*'

'Algie, you remember the underground cow?'

Algernon Stitch looked at Guy with blank benevolence. His wife's introductions were more often allusive than definitive. 'Hullo,' he said. 'Very glad to see you again. You know the Commander-in-Chief, I expect.'

The rich sisters looked at one another, on the spot yet all at sea. Who was this officer of such undistinguished rank? *Son amant, sans doute.* How had their hostess described him? *La vache souterraiue? Ou la vache au Métro?* This, then, was the new chic euphemism. They would remember and employ it with effect elsewhere. '. . . My dear, I believe her chauffeur is her underground cow . . .' It had the tang of the great world.

Besides the Commander-in-Chief there were in the party a young Maharaja in the uniform of the Red Cross, a roving English cabinet minister, and an urbane pasha. Mrs Stitch, never the slave of etiquette, put Guy on her right at table, but thereafter talked beyond him at large. She started a topic.

'Mahmoud Pasha, explain Cavafy to us.'

Mahmoud Pasha, a sad exile from Monte Carlo and Biarritz, replied with complete composure:

'Such questions I leave to His Excellency.'

'Who is Cavafy? What is he?' passed from dark eye to dark eye of the sisters as they sat on either side of their host, but they held their little scarlet tongues.

The roving minister, it appeared, had read the complete works in the Greek. He expounded. The lady on Guy's right said:

'Do they perhaps speak of Constantine Cavafis?' pronouncing the name quite differently from Mrs Stitch. 'We are not greatly admiring him nowadays in Alexandria. He is of the past, you understand.'

The Commander-in-Chief was despondent as he had good reason to be. Everything was out of his control and everything was going wrong. He ate in silence. At length he said:

'I'll tell you the best poem ever written in Alexandria.'

'Recitation,' said Mrs Stitch.

'"They told me, Heraclitus, they told me you were dead . . ."'

'I find it so sympathetic,' said the Greek lady. 'How all your men of affairs are poetic. And they are not socialist, I believe?'

'Hush,' said Mrs Stitch.

'". . . For death he taketh all away, but them he cannot take."'

'Very prettily spoken,' said Mrs Stitch.

'I can do it in Greek,' said the cabinet minister.

'To be Greek, at this moment,' said the lady next to Guy, 'is to live in mourning. My country is being murdered. I come here because I love our hostess. I do not love parties now. My heart is with my people in my own country. My son is there, my two brothers, my nephew. My husband is too old. He has given up cards. I have given up cigarettes. It is not much. It is all we can do. It is – would you say emblematic?'

'Symbolic?'

'It is symbolic. It does not help my country. It helps us a little *here*.' She laid her jewelled hand upon her heart.

The Commander-in-Chief listened in silence. His heart, too, was in the passes of Thessaly.

The Maharaja spoke of racing. He had two horses running next week at Cairo.

Presently they all left the table. The Commander-in-Chief moved across the veranda to Guy.

'Second Halberdiers?'

'Not now, sir. Hookforce.'

'Oh, yes. Bad business about your Brigadier. I'm afraid you fellows have got rather left out of things. Shipping is the trouble. Always is. Well, I'm supposed to be on my way to Cairo. Where are you going?'

'Sidi Bishr.'

'Right on my way. Want a lift?'

The ADC was put in front with the driver. Guy sat in the back with the Commander-in-Chief. They very quickly reached the gates of the camp. Guy made to get out.

'I'll take you in,' said the Commander-in-Chief.

The Catalan refugees were duty-troop that day. They crowded round the Commander-in-Chief's great car with furious, unshaven faces. They poked tommy-guns through the open windows. Then, satisfied that these were temporary allies, they fell back, opened the gates and raised their clenched fists in salutation.

The Brigade Major was smoking in a deck-chair at the flap of his tent when he recognized the flag on the passing car. He leaped to his looking-glass, buckled himself up, pulled himself together, crowned himself with a sun helmet, armed himself with a cane and broke into a double as he approached the sandy space where Guy had that morning drilled his section. The big car was driving away. Guy strolled towards him holding his guide-book.

'Oh, it's you back at last, Crouchback. Thought for a moment that was the C-in-C's car?'

'Yes. It was.'

'What was it doing here?'

'Gave me a lift.'

'The driver had no business to fly the C-in-C's flag without the C-in-C being inside. You should know that.'

'He *was* inside.'

Hound looked hard at Guy.

'You aren't by any chance trying to pull my leg, are you, Crouchback?'

'I should never dare. The C-in-C asked me to apologize to the Colonel. He would have liked to stop but he had to get on to Cairo.'

'Who's mounting guard today?'

'The Spaniards.'

'Oh, God. Did they turn out properly?'

'No.'

'Oh, God.'

Hound stood suspended, anguished by conflicting pride and curiosity. Curiosity won.

'What did he say?'

'He recited poetry.'

'Nothing else?'

'We spoke of the problems of shipping,' said Guy. 'They plague him.' The Brigade Major turned away. 'By the way,' Guy added, 'I think I detected an enemy agent in church today.'

'Most amusing,' said Hound over his shoulder.

132

Holy Saturday in Matchet; Mr Crouchback broke his Lenten fast. He had given up, as he always did, wine and tobacco. During the preceding weeks two parcels had come from his wine merchant, badly pilfered on the railway, but still with a few bottles intact. At luncheon Mr Crouchback drank a pint of burgundy. It was what his merchant cared to send him, not what he would have ordered, but he took it gratefully. After luncheon he filled his pipe. Now that he had no sitting-room, he was obliged to smoke downstairs. That afternoon seemed warm enough for sitting out. In a sheltered seat above the beaches, he lit the first pipe of Easter, thinking of that morning's new fire.

2

No. 6 TRANSIT CAMP, London District, was a camp in name only. It had been a large, unfashionable, entirely respectable hotel. The air was one of easy well-being. No bomb had yet broken a window-pane. Here Movement Control sent lost detachments. Here occasionally was brought a chaplain under close arrest. In this green pasture Trimmer and his section for a time lay down. Here Kerstie Kilbannock elected to do her war-work.

Kerstie was a good wife to Ian, personable, faithful, even-tempered and economical. All the pretty objects in their house had been bargains. Her clothes were cleverly contrived. She was some-times suspected of fabricating the luncheon *vin rosé* by mixing the red and white wines left over from dinner; no more damaging charge was ever brought against her. There were nuances in her way with men which suggested she had once worked with them and competed on equal terms. Point by point she was the anti-thesis of her friend Virginia Troy.

On his going into uniform Ian's income fell by £1,500. Kerstie did not complain. She packed her sons off to their grandmother in Ayrshire and took two friends named Brenda and Zita into her house as paying guests. She took them also, unpaid, into her can-teen at No. 6 Transit Camp, London District. Kerstie was paid, not much but enough. The remuneration was negative; wearing overalls, eating free, working all day, weary at night, she spent nothing. When Virginia Troy, casually met during an air-raid at the Dorchester Hotel, confided that she was hard up and homeless – though still trailing clouds of former wealth and male subservience – Kerstie took her into Eaton Terrace – 'Darling, don't breathe to Brenda and Zita that you aren't paying' – and into her canteen – 'Not a word, darling, that you're being paid.'

Working as waitresses these ladies, so well brought up, giggled and gossiped about their customers like real waitresses. Before she began work Virginia was initiated into some of their many jokes. Chief of these, by reason of his long stay, was the officer they called 'Scottie'. Scottie's diverse forms of utter awfulness filled them with delight.

'Wait till you see him, darling. Just wait.'

Virginia waited a week. All the ladies preferred the 'other ranks' canteen by reason of the superior manners which prevailed there. It was Easter Monday, after Virginia had been there a week, that she took her turn beside Kerstie at the officers' bar.

'Here comes our Scottie,' said Kerstie and, nosy and knowing, Trimmer sauntered across the room towards them. He was aware that his approach always created tension and barely suppressed risibility and took this as a tribute to his charm.

'Good evening, beautiful,' he said in his fine, free manner. 'How about a packet of Players from under the counter?' and then, seeing Virginia, he fell suddenly silent, out of it, not up to it, on this evening of all evenings.

Fine and free, nosy and knowing, Trimmer had seemed, but it was all a brave show, for that afternoon the tortoise of total war had at last overtaken him. A telephone message bade him report next day at HOO HQ at a certain time, to a certain room. It boded only ill. He had come to the bar for stimulus, for a spot of pleasantry with 'les girls' and here, at his grand climacteric, in this most improbable of places, stood a portent, something beyond daily calculation. For in his empty days he had given much thought to his escapade with Virginia in Glasgow. So far as such a conception was feasible to Trimmer, she was a hallowed memory. He wished now Virginia were alone. He wished he were wearing his kilt. This was not the lovers' meeting he had sometimes adumbrated at his journey's end.

On this moment of silence and uncertainty Virginia struck swiftly with a long, cool and cautionary glance.

'Good evening, Trimmer,' she said.

'You two know each other?' asked Kerstie.

'Oh, yes. Well. Since before the war,' said Virginia.

'How very odd.'

'Not really, is it, Trimmer?'

Virginia, as near as is humanly possible, was incapable of shame, but she had a firm residual sense of the appropriate. Alone, far away, curtained in fog – certain things had been natural in Glasgow in November which had no existence in London, in spring, amongst Kerstie and Brenda and Zita.

Trimmer recovered his self-possession and sharply followed the line.

'I used to do Mrs Troy's hair,' he said, 'on the *Aquitania*.'

'Really? I crossed in her once. I don't remember you.'

'I was rather particular in those days what customers I took.'

'That puts you in your place, Kerstie,' said Virginia. 'He was always an angel to me. He used to call himself Gustave then. His real name's Trimmer.'

'I think that's rather sweet. Here are your cigarettes, Trimmer.'

'Ta. Have one?'

'Not on duty.'

'Well, I'll be seeing you.'

Without another glance he sauntered off, disconcerted, perplexed but carrying himself with an air. He wished he had been wearing his kilt.

'You know,' said Kerstie, 'I think that rather spoils our joke. I mean there's nothing very funny about his being what he is when one knows what he is – is there? – if you see what I mean.'

'I see what you mean,' said Virginia.

'In fact, it's all rather sweet of him.'

'Yes.'

'I must tell Brenda and Zita. He won't mind, will he? I mean he won't disappear from our lives now we know his secret?'

'Not Trimmer,' said Virginia.

Next morning at 1000 hours General Whale looked sadly at Trimmer and asked:

'McTavish, what is your state of readiness?'

'How d'you mean, sir?'

'Is your section all present and prepared to move immediately?'

'Yes, sir, I suppose so.'

'Suppose so?' said GSO II (Planning). 'When did you last inspect them?'

'Well, we haven't exactly had any actual inspection.'

'All right, Charles,' interposed General Whale, 'I don't think we need go into that. McTavish, I've some good news for you. Keep it under your hat. I'm sending you on a little operation.'

'Now, sir? Today?'

'Just as soon as it takes the navy to lay on a submarine. They won't keep you hanging about long, I hope. Move to Portsmouth tonight. Make out your own list of demolition stores and check it with Ordnance there. Tell your men it's routine training. All right?'

'Yes, sir. I suppose so, sir.'

'Good. Well, go with Major Albright to the planning-room and he'll put you in the picture. Kilbannock will be with you, but purely as an observer, you understand. You are in command of the operation. Right?'

'Yes, I think so, sir, thank you.'

'Well, in case I don't see you again, good luck.'

When Trimmer had followed GSO II (Planning) and Ian Kilbannock from the room, General Whale said to his ADC, 'Well, he took that quite quietly.'

'I gather there's not much prospect of opposition.'

'No. But McTavish didn't know that, you know.'

Trimmer remained quiet while he was 'put in the picture'. It was significant, Ian Kilbannock reflected while he listened to the exposition of GSO II (Planning) that this metaphoric use of 'picture' had come into vogue at the time when all the painters of the world had finally abandoned lucidity. GSO II (Planning) had a little plastic model of the objective of 'Popgun'. He had air photographs and transcripts of pilots' instructions. He spoke of tides, currents, the phases of the moon, charges of gun-cotton, fuses and detonators. He drafted a move order. He designated with his correct initials the naval authority to whom Popgun Force should report. He gave the time of the train to Portsmouth and the place of accommodation there. He delivered a stern warning about the need for 'security'. Trimmer listened agape but not aghast, in dreamland. It was as though he were being invited to sing in Grand Opera or to ride the favourite in the Derby. Any change from No. 6 Transit Camp, London District, was a change for the worse, but he had come that morning with the certainty that those paradisal days were over. He had expected, at the best, to be sent out to rejoin Hookforce in the Middle East, at the worst to rejoin his regiment in Iceland. Popgun sounded rather a lark.

When the conference was over Ian said: 'The Press will want to know something of your background when this story is released. Can you think up anything colourful?'

'I don't know. I might.'

'Well, let's get together this evening. Come to my house for a drink before the train. I expect you've got a lot to do now.'

'Yes, I suppose I have.'

'You haven't by any chance lost that section of yours, have you?'

'Not exactly. I mean, they must be somewhere around.'

'Well, you'd better spend the day finding them, hadn't you?'

'Yes, I suppose I ought,' said Trimmer gloomily.

This was the day when the ladies in Eaton Terrace kept their weekly holiday. Kerstie had arranged substitutes so that all four could be at liberty together. They slept late, lunched in hotels, did their shopping, went out with men in the evenings. At half past six all were at home. The black-out was up; the fire lighted. The first sirens had not yet sounded. Brenda and Zita were in dressing-gowns. Zita's hair was in curling-pins and a towel. Brenda was painting Kerstie's toe-nails. Virginia was still in her room. Ian intruded on the scene.

'Have we anything to eat?' he asked. 'I've brought a chap I've got to talk to and he's catching a train at half past eight.'

'Well, well, well,' said Trimmer, entering behind him. 'This *is* a surprise for all concerned.'

'Captain McTavish,' said Ian, 'of No. X Commando.'

'Oh, we know him.'

'Do you? Do they?'

'Behold a hero,' said Trimmer. 'Just off to death or glory. Do I understand one of you lovelies is married to this peer of the realm?'

'Yes,' said Kerstie, 'I am.'

'What is all this?' asked Ian, puzzled.

'Just old friends meeting.'

'There's nothing to eat,' said Kerstie, 'except some particularly nasty-looking fish. Brenda and Zita are going out and Virginia says she doesn't want anything. There's some gin.'

'Does Mrs Troy live here too, then?' asked Trimmer.

'Oh yes. All of us. I'll call her.' Kerstie went to the door and shouted: 'Virginia, look what's turned up.'

'There's something here I don't understand,' said Ian.

'Never mind, darling. Give Trimmer some gin.'

'Trimmer?'

'That's what we call him.'

'I think perhaps I won't stay,' said Trimmer, all the bounce in him punctured suddenly at the thought of Virginia's proximity.

'Oh rot,' said Ian. 'There's a lot I want to ask you. We may not have time at Portsmouth.'

'What on earth are you and Trimmer going to do at Portsmouth?'

'Oh, nothing much.'

'Really, how odd they are being.'

Then Virginia joined them, modestly wrapped in a large bath-towel.

'What's this?' she said. 'Guests? Oh, you again? You do get around, don't you?'

'I'm just going,' said Trimmer.

'Virginia, you must be nicer to him. He's off to death or glory, he says.'

'That was just a joke,' said Trimmer.

'Obviously,' said Virginia.

'*Virginia*,' said Kerstie.

'I can get something to eat at the canteen,' said Trimmer. 'I ought to go and make sure that none of my fellows has given me the slip, anyway.'

Ian concluded that he was in the presence of a mystery which like so many others, come war, come peace, was beyond his comprehension.

'All right,' he said. 'If you must. We'll meet at the sea-side to-morrow. I'm afraid you'll never get a taxi here.'

'It isn't far.'

So Trimmer went out into the darkness and the sirens began to wail.

'Well, I must say,' said Ian, returning to them. 'That was all very awkward. What was the matter with you all?'

'He's a friend of ours. We somehow didn't expect him here, that's all.'

'You weren't awfully welcoming.'

'He's used to our little ways.'

'I give it up,' said Ian. 'How about this horrible fish?'

But later when he and Kerstie were alone in their room, she came clean.

'. . . and what's more,' she concluded, 'if you ask me, there's something rum between him and Virginia.'

'How do you mean rum?'

'Darling, how is anything ever rum between Virginia and any-one?'

'Oh, but that's impossible.'

'If you say so, darling.'

'Virginia and McTavish?'

'Well, didn't they seem rum to you?'

'Something was rum. You all were, it seemed to me.'

After a pause Kerstie said: 'Weren't those bombs rather near?'

'No, I don't think so.'

'Shall we go down?'

'If you think that you'd sleep better.'

They carried their sheets and blankets into the area kitchen where iron bedsteads stood along the walls. Brenda and Zita and Virginia were already there, asleep.

'It's important about his having been a hairdresser. A first-class story.'

'Darling, you surely aren't going to write about our Trimmer?'

'I might,' said Ian. 'You never know. I might.'

At Sidi Bishr camp in the brigade office, Tommy Blackhouse said:

'Guy, what's all this about your consorting with spies?'

'What indeed?' said Guy.

'I've a highly confidential report here from Security. They have a suspect, an Alsatian priest, they've been watching. They've identified you as one of his contacts.'

'The fat boy with the broom?' said Guy.

'No, no, an RC priest.'

'I mean was it a fat boy with a broom who reported me?'

'They do not as a rule include portraits of their sources of information.'

'It's true I went to confession in Alexandria on Saturday. It's one of the things we have to do now and then.'

'So I've always understood. But this report says that you went round to the house where he lives and tried to get hold of him out of school.'

'Yes, that's true.'

'What a very odd thing to do. Why?'

'Because as a matter of fact I thought he was a spy.'

'Well, he *was*.'

'Yes, I thought so.'

'Look here, Guy, this may be a serious matter. Why the devil didn't you report it?'

'Oh, I did, at once.'

'Who to?'

'The Brigade Major.'

Major Hound, who was sitting at a neighbouring table relishing what he took to be Guy's discomfiture, started sharply.

'I received no report,' he said.

'I made one,' said Guy. 'Don't you remember?'

'No. I certainly don't.'

'I told you myself.'

'If you had, there would be a note of it in my files. I checked them this morning before you came in, as a matter of fact.'

'The day the C-in-C gave me a lift home.'

'Oh,' said Hound, disconcerted. 'That? I thought that you were trying to pull my leg.'

'For Christ's sake,' said Tommy. 'Did Guy make a report to you or didn't he?'

'I think he did say something,' said Major Hound, 'in the most irregular fashion.'

'And you took no action?'

'No. It was not an official report.'

'Well, you'd better draft an official report to these jokers, letting Guy out.'

'Very good, Colonel.'

So Major Hound wrote in the finest Staff College language that Captain Crouchback had been investigated and the Deputy-Commander of Hookforce was satisfied that there had been no breach of security on the part of that officer. And this letter, together with the original report, was photographed and multiplied and distributed and deposited in countless tin boxes. In time a copy reached Colonel Grace-Groundling-Marchpole in London.

'Do we file this under "Crouchback"?'

'Yes, and under "Box-Bender" too, and "Mugg". It all ties in,' he said gently, sweetly rejoicing at the underlying harmony of a world in which duller minds discerned mere chaos.

Trimmer and his section lay long at Portsmouth. The navy were hospitable, incurious, not to be hurried. Ian travelled up and down to London as the whim took him. The ladies in his house were full of questions. Trimmer had become a leading topic among them.

'You'll hear in good time,' said Ian, further inflaming their interest.

Trimmer's Sergeant knew something about demolition. He made a successful trial explosion in an enclosed fold of the hills. The experiment was repeated a day or two later in the presence of GSO II (Planning) HOO HQ and one of the men was incapacitated. One day Popgun Force was embarked in a submarine and Trimmer explained the projected operation. An hour later they were put ashore again, on a report of new minelaying in the Channel. From that time they were placed virtually under close arrest in the naval barracks. Trimmer's batman, a man long manifestly mutinous, took the occasion to desert. This information was badly received at HOO HQ.

'Strictly speaking of course, sir,' said GSO II (Planning), 'Popgun should be cancelled. Security has been compromised.'

'This is no time for strict speaking,' said DLFHOO, '— security.'

'Quite, sir. I only meant McTavish will look pretty silly if he finds the enemy waiting for him.'

'He looks pretty silly to me now.'

'Yes, sir. Quite.'

So eventually Popgun Force re-embarked, comprising Trimmer, his Sergeant, five men, and Ian. Even thus depleted they seemed too many.

They sailed at midday. The ship submerged and immediately all sense of motion, all sense of being at sea, utterly ceased. It was like being in a tube train, Ian thought, stuck in the tunnel.

He and Trimmer were invited to make themselves comfortable in the comfortless little cell that was called the ward-room. The Sergeant was in the Petty Officers' mess. The men disposed among the torpedoes.

'We shan't be able to surface until after dark,' said the Captain. 'You may find it a bit close by then.'

After luncheon the Third Hand distributed a specific against carbon dioxide poisoning.

'I should try and get some sleep,' he said.

Ian and Trimmer lay on the hard padded seats and presently slept.

Both awoke with headaches when the ship's officers came in for dinner.

'We ought to be at your island in about four hours,' said the Captain.

After dinner the sailors went back to the control-room and the engines. Ian drank. Trimmer composed a letter.

Writing did not come easily to him and this was not an easy letter to write.

I am leaving this to be sent to you in case I do not come back. When I said death or glory it wasn't just a joke you see. I want you to know that I thought of you at the last. Ever since we met I've known I had found the real thing. It was good while it lasted.

He filled three pages of his message pad. He signed it, after cogitation, 'Gustave'. He read it through. As he did so he conjured up the image of Virginia, as he had seen her on the afternoon of his flight from Glasgow, as he had met her again in London; of Virginia not so much as he had seen her, but rather as she had seemed to see him. He re-read the letter under the imagined wide stare of those contemptuous eyes and that infinitesimal particle of wisdom that lay in Trimmer's depths asserted itself. It just would not do, not for Virginia. He folded it small, tore it across and let the pieces fall to the steel deck.

'I think I could do with a spot,' he said to Ian.

'No, no. Later. You have responsibilities ahead.'

Time passed slowly. At last there came a sudden exhilaration. 'What's this?'

'Fresh air.'

Presently the Captain came in and said: 'Well, this is the time we ought to be coming in.'

'Shall I go and stir my chaps up?'

'No, leave them. I doubt if you'll be able to land tonight.'

'Why on earth not?' asked Ian.

'I seem to have lost your bloody island.'

He left them.

'What the hell's he up to?' said Trimmer. 'We can't go back now. They'll all desert if they try and lock us up in those barracks again.'

The Third Hand came into the wardroom.

'What's happening?' asked Ian.

'Fog.'

'Surely with all the gadgets you can find an island?'

'You might think so. We may yet. We can't be far off.'

The ship was on the surface and the trap open. The night had been chosen with the best meteorological advice. The little empty island should have shone out under a gibbous moon. But there was no moon visible that night, no stars, only mist curling into the flats.

Half an hour passed. The ship seemed to be nosing about very slowly in the calm waters. The Captain returned to the wardroom.

'Sorry. It looks as though we've got to pack it up. Can't see anything. It may lift of course as quick as it came down. We've got some time in hand.'

Ian filled his glass. Soon he began to yawn. Then to doze. The next thing he knew the Captain was with them again.

'O.K.', he said. 'We're in luck. Everything is clear as day and here's your island straight ahead. I reckon you've an hour and a half for the job.'

Trimmer and Ian awoke.

Sailors dragged four rubber dinghies into the open night and inflated them on deck from cylinders of compressed air. The demolition stores were lowered. Popgun Force sat two and two, bobbing gently at the ship's side. Low cliffs were clear before them, a hundred yards distant. Popgun Force paddled inshore.

Orders were detailed and lucid, drafted at HOO HQ. Two men, the beach-party, were to remain with the boats. The Sergeant was to land the explosives and wait while Trimmer and Ian reconnoitred for the tower which, in the model, stood on the summit of the island half a mile inland. They would all be in sight of one another's signalling-lamps all the time.

As Ian climbed awkwardly over the rubber gunwale and stood knee deep in the water, which gently lapped the deep fringe of bladder-wrack, he felt the whisky benevolently stirring within him. He was not a man of strong affections. Hitherto he had not greatly liked Trimmer. He had been annoyed at the factitious importance which seemed to surround him in Eaton Terrace. But now he felt a comradeship in arms.

'Hold up, old boy,' he said loudly and genially, for Trimmer had fallen flat.

He gave a heave. Hand in hand he and Trimmer landed on enemy territory. Popgun Force stood on the beach.

'All right to carry on smoking, sir?' asked the Sergeant.

'I suppose so,' said Trimmer. 'I don't see why not. I could do with a fag myself.'

Little flames spurted on the beach.

'Well, carry on according to plan, Sergeant.'

The cliffs presented no problem. They had fallen in half a dozen places and grassy slopes led up between them. Trimmer and Ian walked briskly forward and up.

'We ought to be able to see the place on the skyline,' said Trimmer rather plaintively. 'It all seems much flatter than the model.'

'"Very flat Norfolk,"' said Ian in an assumed voice.

'What on earth do you mean?'

'Sorry. I was quoting from my favourite play.'

'What's that got to do with it?'

'Nothing really, I suppose.'

'It's all very well to be funny. This is serious.'

'Not to me, Trimmer.'

'You're drunk.'

'Not yet. I daresay I shall be before the evening's out. I thought it a wise precaution to bring a bottle ashore.'

'Well, give me a go.'

'Not yet, old boy. I have only your best interests at heart. Not yet.'

He stood in the delusive moonlight and swigged. Trimmer stared anxiously about him. The gentle sound-effects of operation Popgun, the susurrus of the beach, the low mutter of the demolition party, the heavy breathing of the two officers as they resumed their ascent, were suddenly horrifically interrupted by an alien voice, piercing and not far distant. The two officers stopped dead.

'For Christ's sake,' said Trimmer. 'What's that? It sounds like a dog.'

'A fox perhaps.'

'Do foxes bark like that?'

'I don't think so.'

'It can't be a dog.'

'A wolf?'

'Oh, do try not to be funny.'

'You're allergic to dogs? I had an aunt . . .'

'You don't find dogs without people.'

'Ah. I see what you mean. Come to think of it I believe I read somewhere that the Gestapo use bloodhounds.'

'I don't like this at all,' said Trimmer. 'What the hell are we going to do?'

'You're in command, old boy. In your place I'd just push on.'

'Would you?'

'Certainly.'

'But you're drunk.'

'Exactly. If I was in your place I'd be drunk too.'

'Oh God. I wish I knew what to do.'

'Push on, old boy. All quiet now. The whole thing may have been a hallucination.'

'D'you think so?'

'Let's assume it was. Push on.'

Trimmer drew his pistol and continued the advance. They reached the top of a grassy ridge, and saw half a mile to their flank a dark feature that stood out black against the silver landscape.

'There's your tower,' said Ian.

'It doesn't look like a tower.'

'"Moonlight can be cruelly deceptive, Amanda,"' said Ian in his Noel Coward voice. 'Push on.'

They moved forward cautiously. Suddenly the dog barked again and Trimmer as suddenly fired his pistol. The bullet struck the turf a few yards ahead but the sound was appalling. Both officers fell on their faces.

'What on earth did you do that for?' asked Ian.

'D'you suppose I meant to?'

A light appeared in the building ahead. Ian and Trimmer lay flat. A light appeared downstairs. A door opened and a broad woman stood there, clearly visible, holding a lamp in one hand, a shotgun under her arm. The dog barked with frenzy. A chain rattled.

'God. She's going to let it loose,' said Trimmer. 'I'm off.'

He rose and bolted, Ian close behind.

They came to a wire fence, tumbled over it and ran on down a steep bank.

'*Sales Boches!*' roared the woman and fired both barrels in their direction. Trimmer dropped.

'What's happened?' asked Ian, coming up with him where he lay groaning. 'She can't have hit you.'

'I tripped over something.'

Ian stood and panted. The dog seemed not to be in pursuit. Ian looked about him.

'I can tell you what you tripped over. A railway line.'

'A railway line?' Trimmer sat up. 'By God, it is.'

'Shall I tell you something else? There aren't any railways where we ought to be.'

'Oh God,' said Trimmer, 'where are we?'

'I rather think we're on the mainland of France. Somewhere in the Cherbourg area, I daresay.'

'Have you still got that bottle?'

'Of course.'

'Give it to me.'

'Steady on, old boy. One of us ought to be sober and it's not going to be me.'

'I believe I've broken something.'

'Well, I shouldn't sit there too long. A train's coming.'

The rhythm of approaching wheels swelled along the line. Ian gave Trimmer a hand. He groaned, hobbled and sank to the ground. Very soon the glow and spark of the engine came into view and presently a goods-train rolled slowly past. Ian and Trimmer buried their faces in the sooty verge. Not until it was out of sight and almost out of hearing did either speak. Then Ian said: 'D'you know it's only sixteen minutes since we landed?'

'Sixteen bloody minutes too long.'

'We've got plenty of time to get back to the beach. Take it easy. I think we ought to make a slight detour. I didn't like the look of that old girl with the gun.'

Trimmer stood up, resting on Ian's shoulder.

'I don't believe anything is broken.'

'Of course it isn't.'

'Why "of course". It might easily have been. I came the hell of a cropper.'

'Listen, Trimmer, this is no time for argument. I am greatly relieved to hear that you are uninjured. Now step out and perhaps we shall get home.'

'I ache all over like the devil.'

'Yes, I'm sure you do. Step out. Soon over. Damn it, one might think it was you that was drunk, instead of me.'

It took them twenty-five minutes to reach the boats. Trimmer's shaken body seemed to heal with use. Towards the end of the march he was moving fast and strongly but he suffered from cold. His teeth chattered and only a stern sense of duty prevented Ian from offering him whisky. They passed the place where they had left the demolition party but found it deserted.

'I suppose they did a bunk when they heard that shot,' said Trimmer. 'Can't blame them really.'

But when they came to the beach all four dinghies were there with their guards. There was no sign of the rest of the force.

'They went inland, sir, after the train passed.'

'*Inland?*'

'Yes, sir.'

'Oh.' Trimmer drew Ian aside and asked anxiously: 'What do we do now?'

'Sit and wait for them, I suppose.'

'You don't think we can go back to the ship and leave them to follow?'

'No.'

'No. I suppose not. Damn. It's bloody cold here.'

Every two minutes Trimmer looked at his watch, shivering and sneezing.

'Orders are to re-embark at zero plus sixty.'

'Plenty of time to go yet.'

'Damn.'

The moon set. Dawn was still far distant.

At length Trimmer said: 'Zero plus fifty-two. I'm frozen. What the hell does the Sergeant mean by going off on his own like this? His orders were to wait for orders. It's his own look-out if he's left behind.'

'Give him till zero plus sixty,' said Ian.

'I bet that woman's given the alarm. They've probably been captured. There's probably a howling mob of Gestapo looking for us at the moment – with bloodhounds . . . zero plus fifty-nine.'

He sneezed. Ian took a final swig.

'Here, my dear Watson,' he said, 'if I am not mistaken, come our clients – one side or the other.'

Footsteps softly approached. A dimmed torch winked the signal.

'Off we go then,' said Trimmer, not pausing to greet his returning men.

There was a flash and a loud explosion inland behind them.

'Oh God,' said Trimmer. 'We're too late.'

He scrambled for the boat.

'What was that?' Ian asked the Sergeant.

'Gun-cotton, sir. When we saw the train go by, not having heard anything from the Captain, I went up myself and laid a charge. Hop in quiet, lads.'

'Splendid,' said Ian. 'Heroic.'

'Oh, I wouldn't say that, sir. I just thought we might as well show the Jerries we'd been here.'

'In a day or two's time,' said Ian, 'you and Captain McTavish and your men are going to wake up and find yourselves heroes. Can you do with some whisky?'

'Much obliged, sir.'

'For God's sake, come on,' said Trimmer from the boat.

'I'm coming. Be of good comfort, Master Trimmer, and play the man. We shall this day light such a candle by God's grace in England as I trust shall never be put out.'

A signal was made just before dawn briefly announcing the success of the expedition. The submarine dived and the Captain in his cabin began to draft his account of the naval operation. In the wardroom Ian coached Trimmer in the military version. High spirits do not come easily under water. All were content.

Major Albright, GSO II (Planning), HOO HQ, was at Portsmouth to meet them when they came ashore that afternoon. He was effusive, almost deferential.

'What can we do for you? Just say.'

'Well,' said Trimmer, 'how about a spot of leave? The chaps are pretty browned off with Portsmouth.'

'You'll have to come to London.'

'Don't mind if I do.'

'General Whale wants to see you. He'll want to hear your own story, of course.'

'Well, it's more Kilbannock's story really.'

'Yes,' said Ian. 'You'd better leave all that side of it to me.'

And later that night he told the D L F H O O all that he had decided the General should know.

'Jolly good show. Just what was needed. Jolly good,' said the General. 'We must get an M.M. for the Sergeant. McTavish ought to have something. Not quite a D.S.O. perhaps but certainly an M.C.'

'You don't think of putting me in for anything, sir?'

'No. All I want from you is a citation for McTavish. Go and write it now. Tomorrow you can see about a release to the Press.'

In his life in Fleet Street Ian had undertaken many hard tasks for harder masters. This was jam. He returned to General Whale in ten minutes with a typewritten sheet.

'I've pitched it pretty low, sir, for the official citation. Confined myself strictly to the facts.'

'Of course.'

'When we give it to the Press, we might add a little colour, I thought.'

'Certainly.'

General Whale read:

Captain McTavish trained and led a small raiding force which landed on the coast of occupied France. On landing he showed a complete disregard of personal safety which communicated itself to his men. While carrying out his personal reconnaissance he came under small-arms fire. Fire was returned and the enemy post silenced. Captain McTavish pushed farther inland and identified the line of the railway. Observation was kept and heavy traffic in strategic materials was noted. A section of the permanent way was successfully demolished, thereby gravely impeding the enemy's war effort. Captain McTavish, in spite of having sustained injuries in the course of the action, successfully re-embarked his whole force, without casualties, in accordance with the time-table. Throughout the latter phases of the operation he showed exemplary coolness.

'Yes,' said General Whale. 'That ought to do it.'

3

'NOT out,' said Mr Crouchback.

The small batsman at the other end rubbed his knee. Greswold, the fast bowler, the captain of Our Lady of Victory, looked at the umpire in agony.

'Oh, sir.'

'I'm sorry. I just wasn't looking, I'm afraid. Have to give the other fellows the benefit of the doubt, you know.'

He was wearing the fast bowler's sweater, the sleeves knotted round his throat, the body hanging over his thin shoulders, and was glad of the protection against the chill evening wind.

Greswold walked back, tossing the ball crossly from hand to hand. He took a long run; came up at a great pace; Mr Crouchback could not quite see the position of his foot as he delivered the ball. It seemed well over the line. He considered giving a 'no ball' but before he spoke the wicket was down. The little chap was out this time and no mistake. In fact, the whole side was out and the first match of the term was won. Our Lady of Victory's champions returned to the pavilion, gathering round Greswold and thumping him on the back.

'He was out the first time,' said the wicket-keeper.

'Oh, I don't know; Croucher didn't think so.'

'Croucher was watching an aeroplane.'

'Anyway, what's the odds?'

Mr Crouchback walked home to the Marine Hotel with Mrs Tickeridge, who had brought Jenifer and Felix to the match. They walked round by the beach and Jenifer threw sticks into the sea for Felix. Mr Crouchback asked:

'You saw the paper this morning?'

'You mean about the raid on the French railway?'

'Yes. What a splendid young fellow this Captain McTavish must be. You saw he had been a hairdresser?'

'Yes.'

'That's what's so heartening. That's where we've got the

Germans beaten. It was just the same in the first war. We've got no junker class in this country, thank God. When the country needs them, the right men come to the fore. There was this young fellow curling women's hair on a liner, calling himself by a French name; odd trade for a highlander, you might think. There he was. No one suspected what he had in him. Might never have had the chance to show it. Then war comes along. He downs his scissors and without any fuss carries out one of the most daring exploits in military history. It couldn't happen in any other country, Mrs Tickeridge.'

'It wasn't a very attractive photograph of him, was it?'

'He looks what he is – a hairdresser's assistant. And all honour to him. I expect he's a very shy sort of fellow. Brave men often are. My son never mentioned him and they must have been together in Scotland for quite a time. I daresay he felt rather out of it up there. Well, he's shown them.'

When they reached the hotel Miss Vavasour said:

'Oh, Mr Crouchback, I've been waiting to ask you. Would you mind if I cut something out of your newspaper when you've quite finished with it?'

'Of course. Not at all. Delighted.'

'It's the photograph of Captain McTavish. I've got a little frame that will just take it.'

'He deserves a frame,' said Mr Crouchback.

The news of Operation Popgun reached Sidi Bishr first on the BBC news, later in the form of a signal of congratulation to Force HQ from the C-in-C.

'I suppose I'd better pass this on to X Commando?' said Major Hound.

'Of course. To all the units. Have it read out on parade.'

'To the Spaniards too?'

'Particularly the Spaniards. They're always boasting about convents they blew up in their civil war. This'll show 'em we can play the same game. Get that fat interpreter to work.'

'You knew this chap McTavish, Colonel?'

'Certainly. I took him on when I had X Commando. You remember, Guy?'

'Yes, indeed.'

'You and Jumbo Trotter tried to keep him out. Remember? I wish I had a few more officers like McTavish out here. I'd like to have seen old Jumbo Trotter's face when he read the news.'

*

Jumbo in fact had beamed. He had proclaimed to the ante-room of the Halberdier Barracks:

'Poor old Ben Ritchie-Hook; no judge of men. A first-class fighting man, but he had his blind spots, you know. If he took a down on a man, he could be unreasonable. He turned McTavish out of the Corps, you know. Fellow had to join a highland regiment in the ranks. *I* spotted him at once. Not a peacetime soldier, mind you, but no more was Ben. If you ask me, the two of them were a chip off the same block. That's why they never could hit it off. Often happens like that. Seen it dozens of times.'

When Ivor Claire heard the news he merely said: 'Some nonsense of Brendan's, obviously.'

The ladies of Eaton Terrace said:

'What about our Scottie now?'

'What indeed?'

'Were we beastly to him?'

'Not really.'

'Not often.'

'I always had a soft spot.'

'Shall we ask him round?'

'D'you think he'd come?'

'We can try.'

'It would jolly well serve us right if he despised us.'

'I despise myself rather.'

'Virginia. You haven't said anything. Shall we try and get hold of Scottie?'

'Trimmer? Do what you like, my dears, only count me out.'

'Virginia, don't you *want* to make amends?'

'I don't,' said Virginia and left them.

Ty. Lt. A/g Capt. McTAVISH, H. M.C. Future employment of.

'Really,' said the chairman, 'I don't understand why this is a matter for our committee.'

'Minute from the War Cabinet, sir.'

'Extraordinary. I should have thought they had more important things on their minds. What's it all about?'

'Well, sir, you remember McTavish?'

'Yes, yes, of course. Nice bit of work. Excellent young officer.'

'You haven't seen the *Daily Beast*?'

'Of course not.'

'Exactly, sir. You know that Lord Copper has always had it in for the regular army – old school tie, and that sort of rot.'

'I did not,' said the General, filling his pipe. 'I never see the rag.'

'Anyway, they've dug up the story that McTavish began the war as an officer on probation in the Halberdiers and got turned down. They say it was because he'd been a barber.'

'Nothing wrong with that.'

'No, sir. But all the Halberdiers who had anything to do with him are in the Middle East. We've asked for a report, but it will take some time and if, as I presume it is, it's an adverse one, we can't very well use it.'

'What a lot of fuss about nothing.'

'Exactly, sir. The *Daily Beast* are making McTavish an example. Saying the army is losing its best potential leaders through snobbery. You know the kind of thing.'

'I do not,' said the General.

'One of the Labour members has put down a question about him.'

'Oh Lord, has he? That's bad.'

'The Minister wants an assurance that McTavish has been found employment suitable to his merits.'

'Well, that oughtn't to be difficult. It was decided last week to raise three more Commandos. Can't he be given one of those?'

'I don't think he's quite up to it.'

'Really, Sprat, I should have thought he was just the kind of young officer you're always trying to poach. *You* don't object to his having been a barber, do you?'

'Of course not, sir.'

'You were full of his praises last week. Make a note that he is to be found suitable employment in your outfit.'

'Very good, sir.'

'And by suitable I don't mean your ADC.'

'God forbid,' Sprat breathed.

'I mean something that will satisfy those Labour fellows in the House of Commons that we know how to use good men when we find them.'

'Very good, sir.'

DLFHOO returned to his headquarters, as he usually returned from attendance at the War Office, in black despair. He sent for Ian Kilbannock.

'You overdid it,' he said.

Ian knew what he meant.

'Trimmer?'

'Trimmer. McTavish. Whatever he's called. You've gone and got the politicians interested. We're stuck with him now for the rest of the war.'

'I've been giving some thought to the matter.'

'Decent of you.'

'You know,' said Ian, who, since he and his General had become, as it were, accomplices in fraud, had adopted an increasingly familiar tone in the office, 'you'll never get the best out of your subordinates by being sarcastic. I've been thinking about Trimmer and I've learned something. He's got sex appeal.'

'Nonsense.'

'I've seen evidence of it in my own immediate circle – particularly since his outing to France. I've had the Ministries of Information, Supply, Aircraft Production and the Foreign Office after him. They want a hero of just Trimmer's specifications to boost civilian morale and Anglo-American friendship. You can give him any rank you please and second him indefinitely.'

Major-General Whale was silent.

'It's an idea,' he said at length.

'It's particularly important to get him out of London. He's always hanging round my house these days.'

4

CORPORAL-MAJOR LUDOVIC's journal comprised not only *pensées* but descriptive passages which reviewers in their season later commended.

Major Hound is bald and both his face and scalp shine. Early in the morning after shaving there is a dry shine. After an hour he begins to sweat and there is a greasy shine. Major Hound's hands begin to sweat before his face. The top of his head is always dry. The sweat starts two inches above his eyebrows and never extends to his scalp. Does he use a cigarette-holder in order to protect his teeth and fingers from stain, or in order to keep smoke from his eyes? He often tells the orderly to empty his ash-tray. Captain Crouchback despises Major Hound but Colonel Blackhouse finds him useful. I am barely aware of Major Hound's existence. It is in order to fix him in my mind that I have set down these observations.

The defeat in Greece was kept secret until the remnants of the army arrived in Alexandria. They were collected and dispersed for reorganization and equipment. '*We live*,' wrote Corporal-Major Ludovic, '*in the Age of Purges and Evacuation. To empty oneself, that is the task of contemporary man. Cultivate the abhorred vacuum. "The earth is the Lord's and the emptiness thereof."*' Every available unit in the area was sent west into Cyrenaica. Hookforce were the only fighting troops in Alexandria. They found themselves called on to find guards for government buildings and banks. They were assigned a role in the defence of the city in the event of a German break-through. Early in May Tommy Blackhouse, Major Hound and Guy drove out with a Brigadier from Area Command to inspect the sandy ridge between Lake Mariout and the sea where they were expected to hold Rommel's armour with their knives and toggle-ropes and tommy-guns.

'What's to stop him coming round the other side?' asked Tommy.

'According to the plan – the Gyppos,' said the Brigadier.

He laughed, Tommy laughed, they laughed all four.

Guy spent long hours in the club library with bound copies of *Country Life*. Sometimes he joined his old friends of X Commando at the Cecil Hotel or the Union Bar. X Commando had not gone to the trouble of organizing an officers' mess. B Commando dined as punctually and solemnly as Halberdiers in barracks, with Colonel Prentice's great-great-grandfather's sabre displayed on the table. X Commando kept a pile of hard-boiled eggs, oranges and sardines in their tent; they roared at their scuttling and giggling Berber servants for tea and gin, threw down cigar-ends and cigarette-packets and matches and corks and peel and tins round their feet.

'One might be on the Lido,' said Ivor Claire, regarding with disgust the littered sand of the tent floor.

Half a dozen wealthy Greek houses opened their doors to them. And there was Mrs Stitch. Guy did not repeat his visit but her name was everywhere. X Commando felt her presence as that of a beneficent, alert deity, their own protectress. Things could not go absolutely wrong with them while Mrs Stitch was about.

Guy set his intelligence section to make a map of the camp, for Major Hound had returned from one of his trips to Cairo with a case labelled 'intelligence stores' which proved to contain a kindergarten outfit of coloured inks and drawing materials. He fought a daily battle with Major Hound to preserve his men from guard-duties.

So the days passed until in the third week of May war came to Major Hound.

It was heralded by the customary ceremonial fanfare of warning-orders and counter-orders, but before the first of these notes sounded, Mrs Stitch had told Ivor Claire and he had told Guy.

'I hear we're off to Crete at any moment,' Guy said to Major Hound.

'Nonsense.'

'Well. Wait and see,' said Guy.

Major Hound pretended to be busy at his desk. Then he sat back and fitted a cigarette into his holder.

'Where did you hear this rumour?'

'X Commando.'

157

'Both attacks in Crete have been held,' said Major Hound. 'The situation is well under control. I *know* this.'

'Good,' said Guy.

There was another pause during which Major Hound pretended to read his files. Then:

'It doesn't occur to you, I suppose, that we have a priority commitment in the defence of Alexandria?'

'I gathered that Crete was first priority at the moment.'

'The garrison there is larger than they can supply as it is.'

'Well, I dare say I'm wrong.'

'Of course you're wrong. You should know better than to listen to rumours.'

Another pause; this was the witching hour, noted by Corporal-Major Ludovic, when the shine on the Brigade Major's face changed from dry to greasy.

'Besides,' he said, 'this brigade hasn't the equipment for defensive action.'

'Then why are we defending Alexandria?'

'That would be an emergency.'

'Perhaps there's an emergency in Crete.'

'I'm not arguing with you, Crouchback. I'm telling you.'

Silence; then:

'Why doesn't that orderly empty the ash-trays? What do you know about the shipping situation, Crouchback?'

'Nothing.'

'Exactly. Well, for your information we aren't in a position to reinforce Crete even if we wanted to.'

'I see.'

Another pause. Major Hound was not at ease that day. He resorted to his old method of attack.

'How, by the way, is your section employed this morning?'

'Ruling thin red lines. The map of Crete is a straight off-print from the Greek issue, so I am having a half-inch grid put on for our own use.'

'Maps of Crete? Who authorized anyone to draw maps of Crete?'

'I fetched them myself yesterday evening from Ras-el-Tin.'

'You had no business to. That's exactly how rumours start.'

Presently Tommy came into the office. Guy and Major Hound stood up.

'Anything through from Cairo yet?' he asked.

'The mail has gone to the registry, Colonel. Nothing of immediate importance.'

'No one at GHQ starts work before ten. The wires will start buzzing in a few minutes. Meanwhile get out a warning order to the units. I suppose you know we're off?'

'Back to Canal Area for reorganization?'

'Christ, no. Where's that Staff Captain? We must work out a loading table. I met the Flag Officer in command of destroyers at Madame Kaprikis's last night. He's all ready for us. Guy, collect some maps of Crete for issue down to section leaders.'

'That's all laid on, Colonel,' said the Brigade Major.

'Well done.'

At quarter-past ten the telephone from GHQ Cairo began its day-long litany of contradictions. Major Hound listened, noted, relayed with the animation of a stockbroker.

'Yes, sir. Very good, sir. All understood. All informed,' he said to GHQ. 'Get cracking,' he said to the units.

But this show of zeal did not deceive Ludovic.

'*Major Hound seems strangely lacking in the Death-Wish,*' he noted.

It was Major Hound's first operational embarkation, Guy's third. He callously watched the transactions, first earnest, then anxious, then embittered, between Brigade Major, Staff Captain and ESO, the lines of over-burdened, sulky soldiers moving on and off the narrow decks, the sailors fastidiously picking their way among the heaps of military equipment. He knew it all of old and he kept out of it. He talked to a Marine AA gunner who said:

'No air cover. The RAF have packed up in Crete. If we don't make the run in and out in darkness we haven't a hope of getting through. Your chaps will have to be a lot quicker getting ashore than they are coming aboard.'

A mine-laying cruiser and two destroyers were lying in for Hookforce; all bore the scars of the evacuation of Greece. The ship detailed for brigade headquarters was the most battered.

'She needs a month in dock,' said the Marine. 'We'll be lucky if she makes the trip, enemy action apart.'

They sailed at dusk. On board the destroyer with headquarters were three troops of B Commando. The men lay about on the flats and mess decks, the officers in the wardroom. Tommy Blackhouse was invited to the bridge. Peace of a kind reigned.

'Crouchback,' said Major Hound, 'has it occurred to you that Ludovic is keeping a diary?'

'No.'

'It's contrary to regulations to take a private diary into the front line.'

'Yes.'

'Well, you'd better warn him. He's writing something unofficial I'm pretty sure.'

At eight o'clock the Maltese steward laid the table for dinner, setting a bowl of roses in the centre. The captain remained on the bridge. The first officer apologized for him and for the accommodation.

'We aren't equipped for hospitality on this scale,' he said. 'Not enough of anything, I'm afraid.'

The soldiers took out their mugs and canteens and knives and forks. The batmen helped the steward. Dinner was excellent.

'No cause for alarm until dawn,' said the first officer cheerfully as he left them.

The captain had given up his cabin to Tommy and Major Hound and the second-in-command of B Commando. Valises and bed-rolls had been left in camp. The army officers arranged themselves on chairs and benches and floor in the wardroom. Soon they were all asleep.

Guy awoke at dawn and went up into the fresh air; a delicious morning after the breathless night, a calm sea, no other ship in sight, no land, the destroyer steaming rather slowly, it seemed, into the luminous void. Guy met the Marine gunner.

'Is this where our troubles begin?' he asked.

'Not here.' Then as Guy seemed surprised he added: 'Notice anything odd about the sun?'

Guy looked. It was well above the horizon now, ahead on their left, cool and brilliant.

'No,' he said.

'Just where you expected to see it?'

'Oh,' said Guy. 'I see what you mean. It ought to be on the other side.'

'Exactly. We shall be back in Alex in an hour. Engine trouble.'

'That's going to be awkward.'

'She was overdue for an overhaul, as I told you, and she caught a packet in the Aegean. Suits me all right. I haven't had any shore leave this year.'

At breakfast Tommy scowled silently, not so Major Hound who was openly jubilant. He put the nozzle of his Mae West in his mouth and made a little pantomime of playing the bagpipes.

'This is the hell of a thing,' Tommy said to Guy. 'But there's a good chance of their laying on another destroyer in Alexandria.'

'I should rather doubt that, Colonel,' said Major Hound. 'The navy is fully committed.'

'We're one of their commitments. I've made a signal to Prentice on board the cruiser putting him in command until we turn up. I've told him his main job is to keep the brigade intact as a formation. The danger is that they'll try and lump the units into the general reserve of Creforce. Then there'll be trouble winkling them out and getting them together again for our proper role. I hope Prentice is up to it. He hasn't much experience of the tricks of GOCs.'

'Did you mention that matter to Ludovic, Crouchback?'

'Not yet.'

'This will be a good time.'

'What matter?' asked Tommy.

'Just a matter of routine security, Colonel.'

They were in sight of land when Guy found Corporal-Major Ludovic.

'It has come to my ears that you are keeping a diary,' he said.

Ludovic regarded him with his disconcerting grey-pink stare.

'I should hardly call it that, sir.'

'You realize that anything written which is liable to fall into the enemy's hands is subject to censorship.'

'So I have always understood, sir.'

'I'm afraid I must ask to see what it is.'

'Very good, sir.' He took his message-pad from the pocket of his shorts. I have left the typewriter in camp, sir, with the rest of the office equipment. I don't know if you'll be able to read it.'

Guy read:

'*Captain Crouchback has gravity. He is the ball of lead which in a vacuum falls no faster than a feather.*'

'That's all you've written?'

'All I have written since we left camp, sir.'

'I see. Well, I don't think that compromises security in any way. I wonder how *I'm* meant to take it.'

'It was not intended for your eyes, sir.'

'As a matter of fact I have never believed that theory about feathers in a vacuum.'

'No, sir. It sounds totally against nature. I merely employed it figuratively.'

When the ship berthed Tommy and Major Hound went ashore. There were high staff-officers, naval and military, awaiting them on the quay and they went with them to one of the port-offices to confer. The troops leant over the rails, spat and swore.

'Back to Sidi Bishr,' they said.

Quite soon Tommy and Hound returned on board, Tommy cheerful.

'Off again,' he said to Guy. 'They've laid on another destroyer. Here's the latest intelligence. Everything in Crete is under control. The navy broke up the sea landings and sunk the lot. The enemy only hold two pockets and the New Zealanders have got them completely contained. Reinforcements are rolling in every night for the counter-attack. The BGS from Cairo says it's in the bag. We've got a very nice role, raiding lines of communications on the Greek mainland.'

Tommy believed all this. So did Major Hound; no part of his training or previous experience had made him a sceptic. But he remained glum.

The change of ships was quickly done. Like a line of ants the laden men followed one another down one gang plank and up another, swearing quietly. They found quarters indistinguishable from those they had left. New naval officers gave the old greetings and the old apologies. By sunset everyone had settled in.

'We sail at midnight,' said Tommy. 'They don't want to reach the Karso channel until after dark tomorrow. No reason why we shouldn't dine ashore.'

He and Guy went to the Union Bar. It did not occur to them to ask Major Hound to join them. The restaurant seemed as full as ever, despite the notorious crisis in man-power. They ate lobster pilaff and a great dish of quail cooked with Muscat grapes.

'It may be our last decent meal for some time,' Tommy remarked. 'The BGS heard from someone that fresh food is rather short in Crete.'

They ate six birds each and drank a bottle of champagne. Then they had green artichokes and another bottle.

'I dare say in a day or two we shall think of this dinner,' said Tommy, gazing fondly at the leaves which littered their plates, 'and wish we were back here.'

'Not really,' said Guy, washing the butter from his fingers.

'No, not really. Not for all the quail in Egypt.'

They were gay as they drove down to the lightless docks. They found their ship and were asleep before she sailed.

Major Hound awoke to feel his bunk rise and fall, to hear the creaking of plates and the roll and thump of shifting stores. He began to shiver and sweat and swallow. He lay flat on his back, gripping the blankets, open eyed in the darkness, desperately sad. His servant found him thus at seven o'clock when he lurched in with a mug of tea in one hand, a mug of shaving water in the other and a cheerful greeting. Major Hound remained rigid. The man began to polish the boots which still shone from his labours of the previous morning.

'For God's sake,' said Major Hound, 'do that outside.'

'Hard to find anywhere to move, sir.'

'Then leave them.'

'Very good, sir.'

Major Hound cautiously raised himself on one elbow and drank the tea. Immediately the nausea which he had fought through the long small hours returned irresistibly. He reached the wash-basin, clung there and remained for ten minutes with his head resting on the heavy rim. At length he ran some water, dried his eyes and breathing heavily returned to his bed; not, however, before he had seen his face in the little looking-glass. It gave him a further fright.

Rain and spray swept the decks all day, keeping the men below. The little ship wallowed in a heavy long swell.

'This low cloud is a godsend,' said the captain. 'We're near the spot where *Juno* copped it.'

Guy was not often troubled by sea-sickness. He had, however, drunk a quart of wine the previous evening and that, with the movement of the ship, subdued him; not so Tommy Blackhouse, who was in high spirits, now in the wardroom, now on the bridge, now on the troop decks; nor Corporal-Major Ludovic, who early in the afternoon attracted respect in the petty-officers' mess as with a travelling manicure set he prepared his toe-nails for whatever endurances lay ahead.

Lassitude settled on the soldiers.

An hour after dark Tommy Blackhouse fell. He was returning from the bridge when the ship took an unusually heavy plunge; his nailed boots slipped on the steel ladder and he fell to the steel deck with a crash that was clearly heard in the wardroom. Then he was heard shouting and after a minute the first officer announced:

'Your Colonel's hurt himself. Can someone come and help?'

The two troop-leaders of B Commando carried him awkwardly to the sick-bay where the surgeon gave him morphia. He had broken his leg.

From then on Guy went between the prostrate figures of the Brigade Major and the deputy commander. There was little to choose between them as far as ill-looks went.

'That puts the lid on it,' was Major Hound's immediate response to the news. 'There's no point in brigade headquarters landing at all.'

Tommy Blackhouse, in pain, and slightly delirious dictated orders. 'You will be met by liaison officers from Hookforce and Creforce. On disembarkation brigade will immediately set up rear headquarters under Staff Captain, and establish W/T links with units . . . Staff Captain will make contact with the force DQMG and arrange for supplies . . . Forward headquarters consisting of BM and IO will report to Lt-Col. Prentice at B Commando HQ and give him the written orders from GHQ ME defining the special role of Hookforce in harassing enemy L of C . . . Lt-Col. Prentice will report to GOC Creforce and present these orders . . .

His primary task is to prevent Commando units being brigaded with infantry in Creforce reserve ... Deputy commander Hookforce will immediately mount operations under command GOC Creforce ...'

He repeated himself often, dozed, woke and summoned Guy once more to repeat his orders.

The sea abated as the ship rounded the eastern point of Crete and steamed along the north coast. When they came into Suda Bay it was quite calm. A young moon was setting. The first sign of human activity they saw was a burning tanker lying out in the harbour and brightly illuminating it. The destroyer dropped anchor and Major Hound gingerly left his bunk and climbed to the bridge. Guy remained with Tommy. Captain Slimbridge, the signaller, and the officers of B Commando were putting their men in readiness to disembark. Captain Roots the Staff Captain and Corporal-Major Ludovic were in conference. Tommy became fretful.

'What's happening? They've only got two hours to turn round in. A lighter ought to have come out the moment we berthed.' Presently there was a hail alongside. 'There it is. Go and see, Guy.'

Guy went on the dark deck. It was crowded with troops standing-to, heaped with stores, motor-cycles, signalling equipment. A small pulling boat lay alongside and a single figure came aboard. Guy went back to report.

'Go up to the captain and see what's going on.'

Guy found the captain in his cabin with Major Hound and a haggard, unshaven, shuddering Lieutenant-Commander wearing a naval greatcoat and white shorts.

'I've got my orders to pull out and by God I'm pulling out,' the sailor was saying. 'I got my orders this morning. I ought to have gone last night. I've been waiting all day on the quay. I had to leave all my gear behind. I've only got what I stand up in.'

'Yes,' said the captain, 'so we see. What we want to know is whether a lighter is coming out for us.'

'I shouldn't think so. The whole place is a shambles. I'm pulling out. I got my orders to pull out. Got them in writing.' He spoke in a low monotone. 'I could do with a cup of tea.'

'Wasn't there an ESO on the quay?' asked Major Hound.

'No. I don't think so. I found this boat and rowed out. I've got my orders to pull out.'

'We don't seem to get any acknowledgment of our signals,' said the captain.

'It's a bloody shambles,' said the man from Crete.

'Well,' said the captain, 'I wait here two hours. Then I sail.'

'You can't sail too soon for me.' Then he turned to Major Hound and said with an awful personal solicitude. 'You've got to know the password, you know. You can't go anywhere on shore unless you know that. They'll shoot you as soon as look at you, some of these sentries, if you don't know the password.'

'Well, what is it?'

'Changes every night.'

'Exactly; what is it?'

'That I *do* know. That I *can* tell you. I know it as well as I know my own name.'

'What is it?'

The sailor looked with blank, despairing eyes. 'Sorry,' he said. 'It's slipped my mind at the moment.'

Guy and Major Hound left.

'It looks like another false alarm,' said the Major quite cheerfully.

Guy went to report to Tommy.

'God almighty,' he said. 'Christ all bloody mighty. What's come over them all? Has everyone gone to sleep?'

'I don't think it's that,' said Guy.

Three-quarters of an hour passed and then word went crackling over the ship: 'Here it comes.'

Guy went on deck. Sure enough a large dark shape was approaching across the water. The men all round him began to hoist their burdens. The sailors had already thrown a rope net over the side. The troops crowded to the rail. A voice from below called:

'Two hundred walking wounded coming aboard.'

Major Hound cried, 'Who's there? Is there anyone from Movement Control?'

No one answered him.

'I must see the captain,' said Major Hound. 'That MLC must

go back, land the wounded, come back empty for us, land us and then take on the wounded. That's the way it should be done.'

No one heeded him. Very slowly bearded and bandaged figures began to appear along the side of the ship.

'Get back,' said Major Hound. 'You can't possibly come aboard while we're here.'

'Passengers off the car first, please,' said a facetious voice in the darkness.

The broken men clambered on deck and thrust a passage through the waiting troops. Someone in the darkness said: 'For God's sake get this gear out of the way' and the word was taken up: 'Ditch all gear. Ditch all gear.'

'What on earth are they doing?' cried Major Hound. 'Stop them.'

The three troops of B Commando were under control. Headquarters troops were on the other side of the ship. The signallers began throwing their wireless sets overboard. A motor-cycle followed.

Guy found the officer in command of the MLC.

'I cast off fifteen minutes after the last of this party gets on board. You've got to look slippy,' said the sailor. 'I've another journey after this. Two hundred more wounded and a Greek general. Then I sink the boat and come aboard myself and it's good-bye to Crete for yours truly.'

'What's going on?' asked Guy.

'It's all over. Everyone's packing up.'

Guy went below to make a final, brief report to his commander.

'Things have a way of turning out lucky for you, Tommy,' he said without any bitterness.

The sick-bay was crowded now. Two army doctors and the ship's surgeon were dealing with urgent cases. While Guy stood there beside Tommy's bunk a huge, bloody, grimy, ghastly Australian sergeant appeared in the door. He grinned like a figure of death and said: 'Thank God we've got a navy,' then sank slowly to the deck and on the instant passed into the coma of death. Guy stepped over his body and fought his way past the descending line of men; there were many unwounded among them, ragged, unshaven, haggard, but seemingly whole.

'What are you?' he asked one of them.

'Records,' said the man.

Presently without any clear order given Hookforce began climbing down the rope net into the MLC.

The moon was down. The only light was the burning tanker a mile distant.

'Major Hound,' Guy called. 'Major Hound.'

A soft voice beside him said: 'The Major is safely aboard. I found him. He came with me, Corporal-Major Ludovic.'

The MLC chugged up to the quay, a structure so blasted that it seemed like rough, natural rock. Before they could get ashore wounded and stragglers began scrambling into the boat.

'Get back, you bastards,' shouted the captain. 'Cast off there.' The seamen pushed the craft away from the sea-wall. 'I'll shoot any man who tries to come aboard till I'm ready for him. Get back the lot of you. Get the hell off the quay.'

The ragged mob began pushing back in the darkness. 'Now, you pongoes,' said the captain of the MLC, 'jump to it.'

He ran the craft in again and at last the party landed. This event so large to Guy and Major Hound and the rest of them, would be recorded later in the official history:

'A further encouragement was given to the hard-pressed garrison of Crete when at midnight on 26th May HMS *Plangent* (Lt.-Comdr Blake-Blakiston) landed HQ Hookforce plus remainder of B Commando at Suda and took off 400 wounded without incident.'

The MLC captain shouted: 'Can't take any more. Get back, the rest of you. Cast off.'

The crowd of disappointed men sat among the broken stones. The laden boat moved off towards the ship. The newly landed party pushed through the stragglers and fell in.

'Find the liaison officers,' said Major Hound. 'They must be here.'

Guy shouted: 'Anyone from Hookforce?'

A bundle of bandages groaned: 'Oh, pipe down.'

Then two figures emerged from the crowd and identified themselves as troop-leaders from B Commando.

'Ah,' said Major Hound. 'At last. I was beginning to wonder. You're from Colonel Prentice?'

'Well, not exactly,' said one of the officers. He spoke in the same dull undertone as the fugitive sailor. It was a voice which Guy was to recognize everywhere in the coming days; the accent of defeat. 'He's dead, you see.'

'Dead?' said Major Hound crossly as though officiously informed of the demise of an aunt who, he had every reason to suppose, was in good health. 'He can't be. We were in communication with him the day before yesterday.'

'He was killed. A lot of the Commandos were.'

'We should have been informed. Who is in command now?'

'I believe I am.'

'What are you doing here?'

'We heard a ship was coming to take us off. But it seems we were wrong.'

'You *heard*? Who gave orders for your embarkation?'

'We haven't had any orders from anyone for twenty-four hours.'

'Look here,' said the second-in-command of B Commando, 'hadn't we better go somewhere where you can put us in the picture?'

'There's an office over there. We've been sitting in it since the bombing stopped.'

He and Guy and Major Hound and the B Commando second-in-command stumbled among the pits and loose cobbles to a hut marked 'SNO'. Guy laid his map-case on the table and turned his torch on it.

'We've sixty men and four officers, counting me. There may be others straggling. This is all I could collect. They're down here in the port area. You can't move on the roads. And I've got a couple of trucks. Everyone's pinching transport. But they're safe enough down here under guard. All the traffic is moving south to Sphakia.'

'I think you'd better tell us what's happened.'

'I don't know much. It's a shambles. They were moving out last night when we arrived – all the odds and sods, that is. The line was up on what they call 42nd Street. We were put under command of A Commando and rushed straight out to counter-attack at dawn. That was when Prentice was killed. We got right on to the aerodrome. Then we discovered that the Spaniards who were supposed to be on our flank, hadn't shown up. And there was no sign of the people who were supposed to come through and relieve us. So we sat there for an hour being shot at from all directions. Then we moved off again. We lost A Commando. Stukas got most of our transport. We lay in the fields all day being dive-bombed. Then after dark we came down here and here we are.'

'I see,' said Major Hound. 'I see.'

He was turning the problem in his clouded mind, finding no staff solution. At length he said: 'I suppose you know where Creforce headquarters are?'

'They might be anywhere now. They *were* in a monastery building somewhere off the main road.'

'And the other Commandos?'

'C was in the counter-attack with us. I think they're lying up somewhere near HQ. I haven't seen X since we landed. They were sent off on a different job somewhere else.'

Major Hound's good habits began to take control. He took the map.

'*That*,' he said, pointing blindly into the contours behind Suda, 'is assembly point. Rendezvous there forthwith. *That* is brigade headquarters. I will now go forward to Creforce. The GOC must see our orders from C-in-C at once. I shall need a guide. I will see unit commanders at headquarters at 0900 hours. Are you in W/T communication with A, C, and X?'

'No.'

'Pass the message by runner. Any questions?'

The second-in-command of B Commando seemed about to speak. Then his shoulders sagged and he turned about and left.

'You've made a note of those orders, Crouchback?'

'Yes. Do you think they'll be carried out?'

'I presume so. Anyway, they have been given. One can't do more.'

Major Hound dispatched Captains Roots and Slimbridge and the rear headquarters to their map reference in the hills. Then he and Guy with their servants climbed into the three-ton lorry and drove off. A guide from B Commando sat in front with the driver.

As they left the port area they turned into the main road that led from Canea. They drove without lights. The sky was clear and full of stars. They could see a fair way and as far as they could see and as far as they went the road was densely filled with walking men interspersed with motor-vehicles of all kinds, lightless also, moving at walking pace. Some of the men were in short columns of threes, fully equipped, some were wounded, supporting one another, some wandered without arms. The lorry moved against all this traffic, clearing a passage. Occasionally a man would shout at them. One said: 'Wrong way, mate.' Most of the men did not look up. Some walked straight into the bonnet and mudguards. For some miles the flow of men never changed. Then they turned up a lane and a sentry halted them. The driver opened the bonnet and began to work on the engine with a flash-lamp.

'Put out that light,' said the sentry.

'What are you doing?' asked Major Hound.

'Taking the distributor. We don't want this truck pinched.'

The guide led them into a peaceful vineyard. They were challenged again and at length reached some dark buildings. Guy looked at his watch. Half past two.

The batmen sat down outside. Guy and Major Hound pushed back the two blankets which hung over the door of a peasant's two-roomed house. Inside a storm lantern and maps lay on the table. Two men were asleep, sitting on chairs, their heads in their arms on the table. Major Hound saluted. One of the men raised his head.

'Yes?'

'Brigade Headquarters, Hookforce, reporting, sir, with orders from C-in-C ME.'

'What? Who?' The face of the BGS was blank with weariness. 'The GOC is not to be disturbed. We're moving in an hour. Just leave whatever it is you've got. I'll attend to it.'

GSO I slowly sat up.

'Did you say "Hookforce"? The GOC has been waiting for a report from you all day.'

'It's very urgent I should see him.'

'Yes, yes, of course. But not just now. He can't see anyone now. This is the first sleep he's had for two days and we've got to make our move before dawn. Is Colonel Blackhouse with you?'

Major Hound began to explain the situation, to put BGS and GSO I in the picture. It was plain to Guy that they understood nothing. For Major Hound it was enough that the words should be spoken, the correct sounds made even into the void of their utter weariness.

'. . . Based on Canea . . . Raiding tasks on enemy L of C in conjunction with SNO . . .'

'Yes,' said BGS. 'Thank you. Leave it here. The GOC shall see it. Ask Colonel Blackhouse to report at eight.'

He pointed to the map on the talc cover of which the new headquarters were neatly marked in chalk. It was conveniently near the place chosen by Major Hound, Guy noticed, on the forward slopes just off the road where it turned inland for the mountains and the south coast.

They returned to the lorry and as they drove into the main road, going with the stream now, a New Zealand officer stopped them. 'Can you take on some wounded?'

'I don't know where the ADS is,' said Major Hound.

'Nor do I. These are men from the Canea hospital. The Jerries turned them out.'

'That hardly sounds likely.'

'Well, here they are.'

'Oh. Where do they want to go?'

'Anywhere.'

'We're only going three miles.'

'That'll be some help.'

The wounded men began climbing and pulling one another up until the lorry was full.

'Thanks,' said the New Zealander.

'Where are you going yourself?'

'Sphakia, if I can make it.'

Presently they came to a part of the road where the walking and marching men had somehow been directed into the side and there was a clear way ahead. They began bumping along at a fair speed, the wounded men often groaning as they were thrown about.

Guy was being painfully pressed against the backboard. He dug forward with his knees and the man in front edged forward, then turned and peered at him in the darkness. A curious sound emerged:

'Sorry and all that. Bit on the tight side, what?'

It was a preposterous accent, the grossly exaggerated parody of the hot-potato, haw-haw voice; something overheard from Christmas charades. Guy flashed his torch and discerned a youngish man incongruously clothed in service-dress, Sam Browne, and the badges of a Lieutenant-Colonel.

'Are you wounded?' Guy asked.

'Hardly. Jolly sporting of you to give me a lift.'

'Where are you going?'

'Following the jolly old crowd, don't you know. It's *sauve qui peut* now, as the French say.'

'Do they? Is it? May I ask who you are?'

'I'm OC Transit Camp. Or rather I was, what? Nothing *we* could do, don't you know? Our orders are to find our own way to the coast.'

The lorry slowed among another block of walking men. Guy began to wonder about this man next to him. It was a device of German parachute troops, he had been told, to infiltrate in enemy uniforms and spread subversive rumours.

'Was it part of your orders to tell everyone it's *sauve qui peut*?'

'Hardly.'

Major Hound was separated from them by half a dozen hunched and prostrate men. Guy crawled and pushed towards him.

'Who's this chap at the back?' he whispered. 'Do you think he's all right?'

'I don't know why not.'

'He's got a very odd way of speaking and he's saying some very odd things.'

'He seems perfectly normal to me. Anyway, this is as far as we can take him.'

They had reached the high ground where Major Hound had sited his headquarters. All was in order here. A signaller stood at the side of the road as sentry and guide. As they stopped, stragglers gathered round. 'Room for another, mate?'

'Get out. Everyone out,' said Major Hound.

Sergeant Smiley joined them.

'Move to it,' he shouted.

Uncomplaining, unquestioning, the wounded men managed their descent and silently limped off among the moving crowd.

'Thanks no end,' said the OC Transit Camp.

The lorry was driven off the road among boulders and trees; its distributor was again removed, its camouflage-net correctly spread.

Corporal-Major Ludovic appeared in the glimmer.

'Everything in order, Corporal-Major?'

'Sir.'

'Captain Roots here?'

'He went in the truck with Captain Slimbridge to look for rations.'

'Good. All-round defence posted?'

'Sir.'

'Well, I think I'll turn in. It'll be light in an hour. Then we shall know better how we stand.'

Whatever strange tides were flowing round him, Major Hound still kept afloat, like Noah, sure in his own righteousness. But he did not sleep.

Guy made his bed behind a boulder among thorny sweet shrubs. He too lay awake. That strange man in service dress, he decided, was not a German paratrooper; merely a private soldier who had stolen officer's uniform the better to effect his escape.

And quarter of a mile distant on the road to the mountains the silent men stumbled and the blind cars rattled.

Major Hound had eaten nothing since he put to sea. His first thought, as headquarters came to life at dawn, was of food.

'Time we were brewing up, Corporal-Major.'

'Captain Roots and his ration-party have not returned, sir.'

'No tea?'

'No tea, sir. No water except what's in our bottles. I was advised not to light a fire, sir, on account of the hostile aircraft.'

Major Hound's second thought was of his personal appearance. He opened his haversack, propped a looking-glass against a boulder, smeared his face with sticky matter from a tube and began to shave.

'Crouchback, are you awake?'

'Yes.'

'We've got a conference this morning.'

174

'Yes.'

'Better spruce up a bit. Have you any shaving-cream?'

'Never use it.'

'I can lend you some of mine. You don't need much.'

'Thanks awfully, I'll wait for hot water. From what I could see last night there isn't a great deal of shaving done on this island.'

Major Hound wiped his face and razor, and handed it and his towel to his batman. He studied the crowded road through his binoculars.

'I can't think what's happened to Roots.'

'While we were waiting last night, sir,' said Corporal-Major Ludovic, 'I got into conversation with an Australian Sergeant. Apparently in the last day or two there have been many cases of men shooting officers and stealing their motor-vehicles. In fact, he suggested that he and I should adopt the practice, sir.'

'Don't talk nonsense, Corporal-Major.'

'I rejected the suggestion, sir, with scorn.'

Major Hound looked hard at Ludovic, then he rose and strolled slowly towards the risen sun.

'Crouchback,' he called. 'Would you come over here a minute?'

Guy joined him and walked behind up the little white goat-track until they were out of earshot, when Major Hound said:

'Does Ludovic strike you as queer?'

'He always has.'

'Was he trying to be insolent just now?'

'I think perhaps he was trying to be funny.'

'It's going to be awkward if he cracks up.'

'Very.'

They stood silent among a little group of umbrella pines watching the procession on the road. It had thinned now, no longer the solid block of the hours of darkness; men trudged along apart in pairs and clusters. One lorry only was in sight, slowly climbing the slope towards them.

Hound said rather quickly as though he had been rehearsing the question: 'I say, do you mind if I call you "Guy"?'

'Not particularly.'

'My friends usually call me "Fido".'

'Philo?'

'Fido.'

'Oh. Yes. I see.'

A pause.

'I don't altogether like the look of things, Guy.'

'Neither do I, Fido.'

'What's more, I'm damned hungry.'

'So am I.'

'You don't really think they can have murdered Roots and gone off with our lorry?'

'No.'

As they spoke in low confidential tones there came to them from the bright morning sky the faint, crescent hum of an aeroplane and with it a nearer, louder, more doleful, scarcely more human sound, echoed from man to man along the dusty road: 'Aircraft. Take cover. Take cover. Take cover. Aircraft.'

At once the whole aspect was transformed. All the men stumbled off the road, flung themselves down face forward and totally disappeared among the scrub and rock. The dust subsided behind them. The lorry drove straight to the cover of the pines where Guy and Fido stood, stopped when it could go no deeper. A dozen men climbed out and ran from it, falling flat among the tactically dispersed elements of Hookforce headquarters.

'This won't do,' said Fido.

He walked towards them.

'Look here, you men, this is Brigade Headquarters area.'

'Aircraft,' they said. 'Take cover.'

The little, leisurely reconnaissance plane grew from a glint of silver to a recognizable machine. It flew low above the road, dwindled, turned, grew again, turned its attention to the lorry and fired a burst, wide by twenty yards, circled, mounted and at length disappeared to seawards into the silent quattrocento heaven.

Guy and Fido had lain down when the bullets fell. They stood up and grinned at one another, accomplices in indignity.

'You'd better move on now,' said Fido to the men from the truck.

None of them answered.

'Who's in command of this party?' asked Fido. 'You, Sergeant?'

The man addressed said sulkily. 'Not exactly, sir.'

'Well, you'd better take command and move on.'

'You can't move, not in daytime. There's Jerries over all the time. We've had a week of it.'

All round now heads were bobbing up in the bushes but no one moved on the road. The Sergeant swung his pack forward and took out a tin of biscuits and a tin of bully-beef. He hacked the meat open with his bayonet and began carefully dividing it.

Fido watched. He craved. Not Guy nor the ragged, unshaven Sergeant, not Fido himself who was dizzy with hunger and lack of sleep, nor anyone on that fragrant hillside could know that this was the moment of probation. Fido stood at the parting of the ways. Behind him lay a life of blameless professional progress; before him the proverbial alternatives: the steep path of duty and the heady precipice of sensual appetite. It was the first great temptation of Fido's life. He fell.

'I say, Sergeant,' he said in an altered tone, 'have you any of that to spare?'

'Not to spare. Our last tin.'

Then one of the other men spoke, also gently:

'You don't happen to have a smoke on you, sir?'

Fido felt in his pocket, opened his cigarette case and counted.

'I might be able to spare a couple,' he said.

'Make it four and you can have my bully. I'm queer in the stomach.'

'And two biscuits.'

'No, I can eat biscuit. It's bully I never have fancied.'

'One biscuit.'

'Five fags.'

The deal was done. Fido took his price of shame in his hand, the little lump of the flaky, fatty meat and his single biscuit. He did not look at Guy, but went away out of sight to eat. It took a bare minute. Then he returned to the centre of his groups and sat silent with his map and his lost soul.

5

THE 'tactical dispersal' of Hookforce headquarters, modified by the defection of Captains Roots and Slimbridge and their ration-party and the incursion of various extraneous elements, had an appearance of being haphazard. The 'all-round defence' comprised four signallers outlying with rifles at the points of the compass. Under their guard little groups rested among scrub and boulder. The Brigade Major sat alone in the centre, Guy some distance away. The warmth of the early sun comforted them all.

Guy's servant approached with a mess-tin containing cold baked beans, biscuits and jam.

'All I could scrounge, sir.'

'Splendid. Where did it come from?'

'Our section, sir. Sergeant Smiley had a look round on the quay last night.'

Guy joined his men who were eating with caution, out of sight of the improvident clerks and signallers. They greeted him cheer-fully. This was their picnic, he their guest; it was not for him officiously to ordain a general distribution of their private spoils.

'I don't see any immediate intelligence task,' he said. 'The best thing we can do is to make a recce for water. There ought to be a spring in one of these gullies.'

Sergeant Smiley handed round cigarettes.

'Go carefully with those,' said Guy. 'We may find them valuable for barter.'

'I got ten tins off the navy, sir.'

Guy sent two men to look for water. He marked his map. He noted on his pad. '*28/6/41. Adv. Bde HQ established on track west of road 346208 0500 hrs. Enemy recce plane 0610.*' It occurred to him on that morning of uncertainty that he was behaving pretty much as a Halberdier snould. He wished that Colonel Tickeridge could be there to see him, and even as he cherished this remote whim, Colonel Tickeridge in fact appeared.

Not recognizably at first; a mere speck in the empty road, then, as he drew nearer, two specks. In the words of the *Manual of Small Arms*, at six hundred yards the heads were dots, the bodies tapered; at three hundred yards the faces were blurred; at two hundred yards all parts of the body were distinctly seen; his old commander's great moustache was unmistakable.

'Hi,' Guy shouted, hastening towards the road. 'Colonel Tickeridge, sir. Hi.'

The two Halberdiers halted. They were as cleanshaven as Fido, all their equipment in place, just as they had appeared during battalion exercises at Penkirk.

'Uncle. Well, I'll be damned! What are you up to? You aren't Creforce headquarters by any happy chance?'

It was no time for detailed reminiscence. They exchanged some essential military information. The Second Halberdiers had come out of Greece without firing a shot and lived in billets between Retino and Suda, waiting for orders. At last Colonel Tickeridge had been summoned to headquarters. He was in complete ignorance of the progress of the battle. Nor had he yet heard of the loss of Ben Ritchie-Hook. Guy began to put him in the picture.

Fido was not yet so sunk in dishonour that he could bear to see a junior officer speak to a senior without intervening. He bustled up and saluted.

'You're looking for Force Headquarters, sir? They should be on the reverse slope. I'm reporting there at eight myself.'

'I was called for eight but I'm going while things are quiet. The Germans work a strict time-table. At eight o'clock sharp they start throwing things. They knock off for lunch, then carry on until sunset. Never varies. What's the G O C doing back here? Who are all these frightful-looking fellows I see all over the shop? What's going on?'

'They say it's *sauve qui peut* now,' said Fido.

'Don't know the expression,' said Colonel Tickeridge.

It was twenty past seven.

'I'm pushing on. They never by any chance hit anyone with their damned bombs, but they make me nervous.'

'We'll come too,' said Fido.

No one else moved over the roads. The men who had tramped all night lay deep in the scrub, feeling the sun, breathing the spicy air, hungry and thirsty and dirty, waiting for the long dangerous day to bring another laborious night.

Punctually at eight the sky filled with aeroplanes. The GOC's conference was just beginning. A dozen officers squatted round him in a booth of blankets and boughs and camouflage-net. Some of them, who had been heavily bombed in the last week, hunched their shoulders and, as a machine approached, seemed deaf to other sounds. No bombs or bullets came near them.

'I regret to inform you, gentlemen,' said the GOC,' that the decision has been taken to abandon the island.' He proceeded to give a summary of the situation . . . 'This brigade and that brigade have borne the brunt of the fighting and are severely mauled. . . . I have therefore withdrawn them from the action and ordered them to embarkation points on the south coast.' That was the rabble of the previous night, Guy thought; those are the drowsy, footsore men in the bushes. . . . 'I have withdrawn them from the action . . .'

The General proceeded to the details of a rear-guard. Hook-force and the Second Halberdiers, it appeared, were the only units now capable of fighting. The General indicated lines to be held.

'Is this a last-man, last-round defence?' asked Colonel Ticker-idge cheerfully.

'No. No. A planned withdrawal . . .' So-and-so was to fall back through such-and-such . . . This bridge and that were to be blown behind the last sub-unit.

'I don't seem to have much on my flanks,' said Colonel Ticker-idge presently.

'You needn't worry about them. The Germans never work off the roads.'

At length he said: 'It must be accepted that administration has to some extent broken down. . . . Dumps of ammunition and rations will be established at various points on the road. . . . It is hoped that more may be flown in tonight. . . . Some improvisation may be necessary. . . . I will move my headquarters tonight to Imbros. . . . Traffic to present headquarters must be kept to a minimum. You will leave singly, avoiding making tracks. . . .'

By nine o'clock Guy and Fido were back where they had started. Twice on the return journey they took cover as an aeroplane swooped low over their heads. Once or twice as they walked the open road voices from the bush admonished them: 'Keep down, can't you,' but mostly they moved through a land seemingly devoid of human life. When they reached their headquarters Fido busied himself in transcribing the General's orders. Then he said:

'Guy, do you think the unit commanders will turn up at my conference?'

'No.'

'It's their own fault if they don't.' He looked hopelessly about him with his keen eyes. 'No one moving anywhere. I think you'd better take the truck and distribute orders personally.'

'Where?'

'Here,' said the Brigade Major, pointing to the chalk marks on his map, 'and here, and here. Or somewhere,' he added in blank despair.

'Corporal-Major, where's our driver?'

The driver could not be found. No one remembered seeing him that morning. He was not a Commando man, but one of the transport pool attached to them in this island of disillusion.

'What the devil can have happened to him, Corporal-Major?'

'I conclude, sir, that finding it impossible to drive away, he preferred to walk. The moment I saw him, sir, I formed the impression that his heart was not in the fight and, fearing to lose another vehicle, I took possession of the distributor.'

'Excellent work, Corporal-Major.'

'Transport of all kinds being, sir, in the cant expression of the Australian I mentioned, gold dust, sir.'

'I'm worried about Roots,' said the Brigade Major. 'Keep an eye out for him.'

A Stuka came near them, spotted the intruders' truck, circled, dived and dropped three bombs on the farther side of the road among the invisible stragglers, then lost interest and soared away to the west. Guy, Fido and Ludovic rose to their feet.

'I shall have to move headquarters,' said Fido. 'They'll all see that damned truck.'

'Why not move the truck?' said Guy.

Ludovic, without waiting for an order, mounted the vehicle, got it going, backed into the road and drove half a mile. The stragglers roused themselves to shout abusively after him. As he returned on foot carrying a tin of petrol in each hand another Stuka appeared, dived on the truck and, luckier than its predecessor, toppled it over with a near miss.

'There goes your —ing transport,' said Ludovic to the straggler Sergeant. He had the manservant's gift of tongues, speaking now in strong plebeian tones; when he turned to the Brigade Major he was his old fruity self. 'May I suggest, sir, that I take a couple of men and go with Captain Crouchback? We might be able to pick up some rations somewhere.'

'Corporal-Major,' said Guy, 'you don't by any chance suspect I might make off alone with our truck?'

'Certainly not, sir,' said Ludovic demurely.

Fido said: 'No. Yes. Well. Whatever you think best. Only get on with it, for God's sake.'

Guy found a volunteer driver from his section and soon they set off, he in the cab, Ludovic and two men in the back, down the road they had travelled in darkness.

Sea and land seemed empty; the sky alone throbbed with life. But the enemy had lost interest in trucks for the moment. The aeroplanes were no longer roaming at large. Instead they had some insect-plan a mile or more away in the hills south of the harbour. They followed an unvarying course, coming in from the sea at five-minute intervals, turning, diving, dropping bombs, machine-gunning, circling, diving, bombing, firing, three times each along the same line, then out to sea again to their base on the mainland. As they performed this rite Guy and his truck went about their business undisturbed.

Trampled gardens, damaged and deserted villas gave place to gutted terraces along the road; then villas again into the country beyond Suda.

'Stop here a moment,' said Guy. 'We ought to be near X Commando.'

He studied his map, he studied the surviving landmarks. There was a domed church on the left among olive trees, some of them burned and splintered, most of them full and placid as the groves of Santa Dulcina.

'This must be it. Draw into cover and wait here.'

He got down and walked alone into the plantation. It was full, he found, of trenches and the trenches were full of men. They sat huddled, half asleep, and few looked up when Guy questioned them. Sometimes one or another said, in the flat undertone of Creforce: 'Keep down, for God's sake. Take cover, can't you?' They were pay-clerks and hospital-orderlies and aerodrome ground-staff, walking-wounded, RASC, signallers, lost sections of infantry, tank-crews without tanks, gunners without guns; a few dead bodies. They were not X Commando.

Guy returned to his truck.

'Drive on slowly. Keep a look-out at the back. They'll have a sentry posted on the road.'

They drove on and presently came to two men in foreign uniforms working with spades at the side of the road, one old, one young. The old man was rather small, very upright, very brown, very wrinkled, with superb white moustaches and three lines of decorations. The young man threw down his spade and ran into the road to stop the lorry while the old man stood looking at the heap they had made and then crossed himself three times in the Greek manner.

'It is General Miltiades,' said the young man in clear English. 'We have been separated from the Household a week now. Would you be so kind as to take us to the harbour? The General is to take an English ship to Egypt. We should have been there last night, but an aeroplane shot our car and wounded the driver. The General would not leave him. He died two hours ago and we have just buried him. Now we must go on.'

'That was the last ship from Suda. He must go to Sphakia.'

'Can you take us?'

'I can take you a few miles. Jump in, if you don't mind my doing a few errands on the way.'

They began to drive on but the interpreter beat on the back of the cab, saying: 'That is the wrong way. Only Germans that way,' and in confirmation of his opinion a motor-cyclist suddenly appeared and stopped in front of them. He wore a grey uniform and a close-fitting helmet. He stared at Guy through his goggles with blank young eyes, then hastily turned about and drove off.

'I say,' said Guy to his driver, 'what do you imagine that was?'

'Looked like a Jerry, sir.'

'We *have* come too far. About turn.'

Unmolested they backed and turned and drove away. After half a mile Guy said: 'I ought to have had a shot at that man.'

'Didn't give us much time, sir.'

'He ought to have had a shot at us.'

'I reckon he was taken by surprise same as we were. I never thought somehow to see a Jerry so close.'

Ludovic could not have seen the cyclist; that, in a way, was a comfort. They passed the Greek staff-car; they passed the church.

'The stragglers seem to be in front of the firing-line in this battle,' Guy remarked.

They drove slowly, looking for signs of Hookforce. Soon there was a beating on the back of the cab.

'Sir,' said Ludovic, 'this General knows where there are rations, and petrol.'

Directed from behind they drove back into Suda and near the port stopped at a warehouse. Most of it was burned, but on the far side of the yard stood a pile of petrol tins and two Greek soldiers guarding a little heap of provisions. They greeted the general staff with warmth. There was wine among the stores and many empty flasks lying about.

'You can give these good men a lift also?' asked the interpreter. 'They are a little drunk, I believe, and not able to march.'

'Jump in,' said Guy.

Ludovic examined the provisions. There were bales of hay, sacks of rice and macaroni and sugar and coffee, some dried but reeking fish, huge, classical jars of oil. These were not army rations but the wreckage of private enterprise. He chose a cheese, two boxes of ice-cream cornets and a case of sardines. These and wine alone were useful without the aid of fire.

They drove slowly back. The aeroplanes still pounded away at their invisible target in the hills. The Greek soldiers fell asleep. The General changed his boots.

The sun was high and hot, and as Guy's truck reached the point where the road turned inland the succession of aeroplanes ceased. The last of them dwindled and vanished, a hush fell, perceptible even in the rattling cab, and suddenly all over the roadside figures appeared, stretching and strolling. This was the luncheon recess.

'That looks like our lot,' said the driver, pointing to two men with an anti-tank rifle at the side of the road.

Here at last was Hookforce, in slit trenches interspersed with stragglers in a wide vineyard. The trees were old and gnarled and irregular, full of tiny green fruit just formed. The COs were together squatting in the shade of a cart-house, A, C, and X Commandos and the Major from B Commando who had landed from the destroyer the night before.

Guy approached and saluted.

'Good morning, sir; good morning, sir. Good morning, Tony.'

Since Tommy's promotion, X had been commanded by a Coldstreamer named Tony Luxmore, a grave, cold young man consistently lucky at cards. He greeted Guy crossly.

'Where the hell have you been? We've just sweated up to brigade headquarters and back looking for you.'

'Looking for *me*, Tony?'

'Looking for orders. What's happened to your Brigade Major? We woke him up but we couldn't get any sense out of him. He kept repeating that everything was laid on. Orders were being distributed by hand of officer.'

'He's hungry.'

'Who isn't?'

'He hasn't had any sleep.'

'Who has?'

'He had a bad crossing. Anyway, here are your orders.'

Tony Luxmore took the pencilled sheets and while he and the other commanders studied them, Guy filled his water-bottle at the well. Cistus and jasmine flowered among the farm buildings, but there was a sour smell in the air, exhaled by the dirty men.

'These don't make any sense,' said the CO of A Commando.

Guy tried to elucidate the planned withdrawal. Hookforce, he learned, had done their own regrouping that morning, dissolving the remains of B Commando and attaching them by troops and sections to replace the losses of A and C. X Commando alone was up to strength. The orders were amended. Guy made notes in his pocket-book and marks on his map-cover, taking a dry relish in punctiliously observing the forms of procedure. Then he prepared to leave the weary men, deeply weary himself and out of temper with them.

General Miltiades meanwhile had been sitting calmly in the back of the truck. Suddenly Tony Luxmore noticed him. He was a man who, once seen, was not easily forgotten.

'General Miltiades,' he cried. 'Hullo, sir. You wouldn't remember me. You came with the King to stay with my parents at Wrackham.'

The General smiled in all his wrinkles. He did not remember Tony or Tony's parents, the wintry pillared house where he had slept, the farm where he had eaten Irish-stew, or the high bare coverts where in another age not long ago he had shot pheasant. He was past seventy. In youth he had fought the Turks and been often wounded. In middle life the politicians had often sent him into exile. In old age he was homeless again, finally it might seem, still following his king. Barracks, boarding-houses, palaces, English country houses, stricken battlefields – all were the same to General Miltiades.

He climbed down with agility. His liaison officer followed, carrying a straw-covered flask in each hand.

'The General asks you to take wine with him.'

Mugs were filled. The General had some English. He proposed a toast; with no shade of irony in his steady, pouchy eyes; the single word: 'Victory.'

'How about you, Corporal-Major?' Guy asked.

'Thank you, sir. I have already refreshed myself.'

There was saluting and hand-shaking. Then Guy's party boarded the lorry again and drove away.

'*Captain Crouchback*,' Corporal-Major Ludovic noted, '*is pleased because General Miltiades is a gentleman. He would like to believe that the war is being fought by such people. But all gentlemen are now very old.*'

Ludovic sat on a hot boulder some little distance apart. The cheese, the wafers, the sardines had been divided. Some men ravenously ate all at once. Ludovic had stowed away a substantial part – 'The unexpired portion' of how many days' ration? Everyone had had a mug of wine. Now they spread blankets to protect

186

their knees against the fierce sun and were one by one falling asleep. General Miltiades had tried to explain, with map and interpreter, various peculiarities of the terrain which might be exploited to the enemy's discomfort. Major Hound proved an inattentive audience. He said petulantly to Guy, when the General briefly pottered away alone into the cover, 'What did you want to bring him here for? How are we going to get rid of him?'

'I suggest we give him a lift to the GOC later in the day.'

'I've got to think about moving headquarters.'

Guy tried to explain the readjustments among the units. Major Hound said: 'Yes, yes. It's their responsibility.'

He had taken in nothing.

Then Guy, too, lay down to sleep. The General returned and lay down. Ludovic slept. Fido alone kept open his keen bewildered eyes.

They did not sleep long. Sharp at two o'clock came the drone of engines and the dismal cry repeated across the hillside. 'Aircraft. Take cover. Take cover. Take cover.'

Major Hound became suddenly animated.

'Cover all metal objects. Put away all maps. Hide your knees. Hide your faces. Don't look up.'

The Stukas came over in formation. They had another insect-plan for the afternoon. Just below Hookforce headquarters lay a circular fertile pocket of young corn, such as occur unaccountably in Mediterranean hills. This green patch had been chosen by the airmen as a landmark. Each machine flew straight to it, coming very low, then swung east to a line a mile away off the road, dropped bombs, fired its machine-gun, turned again and headed for the sea. It was the same kind of operation as Guy had watched on the other side of the road that morning. One after another the aeroplanes roared down.

'What on earth are they after?' Guy asked.

'For God's sake keep quiet,' said Fido.

'They can't possibly hear us.'

'Oh, do keep quiet.'

'Fido, if we stuck a Bren on a tripod we couldn't miss.'

'Don't move,' said Fido. 'I forbid you to move.'

'I'll tell you what they're doing. They're clearing a way for their infantry to come round our flanks.'

'Oh, do shut up.'

The General slept on. Everyone else was awake, motionless, numb, as though mesmerized by the monotonous mechanical procession.

Hour after hour the bombs thumped. When to the cowering and torpid men the succession seemed interminable, it abruptly ceased. The drone of the last aeroplane faded into silence and the hillside came to life. Everywhere men began lacing their boots and collecting whatever equipment they still had with them. The stragglers in headquarters area silently took the road. Fido raised his muzzle.

'I've been thinking,' he said. 'I don't believe we're going to see Roots and Slimbridge again, or their lorry. We're simply left in the air with no rear headquarters.'

'Well, we've no Brigade Commander either. I don't know why you want an advanced headquarters, for that matter.'

'No,' said Fido, 'neither do I.'

His tail was right down. Now he was not fair game.

'I dare say we can be some help coordinating,' said Guy in an attempt to console.

'I don't know exactly what you mean by that.'

'Neither do I, Fido. Neither do I. I'm going to sleep.'

'I think I'd better send the General to the General, don't you?'

'Whatever you like.'

'In the lorry?'

'Yes. It can come back for us.'

Guy moved away and found a place with few thorns. He lay looking up into the sky. The sun was not yet down but the moon rode clear above them, a fine, opaque, white brush-stroke on the rim of her disc of shadow. Guy was aware of the movement round him, of the Greeks and the lorry and Ludovic, and then was deep asleep.

When he awoke the moon had travelled far among the stars. Fido was scratching and snuffling at him.

'I say, Guy, what's the time?'

'For Christ's sake, Fido, haven't you got a watch?'

'I must have forgotten to wind it.'

'Half past nine.'

'Only that. I thought it was much later.'

'Well, it isn't. D'you mind if I go to sleep again?'

'Ludovic isn't back yet with the truck.'

'Then there's no point in waking up.'

'What's more, he's taken my batman with him.'

Guy slept again, it seemed very briefly. Then Fido was pawing him again.

'I say, Guy, what's the time?'

'Didn't you put your watch right when I told you last time?'

'I can't have, somehow I must have forgotten. It's ticking but it says seven fifteen.'

'Well, it's a quarter past ten.'

'Ludovic's not back yet.'

Guy turned over and slept again, more lightly this time. He kept waking and turning. His ears caught an occasional truck on the road. Later he heard rifle fire some distance away and a motorcycle stop; then loud excited conversation. He looked at his watch; just on midnight. He needed more sleep but Fido was standing beside him shouting, 'Where's Sergeant Smiley? Get brigade headquarters fallen in on the road. Get cracking, everyone.'

'What on earth's the matter?'

'Don't bother me with questions. Get cracking.'

Hookforce headquarters comprised eight men now. Fido looked at them in the starlight.

'Where's everyone else?'

'Went with the Corporal-Major, sir.'

'We shan't see them again,' said Fido bitterly. 'Forward.'

It was not forward they went but backward; back a long way, Fido ahead setting a strenuous pace over the rough road. Guy was at first too dazed to do more than keep step beside him; after a mile he tried to talk.

'What on earth's happened?'

'The enemy. All round us. Closing in on the road from both flanks.'

'How do you know?'

'The Commandos are engaging them lower down.'

Guy asked no further questions then. All his breath was needed for the march. Sleep had brought no refreshment. The past twenty-four hours had wearied and weakened them all, and Guy was ten years older than most of the men. Fido was putting out all his strength, staring straight ahead into the uncertain star-gloaming. The young moon had set. The pace was slower than a route march, faster than anything else on the road that night. They passed ghostly limping couples, and the ghosts of formed bodies of troops dragging slowly in the same blind flight. They passed peasants with donkeys. After an hour by Guy's watch, he said: 'Where are we going to halt, Fido?'

'Not here. We must get as far as we can before day-break.'

They passed an empty village.

'How about here?'

'No. An obvious target. We must push on.'

The men were beginning to drop behind.

'I must rest for ten minutes,' said Guy. 'Let the men catch up.'

'Not here. There's no cover.'

The road at this point was a scratched contour round the side of a hill, with precipitous slopes up and down on either hand.

'Once we halt we shan't get on again tonight.'

'There's something in that, Fido. Anyway, take it easy a bit.'

But Fido would not take it easy. He led on through another deserted village; going slow, but with all his powers, then there were trees at the roadside and a suggestion of open country beyond. It was nearly four o'clock.

'For God's sake let's stop here, Fido.'

'We've a good hour of darkness still. We must push on while we can.'

'Well, I can't. I'm stopping here with my section.'

Fido did not demur. He turned abruptly off the road and sat down in what seemed to be an orchard. Guy waited on the road while the men one by one came up.

'We're setting up headquarters here,' he said fatuously.

The men stumbled off the road, over the wall, into the grove of fruit trees.

Guy lay down and slept fitfully.

Fido did not sleep until dawn; in a dream untroubled of hope, he brooded, clasping his knees. He had fallen among thieves. He considered the plain treachery of Ludovic, the suspected treachery of Roots and Slimbridge and he began framing the charges for a court-martial. He considered the probabilities of such a court ever being convened, of himself ever being available to give evidence and found them nugatory. Presently the sun rose, the wayfarers, much sparser now, sought cover, and Fido snoozed.

He awoke to a strange spectacle. The road beside him was thronged with hairy men – not merely unshaven but fully bearded with fine dark locks – a battalion of them in numbers, waving a variety of banners, shirts and scraps of linen on sticks; some of them bore whole sheets of bed linen as canopies over their heads. They were dressed in motley. Guy Crouchback was talking to the leading man in a foreign language.

Fido raised his head over the wall and called: 'Guy, Guy. Who are they?'

Guy went on talking and presently returned, smiling.

'Italian prisoners,' he explained. 'Not a happy party. They surrendered to the Greeks weeks ago on the Albanian frontier. Since then they've been marched from place to place until they managed to infiltrate into the retreat and got here. Now they've been told to join up with the Germans and they're full of indignation that we won't transport them to Egypt. They've got a very fierce doctor in charge who says it's contrary to international convention to turn unwounded prisoners loose until the end of hostilities. What's more, he has an idea that the island is full of furious Australians who will murder them if they catch them. He was demanding an armed escort.'

Fido was not amused. He merely said:

'I don't know of any international convention which prescribes that.'

In a year or two of war 'Liberation' would acquire a nasty meaning. This was Guy's first meeting with its modern use.

The procession shuffled dismally past and was still in sight when the first aeroplane of the day roared down on them. Some stood their ground and waved their white flags; others scattered. These were the wiser. The German fired a line of bullets through them;

several fell; the remainder scattered for cover as the airman returned and fired again.

'The Australians *will* murder them if they start attracting attention,' said Guy.

Then the German roared away to seek other targets. The irate doctor returned to the road and examined the fallen. He shouted for help and presently two Italians and an Englishman joined him. Together they moved the wounded and dying into the shade. The white flags lay unregarded in the dust.

Guy sat down beside Fido.

'We came a long way last night.'

'Twelve miles, perhaps. I ought to find the GOC and report.'

'Report what? Don't you think we'd better know what's really happening?'

'How can we?'

'I can go and find out.'

'Yes. Did you eat all your rations yesterday? I did.'

'I too. What's more, I'm thirsty.'

'Perhaps there might be something in that village we passed, eggs or something. I believe I heard a cock crowing once. Why not take your servant and Sergeant Smiley and send them back with anything you find.'

'I'd sooner go alone.'

Fido did not find it in his heart to order a foraging party.

Guy left him in command of a clerk, three signallers and the intelligence section. There seemed to be no orthodox tactical disposal for this force which was scattered and asleep. Fido gazed about him. At a short distance the ground fell away to a gully in which lay a stagnant pool. Two or three men – not his – were bathing their feet there. Fido joined them and dabbled in the night-cool stagnant water.

'I shouldn't drink that,' he said to one of the men who was lapping near him.

'Got to, chum. Threw my bottle away yesterday when it was empty. How far is it now?'

'To Sphakia? Not more than twenty miles, I think.'

'That's not so bad.'

'There's a biggish climb ahead.'

The man examined his boots carefully.

'I think they'll hold out,' he said. 'I can if they do.'

Fido let his feet dry. He threw away his socks and put on a clean pair which he had kept in his pack. He then examined his boots; nothing wrong with them; they would last for weeks more; but would Fido? He felt dizzy and inert. Every movement required forethought, decision and effort. He looked about him and saw quite close a culvert which ran under the road and in time of rain carried the stream of which this puddle was a relic. It was wide, clean, dry now and keenly inviting. Carrying his boots, Fido padded to the mouth on his clean socks. He could see at the far end a deliciously remote, framed picture of a green and dun valley; between him and it everything was dark and empty. Fido crept in. He went half-way until both bright landscapes were the same size. He unbuckled his equipment and put it beside him. He found the curve of the drain comfortable to his aching back; like a hunted fox, like an air marshal under a billiard-table, he crouched in torpor.

Nothing disturbed him. The Germans were busy that day land-ing reinforcements and searching for rescue-ships. There were no bombs or bullets here. All that was left of Hookforce rolled down the road overhead, but Fido did not hear. No sound penetrated to his kennel and in the silence two deep needs gnawed at him – food and orders. He must have both or perish. The day wore on. To-wards evening an intolerable restlessness possessed him; hoping to stay his hunger, he lit his last cigarette and smoked it, slowly, greedily sucking until the glowing stub began to burn the tips of his fingers. Then he took one last deep breath and, as he did so, the smoke touched some delicate nerve of his diaphragm and he began to hiccup. The spasms tortured him in his cramped position; he tried lying full length; finally he crawled into the open. For all his agitation he moved laboriously and crazily like a man photo-graphed in 'slow motion'; thus he climbed to the road and sat beside it on the wall. Men were on the move again, trudging past, some with their eyes in the dust, some fixed on the mountains ahead. It was the moment of evening when the milky wisp of moon became sharp and luminous. Fido saw none of this; each regular hiccup took him by surprise and was at once forgotten; between hiccups his mind was dull and empty, his eyes dazzled and fogged; there was a continuous faint shrilling in his ears as though from distant grasshoppers.

Presently there was an intrusion from the exterior world. A car approached. It came very slowly, and when Fido stood in the road, waving, it stopped. It was a small shabby sports-car, once doubtless the pride of some gilded Cretan youth. Sprawled in the back, upheld by a kneeling orderly, as though in gruesome parody of a death scene from grand opera, lay a dusty and bloody New Zealand officer. In front sat a New Zealand Brigadier and a young officer driving, both haggard. The Brigadier opened his eyes and said:

'Drive on. Can't stop.'

'I've got to get to Headquarters,' said Fido.

'No room. My Brigade Major's in a bad way. Must get him to a dressing-station.'

'I'm a Brigade Major. Hookforce. I've an urgent personal report for the GOC.'

The Brigadier blinked and squinnied and collected his powers of thought.

'Hookforce?' he said. 'Hookforce. You're finding the rear-guard?'

'Yes, sir. I know the GOC wants my report at once.'

'That makes a difference,' said the Brigadier. 'I reckon that gives you priority. Hop out, Giles; I'm sorry but you'll have to walk from here.'

The haggard young officer said nothing. He looked desperate. He climbed out and the Brigadier moved into his place at the wheel. He leaned against the warm stone wall and watched the car drive slowly towards the mountains.

For a time no one spoke except the wounded man who babbled in delirium. Fatigue had brought the Brigadier to a condition resembling senility, in which comatose periods alternated with moments of sharp vexation. For the moment his effort of decision had exhausted him. One tiny patch in his mind remained alive, and with this he steered, braked, changed gear. The road ran zigzag and the darkness deepened.

Fido as though in bed between the opening of the door and the drawing of the curtains recalled the nightmare march of the preceding night and measured each slow mile in terms of blisters and sweat and hunger and thirst and lassitude. He was moving effortlessly in the right direction, passing the ragged men who had gone by as he sat on the wall. Every minute he hiccuped.

Suddenly the Brigadier said: 'Shut up.'

'Sir?'

'How can I drive when you keep making that infernal noise?'

'I'm sorry, sir.'

The other Brigade Major kept saying: 'The returns aren't in from the units. Why aren't the returns in?'

The Brigadier fell silent again. His mind seemed to gape and close like the mouth of a goldfish. Presently he said:

'Bloody good rear-guard. We got caught with our trousers down all right. Before we'd even had breakfast there were fellows shooting at us with a damned mortar. That's how Charlie copped it. Where was your bloody rear-guard? What's happening? Put me in the picture.'

Fido roused himself from his happy trance. He said whatever came to mind.

'The situation is fluid,' he said; he hiccuped and continued. 'Out-flanked. Infiltrated. Patrol activity. Probing. Break through in strength. Element of surprise. Coordinated withdrawal.'

The Brigadier was not listening.

'Oh,' he said, 'so that's the long and short of it?'

Two miles of dreamland. Then: 'What exactly are you going to report to the General?'

'Sitrep,' said Fido simply. 'Every hour at the hour; orders,' he continued, 'reporting for orders. Information. Intention. *Method*,' he suddenly shouted.

'Quite correct,' said the Brigadier. 'Quite correct.'

He was leaning heavily on the steering-wheel, staring into the darkness. They were climbing steeply now, back and forward along the face of the precipice, with groups of shadowy men straggling everywhere. The Brigadier enjoyed the peculiar immunity from accident that is granted to sleep-walkers.

It seemed to Fido that the moment of unpleasantness was past, but when at length the Brigadier spoke it was with unmistakable malevolence.

'Get out, bastard,' he said.

'Sir?'

'Who in hell d'you think you are, taking Giles's place? Giles is worth six of you. Get out and walk, bastard.'

'Me, sir?'

'You are a bastard, aren't you?'

'No, sir.'

Fido's hiccups ceased suddenly.

'Oh.' The Brigadier seemed disconcerted by this denial. 'My mistake. Sorry. Still, you can bloody well get out and walk, just the same – bastard.'

But he did not stop and soon he began to whistle through his teeth. Fido dozed. Thus they came to the head of the pass where they were suddenly jolted into consciousness. They had collided with something large and black and solid.

'What the hell?' said the Brigadier.

They had not been travelling fast enough to incur much damage. The horn at least was working and the Brigadier pierced the fastness with its ignoble note.

'Aw, pipe down,' came in feeble protest from the darkness.

'What the devil have they stopped for? Go and move them on.'

Fido climbed out and felt his way round the obstruction. It was an empty lorry. Another stood in front of it and beyond that another. Fido groped forward, finding himself one of an ant-line of toiling men who were climbing off the road into the rugged mountain-side. He discerned that the cliff was down on one side and on the other the road had fallen away into the valley leaving a single steep, precarious mass of broken rock. Beyond it the road led down. An officer was rolling stones down the precipice, calling: 'I want men for a working-party. We've got to get this clear. I want volunteers.'

No one heeded him.

Fido stopped and said, 'What's this? A bomb?'

'Sappers. Blew the road without orders and cleared out. I'll have 'em court-martialled if it's the last thing I do. If I have to wait the whole bloody war in prison to do it. I'll get their names. Lend a hand, for Christ's sake.'

'You'll never do it,' said Fido.

'I must. There's five thousand men got to come through.'

'I'll report it,' said Fido. 'I'm on my way to headquarters now. I'll see the General hears about it personally.'

'You'd do better to stay and help.'

'Must push on,' said Fido.

He pushed on over the landslide, down the road to the plain, to the plain which led to the sea, and as he pushed he left behind him all memory of the frantic, forlorn road-mender, of the irascible New Zealand Brigadier and the dying Major. His mind curled up and slept and the swing of his body carried him from one numb foot to the other, one after the other, on and down towards the sea.

Creforce HQ was a line of caves. Fido found them soon after midnight. Good order prevailed there and military discipline; a sentry challenged him and having heard his account of himself directed him where to go. Fido paused on the goat-track like a drunkard composing himself before entering sober company. Now that his weary quest was at length accomplished it was borne in on him that he had nothing to report, nothing to ask, no reason to be there at all. He had been led by instinct, nosing out his master. He brought no propitiatory rat. He was a bad dog; he had been off on his own, rolling in something nasty. He wanted to fawn and lick the correcting hand.

This would not do. Gradually Fido's slumbrous mind came alive with humanity as the Cretan hillsides had done when the last aeroplane departed.

The mouths of the caves had been roughly walled with loose stones and screens of blankets propped against them. He peered into the first and found a section of signallers round a storm lantern and a wireless set, vainly calling Cairo. The next was in darkness. Fido flashed his torch and saw half a dozen sleeping men and beyond them on a natural shelf of rock a tin of familiar aspect. Cautiously and, it seemed to him, very courageously, Fido stepped across and stole six biscuits – all that remained. He ate them luxuriously in the star-light and wiped the crumbs from his lips. Then he entered the presence of the GOC.

The roof of the cave was too low to allow Fido to stand to attention. He struck his head painfully, then bent and saluted the dust before his feet.

The headmen of the defeated tribe huddled on their haunches like chimps in a zoo. The paramount-chief seemed to recognize Fido.

'Come in,' he said. 'Everything going well?'

'Yes, sir,' said Fido desperately.

'They'll be able to take off their full thousand tonight? The check points are functioning satisfactorily? Priorities being observed as laid down, eh?'

'I've come from Hookforce, sir.'

'Oh. I thought you were from the beach. I want a report from the beach.'

The BGS said: 'We got a sitrep from the Halberdiers three hours ago. As you know, they are holding the line at Babali Inn. They fall back through you before dawn. Your men all in position?'

'Yes, sir,' Fido lied.

'Good. The navy landed stores tonight. They're dumped at the approaches to Sphakia. The DQMG will issue chits for you to draw on them. There ought to be plenty to see you through until the Germans have taken over the job of feeding you.'

'But aren't *we* being taken off, sir?'

'No,' said the General. 'No. I'm afraid that won't be possible. The navy are doing what they can, doing magnificently. Someone's got to stay behind and cover the final withdrawal. Hookforce were last on, so I'm afraid you're the last off. Sorry, but there it is.'

This was not a people among whom toothless elders were held in honour. Strong yellow fangs gnawed the human sacrifice.

One of the staff said: 'Are you all right for money?'

'Sir?'

'Some of you may be able to make your own ways in small parties to Alexandria. Buy boats along the coast. "Caiques" they call them. You'll need drachmas.' He opened a suitcase and revealed what might have been the spoils of a bank robbery. 'Help your-self.'

Fido took two great bundles of 1,000-drachma notes.

'Remember,' continued the staff officer, 'wherever the enemy shows his head, give him a bloody nose.'

'Yes, sir.'

'Sure you have enough drachmas?'

'Yes, I think so, sir.'

'Well, good luck.'

'Good luck. Good luck. Good luck,' echoed the headmen as Fido saluted his toes and made his way into the open air.

As he passed the sentry he left the world of good order and military discipline and was on his own in the wilderness. Somewhere not far away, in easy walking distance, lay the sea and the navy. He had only to keep moving downhill. His torch was dying. He lit his footsteps with occasional flickers, provoking protests from the surrounding scrub. 'Put that bloody light out.'

He plunged on and down.

'Put that bloody light out.'

Suddenly quite near him there was a rifle shot. He heard the crack and smack and whistling ricochet among the rocks behind him. He dropped his torch and began feebly to trot. He lost the path and stumbled from boulder to boulder until treading on something which seemed smooth and round and solid in the starlight he found himself in the top of a tree which grew twenty feet below. Scattering Greek currency among the leaves, he subsided quite gently from branch to branch and when he reached ground continued to roll over and over, down and down, caressed and momentarily stayed by bushes until at length he came to rest as though borne there by a benevolent Zephyr of classical myth, in a soft, dark, sweet-smelling, empty place where the only sound was the music of falling water. And there for a time his descent ended. Out of sight, out of hearing, the crowded boats put out from the beach; the men-o'-war sailed away and Fido slept.

Sage and thyme, marjoram and dittany and myrtle grew all about Fido's mossy bed and, as the sun mounted over the tufted precipice, quite overcame the sour sweat of his fear.

The spring had been embellished, consecrated and christianized; the water glittered and bubbled through two man-made basins and above it an arch had been cut in the natural rock. Above the arch, in a flat panel, the head of a saint, faded and flaked, was still discernible.

Fido awoke in this Arcadian vale to find standing near him and gazing fiercely down a figure culled straight from some ferocious folk-tale. His bearing was patriarchal, his costume, to Fido's eyes, phantasmagoric – a goat-skin jacket, a crimson sash stuck full of antique weapons, trousers in the style of Abdul the Damned, leather puttees, bare feet. He carried a crooked staff.

'Good morning,' said Fido. 'I am English, an ally. I fight the Germans. I am hungry.'

The Cretan made no answer. Instead he reached forward with his crosier, deftly hooked Fido's pack from beside him and drew it away.

'Here. I say. What d'you think you're doing?'

The old man removed and examined Fido's possessions, transferring them one by one to his own pouch. He took even the safety-razor and the tube of soap. He turned the pack upside down and shook it, made as though to throw it away, thought better and hung it round his massive neck. Fido watched, fascinated. Then he shouted: 'Stop that, damn you. Give those things back.'

The old man regarded him as though he were a fractious great-grandson. Fido drew his pistol.

'Give those back or I'll shoot,' he cried wildly.

The Cretan studied the weapon with renewed interest, nodded gravely and stepped forward.

'Stop,' cried Fido. 'I'll shoot.'

But his finger lay damp and limp on the trigger. The old man leant forward. Fido made no movement. The horny hand touched his and gently loosened his grip on the butt. The old man studied the pistol for a moment, nodding, then tucked it beside his daggers in the red sash. He turned and silently, surely, climbed away up the hillside.

Fido wept.

He lay there all the morning long, quite devoid of the power and will to move. Sometimes he dreamed horribly, sometimes through his waking maze he tried to consider his situation. Enemies encompassed him. Someone had tried to shoot him the night before – German, Australian, Cretan, it did not signify; every hand was against him. At noon he crawled to the fountain and put his bald head under the jet. It brought him sharply to a realization of his hunger. There had been talk last night of dumps of food on the beaches. The stream must lead to the sea, to the beaches, to the dumps of food. He had somewhere about him a chit from the DQMG. He did not, even in his extremity, quite abandon his faith in the magic of official forms. In bumf lay salvation. He stood and groggily pursued his course.

Soon the way narrowed and became a gorge, with the path straying in and out of the water. He moved very slowly, often pausing to lean against the rock-wall. Into the stillness of one of these pauses struck a horripilant sound. Someone was coming. There was no escape on either hand; the cliffs rose sheer. He could only turn or stand and wait his fate. Fido stood. The steps came very close. Fido could wait no longer. He ran forward to meet whatever was coming, his hands up, crying: 'I surrender. I am unarmed, I'm a non-combatant. Don't shoot.'

He shut his eyes. Then a voice said: 'Major Hound, sir. You're not yourself. Try some of this, sir.'

Fido subsided. He was dimly aware of an icy sit-upon and a burning head. It seemed to him that he was squatting in the brook while over him there stood the phantasm of Corporal-Major Ludovic proffering a bottle. Tart, tepid wine poured down his throat and dribbled on his chin and chest. He gulped and panted and blubbed a little and gradually recovered some possession of himself while Ludovic, a firmer image with each passing moment, leaned on the opposing wall and watched.

'A fortunate meeting, if I may say so, sir. Can you manage another mile? Dinner's ready.'

Dinner. Fido felt in the pockets of his bush-shirt. Forty or fifty thousand drachmas fluttered between his trembling fingers. Then he found what he wanted, his chit from the DQMG.

'Dinner,' he affirmed.

Ludovic examined it, smoothed it and tucked it away. He

collected the bank-notes. He held out a hand and drew Fido firmly to his feet. Then he turned and led.

The gorge soon widened and became a little cultivated plain bounded by receding cliffs and opening on the sea. Ludovic's way led off the path and the stream, following the rocky margin. It was hard going and Fido lagged and staggered until after half an hour he whispered, 'Corporal-Major. Wait for me. I can't go on,' so faintly that the words were lost in the sound of his stumbling boots. Ludovic strode on. Fido stood with hanging head and closed eyes, out on his feet. And in that moment of prayerless abandonment, succour was vouchsafed. Tiny, delicious, doggy perceptions began to flutter in the void. He raised his bowed nose and sniffed. Clear as the horn of Roland a new note was recalling him to life. Unmistakable and compelling, above the delicate harmony of bee-haunted flower and crushed leaf a great new smell was borne to him; the thunderous organ-tones of Kitchen. Fido was suffused, inebriated, transported. He pressed forward, he overtook Ludovic, he passed him, wordlessly, following his nose in and out of boulders, up treacherous scree, the scent stronger with every frantic step; until at length he came to a wide cave high in the cliff face and he stumbled into the cool gloom where amid steam and wood-smoke a group of shadowy men sat round an iron cauldron; in it there seethed chickens and hares and kids, pigs and peppers and cucumbers and garlic and rice and crusts of bread and dumplings and grated cheese and pungent roots and great soggy nameless white tubers and wisps of succulent green and sea-salt and a good deal of red wine and olive oil.

Fido was bereft of knife, fork, spoon, and tin. He squinnied round the congregation and discerned the semblance of his batman about to tuck in. He snatched. The man held fast.

'Here, what's the idea?'

Fido pulled, the man pulled back, their thumbs deep in the hot grease. Then from behind them Ludovic, in the voice of comradeship, said persuasively: 'Give over, Syd. Anyone with eyes in his head can see the Major's all in. We can't have him going sick on us now we've found him, can we, Syd?'

So Fido took possession of the tin and silently feasted.

The cave was commodious; from its modest mouth it opened

into a spacious chamber and branched into dim, divergent passages; from somewhere in its depths came the sound of running water. It held without overcrowding three women, some assorted live-stock and more than fifty men, mostly Spaniards.

These wanderers had got away to a good start. They were familiar with defeat in all its aspects, versed in its stratagems, sharp to recognize its portents. Before their lighter touched shore they had sniffed the air of disaster and twelve hours before the rout began had resumed their migration, passing through villages still unravaged by war, looting with practised hands. Theirs was the cauldron and its rich contents, theirs the women, theirs the brass bedstead and other pieces of domestic furniture which gave an impression of cosy settled occupation to their place of refuge. But they were heirs of a tradition of hospitality. Fiercely resistant of other intruders, they had greeted their old comrades of Hookforce, when out foraging they fortuitously met, with happy smiles, raised fists and sentiments of proletarian solidarity.

They retained their arms but had shed all but the rudiments of their British uniforms in favour of a variety of Cretan hats, scarves and jackets. When Fido paused in his eating and looked about him, he took them for local brigands, but he was known to them. He had not been a favourite of theirs at Sidi Bishr. Had he come possessed of any pretence of authority or equipped with any desirable property they would have made short work of him. But destitute, he was their kin and their guest. They watched him benevolently.

Presently Ludovic said: 'I shouldn't eat any more just at present, sir.' He rolled a cigarette and handed it to Fido. 'I've always considered it a mystery, sir, that one immediately revives after eating. According to science, several hours of digestion must pass before any real physical nourishment is obtained.'

The speculation did not interest Fido. Replete and fortified, he began to resume the habits of his calling.

'I'm not quite clear, Corporal-Major, how you come to be here?'

'Much the same way as yourself, I think, sir.'

'I expected you to report back to headquarters.'

'There, sir, we both made a miscalculation. I thought I should be safely back in Egypt by this time, but I encountered difficulties, sir. I found check points at all the approaches to the beach. Only formed bodies of men under their officers were allowed through. There was what you might call a shambles last night in the dark. Men looking for officers, officers looking for men. That was why I was so particularly pleased to meet you today. I was looking for an unattached officer. I hardly hoped it would be you, sir. With your help we shall get off very nicely, I believe. I've got the men all lined up for parade tonight – rather a motley crowd, I fear, sir, representing all arms of the service. Not quite what we're used to at Knightsbridge or Windsor. But they'll pass in the dark. The Spaniards have decided to stay on.'

'What you're suggesting is entirely irregular, Corporal-Major.'

Ludovic regarded him softly.

'Come, come, Major Hound, sir. Don't you think we might drop all that? Just between ourselves, sir. Tonight when we embark our party, later when we get back to Alex – it will be quite appropriate then; but just at the moment, as we are here, after what's happened, sir, don't you think it will be more suitable,' and his voice changed suddenly from its plummy to its plebeian mode – 'to shut your bloody trap.'

Suddenly, for no human reason, a great colony of bats came to life in the vault of the cave, wheeled about, squeaking in the smoke of the fire, fluttered and blundered and then settled again, huddled head-down, invisible.

6

GUY was weary, hungry and thirsty, but he had fared better than Fido in the last four days and, compared with him, was in good heart, almost buoyant, as he tramped alone, eased at last of the lead weight of human company. He had paddled in this lustral freedom on the preceding morning when he caught X Commando among the slit trenches and olive trees. Now he wallowed.

Soon the road ran out and round the face of a rocky spur – the place where Fido had found no cover – and here he met a straggling platoon of infantry coming fast towards him, a wan young officer well ahead.

'Have you seen anything of Hookforce?'

'Never heard of them.'

The breathless officer paused as his men caught up with him and formed column. They still had their weapons and equipment.

'Or the Halberdiers?'

'Cut off. Surrounded. Surrendered.'

'Are you sure?'

'Sure? For Christ's sake, there are parachutists everywhere. We've just been fired on coming round that corner. You can't get up the road. A machine-gun, the other side of the valley.'

'Where exactly?'

'Believe you me, I didn't wait to see.'

'Any casualties?'

'I didn't wait to see. Can't wait now. I wouldn't try that road if you know what's healthy.'

The platoon scuffled on. Guy looked down the empty exposed road and then studied his map. There was a track over the hill which rejoined the road at a village two miles on. Guy did not greatly believe in the machine-gun but he chose the short cut and painfully climbed until he found himself on the top of the spur. He could see the whole empty, silent valley. Nothing moved anywhere except the bees. He might have been standing in the hills behind Santa Dulcina any holiday morning of his lonely boyhood.

Then he descended to the village. Some of the cottage doors and windows were barred and shuttered, some rudely broken down. At first he met no one. A well stood before the church, built about with marble steps and a rutted plinth. He approached thirstily but found the rope hanging loose and short from its bronze staple. The bucket was gone and leaning over he saw far below a little shaving-glass of light and his own mocking head, dark and diminished.

He entered an open house and found an earthenware jar of classic shape. As he removed the straw stopper he heard and felt a hum and, tilting it to the light, found it full of bees and a residue of honey. Then looking about in the gloom he saw an old woman gazing at him. He smiled, showed his empty water-bottle, made signs of drinking. Still she gazed, quite blind. He searched his mind for vestiges of Greek and tried: '*Hudor. Hydro. Dipsa.*' Still she gazed, quite deaf, quite alone. Guy turned back into the sunlight. There a young girl, ruddy, bare-footed and in tears, approached him frankly and took him by the sleeve. He showed her his empty bottle, but she shook her head, made little inarticulate noises and drew him resolutely towards a small yard on the edge of the village, which had once held live-stock but was now deserted except by a second, similar girl, a sister perhaps, and a young English soldier who lay on a stretcher motionless. The girls pointed helplessly towards this figure. Guy could not help. The young man was dead, undamaged it seemed. He lay as though at rest. The few corpses which Guy had seen in Crete had sprawled awkwardly. This soldier lay like an effigy on a tomb – like Sir Roger in his shadowy shrine at Santa Dulcina. Only the bluebottles that clustered round his lips and eyes proclaimed that he was flesh. Why was he lying here? Who were these girls? Had a weary stretcher-party left him in their care and had they watched him die? Had they closed his eyes and composed his limbs? Guy would never know. It remained one of the countless unexplained incidents of war. Meanwhile, lacking words the three of them stood by the body, stiff and mute as figures in a sculptured Deposition.

To bury the dead is one of the corporal works of charity. There were no tools here to break the stony ground. Later, perhaps, the enemy would scavenge the island and tip this body with others into a common pit and the boy's family would get no news of him and wait and hope month after month, year after year. A precept came to Guy's mind from his military education: 'The officer in command of a burial party is responsible for collecting the red identity discs and forwarding them to Records. The green disc remains on the body. If in doubt, gentlemen, remember that green is the colour of putrefaction.'

Guy knelt and took the disc from the cold breast. He read a number, a name, a designation, *RC*. 'May his soul and the souls of all the faithful departed, in the mercy of God, rest in peace.'

Guy stood. The bluebottles returned to the peaceful young face. Guy saluted and passed on.

The country opened and soon Guy came to another village. Toiling beside Fido in the darkness, he had barely noticed it. Now he found a place of some size, other roads and tracks converged on a market square; the houses had large barns behind them; a domed church stood open. Of the original inhabitants there was no sign; instead, English soldiers were posted in doorways – Halberdiers – and at the cross-roads sat Sarum-Smith, smoking a pipe.

'Hullo, uncle. The CO said you were about.'

'I'm glad to find you. I met a windy officer on the road who said you were all in the bag.'

'It doesn't look like it, does it? There was something of a schemozzle last night but we weren't in that.'

Since Guy last saw him in West Africa, Sarum-Smith had matured. He was not a particularly attractive man, but man he was. 'The CO's out with the Adj, going round the companies. You'll find the second-in-command at battalion headquarters, over there.'

Guy went where he was directed, to a farm-house beside the church. Everything was in order. One notice pointed to the regimental aid post, another to the battalion-office. Guy passed the RSM and the clerks and in the further room of the house found Major Erskine. An army blanket had been spread on the kitchen table. It was, in replica, the orderly room at Penkirk.

Guy saluted.

'Hullo, uncle, you could do with a shave.'

'I could do with some breakfast, sir.'

'Lunch will be coming up as soon as the CO gets back. Brought us some more orders?'

'No, sir.'

'Information?'

'None, sir.'

'What's headquarters up to then?'

'Not functioning much at the moment. I came to get information from you.'

'We don't know much.'

He put Guy in the picture. The Commandos had lost two troops somehow during the night. An enemy patrol had wandered in from the flank during the morning and hurriedly retired. The Commandos were due to come through them soon and take up positions at Imbros. They had motor transport and should not have much difficulty in disengaging. The Second Halberdiers were to hold their present line till midnight and then fall back behind Hookforce to the beach perimeter. 'After that we're in the hands of the navy. Those are the orders as I understand them. I don't know how they'll work out.'

A Halberdier brought Guy a cup of tea.

'Crock,' said Guy, 'I hope you remember me?'

'Sir.'

'Rather different from our last meeting.'

'Sir,' said Crock.

'The enemy aren't attacking in any strength yet,' Major Erskine continued. 'They're just pushing out patrols. As soon as they bump into anything, they stop and try working round. All quite elementary. We could hold them for ever if those blasted Q fellows would do their job. What are we running away for? It's not soldiering as I was taught it.'

A vehicle stopped outside and Guy recognized Colonel Tickeridge's large commanding voice. He went out and found the Colonel and the Adjutant. They were directing the unloading from a lorry of three wounded men, two of them groggily walking, the third lying on a stretcher. As this man was carried past him he turned his white face and Guy recognized one of his former company. The man lay under a blanket. His wound was fresh and he was not yet in much pain. He smiled up quite cheerfully.

'Shanks,' said Guy. 'What have you been doing to yourself?'

'Must have been a mortar bomb, sir. Took us all by surprise, bursting right in the trench. I am lucky, considering. Chap next to me caught a packet.'

This was Halberdier Shanks who, Guy remembered, used to win prizes for the Slow Valse. In the days of Dunkirk he had asked for compassionate leave in order to compete at Blackpool.

'I'll come and talk when the MO's had a look at you.'

'Thank you, sir. Nice to have you back with us.'

The other two men had limped off to the RAP. They must be from D Company too, Guy supposed. He did not remember them; only Halberdier Shanks, because of his Slow Valse.

'Well, uncle, come along in and tell me what I can do for you.'

'I was wondering if there was anything *I* could do for *you*, Colonel.'

'Yes, certainly. You will lay on hot dinners for the battalion, a bath for me, artillery support and a few squadrons of fighter aircraft. That's about all we want this morning, I think.' Colonel Tickeridge was in high good humour. As he entered his headquarters he called: 'Hi, there. Bring on the dancing-girls. Where's Halberdier Gold?'

'Just coming up, sir.'

Halberdier Gold was an old friend, since the evening at Matchet when he had carried Guy's bag from the station, before the question even arose of Guy's joining the corps. He smiled broadly.

'Good morning, Gold; remember me?'

'Good morning, sir. Welcome back to the battalion.'

'Vino,' called Colonel Tickeridge. 'Wine for our guest from the higher formation.'

It was said with the utmost geniality but it struck a slight chill after the men's warmer greeting.

Gold laid a jug of wine on the table with the biscuits and bully beef. While they ate and drank, Colonel Tickeridge told Major Erskine:

'Quite a bit of excitement on the left flank. We were up with D Company and I was just warning Brent to expect fireworks in half an hour or so when the Commandos pull out, when I'm blessed if the blighters didn't start pooping off at us with a heavy mortar from the other side of the rocks. De Souza's platoon caught it pretty hot. Lucky we had the truck there to bring back the pieces. We just stopped to watch Brent winkle the mortar out. Then we came straight home. I've made some nice friends out there – a company of New Zealanders who rolled up and said please might they join in our battle – first-class fellows.'

This seemed the moment for Guy to say what had been in his mind since meeting Shanks.

'That's exactly what I want to do, Colonel,' he said. 'Isn't there a platoon you could let me take over?'

Colonel Tickeridge regarded him benevolently. 'No, uncle, of course there isn't.'

'But later in the day, when you get casualties?'

'My good uncle, you aren't under my command. You can't start putting in for a cross-posting in the middle of a battle. That's not how the army works, you know that. You're a Hookforce body.'

'But, Colonel, those New Zealanders –'

'Sorry, uncle. No can do.'

And that, Guy knew from of old, was final.

Colonel Tickeridge began to explain the details of the rear-guard to Major Erskine. Sarum-Smith came to announce that the Commandos were coming through and Guy followed him out into the village and saw a line of dust and the back of the last Hookforce lorry disappearing to the south. There was a little firing, rifles and light machine-guns, and an occasional mortar bomb three-quarters of a mile to the north where the Halberdiers held their line. Guy stood between his friends, isolated.

A few hours earlier he had exulted in his loneliness. Now the case was altered. He was a 'guest from the higher formation', a 'Hookforce body', without place or function, a spectator. And all the deep sense of desolation which he had sought to cure, which from time to time momentarily seemed to be cured, overwhelmed him as of old. His heart sank. It seemed to him as though literally an organ of his body were displaced, subsiding, falling heavily like a feather in a vacuum jar; Philoctetes set apart from his fellows by an old festering wound; Philoctetes without his bow. Sir Roger without his sword.

Presently Colonel Tickeridge cheerfully intruded on his despondency.

'Well, uncle, nice to have seen you. I expect you want to get back to your own people. You'll have to walk, I'm afraid. The Adj and I are going round the companies again.'

'Can I come too?'

Colonel Tickeridge hesitated, then said: 'The more the merrier.'

As they went forward he asked news of Matchet. 'You staff wallahs get all the luck. We've had no mail since we went into Greece.'

The Second Halberdiers and the New Zealanders lay across the main road, their flanks resting on the steep scree that enclosed the valley. D Company were on the far right flank, strung out along a water-course. To reach them there was open ground to be crossed.

As Colonel Tickeridge and his party emerged from cover a burst of fire met them.

'Hullo,' he said, 'the Jerries are a lot nearer than they were this morning.'

They ran for some rocks and approached cautiously and circuitously. When they finally dropped into the ditch they found Brent and Sergeant-Major Rawkes. Both were preoccupied and rather grim. They acknowledged Guy's greeting and then turned at once to their CO.

'They've brought up another mortar.'

'Can you pin-point it?'

'They keep moving. They're going easy with their ammunition at present but they've got the range.'

Colonel Tickeridge stood and searched the land ahead through his field-glasses. A bomb burst ten yards behind; all crouched low while a shower of stone and metal rang overhead.

'We haven't anything to spare for a counter-attack,' said Colonel Tickeridge. 'You'll have to give a bit of ground.'

In training Guy had often wondered whether the exercises at Penkirk bore any semblance to real warfare. Here they did. This was no Armageddon, no torrent of uniformed migration, no clash of mechanical monsters; it was the conventional 'battalion in defence', opposed by lightly armed, equally weary small forces. Ritchie-Hook had done little to inculcate the arts of withdrawal, but the present action conformed to pattern. While Colonel Tickeridge gave his orders, Guy moved down the bank. He found de Souza and his depleted platoon. He had a picturesque bandage round his head. Under it his sallow face was grave.

'Lost a bit of my ear,' he said. 'It doesn't hurt. But I'll be glad when today is over.'

'You're retiring at midnight, I gather.'

'"Retiring" is good. It sounds like a maiden aunt going to bed.'

'I dare say you'll be in Alexandria before me,' said Guy. 'Hookforce is last out, covering the embarkation. I don't get the impression that the Germans are anxious to attack.'

'D'you know what I think, uncle? I think they want to escort us quietly into the ships. Then they can sink us at their leisure from the air. A much tidier way of doing things.'

211

A bomb exploded short of them.

'I wish I could spot that damned mortar,' said de Souza.

Then an orderly summoned him to company headquarters. Guy went with him and rejoined Colonel Tickeridge.

It took little time to mount the withdrawal on the flank. Guy watched the battalion adjust itself to its new line. Everything was done correctly. Colonel Tickeridge gave his orders for the hours of darkness and for the final retreat. Guy made notes of times and lines of march in which the Halberdiers and New Zealanders would pass through Hookforce. Then he took his leave.

'If you run across any blue jobs,' said Colonel Tickeridge, 'tell them to wait for us.'

For the third time Guy followed the road south. Night fell. The road filled with many men. Guy found the remnants of his head-quarters where he had left them. He did not inquire for Major Hound. Sergeant Smiley offered no information. They fell in and set out into the darkness. They marched all night, one silent component of the procession of lagging, staggering men.

Another day; another night.

'Night and day,' crooned Trimmer, 'you are the one. Only you beneath the moon and under the sun, in the roaring traffic's boom –'

'Listen,' said Ian Kilbannock severely, 'you are coming to the Savoy to meet the American Press.'

'In the silence of my lonely room I think of you.'

'*Trimmer.*'

'I've met them.'

'Not these. These are Scab Dunz, Bum Schlum, and Joe Mulligan. They're great fellows, Scab, Bum, and Joe. Their stories are syndicated all over the United States. Trimmer, if you don't stop warbling I shall recommend your return to regimental duties in Iceland. Bum and Scab are naturally antifascist. Joe is more doubtful. He's Boston Irish and he doesn't awfully care for us.'

'I'm sick of the Press. D'you see what the *Daily Beast* are calling me – "The Demon Barber"?'

'Their phrase, not ours. I wish I'd thought of it.'

'Anyway, I'm lunching with Virginia.'

'I'll get you out of that.'

'It isn't exactly a hard date.'

'Leave it to me.'

Ian picked up the telephone and Trimmer lapsed into song.

'There's oh such a burning, yearning, churning under the hide of me.'

'Virginia? Ian. Colonel Trimmer regrets he's unable to lunch today, madam.'

'The demon barber? It never occurred to me to lunch with him. Ian, do something, will you? for an old friend. Persuade your young hero that he utterly nauseates me.'

'Is that quite kind?'

'There are dozens of girls eager to go out with him. Why must he pick on me?'

'He says there's a voice within him keeps repeating, "You, you, you."'

'Cheek. Tell him to go to hell, Ian, like an angel.'

Ian rang off.

'She says you're to go to hell,' he reported.

'Oh.'

'Why don't you lay off Virginia? There's nothing in it for you.'

'But there is, there was. She can't put on this stand-offish turn with me. Why, in Glasgow –'

'Trimmer, you must have seen enough of me to know that I'm the last man in the world you should choose to confide in – particularly on questions of love. You must forget all about Virginia, all about all these London girls you've been going about with lately. I've got a great treat in store for you. I'm going to take you round the factories. You're going to boost production. Lunch-hour talks. Canteen dances. We'll find you all kinds of delicious girls. You're in for a lovely time, Trimmer, in the midlands, in the north, far away from London. But meanwhile you must do your bit for Anglo-American relations with Scab and Bum and Joe. There's a war on.'

In the staff-car which took them to the Savoy, Ian tried to put Trimmer in the picture.

'. . . You won't find Joe much interested in military operations, I'm glad to say. He's been brought up to distrust the "red coats".

213

He looks on us all as feudal colonial oppressors, which, I will say for you, Trimmer, you definitely are not. We've got to sell him the new Britain that is being forged in the furnace of war. Dammit, Trimmer, I don't believe you're listening.'

Nor was he. A voice within him kept forlornly repeating, 'You, you, you.'

Ian Kilbannock, like Ludovic, had a gift of tongues. He spoke one language to his friends, another to Trimmer and General Whale, another to Bum, Scab, and Joe.

'Hiya, boys,' he cried, entering the room. 'Look what the cat's brought in.'

It was not for economy that these three fat, untidy men lived cheek by jowl together; their expense accounts were limitless. Nor was it, as sometimes in the past, for motives of professional rivalry; in this city of communiqués and censorship there were no scoops to be had, no need to watch the opposition. It was the simple wish for companionship; their common condition of exile; the state of their nerves. Low diet, deep drinking and nightly alarms had transformed them, or rather had greatly accelerated processes of decay that were barely noticeable in the three far-feared ace reporters who had jauntily landed in England more than a year ago. They had covered the fall of Addis Ababa, of Barcelona, of Vienna, of Prague. They were here to cover the fall of London and the story had somehow gotten stale. Meanwhile they were subject to privations and dangers which, man and boy, they had boastfully endured for days at a time, but which, prolonged indefinitely and widely shared, became irksome.

Their room overlooked the river but the windows had been criss-crossed with sticking plaster and few gleams of sunshine penetrated them. Inside, the electric light burned. There were three typewriters, three cabin-trunks, three beds, a tumbled mass of papers and clothes, numberless cigarette-ends, dirty glasses, clean glasses, empty bottles, full bottles. Three pairs of bloodshot eyes gazed at Trimmer from three putty-coloured faces.

'Bum, Scab, Joe, this is the boy you've all been wanting to meet.'

'Is that a fact?' asked Joe.

'Colonel McTavish, I'm pleased to meet you,' said Bum.

'Colonel Trimmer, I'm pleased to meet you,' said Scab.

'Hey,' said Joe. 'Who is this joker? McTavish? Trimmer?'

'That is still being discussed at a high level,' said Ian. 'I'll let you know for certain before your story is released.'

'What story?' asked Joe balefully.

Scab came to the rescue.

'Don't mind Joe, Colonel. Let me fix you a drink.'

'Joe isn't feeling too hot this morning,' said Bum.

'I just asked what's the guy's name and what's the story. What's not too hot about that?'

'What say we all have a drink?' said Bum.

Of Trimmer's abounding weaknesses hard drinking was not one. He did not enjoy whisky before luncheon. He refused the glass thrust upon him.

'What's wrong with the guy?' asked Joe.

'Commando training,' said Ian.

'Is that so? Well, I'm just a goddam newsman and I don't train. When a guy won't drink with me, I drink alone.'

Scab was the most courtly of the trio.

'I can guess where you want to be right now, Colonel,' he said.

'Yes,' said Trimmer, 'Glasgow, in the station hotel, in a fog.'

'No, sir. Where you want to be right now is in Crete. Your boys are putting up a wonderful fight there. You heard the Old Man on the radio last night? There is no question, he said, of evacuating Crete. The attack has been held. The defence is being reinforced. It's a turning-point. There's going to be no more withdrawal.'

'We're with you in this,' said Bum generously, 'all the way. I don't say there haven't been times I've hated you limeys' guts. Abyssinia, Spain, Munich, that's all done with, Colonel. What wouldn't I give to be in Crete. That's where the news is today.'

'You may remember,' said Ian, 'you asked me to bring Colonel McTavish to lunch. You thought he could give you a story.'

'That's right. We did, didn't we? Well, how about we have another drink first, even if the Colonel can't join us?'

They drank and they smoked. The hands which lit the cigarettes became steadier with each glass, the genial tones more emotional.

'I like you, Ian, even if you are a lord. Hell, a man can't help it if he's a lord. You're all right, Ian, I like you.'

'Thank you, Bum.'

'I like the Colonel too. He don't say much and he don't drink any but I like him. He's a regular guy.'

Even Joe softened enough to say: 'Anybody says the Colonel isn't all right, I'll punch his teeth in.'

'Everyone says the Colonel's all right, Joe.'

'They better.'

Presently the time for luncheon passed.

'There isn't anything fit to eat around here, anyway,' said Joe.

'I'm not hungry right now myself,' said Bum.

'Food? I can take it or leave it,' said Scab.

'Now, boys,' said Ian. 'Colonel McTavish is a pretty busy man. He's here to give you his story. How about asking him anything you want now?'

'All right,' said Joe. 'What else have you done, Colonel? That raid of yours was good copy. They ate it up back home. You got decorated. You got made Colonel. So what? Where else have you been? Tell us what you did this week and the week before. How come you're not in Crete?'

'I've been on leave,' said Trimmer.

'Well, that's a hell of a story.'

'Here's the angle, boys,' said Ian. 'The Colonel here is a portent – the new officer which is emerging from the old hide-bound British Army.'

'How do I know he's not high-bound?'

'Joe, you don't have to be so suspicious,' said Scab. 'Anyone with eyes in his head can see he isn't hide-bound.'

'He doesn't *look* high-bound,' Joe conceded, 'but how do I know he *isn't*. Are you high-bound?'

'He's not hide-bound,' said Ian.

'Why don't you let the Colonel answer for himself? I put it to you, Colonel, are you or are you not high-bound?'

'No,' said Trimmer.

'That's all I wanted to know,' said Joe.

'You asked him. He told you,' said Bum.

'Now I know. So what the hell?'

Presently through the fumes of tobacco and whisky a great earnestness enveloped Scab.

'You're not hide-bound, Colonel, and I'll tell you why. You've had advantages these stuff-shirts haven't had. You've worked, Colonel. And where have you worked? On an ocean liner. And who have you worked for? For American womanhood. Am I right or am I right? It all ties in. I can make a great piece out of this. How it's the casual personal contacts that make international alliances. The beauty parlour as the school of democracy. You must have had some very very lovely contacts on that ocean liner, Colonel.'

'I had the pick of the bunch,' said Trimmer.

'Tell them,' said Ian, 'about your American friends.'

A small pink gleam of professional interest broke in the journalists' eyes while Trimmer by contrast lapsed into trance.

'There was Mrs Troy,' he began.

'I don't think that's quite what the boys want,' said Ian.

'Not every voyage, of course, but two or three times a year. Four times in 1938 when half our regulars were keeping away because of the situation in Europe. *She* wasn't afraid,' mused Trimmer. 'I always looked for her name on the passenger list. Before it was printed I used to slip into the office and take a dekko. There was something about her – well, you know how it is – like music. When she had a hangover I was the only one who could help. There was something about me, she said, the way I massaged the back of her neck.'

'But you must have met other, more typical Americans?'

'She isn't typical. She isn't American except she married one and she hadn't any use for him. She's something quite apart.'

'They aren't interested in Mrs Troy,' said Ian. 'Tell them about the others.'

'Old trouts mostly,' said Trimmer. 'Mrs Stuyvesant Oglander. There were smart ones too, of course, Astors, Vanderbilts, Cuttings, Whitneys – they all came to me, but nobody was like Mrs Troy.'

'What I had in mind for my readers, Colonel, was something a little more homy.'

Trimmer had his pride. He awoke now from his reverie, sharply piqued.

'I never touched the homy ones,' he said.

'Goddammit,' cried Joe in triumph. 'What d'you know? The Colonel *is* high-bound.'

Then Ian abandoned this phase of Anglo-American friendship and within a few minutes he and Trimmer stood in the Strand vainly searching for a taxi. It was the moment of Guy's despair at Babali Hani. Their prospect, too, was dismal. The London crowd shuffled past, men in a diversity of drab uniforms, women in the strange new look of the decade – trousered, turbaned, cigarettes adhering and drooping from grubby weary faces; all of them surfeited with tea and Woolton pies, all of them bearing gas-masks which bumped and swung to their ungainly tread.

'You didn't do very well,' said Ian severely.

'I'm hungry.'

'You won't find anything to eat at this time of day. I'm going home.'

'Shall I come with you?'

'No.'

'Will Virginia be there?'

'I shouldn't think so.'

'She was when you telephoned.'

'She was just going out.'

'I haven't seen her for a week. She's given up her job at the Transit Camp. I've asked the other girls. They won't say where she's working. You know how girls are.'

Ian looked sorrowfully at his protégé. It was in his mind to offer some sort of exhortation, to remind him of the coming delights of the armament industry, but Trimmer looked so sorrowfully back at him that he merely said: 'Well, I'm walking to HOO HQ. You'll be hearing from me,' and turning, set off towards Trafalgar Square.

Trimmer followed as far as the Tube station, then broke off without a word and descended, a sad little song in his heart, to a platform lined with bunks where he waited long for a crowded train.

At Marchmain House HOO HQ, revitalized by the new exalted enthusiasm for Special Service troops, was expanding. More flats were added and more faces. It was here, in Ian's office, that Virginia Troy had taken refuge.

'Have you shaken off the Demon?' she asked.

'He just melted away, humming horribly. Virginia, I've got to talk to you seriously about Trimmer. The welfare of the department is at stake. Do you realize that he constitutes our sole contribution to the war effort to date? I have never seen a man so changed by success. A month ago he was all bounce. With that accent, that smile and that lock of hair he was absolutely cut out to be a great national figure. Look at him today. I doubt if he'll last the summer. I've already seen Air Marshal Beech break up under my eyes. I know the symptoms. It musn't happen again. I shall get a bad name in the service and this time it isn't my fault at all. As the victim has remarked, it's you, you, you. Do I have to remind you that you came to me with tears and made my home life hideous until I got you this job? I expect a little loyalty in return.'

'But, Ian, why d'you suppose I wanted to leave the canteen except to get away from Trimmer?'

'I thought you were bored with Brenda and Zita.'

'Only because they always had Trimmer around.'

'Ah,' said Ian. 'Oh.' He twiddled with things on his desk. 'What's all this about Glasgow?' he asked.

'Oh, *that*,' she said. 'That was nothing. That was fun. Not a bit like what's going on now.'

'Now the poor beast thinks he's in love.'

'Yes, it's too indecent.'

On 31 May, Guy sat in a cave overhanging the beach of Sphakia where the final embarkation was shortly to begin. By his watch it was not yet ten o'clock but it seemed the dead of night. Nothing stirred in the moonlight. In the crowded ravine below the Second Halberdiers stood in column of companies, every man in full marching order, waiting for the boats. Hookforce was deployed on the ridge above, holding the perimeter against an enemy who since sunset had fallen silent. Guy had brought his section here late that afternoon. They had marched all the previous night and most of that day, up the pass, down to Imbros, down a gully to this last position. They dropped asleep where they halted. Guy had sought out and found Creforce headquarters and brought from them to the Hookforce commanders the last grim orders.

He dozed and woke for seconds at a time, barely thinking.

There were footsteps outside. Guy had not troubled to post a look-out. Ivor Claire's troop was a few hundred yards distant. He went to the mouth of the cave and in the moonlight saw a familiar figure and heard a familiar voice: 'Guy? Ivor.'

Ivor entered and sat beside him.

They sat together, speaking between long pauses in the listless drawl of extreme fatigue.

'This is a damn fool business, Guy.'

'It will all be over tomorrow.'

'Just beginning. You're sure Tony Luxmore hasn't got the wrong end of the stick? I was at Dunkirk, you know. Not much fuss about priorities there. No inquiries afterwards. It doesn't make any sense, leaving the fighting troops behind and taking off the rabble. Tony's all in. I bet he muddled his orders.'

'I've got them all in writing from the GOC. Surrender at dawn. The men aren't supposed to know yet.'

'They know all right.'

'The General's off in a flying-boat tonight.'

'No staying with the sinking ship.'

'Napoleon didn't stay with his army after Moscow.'

Presently Ivor said: 'What does one *do* in prison?'

'I imagine a ghastly series of concert parties – perhaps for years. I've a nephew who was captured at Calais. D'you imagine one can do anything about getting posted where one wants?'

'I presume so. One usually can.'

Another pause.

'There would be no sense in the GOC sitting here to be captured.'

'None at all. No sense in any of us staying.'

Another pause.

'Poor Freda,' said Ivor. 'Poor Freda. She'll be an old dog by the time I see her again.'

Guy briefly fell asleep. Then Ivor said: 'Guy, what would you do if you were challenged to a duel?'

'Laugh.'

'Yes, of course.'

'What made you think of that now?'

'I was thinking about honour. It's a thing that changes, doesn't it? I mean, a hundred and fifty years ago we would have had to fight if challenged. Now we'd laugh. There must have been a time a hundred years or so ago when it was rather an awkward question.'

'Yes. Moral theologians were never able to stop duelling – it took democracy to do that.'

'And in the next war, when we are completely democratic, I expect it will be quite honourable for officers to leave their men behind. It'll be laid down in King's Regulations as their duty – to keep a *cadre* going to train new men to take the place of prisoners.'

'Perhaps men wouldn't take kindly to being trained by deserters.'

'Don't you think in a really modern army they'd respect them the more for being fly? I reckon our trouble is that we're at the awkward stage – like a man challenged to a duel a hundred years ago.'

Guy could see him clearly in the moonlight, the austere face, haggard now but calm and recollected, as he had first seen it in the Borghese Gardens. It was his last sight of him. Ivor stood up saying: 'Well, the path of honour lies up the hill,' and he strolled away.

And Guy fell asleep.

He dreamed continuously, it seemed to him, and most prosaically. All night in the cave he marched, took down orders, passed them on, marked his map, marched again, while the moon set and the ships came into the bay and the boats went back and forth between them and the beach, and the ships sailed away leaving Hookforce and five or six thousand other men behind them. In Guy's dreams there were no exotic visitants among the shades of Creforce, no absurdity, no escape. Everything was as it had been the preceding day, the preceding night, night and day since he had landed at Suda, and when he awoke at dawn it was to the same half-world; sleeping and waking were like two airfields, identical in aspect though continents apart. He had no clear apprehension that this was a fatal morning, that he was that day to resign an immeasurable piece of his manhood. He saw himself dimly at a great distance. Weariness was all.

'They say the ships left food on the beach,' said Sergeant Smiley.

'We'd better have a meal before we go to prison.'

'It's true then, sir, what they're saying, that there's no more ships coming?'

'Quite true, Sergeant.'

'And we're to surrender?'

'Quite true.'

'It don't seem right.'

The golden dawn was changing to unclouded blue. Guy led his section down the rough path to the harbour. The quay was littered with abandoned equipment and the wreckage of bombardment. Among the scrap and waste stood a pile of rations – bully beef and biscuit – and a slow-moving concourse of soldiers foraging. Sergeant Smiley pushed his way through them and passed back half a dozen tins. There was a tap of fresh water running to waste in the wall of a ruined building. Guy and his section filled their bottles, drank deep, refilled them, turned off the tap; then breakfasted. The little town was burned, battered and deserted by its inhabitants. The ghosts of an army teemed everywhere. Some were quite apathetic, too weary to eat; others were smashing their rifles on the stones, taking a fierce relish in this symbolic farewell to their arms; an officer stamped on his binoculars; a motor bicycle was burning; there was a small group under command of a sapper Captain doing something to a seedy-looking fishing-boat that lay on its side, out of the water, on the beach. One man sat on the sea-wall methodically stripping down his Bren and throwing the parts separately far into the scum. A very short man was moving from group to group saying: 'Me surrender? Not bloody likely. I'm for the hills. Who's coming with me?' like a preacher exhorting a doomed congregation to flee from the wrath to come.

'Is there anything in that, sir?' asked Sergeant Smiley.

'Our orders are to surrender,' said Guy. 'If we go into hiding the Cretans will have to look after us. If the Germans found us we should only be marched off as prisoners of war – our friends would be shot.'

'Put like that, sir, it doesn't seem right.'

Nothing seemed right that morning, nothing seemed real.

'I imagine a party of senior officers have gone forward already to find the right person to surrender to.'

An hour passed.

The short man filled his haversack with food, slung three water-bottles from his shoulders, changed his rifle for the pistol which an Australian gunner was about to throw away, and bowed under his load, sturdily strutted off out of their sight. Out to sea, beyond the mouth of the harbour, the open sea calmly glittered. Flies everywhere buzzed and settled. Guy had not taken off his clothes since he left the destroyer. He said: 'I'll tell you what I'm going to do, Sergeant. I'm going to bathe.'

'Not in *that*, sir?'

'No. There'll be clean water round the point.'

Sergeant Smiley and two men went with him. There was no giving of orders that day. They found a cleft in the rocky spur that enclosed the harbour. They strolled through and came to a little cove, a rocky foreshore, deep clear water. Guy stripped and dived and swam out in a sudden access of euphoria; he turned on his back and floated, his eyes closed to the sun, his ears sealed to every sound, oblivious of everything except physical ease, solitary and exultant. He turned and swam and floated again and swam; then he struck out for the shore, making for the opposite side. The cliffs here ran down into deep water. He stretched up and found a handhold in a shelf of rock. It was already warm with the sun. He pulled up, rested luxuriously on his fore-arms with his legs dangling knee deep in water, paused, for he was feebler than a week ago, then raised his head and found himself staring straight into the eyes of another, a man who was seated above him on the black ledge and gazing down at him; a strangely clean and sleek man for Creforce; his eyes in the brilliant sunshine were the colour of oysters.

'Can I give you a hand, sir?' asked Corporal-Major Ludovic. He stood and stooped and drew Guy out of the sea. 'A smoke, sir?'

He offered a neat, highly pictorial packet of Greek cigarettes. He struck a light. Guy sat beside him, naked and wet and smoking.

'Where on earth have you been, Corporal-Major?'

'At my post, sir. With rear headquarters.'

'I thought you'd deserted us?'

'Did you, sir? Perhaps we both made a miscalculation.'

'Have you seen Major Hound?'

'Oh yes, sir. I was with him until – as long as he needed me, sir.'

'Where is he now? Why have you left him?'

'Need we go into that, sir? Wouldn't you say it was rather too early or rather too late for inquiries of that sort?'

'What are you doing here?'

'To be quite frank, sir, I was considering drowning myself. I am a weak swimmer and the sea is most inviting. You know something of theology, I believe, sir, I've seen some of your books. Would moralists hold it was suicide if one were just to swim out to sea, sir, in the fanciful hope of reaching Egypt? I haven't the gift of faith myself, but I have always been intrigued by theological speculation.'

'You had better rejoin Sergeant Smiley and the remains of headquarters.'

'You speak as an officer, sir, or as a theologian?'

'Neither really,' said Guy.

He stood up.

'If you aren't going to finish that cigarette, may I have it back?' Corporal Ludovic carefully pinched off the glowing end and returned the half to its packet. 'Gold-dust,' he said, relapsing into the language of the barracks. 'I'll follow you round, sir.'

Guy dived and swam back. By the time he was dressed, Corporal-Major Ludovic was among them. Sergeant Smiley nodded dully. Without speaking, they strolled together into Sphakia. The crowd of soldiers had grown and was growing as unsteady files shuffled down from their hiding-places in the hills. Nothing remained of the ration dump. Men were sitting about with their backs against the ruined walls eating. The point of interest now was the boating party who were pushing their craft towards the water. The sapper Captain was directing them in a stronger voice than Guy had heard for some days.

'Easy ... All together, now, heave ... steady ... keep her moving ...' The men were enfeebled but the boat moved. The beach was steep and slippery with weed. '... Now then, once more all together ... she's off ... let her run ... What ho, she floats ...'

Guy pushed forward in the crowd.

'They're barmy,' said a man next to him. 'They haven't a hope in hell.'

The boat was afloat. Three men, waist deep, held her; the Captain and the rest of his party climbed on board and began bailing out and working on the engine. Guy watched them.

'Anyone else coming?' the sapper called.

Guy waded to him.

'What are your chances?' he asked.

'One in ten, I reckon, of being picked up. One in five of making it on our own. We're not exactly well found. Coming?'

Guy made no calculation. Nothing was measurable that morning. He was aware only of the wide welcome of the open sea, of the satisfaction of finding someone else to take control of things.

'Yes. I'll just talk to my men.'

The engine gave out a puff of oily smoke and a series of small explosions.

'Tell them to make up their minds. We'll be off as soon as that thing starts up.'

Guy said to his section: 'There's one chance in five of getting away. I'm going. Decide for yourselves.'

'Not for me, sir, thank you,' said Sergeant Smiley. 'I'll stick to dry land.'

The other men of his Intelligence section shook their heads.

'How about you, Corporal-Major? You can be confident that no moral theologian would condemn this as suicide.'

Corporal-Major Ludovic turned his pale eyes out to sea and said nothing.

The sapper shouted: 'Liberty boat just leaving. Anyone else want to come?'

'I'm coming,' Guy shouted.

He was at the side of the boat when he noticed that Ludovic was close behind him. The engine started up, drowning the sound which Ludovic had heard. They climbed on board together. One of the watching crowd called, 'Good luck, chums,' and his words were taken up by a few others, but did not carry above the noise of the engine.

The sapper steered. They moved quite fast across the water, out

225

of the oil and floating refuse. As they watched they saw that the crowd on shore had all turned their faces skyward.

'Stukas again,' said the sapper.

'Well, it's all over now. I suppose they've just come to have a look at their spoils.'

The men on shore seemed to be of this opinion. Few of them took cover. The match was over, stumps drawn. Then the bombs began to fall among them.

'Bastards,' said the sapper.

From the boat they saw havoc. One of the aeroplanes dipped over their heads, fired its machine-gun, missed and turned away. Nothing further was done to molest them. Guy saw more bombs burst on the now-deserted water-front. His last thoughts were of X Commando, of Bertie and Eddie, most of all of Ivor Claire, waiting at their posts to be made prisoner. At the moment there was nothing in the boat for any of them to do. They had merely to sit still in the sunshine and the fresh breeze.

So they sailed out of the picture.

7

SILENCE was all. Ripeness was all. Silence swelled lusciously like a ripening fig, while through the hospital the softly petulant northwest wind, which long ago delayed Helen and Menelaus on that strand, stirred and fluttered.

This silence was Guy's private possession, all his own work.

There were exterior sounds in plenty, a wireless down the corridor, another wireless in the block beyond the window, the constant jingle of trolleys, footsteps, voices; that day as each preceding day people came into Guy's room and spoke to him. He heard them and understood and was as little tempted to answer as to join in the conversation of actors on a stage; there was an orchestra pit, footlights, a draped proscenium, between him and all these people. He lay like an explorer in his lamp-lit tent while in the darkness outside the anthropophagi peered and jostled.

There had been a silent woman in Guy's childhood named Mrs

Barnet. He was often taken to visit her by his mother. She lay in the single upper room of a cottage which smelled of paraffin and geraniums and of Mrs Barnet. Her niece, a woman of great age by Guy's standards, stood and answered his mother's inquiries. His mother sat on the only chair by the bedside and Guy stood beside her, watching them all and the pious plaster statues which clustered everywhere round Mrs Barnet's bed. It was the niece who said thank you for the provisions Guy's mother brought and said, when they left: 'Auntie does so appreciate your coming, ma'am.'

The old woman never spoke. She lay with her hands on the patchwork quilt and gazed at the lamp-stained paper on the ceiling, a paper which, where the light struck it, revealed a sheen of pattern like the starched cloth on the dining-room table at home. Her head lay still but she moved her eyes to follow the movements in her room. Her hands turned and twitched, ceaselessly but very slightly. The stairs were precipitous and enclosed top and bottom by thin, grained doors. The old niece followed them down into the parlour and into the village street, thanking them for their visit.

'Mummy, why do we visit Mrs Barnet?'

'Oh, we have to. She's been like that ever since I came to Broome.'

'But does she know us, Mummy?'

'I'm sure she'd miss it, if we didn't come.'

His brother Ivo had been silent, too, Guy remembered, in the time before he went away, sitting all day sometimes in the long gallery doing nothing, sitting aloof at the table while others were talking, quite alert and quite speechless.

In the nursery Guy had had his own periods of silence. 'Swallowed your tongue, have you?' Nannie would ask. It was in similar tones that the Sister addressed him, coming in four or five times in the day with a cheerful rallying challenge. 'Nothing to say to us today?'

The lame Hussar who brought round the whisky-and-soda at sundown lost patience sooner. At first he had tried to be friendly. 'Tommy Blackhouse is two doors down asking for you. I've known Tommy for years. Wish I could have joined his outfit. Rotten show their all getting put in the bag ... I caught my little packet at Tobruk ...' and so on. But when Guy lay mute, he gave it up and now stood equally silent with his tray of glasses waiting while Guy drank.

Once the Chaplain had come.

'I've got you listed as Catholic – is that right?'

Guy did not answer.

'I'm sorry to hear you aren't feeling too good. Anything you want? Anything I can do? Well, I'm always about. You've only to ask for me.' Still Guy did not answer. 'I'll just leave this with you,' said the priest, putting a rosary into his hands, and that was relevant to Guy's thoughts for the last thing he remembered was praying. They had all prayed in the boat in the days of extremity, some offering to do a deal: 'Get me out of here, God, and I'll live different. Honest I will,' others repeating lines of hymns remembered from childhood; all save Ludovic, godless at the helm.

There was one clear moment of revelation between great voids when Guy discovered himself holding in his hand, not, as he supposed, Gervase's medal, but the red identity disc of an unknown soldier, and heard himself saying preposterously: 'Saint Roger of Waybroke defend us in the day of battle and be our safeguard against the wickedness and snares of the devil . . .'

After that all was silence.

Guy lay with his hands on the cotton sheet rehearsing his experiences.

Could there be experience without memory? Could there be memory where fact and fancy were indistinguishable, where time was fragmentary and elastic, made up of minutes that seemed like days, of days like minutes? He could talk if he wished to. He must guard that secret from them. Once he spoke he would re-enter their world, he would be back in the picture.

There had been an afternoon in the boat, in the early days of anxiety and calculation, when they had all sung 'God save the King'. That was in thanksgiving. An aeroplane with RAF markings had come out of the sky, had changed course, circled and hurtled over their heads, twice. They had all waved and the machine had soared away to the south towards Africa. Deliverance seemed certain then. The sapper ordered watches; all next day they kept a look-out for the boat which must be on its way, which never came. That night hope died and soon the pain of privation gave place to inertia. The sapper who had been so brisk and busy lapsed into a daze. Fuel had given out. They had hoisted the sail. It needed little management. Sometimes it hung slack, sometimes it filled to the breeze. The men sprawled comatose, muttering and snoring. Suddenly the sapper shouted frantically. 'I know what you're up to.' No one answered him. He turned to Ludovic and cried, 'You thought I was asleep, but I heard you. I heard everything.'

Ludovic gazed palely and silently. The sapper said with intense malevolence:

'Understand this. If I go, you go with me.'

Then, exhausted, he sank his head on his blistered knees. Guy between dozing and waking, prayed.

Later – that day? the next? the day after? – the sapper moved to a place beside Guy and whispered: 'I want your pistol, please.'

'Why?'

'I threw mine away before I found this boat. I'm skipper here. I'm the only man entitled to arms.'

'Nonsense.'

'Are you in this too?'

'I don't know what you're talking about.'

'No, that's right, isn't it? You were asleep. But I heard them, while you were asleep. I know their plans, *his* plan,' he said, nodding towards Ludovic. 'So, you see, don't you, I *must* have your pistol, *please*.'

Guy looked into the wild eyes and took the pistol from his holster.

'If you fall asleep again *he*'ll get hold of it. That's his plan. I'm the only man who can stay awake. I've got to keep awake. If I go to sleep, *he*'s got us all.' The mad eyes were full of pleading. 'So you see, please, I must have the pistol.'

Guy said: 'That's the best place for it,' and dropped the weapon over the side of the boat.

'Oh, you fool, you bloody fool. He's got us now.'

'Lie down,' said Guy. 'Keep quiet. You'll make yourself ill.'

'One against the lot of you,' said the sapper. 'All alone.'

And that night between moonset and sunrise he disappeared. At dawn the sail hung limp. There was no fixed point anywhere on the horizon to tell them whether they were motionless or drifting with the current and there was no sign of the sapper.

What else was real? The bugs. They were a surprise at first. Guy had always thought of the sea as specially clean. But all the old timbers of the boat were full of bugs. At night they swarmed everywhere, stabbing and stinking. By day they crawled into the shady places of the body, behind the knees, on the back of the neck, on the under cheek. They were real. But what of the whales? There was an hour of moonlight quite clear in Guy's mind when he had awoken to hear all the surrounding water singing with a single low resonant note and to see all round them huge shining humps of meat heaving and wallowing. Had they been real? Had the fog been real that descended and enclosed them and vanished again as swiftly as it came? And the turtles? That night or another, after the moon had set, Guy saw the calm plain fill with myriads of cats' eyes. There was some life still, which Guy was husbanding, in the battery of his torch. He cast a dim beam outward and saw the whole surface of the water encrusted with carapaces gently bobbing one against the other and numberless ageless lizard-faces gaping at him as far as his light reached.

Guy still cogitated these dubious episodes while his health waxed as though the sap were rising vernally in a dry twig. They had tended him carefully. At first while he was still dazed with morphia, they suspended a jar of salts above him and ran a rubber tube from it into the vein of his arm just as gardeners fatten vegetable marrows for the Flower Show, and his horrible tongue had become small and red and wet once more as the liquid surged through him. They had oiled him like a cricket-bat and his old, wrinkled skin grew smooth. Very soon the hollow eyes that glared so fiercely from the shaving-glass had resumed their habitual soft melancholy. The wild illusions of his mind had given place to intermittent sleep and vague, calm consciousness.

In his first days he had gratefully drunk the fragrant cups of malty beverages and the tepid rice-water. Appetite lagged behind his physical advance. They put him on 'light diet', boiled fish and sago, and he ate nothing. They promoted him to tinned herrings, bully beef and great boiled potatoes, blue and yellow, and cheese.

'How's he eating?' the inspecting Colonel always asked.

'Only fair,' the Sister reported.

Guy was a nuisance to this stout, kindly and rather breathless officer. He knew it and was sorry.

The Colonel tried many forms of appeal from the peremptory, 'Come along, Crouchback. Snap out of it,' to the solicitous: 'What you need is sick leave. You could go anywhere – Palestine if you liked. Feed yourself up. Just make the effort.' The Colonel sent a psychiatrist to him, a neurotic whom Guy easily baffled by his unbroken silence. At last the Colonel said: 'Crouchback, I have to tell you that your papers have come through. Your temporary appointment ceased on the day of the capitulation in Crete. As from the first of this month you revert to Lieutenant. Can't you understand, man,' he cried in exasperation; 'you're losing *money* lying there?'

There was real urgency in the appeal. Guy would have liked to reassure him, but by now he had lost the knack, just as once on a visit to England before the war, when he was very tired, he had unaccountably found himself impotent to tie his bow tie. He had repeated what seemed to be the habitual movements; each time the knot either fell apart or else produced a bow that stood rigidly perpendicular. For ten minutes he had struggled at his glass before ringing for help. Next evening and on all subsequent evenings he had performed the little feat of dexterity without difficulty. So now, moved by the earnestness of the senior medical officer, he wished to speak and could not.

The senior medical officer examined the charts on which were recorded Guy's normal temperature, his steady pulse and the regular motions of his body.

The senior officer handed the charts to a Sister in a red cape, who handed them to a Sister in a striped cape, and the procession left him alone.

Outside the door he spoke anxiously and reluctantly about moving Guy to an 'observation ward'.

But mad or sane, Guy offered no scope for an observer. He lay like Mrs Barnet with his hands on the cotton sheet, scarcely moving.

When release came it was not through official channels.

Quite suddenly one morning a new clear voice called Guy irresistibly to order.

'*C'e scappato il Capitano.*'

Mrs Stitch, a radiant contrast to the starched and hooded nurses who had been Guy's only visitants, stood at his door. Without effort or deliberation Guy replied: '*No Capitano oggi, signora, Tenente.*'

She came and sat on the bed and immediately plunged into the saga of a watch which the King of Egypt had given her and how Algie Stitch had doubted whether she should accept it and how the Ambassador had been in no doubts at all and what the Commander-in-Chief's sister had said. 'I can't help it, I *like* the King.' And she produced the watch from her bag – not the basket today, something fresh and neat from New York – and set it to do its tricks. It was a weighty, elaborately hideous mechanism of the Second Empire, jewelled and enamelled and embellished with cupids which clumsily gavotted as the hours struck, and Guy found himself answering easily.

Presently Mrs Stitch said: 'I've just been talking to Tommy Blackhouse. He's down the passage with his leg strung up to the roof. I wanted to take him home with me but they won't let him move. He sent you all sorts of messages. He wants your help writing to next-of-kin of his Commando. That was an awful business.'

'Yes, Tommy was lucky to be out of it.'

'Eddie and Bertie – all one's friends.'

'And Ivor.'

Guy had thought long of Ivor in his silent days, that young prince of Athens sent as sacrifice to the Cretan labyrinth.

'Oh, Ivor's all right,' said Mrs Stitch. 'Never better. He's just been staying with me.'

'*All right?* How? In a boat like me?'

'Well, not quite like you. More comfortable. Trust Ivor for that.'

Like the saline solution which had dripped through the rubber tube into his punctured arm, this news of Ivor oozed through Guy, healing and quickening.

'That's lovely,' he said. 'That's really delightful. It's the best thing that's happened.'

'Well, of course *I* think so,' said Mrs Stitch. 'I'm on Ivor's side always.'

Guy did not notice any qualification in her tone. He was too much exhilarated by the thought of his friend's escape.

'Is he about? Make him come and see me.'

'He's not about. He left yesterday, in fact, for India.'

'Why India?'

'He was sent for. The Viceroy is a sort of cousin. He claimed him.'

'I can't imagine Ivor being made to do anything he didn't want.'

'I think he wanted to go, all right – after all, it's about the only place left where there's plenty of horses.'

At that moment the Sister brought in the tray.

'I say, is that what they give you to eat? It looks revolting.'

'It is.'

Mrs Stitch took a spoon and sampled the luncheon.

'You can't eat this.'

'Not very well. Tell me about Ivor. When did he get out?'

'More than a week ago. With all the others.'

'What others? *Did* any of Hookforce get away?'

'I think so. Tommy told me there were some signallers and a Staff Captain.'

'But X Commando?'

'No. I don't think there were actually any others of them.'

'But I don't quite understand. What was Ivor doing?'

'It's a saga. I can't embark on it now.' She rang a chime on her watch and set the cupids dancing. 'I'll come back. It's lovely seeing you so well. They gave me quite a different account of you.'

'I was with Ivor the last evening in Crete.'

'Were you, Guy?'

'We had a long gloomy talk about the surrender. I can't understand what happened after that.'

'I imagine everything was pretty complete chaos.'

'Yes.'

'And everyone too tired and hungry to remember anything.'

'More or less everyone.'

'No one making much sense.'

'Not many.'

'No one with much reason to be proud of themselves.'

'Not a great many.'

'Exactly what I've said all along,' said Mrs Stitch triumphantly. 'Obviously, by the end there *weren't* any orders.'

It was Guy's first conversation since his return to consciousness. He was a little dizzy, but it came to him, nevertheless, that an attempt was being made at – to put it in its sweetest form – cajolery.

'There were orders, all right,' he said, 'perfectly clear ones.'

'Were there, Guy? Are you sure?'

'Quite sure.'

Mrs Stitch seemed to have lost her impatience to leave. She sat very still, with the funny watch in her hands. 'Guy,' she said,'I think I'd better tell you, there are a lot of beastly people about at the moment. They aren't all being awfully nice about Ivor. As you remember them, there wasn't anything in those orders to give the impression Ivor was meant to stay behind and be taken prisoner, was there?'

'Yes.'

'Oh . . . I don't suppose you remember them very well.'

'I've got them written down.'

Her splendid eyes travelled over the poor little room and came to rest on the locker which held all Guy's possessions.

'In there?'

'Presumably. I haven't looked.'

'I suppose they were countermanded.'

'I don't know who by. The General had left.'

'What happened,' said Julia as though at repetition in the schoolroom, 'was an order from the beach for Hookforce to embark immediately. Ivor was sent down to verify it. He met the naval officer in charge who told him that guides had been sent back and that Hookforce was already on its way. His ship was just leaving. There was another staying for Hookforce. He ordered him into the boat straight away. Until Ivor reached Alexandria he thought the rest of Hookforce was in the other cruiser. When he found it wasn't, he was in rather a jam. That's what happened. So you see no one can blame Ivor, can they?'

'Is that his story?'

'It's our story.'

'Why did he run off to India?'

'That was my idea. It seemed just the ticket. He had to go somewhere. Tommy's Commando doesn't exist any more. Ivor's regiment's not here. He couldn't spend the rest of the war in the Mohamed Ali Club, I mean. It was seeing him so much about, made people gossip. Of course,' she added, 'there was no reason then to expect anyone from Hookforce to turn up until after the war. What are you going to do with those notes of yours?'

'I suppose someone will want to see them.'

'Not Tommy.'

She was right in that. After she left, Guy walked down the passage to Tommy's room. He passed the Sister on the way.

'I was just going to talk to Colonel Blackhouse.'

'*Talk?*' she said. '*Talk?* It's plain to see *you*'ve had a visitor.'

Tommy lay with his leg in plaster, suspended on a line from a pulley. He greeted Guy with delight.

'They ought to recommend you for an MC or something,' he said. 'Trouble is, of course, Crete wasn't all that successful. They prefer handing out decorations after a victory. Were you ever actually in command of the party?'

'No. There was a sapper who did everything at first. After we lost him, we more or less drifted, I think.'

'What became of Hound?'

'I've no idea. Ludovic is the only man who can tell you that.'

'I gather Ludovic turned out well.'

'Did he?'

'First class. It was he who carried you ashore at Sidi Barani, you know.'

'I didn't know.'

'He must be strong as a horse. He was only in hospital two days. I've put him in for a commission. I can't say I ever liked the fellow much, but clearly I was wrong, as usual. The nurses told me you were off your head, Guy. You seem all right to me.'

'Julia Stitch called this morning.'

'Yes, she told me on her way out. She's going to try and get you moved up to her house.'

'She told me about Ivor.'

'Yes. So she said.' The professional wariness which Guy well knew in Tommy now clouded his frank and friendly expression. 'Ivor was in great form. They wouldn't let him go and see you. He was full of congratulations on your getting away. Pity he had to go off so soon.'

'Did he tell you the story of his own escape?'

'One version of it.'

'You didn't believe it?'

'My dear Guy, what d'you take me for? No one believes it, least of all Julia.'

'You aren't going to do anything about it?'

'*I?* It's nothing to do with me, thank God. My position at the moment is Major, waiting re-posting on discharge from hospital. Ivor's put up a pretty poor show. *We* know that – you won't find me applying for him a second time. Julia's got him out of the way. She had to work hard to do it, I can tell you. Now the best thing is for everyone to keep quiet and forget the whole business. It's far too big a thing for anyone to *do* anything about. He might have to stand court-martial for desertion in the face of the enemy. That would be the bloody hell of a thing. They shot people for it in the last war. Of course no one's going to *do* anything. Come to think of it, it's a lucky thing for Ivor we haven't your Brigadier Ritchie-Hook with us. *He*'d do something.'

Guy did not mention the notes in his locker. Instead they talked of the future.

'It looks as if Commandos are off as far as the Middle East is concerned,' said Tommy. 'We're both lucky. We shan't get pushed about. We've got battalions of our own regiments out here. You'll go back to the Halberdiers, I take it?'

'I hope so. There's nothing I ask better.'

That afternoon Guy was transported to Mrs Stitch's. The hospital sent him there in an ambulance. Indeed, they insisted on carrying him in and out of that vehicle on a stretcher, but before leaving he walked from place to place making his farewells.

'You'll be in clover up there,' said the senior medical officer, signing him off the strength. 'Nothing like a bit of home comfort to pull you round.'

'What it is to have influence!' said the Sister.

'She tried to kidnap me,' said Tommy. 'I love Julia, but you have to be jolly well to stay with her.'

Guy had heard this warning on Ivor's lips and discounted it. Coming from the sturdier Tommy it made him hesitate, but it was then too late. The stretcher-bearers stood remorsely at his side. Within half an hour he was at Mrs Stitch's luxurious official residence.

Her grandparents had spent their lives in the service of Queen Victoria and in that court had formed standards of living which projected themselves over another generation and determined Mrs Stitch's precocious but impressionable childhood. Mrs Stitch grew up with the conviction that comfort was rather common. She enjoyed the sumptuous and, within certain incalculable limits, the profuse – no one at her table could ever be quite sure which course of a seemingly classic dinner might not disconcertingly prove to be the last; she enjoyed change and surprise, crisp lettuce-freshness and hoary antiquity, but she did not like male guests to live soft.

This was apparent when she led the stretcher-party down to the room prepared for Guy; down it was, well below ground-level. Mrs Stitch danced lightly from cockroach to cockroach across the concrete floor, squashing six on her way to the window. This she threw open on the kitchen yard. At eye level the bare feet of Berber servants passed to and fro. One squatted near, plucking a goose whose feathers caught by the north-west breeze floated in among them.

'There,' she said. 'Lovely. What more could anyone ask? – I know, flowers.' She was gone. She was back, laden with tuberoses. 'Here,' she said, putting them in the basin. 'If you want to wash, use Algie's loo.' She surveyed the room with unaffected pleasure. 'All yours,' she said. 'Join us when you feel like it.' She was gone. She was back. 'Fond of cats? Here's some. They'll keep down the beetles.' She threw in two tiger-like animals and shut the door. They stretched and scornfully left by the window.

Guy sat on the bed feeling that things had been too much for him that day. He still wore the pyjamas and dressing-gown which seemed to be the correct rig for this move. The stretcher-bearers now returned with his luggage.

'Can we help with your gear, sir? There doesn't seem anywhere to put anything much, does there, really?'

No cupboard, no drawer; a peg. One of the men hung up his equipment; they saluted and left.

Guy's kit had followed him – much pilfered, it transpired – from camp to hospital. There was also the bundle containing the laundered rags he had worn in Crete and the neat packet of possessions taken from his pockets and haversack; with the red identity disc lay his manumission from Chatty Corner and the pocket-book in which he had kept the notes for his War Diary. The elastic band had gone. The covers were blistered and limp and creased and tattered, some of the pages stuck together. Guy carefully separated them with a razor-blade. It was all there. On the blotched maths-paper he could follow in the deterioration of his writing the successive phases of exhaustion. As he grew feebler he had written larger and more heavily. The last entry was a deep scrawl, covering a sheet, recording the appearance of an aeroplane over the boat. This was his contribution to History; this perhaps the evidence in a notorious trial.

Guy lay on his bed, too much shaken by the physical events of the day to concentrate on the moral issues. For Julia Stitch there was no problem. An old friend was in trouble. Rally round. Tommy had his constant guide in the precept: never cause trouble except for positive preponderant advantage. In the field, if Ivor or anyone else were endangering a position, Tommy would have had no compunction in shooting him out of hand. This was another matter. Nothing was in danger save one man's reputation. Ivor had behaved abominably but he had hurt no one but himself. He was now out of the way. Tommy would see to it that he was never again in a position to behave as he had done in Crete. His troop was out of the way too, until the end of the war. It did not much matter, as far as winning the war went, what they said in their prison camp. Perhaps in later years when Tommy met Ivor in Bellamy's he might be a shade less cordial than of old. But to instigate a court-martial on a capital charge was inconceivable; in the narrowest view it would cause endless professional annoyance and delay; in the widest it would lend comfort to the enemy.

Guy lacked these simple rules of conduct. He had no old love for

Ivor, no liking at all, for the man who had been his friend had proved to be an illusion. He had a sense, too, that all war consisted in causing trouble without much hope of advantage. Why was he here in Mrs Stitch's basement, why were Eddie and Bertie in prison, why was the young soldier lying still unburied in the deserted village of Crete, if it was not for Justice?

So he lay pondering until Mrs Stitch called him up to cocktails.

Days passed while Guy lay in the chaise-longue beside the strutting and preening peacocks. Guests came and went singly and in large parties, pashas, courtiers, diplomats, politicians, generals, admirals, subalterns, Greek and Egyptian and Jewish and French, but Mrs Stitch never neglected Guy. Three or four times a day she was at his side with the hypodermic needle of her charm.

'Isn't there anybody you'd like me to ask?' she said one day, planning dinner.

'Well, there is one. Colonel Tickeridge. I hear he's in camp at Mariout. You won't know him but you couldn't help liking him.'

'I'll find him for you.'

That was early in the morning of 22 June – a day of apocalypse for all the world for numberless generations, and for Guy among them, one immortal soul, a convalescent Lieutenant of Halberdiers.

Algernon Stitch brought the news of the invasion of Russia when he returned for luncheon. Only Mrs Stitch and Guy and two secretaries were there.

'Why couldn't the silly fellow have done it to start with?' Algernon Stitch asked, 'instead of landing the lot of us in the soup first.'

'Is it a Good Thing?' Mrs Stitch asked the simple question of the schoolroom.

'Can't tell. The experts don't believe the Russians have a chance. And they've got a lot of things the Germans will find useful.'

'What's Winston going to say?'

'Welcome our new allies, of course. What else can he?'

'It's nice to have one ally,' said Mrs Stitch.

Nothing else was spoken of at luncheon – the Molotov pact, the partition of Poland, the annexation of the Baltic republics, the resources of the Ukraine, the numbers of aeroplanes, of divisions, transport and oil, Tilsit and Tolstoi, American popular opinion, Japan and the Anti-Comintern Pact – all the topics that were buzzing everywhere in the world at that moment. But Guy remained silent.

Mrs Stitch briefly held his hand on the tablecloth. 'Feeling low today?'

'Awfully.'

'Cheer up. Your chum is coming to dinner.'

But Guy needed more than Colonel Tickeridge.

It was just such a sunny, breezy Mediterranean day two years before when he read of the Russo-German alliance, when a decade of shame seemed to be ending in light and reason, when the Enemy was plain in view, huge and hateful, all disguise cast off; the modern age in arms.

Now that hallucination was dissolved, like the whales and turtles on the voyage from Crete, and he was back after less than two years' pilgrimage in a Holy Land of illusion in the old ambiguous world, where priests were spies and gallant friends proved traitors and his country was led blundering into dishonour.

That afternoon he took his pocket-book to the incinerator which stood in the yard outside the window, and thrust it in. It was a symbolic act; he stood like the man at Sphakia who dismembered his Bren and threw its parts one by one out into the harbour, splash, splash, splash, into the scum.

Colonel Tickeridge was cheerful that evening, unworried by issues of right and wrong. The more fellows shooting Germans the better, obviously. Rotten sort of government the Russian. So it had been last time. And the Russians changed it. Probably they would again. He explained these points to Guy before dinner. Colonel Tickeridge was content and only slightly bemused. He supposed so large a party must be celebrating something; what, he never learned. He was a little awed by the eminence of some of his fellow guests, the generals in particular. He was not attracted by the lady on either side. He couldn't understand it when they broke into French. But he tucked in. It was decent of Uncle Crouchback to get him brought here. And later in the evening as he and Guy sat together under the palm trees Mrs Stitch joined them.

'Have you your pistols?' she quoted. 'Have you your sharp-edged axes? Halberdiers! O Halberdiers!'

'Eh?' said Colonel Tickeridge. 'Sorry, I'm not quite there.'

'What have you been talking about?'

'I've been arranging my future,' said Guy. 'Very satisfactorily. The Colonel is taking me back.'

'We lost a lot of good fellows over there, you know. We're busy reforming at the moment. Don't want to take replacements out of the pool, if we can help it. Glad to have one of the old lot back again. Only hope the Brigadier won't snap him up.'

'The Brigadier?' asked Mrs Stitch, politely, vaguely. 'Who is he?'

'Ben Ritchie-Hook. You must have heard of him.'

Mrs Stitch was suddenly alert. 'I think I have. Isn't he dead? I thought that was how Tommy Blackhouse came to command whatever it was.'

'He was lost. Not dead. Far from it. He turned up in western Abyssinia leading a group of wogs. Wanted to go on with them, of course, but the powers that be wouldn't stand for that. They winkled him out and got him to Khartoum. He's due in Cairo this week. We only just heard. It's been a day of all-round good news, hasn't it?'

'Isn't he something of a martinet?'

'Oh, I wouldn't say that exactly. I'd say more of a fizzer, really.'

'Tommy mentioned him the other day, talking about – about something. Hasn't he rather the reputation of a trouble-maker?'

'Only for those who need it,' said Colonel Tickeridge.

'I think I know what you mean,' said Guy.

'There was some fellow in the last war let him down,' said Colonel Tickeridge. 'Not one of ours, of course. Ben was only a company commander then and this fellow was on the staff. Ben got hit immediately after and was in hospital for months. By the time he came out the fellow had got posted into an entirely different show. But Ben never let up on him. He hounded him down and got him broken. It's the big-game hunter in him.'

'I see. I see,' said Mrs Stitch. 'And he's really been in command of Tommy's force all the time?'

'On paper.'

'And he's due when?'

'Before the end of the week, I gather.'

'I see. Well now, I must go and help Algie.'

Two days later Guy and Mrs Stitch sat in the sunlight with orange-juice and melon and coffee and crescent rolls when the peace of the early morning was broken by a motor-bicycle and the odorous garden was affronted with a cloud of greasy smoke. A military dispatch-rider presented a letter. It was a move order, posting Guy to a transit camp at Suez for immediate return to the United Kingdom. It emanated from Movement Control, District Headquarters. He passed it over the table to Mrs Stitch.

'Oh, dear,' she said. 'We shall miss you.'

'But I don't understand. I was due for a medical at the end of the week. They would have passed me fit to join the battalion.'

'Don't you *want* to go home?'

'Of course not.'

'Everybody else seems to.'

'There's been some mistake. D'you think I could have the car for half an hour and straighten it out?'

'Do. If you really think it's worth while.'

Guy drove to headquarters and found the Major who had signed the letter. Guy explained. '. . . Medical on Saturday . . . CO 2nd Halberdiers has applied for posting . . . Ritchie-Hook on the way . . .'

'Yes,' said the Major. 'It looks as though something's gone wrong. Most of my day is spent arguing with chaps who *want* to go back. Homes bombed, wives unfaithful, parents insane – they'll throw any line. It ought to be easy enough to *keep* someone here. I don't quite see,' he said, turning the file, 'where this order originated. Officially you're simply on sick leave. This seems to have come from GHQ Cairo. What's it got to do with them? It isn't as though they were in any hurry to have you at home. You're booked for the slowest possible route. *Canary Castle*. She's unloading at Suez now. Awful old hulk. She's going into dry dock in Durban on the way back. You'll be weeks. Have you been blotting your copy-book by any chance?'

'Not that I know of.'

'Got TB or anything?'

'No.'

'Well, it can't be anything we can't straighten out. Ring me back this afternoon.' He gave Guy the number of his extension.

Julia was still at home when he returned.

'Everything fixed?'

'I think so.'

'Good. No one's in to luncheon. Like to be dropped at the Union Bar?'

Later that afternoon Guy succeeded in speaking to the Major whose number had until then been engaged.

'I asked about you, Crouchback. Nothing I can do, I'm afraid. That order came from right up at the top.'

'But why?'

'That's a thing you probably know more about than I do.'

'Anyway, I can wait until my Brigadier arrives, can't I? He'll be able to do something.'

'Sorry, old boy. Your orders are to embus for Suez 0700 hours tomorrow. Report here at 0615. I shan't be here myself but there'll be someone about. Hope you have a good trip. The old *Canary*'s quite steady. You'll find her full of wop prisoners.'

That night there was a large party. Most of the Greek royal family were there. Guy found it unusually difficult to get a word alone with Mrs Stitch. When he did, he said: 'Julia, you can do anything. Fix this thing for me.'

'Oh, no, Guy, I never interfere with the military. Algie wouldn't like it at all.'

Later that night, as Guy packed, he found the red identity disc he had carried out of Crete. He did not know the correct procedure, where he should send it, how addressed. Finally he wrote on a sheet of Mrs Stitch's thick paper: '*Taken from the body of a British soldier killed in Crete. Exact position of grave unknown*,' folded it unsigned and addressed the envelope simply *G H Q M E*. Eventually, he supposed, it would reach the right department.

But next morning when he found Mrs Stitch up and dressed and waiting to see him off, he thought of a more satisfactory way of paying his debt.

'Julia,' he said, 'do you think Algie could possibly get one of his staff to deal with this for me?'

'Of course. What is it?'

'Just a bit of unfinished business from Crete. I don't know the right man to send it to. Algie's secretary will know.'

Mrs Stitch took the envelope. She noted the address. Then she fondly kissed Guy.

As he drove away she waved the envelope; then turned indoors and dropped it into a waste-paper basket. Her eyes were one immense sea, full of flying galleys.

'GOOD evening, Job.'

'Good evening, sir. Very glad to see you back.'

'Things seem pretty quiet.'

'Oh, I wouldn't say that, sir.'

'No air raids, I mean.'

'Oh, no, sir. That's all over now. Hitler needs all he's got for the Russians.'

'Has Mr Box-Bender arrived yet?'

'Yes, sir. Inside.'

'Hullo, Guy, you back?'

'Hullo, Guy, where have you been?'

'I say, Guy, weren't you with Tommy? Awful business about Eddie and Bertie.'

'Bad luck Tony Luxmore got caught.'

'Anyway, you got away.'

'And Tommy?'

'And Ivor?'

'I was awfully pleased to hear Ivor was all right.'

'Did you see Algie and Julia?'

'Ah, there you are, Guy,' said Box-Bender. 'I've been waiting for you. We'll go straight up and start dinner, if you don't mind. I've got to get back to the House. Besides, everything gets eaten these days if you don't look sharp.'

Guy and his brother-in-law struggled through and up to the coffee-room. Under the chandeliers waitresses distributed the meagre dinner. It was barely half past seven, but already most of the tables were taken. Guy and Box-Bender had to sit in the middle of the room.

'I hope we keep this to ourselves. There's something I particularly want to talk to you about. Better have the soup. The other thing is made of dried eggs. Good trip home?'

245

'Eight weeks.'

'*Eight weeks*. Did you bring anything back with you?'

'I had some oranges. They went bad on the voyage.'

'Oh. Don't look. Elderbury's trying to find somewhere to sit . . . Hullo, Elderbury, you joining us?'

Elderbury sat with them.

'Heard the results of the Tanks for Russia Week?'

'Yes,' said Box-Bender.

'Great idea of Max's.'

'I should like to have seen Harold Macmillan standing to attention while they sang the Red Flag.'

'I saw it on the news-reel. And Mrs Maisky unveiling the picture of Stalin.'

'Well, it's worked,' said Box-Bender. 'Production was up twenty per cent. Twenty per cent – and they were supposed to be working all-out before.'

'And that strike in Glasgow. "Aid to Russia" stopped that.'

'So the *Express* said.'

'Tanks for Russia?' asked Guy. 'I'm afraid all this is new to me. They want tanks pretty badly in the desert.'

'They'll get them, too, don't you worry,' said Box-Bender. 'Naturally the workers are keen to help Russia. It's how they've been educated. It doesn't do any harm to let them have a pot of red paint and splash round with hammers and sickles and "Good old Uncle Joe". It'll wash off. The tanks will get to the place they're most needed. You can be sure of that.'

'Mind you, I'm all for the Russians,' said Elderbury. 'We've had to do a lot of readjustment in the last few weeks. They're putting up a wonderful fight.'

'Pity they keep retreating.'

'Drawing them on, Guy, drawing them on.'

Neither Elderbury nor the dinner conduced to lingering.

'Look,' said Box-Bender briskly, when he and Guy were alone in a corner of the billiard-room. 'I haven't much time. This is what I wanted to show you.' He took a typewritten paper from his pocket-book and handed it to Guy. 'What d'you make of that?'

Guy read:

The Spiritual Combat by Francis de Sales.

Christ the Ideal of the Monk by Abbot Marmion.
Spiritual Letters of Don John Chapman.
The Practice of the Presence of God by Lawrence.

'I think it ought to be "Dom John" not "Don John",' he said.

'Yes, yes, very likely. My secretary copied them. But what d'you make of it?'

'Most edifying. I can't say I've read them much myself. Are you thinking of becoming a monk, Arthur?'

The effect of the little quip was remarkable.

'*Exactly*,' said Box-Bender. 'That's exactly what I expected you to say. It's what other people have said when I showed them.'

'But what is this list?'

'They're the books Tony has sent for from prison. *Now*. What d'you say to that?'

Guy hesitated. 'It's not like him,' he said.

'Shall I tell you what I think? *Religious mania*. It's as plain as a pikestaff the poor boy's going off his head.'

'Why "mania", Arthur? Lots of quite sane people read books like that.'

'Not Tony. At his age. Besides, you know, one's got to remember Ivo.'

There it was, out in the open for a moment's airing, the skeleton from Box-Bender's cupboard. Box-Bender remembered Ivo every day of his busy prosperous life.

Tension quickly resolves in Bellamy's.

'Mind if I join you again?' said Elderbury, carrying a cup of coffee. 'Nowhere else to sit.' And shortly afterwards Guy saw Ian Kilbannock and made his escape.

'What's all this about Ivor Claire?' he asked.

'I've no idea. I've been at sea for eight weeks. The last I heard of him, he'd gone to India.'

'Everyone's saying he ran away in Crete.'

'We all did.'

'They say Ivor ran much the fastest. I thought you might know.'

'I don't, I'm afraid. How's HOO HQ?'

'Seething. We've moved into new premises. Look at these.'

He showed the rings on his cuff.

'There seem more of them.'

'They keep coming. I've got a staff of my own – including Virginia, incidentally. She'll be delighted to hear you're back. She's always talking of you. She's away with Trimmer at the moment.'

'Trimmer?'

'You remember him. McTavish. He's officially named Trimmer now. They couldn't decide for weeks. In the end it went to the Minister. He decided there were too many Scots heroes. Also, of course, Trimmer's so tremendously not Scottish. But he's doing a great job. We've had our noses out of joint a bit this last week. There's a female Soviet sniper going the rounds and getting all the applause. That's why I sent poor Virginia to put some ginger into our boy. He was pining rather. Now things are humming again – except for Virginia, of course. She was sick as mud at having to go – Scunthorpe, Hull, Huddersfield, Halifax . . .'

Next day Guy reported at the Halberdier barracks. His old acquaintance was still in the office, promoted Major once more.

'Back again,' he said. 'Quite an annual event. You come with the fall of the leaf, ha ha.' He was much jollier now he was a Major. 'Everything in order, too, this time. We've been expecting you for weeks. I expect you'd like a spot of leave?'

'Really,' said Guy, 'I don't think I would. I've been sitting about in a ship since the end of June. I might as well get to work.'

'The Captain-Commandant said something about putting you on the square for a fortnight to smarten up.'

'That suits me.'

'Sure? It seemed a bit rough to me. Returned hero and all that. But the Captain-Commandant says people forget everything on active service. I'd better take you to him this morning. Haven't you any gloves?'

'No.'

'We can probably find a pair in the Officers' House.'

They did. They also found Jumbo.

'I've read about your escape,' he said. 'It got in the papers.'

He spoke with gentle, genial reproof. It was not the business of a Halberdier officer to get his name in the papers, but Guy's exploit had been wholly creditable.

At noon, gloved, Guy was marched in to the Captain-Commandant. Colonel Green had aged. 'Mr Crouchback reporting from Middle East, sir,' said the Adjutant.

Colonel Green looked up from his table and blinked.

'I remember you,' he said. 'One of the first batch of young temporary officers. I remember you very well. Apthorpe, isn't it?'

'Crouchback,' said the Adjutant more loudly, putting the relevant papers into the hands of the Captain-Commandant.

'Yes, yes, of course . . .' He reviewed the papers. He remembered the good things he knew of Guy . . . 'Crouchback. Middle East . . . Bad luck you couldn't stay out there and join to second battalion. They wanted you, I know. So did your Brigadier. Old women, these medicos. Still, one has to go by what they say. I've got their report here. They as good as say you're lucky to be alive . . . change of climate essential . . . well, you look fit enough now.'

'Yes, sir, thank you. I'm quite fit now.'

'Good. Excellent. We shall be seeing something of one another, I hope . . .'

That afternoon Guy paraded on the square with a mixed squad of recruits and officers in training under Halberdier Colour-Sergeant Oldenshaw.

'. . . I'll just run through the detail. The odd numbers of the front rank will seize the rifles of the even numbers of the rear rank with the left hand crossing the muzzles – all right? – magazines turned outward – all right? – at the same time raising the piling swivels with the forefinger and thumb of both hands – all right? . . .'

All right, Halberdier Colour-Sergeant Oldenshaw. All right.

FOR THE BEST IN PAPERBACKS, LOOK FOR THE 🐧

In every corner of the world, on every subject under the sun, Penguin represents quality and variety – the very best in publishing today.

For complete information about books available from Penguin – including Puffins, Penguin Classics and Arkana – and how to order them, write to us at the appropriate address below. Please note that for copyright reasons the selection of books varies from country to country.

In the United Kingdom: Please write to *Dept E.P., Penguin Books Ltd, Harmondsworth, Middlesex, UB7 0DA.*

If you have any difficulty in obtaining a title, please send your order with the correct money, plus ten per cent for postage and packaging, to *PO Box No 11, West Drayton, Middlesex*

In the United States: Please write to *Dept BA, Penguin, 299 Murray Hill Parkway, East Rutherford, New Jersey 07073*

In Canada: Please write to *Penguin Books Canada Ltd, 2801 John Street, Markham, Ontario L3R 1B4*

In Australia: Please write to the *Marketing Department, Penguin Books Australia Ltd, P.O. Box 257, Ringwood, Victoria 3134*

In New Zealand: Please write to the *Marketing Department, Penguin Books (NZ) Ltd, Private Bag, Takapuna, Auckland 9*

In India: Please write to *Penguin Overseas Ltd, 706 Eros Apartments, 56 Nehru Place, New Delhi, 110019*

In the Netherlands: Please write to *Penguin Books Netherlands B.V., Postbus 195, NL–1380AD Weesp*

In West Germany: Please write to *Penguin Books Ltd, Friedrichstrasse 10–12, D–6000 Frankfurt Main 1*

In Spain: Please write to *Longman Penguin España, Calle San Nicolas 15, E–28013 Madrid*

In Italy: Please write to *Penguin Italia s.r.l., Via Como 4, I-20096 Pioltello (Milano)*

In France: Please write to *Penguin Books Ltd, 39 Rue de Montmorency, F-75003 Paris*

In Japan: Please write to *Longman Penguin Japan Co Ltd, Yamaguchi Building, 2–12–9 Kanda Jimbocho, Chiyoda-Ku, Tokyo 101*

CLASSICS OF THE TWENTIETH CENTURY

The Outsider Albert Camus

Meursault leads an apparently unremarkable bachelor life in Algiers, until his involvement in a violent incident calls into question the fundamental values of society. 'The protagonist of *The Outsider* is undoubtedly the best achieved of all the central figures of the existential novel' – *Listener*

Dark as the Grave wherein my Friend is Laid Malcolm Lowry

A Dantesque descent into hell: into Lowry's infernal landscape of Mexico – the Mexico of his masterpiece, *Under the Volcano* – and into Lowry's own personal abyss, reverberating with mental terrors and spiritual chasms.

I'm Dying Laughing Christina Stead

A dazzling novel set in the 1930s and 1940s when fashionable Hollywood Marxism was under threat from the savage repression of McCarthyism. 'The Cassandra of the modern novel in English … reading her seems like plunging into the mess of life itself' – Angela Carter

The Desert of Love François Mauriac

Two men, father and son, share a passion for the same woman – attractive, intelligent and proud, but an outcast from respectable society because of her position as a 'kept woman'. 'He writes with an intense, almost tempestuous force about the life of the emotions' – Olivia Manning

The Expelled and Other Novellas Samuel Beckett

Rich in verbal and situational humour, these four stories offer the reader a fascinating insight into Beckett's preoccupation with the helpless individual consciousness, a preoccupation which has remained constant throughout his work.

Chance Acquaintances and Julie de Carneilhan Colette

Two contrasting works in one volume. Colette's last full-length novel, *Julie de Carneilhan* was 'as close a reckoning with the elements of her second marriage as she ever allowed herself'. In *Chance Acquaintances*, Colette visits a health resort, accompanied only by her cat.

CLASSICS OF THE TWENTIETH CENTURY

Petersburg   Andrei Bely

'The most important, most influential and most perfectly realized Russian novel written in the twentieth century' (*The New York Times Book Review*), *Petersburg* is an exhilarating search for the identity of the city, presaging Joyce's search for Dublin in *Ulysses*.

The Miracle of the Rose   Jean Genet

Within a squalid prison lies a world of total freedom, in which chains become garlands of flowers – and a condemned prisoner is discovered to have in his heart a rose of monstrous size and beauty. Of this profoundly shocking novel Sartre wrote: 'Genet holds the mirror up to us: we must look at it and see ourselves.'

Labyrinths   Jorge Luis Borges

Seven parables, ten essays and twenty-three stories, including Borges's classic 'Tlön, Uqbar; Orbis Tertius', a new world where external objects are whatever each person wants, and 'Pierre Menard', the man who rewrote *Don Quixote* word for word without ever reading the original.

The Vatican Cellars   André Gide

Admired by the Dadaists, denounced as nihilist, defended by its author as a satirical farce: five interlocking books explore a fantastic conspiracy to kidnap the Pope and place a Freemason on his throne. *The Vatican Cellars* teases and subverts as only the finest satire can.

The Rescue   Joseph Conrad

'The air is thick with romance like a thunderous sky...' 'It matters not how often Mr Conrad tells the story of the man and the brig. Out of the million stories that life offers the novelist, this one is founded upon truth. And it is only Mr Conrad who is able to tell it us' – Virginia Woolf

Southern Mail/Night Flight   Antoine de Saint-Exupéry

Both novels in this volume are concerned with the pilot's solitary struggle with the elements, his sensation of insignificance amid the stars' timelessness and the sky's immensity. Flying and writing were inextricably linked in the author's life and he brought a unique sense of dedication to both.

Brideshead Revisited

In *Brideshead Revisited* Evelyn Waugh narrates the fortunes of the eccentric but accomplished family of Lord Marchmain, in a social panorama that ranges from Oxford to Venice. And through the bright, delicate beauty of Sebastian Flyte, the heartaches and sufferings of Lady Julia and the disappointments of Charles Ryder, he draws an unforgettable portrait of a doomed aristocracy – at the end of a brilliant, frenetic era.

Vile Bodies

Here, as in *Decline and Fall*, we are in the fashionable Mayfair of the twenties, when the Bright Young Things exercised their inventive minds (and Vile Bodies) in every kind of scandalous escapade. The plot is a deft jigsaw of amusing situations; the characters a vivid assortment of those who inhabit the social domain that lies between Park Lane and Bond Street.

Black Mischief
Decline and Fall
A Handful of Dust
Helena
The Loved One
The Ordeal of Gilbert Pinfold
Put Out More Flags
Scoop
Waugh in Abyssinia
When the Going Was Good
Work Suspended and Other Stories

and

The Diaries of Evelyn Waugh
Edited by Michael Davie
The Letters of Evelyn Waugh
Edited by Marc Amory

and his autobiography
A Little Learning

Completing Waugh's *Sword of Honour* Trilogy

Men At Arms

'Unquestionably the finest novel to have come out of the war'
– Cyril Connolly in the *Sunday Times*

Guy Crouchback, determined to get into the war, takes a commission in
the Royal Corps of Halberdiers. His spirits high, he sees all the
trimmings but none of the action. And his first campaign, an abortive
affair on the West African coastline, ends with an escapade which
seriously blots his Halberdier copybook.

'Waugh's characters have inexorably established themselves among the
enduring fictions . . . In this respect Waugh is in direct line with
Shakespeare and Dickens'
– Clive James in *The New York Review of Books*

Unconditional Surrender

The Crouchback who soldiers on in *Unconditional Surrender* has lost his
Halberdier idealism but gained in human sympathy. Two years at the
London H.Q. of Hazardous Offensive Operations are neither hazardous
nor offensive, but they offer Guy the chance of reconciliation with his
former wife. Then, sent to Jugoslavia, Guy the Catholic finds himself
officially aiding the Communist take-over, but unofficially ministering to
a ragged little group of Jews.

Moments of farce recur, but with a sharper edge. The reader, like Guy
himself, discovers that the action and comedy of Crouchback's war have
given way to a sober awareness of its ultimate futility and harshness.